Praise for *The Two-Family House*

"It's hard to believe *The Two-Family House* is Lynda Cohen Loigman's debut novel. A richly textured, complex, yet entirely believable story, it draws us inexorably into the lives of two brothers and their families in 1950s Brooklyn, New York. . . . As compelling as the story line are the characters that Loigman has drawn here. None is wholly likable nor entirely worthy of scorn. All are achingly human, tragically flawed, and immediately recognizable. We watch them change and grow as the novel spans more than twenty years. . . . Engrossing from beginning to end."
— Associated Press, as seen on ABCNews.com and in *The San Diego Union-Tribune*, *Daily Mail* (UK), and *The Daily Journal*

"In this spellbinding family saga, two women share a terrible secret that binds them for life, yet has the power to destroy everything they love most. With masterful control, Lynda Cohen Loigman boldly explores the anguish and joys of families united by blood and shared loyalties, even as they are divided by jealousy, passion, and mistrust. *The Two-Family House* is that rare, old-fashioned read you never want to end!"   — Cassandra King, national bestselling author of *The Sunday Wife*

"I read the short, gripping prologue, then immediately reread it to bask again in the delicious sense of mystery. *The Two-Family House* explores the impact of a split-second decision on the lives of two related families. I was fascinated by the intriguing blend of personalities as the characters experienced both tragedy and joy, inextricably bound together by blood and deception. With great skill and compassion, Lynda Cohen Loigman turns a story about complex family dynamics into a novel you won't be able to put down."
— Diane Chamberlain, *New York Times* and international bestselling author of *The Secret Life of CeeCee Wilkes* and *Pretending to Dance*

"In *The Two-Family House*, young sisters-in-law are thrown together in a single home, where their children live as near siblings in what on the surface seems an ideal life. Lynda Cohen Loigman plumbs the hidden world beneath the happy faces with insight, honesty, and compassion, and in doing so explores universal truths about family, and love, and loss. I will certainly be giving a copy of this utterly charming novel to my own dearest sister-in-law."

—Meg Waite Clayton, author of *The Wednesday Sisters* and *The Race for Paris*

"No good deed goes unpunished. In a single, intensely charged moment, two women come to a private agreement meant to assure each other's happiness. But as Lynda Cohen Loigman deftly reveals, life is not so simple, especially when it involves two families, tightly intertwined. *The Two Family House* is sympathetically observed and surely plotted all the way through to its deeply satisfying conclusion."

—Christina Schwarz, author of *Drowning Ruth* (an Oprah's Book Club pick) and national bestseller *The Edge of the Earth*

"Where Loigman excels is in capturing the time period—1950s Brooklyn. She draws gender roles accurately, even capturing the frustration of Mort and Rose's eldest daughter, Judith, whose gender constrains her life choices. Loigman nails the way family members, especially parents and children, inadvertently pierce one another with careless comments or subtle looks. As the story unfolds, we are reminded of how a split-second decision can reverberate for decades, even for generations. . . . The real strength of Loigman's debut effort is her characters, to whom you find your loyalty shifting as the story unfolds."

—*The Jerusalem Post*

"But instead of detracting from the book, my uncovering of the 'secret' enhanced my enjoyment of this novel—one of the best I've read in a long time. . . . Who, how, and why is the subject of this well-written, insightful study of human behavior. It is a debut novel for Lynda Cohen Loigman, and promises good things to come."

—*Washington Jewish Week*

"*The Two-Family House* by Lynda Cohen Loigman is an outsider's look into a world filled with tension and mistrust—and most of all, secrets. [It] will make you question and make you angry—but mainly, it will make you rethink your own family history, until you are left wondering—how much do you know about your own past? And how sure are you that, without warning, your world might not be blown apart?"   —Jewish Book Council

"This absolutely riveting book reads like a suspense novel; although many clues are peppered throughout, the reader, like the families, is not invited to share in the shocking secret that binds the two women. The underlying complexities of friendship, the intricacies of marriage, and the disintegration of family are explored in this gem of a family saga. The characters are fully drawn, and the writing is superb. This is a book that is sure to become a popular choice for book clubs."   —Historical Novel Society

"In her first novel, Loigman uses complex characters to deconstruct the anatomy of family relationships and expose deep-rooted emotions, delivering a moving story of love, loss, and sacrifice."

—*Booklist*

"Peeling back the layers that surround an irreversible, life-altering secret, this novel weaves a complex and heartbreaking story about lies and love, forgiveness and family. Written from alternating perspectives of the different family members over more than two decades, the deeply developed voices will bring tears and awe, settling snugly into the heart and mind. It's a reminder that love is always forgiving."   —*RT Book Reviews*

"Two families, both living in one house, drive an exquisitely written novel of love, alliances, the messiness of life, and long-buried secrets. Loigman's debut is just shatteringly wonderful and I can't wait to see what she does next."

—Caroline Leavitt, *New York Times* bestselling author of *Is This Tomorrow* and *Pictures of You*

"*The Two-Family House* takes you on a tour of dysfunction and deep and abiding love in a way that reflects the entanglements that come with a close-living family. . . . Its examination of generations of a family with their own high expectations to live up to resonates on several different levels. . . . This very literary tale actually gives readers so much more than it may seem at first."   —*Bookreporter*

The
Two-Family
House

The Two-Family House

LYNDA COHEN LOIGMAN

ST. MARTIN'S GRIFFIN ☙ NEW YORK

THE TWO-FAMILY HOUSE. Copyright © 2016 by Lynda Cohen Loigman. All rights reserved. Printed in the United States of America. For information, address St. Martin's Press, 175 Fifth Avenue, New York, N.Y. 10010.

www.stmartins.com

The Library of Congress has cataloged the hardcover edition as follows:

Names: Loigman, Lynda Cohen, author.
Title: The two-family house : a novel / Lynda Cohen Loigman.
Description: First edition. | New York : St. Martin's Press, 2016.
Identifiers: LCCN 2015042915| ISBN 9781250076922 (hardcover) |
    ISBN 9781466888883 (e-book)
Subjects: LCSH: Sisters—Fiction. | Jewish fiction. | Domestic fiction. |
    Brooklyn (New York, N.Y.)—Social life and customs—20th century—
    Fiction | BISAC: FICTION / Historical. | FICTION / Jewish.
Classification: LCC PS3612.O423 T96 2016 | DDC 813/.6—dc23
LC record available at http://lccn.loc.gov/2015042915

ISBN 978-1-250-11816-5 (trade paperback)

Our books may be purchased in bulk for promotional, educational, or business use. Please contact your local bookseller or the Macmillan Corporate and Premium Sales Department at 1-800-221-7945, extension 5442, or by e-mail at MacmillanSpecialMarkets@macmillan.com.

First St. Martin's Griffin Edition: March 2017

10 9 8 7 6 5 4 3 2 1

For Bob, Ellie, and Charlie

Acknowledgments

This book is for the women of my mother's family—for my mother, Janice Cohen, whose recipe box I really do talk to; for my grandmother, Tillie Sack, whose unconditional love for every one of her grandchildren made us all believe that we really were that beautiful, that handsome, that smart, and that talented; and for my aunts, Shelley Marcus and Barbara Wisnefsky, who have been my cheering section always. Thanks to the four of them for sharing the stories that have always comforted and inspired me.

I could not have written this book without the constant help and friendship of two brilliant and special writers and women. New friendship in one's forties is an unexpected gift, one that Elisabeth Bassin and Susan Kleinman have given me. Without them, I would have shut my laptop long ago.

Five years ago I had the good fortune of walking into Steve Schnur's class at the Sarah Lawrence College Writing Institute, and my life was forever changed. I must thank my classmates, past and present, for all they have taught me. And to Steve, special thanks for his encouragement and kindness.

Thanks to Leslie Powell, sister of my heart, and to all of my Westchester girlfriends for sharing motherhood and madness with me for the past sixteen years. Thanks to my father, Harris Cohen; my brother, Robert Cohen, and my husband's parents, Carol and Barry Loigman, for all of their enthusiasm. If my brother-in-law, Mark Loigman, was still with us, I have no doubt that he would be the most excited of all.

I have always had a soft spot for fairy tales, and when my agent, Marly Rusoff, called me for the first time, I felt like I had stepped into one. A million thanks to Marly for believing in my characters, for helping me to create the best possible version of this story, and for welcoming me into her magical world. Without Marly and Michael Radulescu, this book would still be just a lonely file on my laptop.

With all the novels out there waiting to be read, I am so grateful to my editor, Jennifer Weis, for choosing mine. Thanks to Jen and Sylvan Creekmore for their enthusiasm, guidance, and hard work. Thanks also to everyone at St. Martin's Press who helped to bring this book to life: Sally Richardson, Jen Enderlin, Brant Janeway, Lisa Senz, Jessica Preeg, Angela Craft, and Olga Grlic.

Thank you to Lynn Goldberg and Kathleen Carter Zrelak for their energy, their guidance, and their positivity.

The Two-Family House is a story rooted deep within me, but I could never have written it without first being a mother. Thanks to my daughter, Ellie, for her love of reading and language, and for sharing so much of herself with me. Thanks to my son, Charlie, for making me laugh and for being the sweetest cure to anything that ails me. How fortunate I am to have one of each.

The very last thank you is for my husband and best friend. Love and gratitude to Bob always for listening to me read my stories at night when all he wants is to sleep, for believing in me even when I don't, for loving me when I am at my worst, and for singing with me in the car, as promised.

The
Two-Family
House

Prologue

She walked down the stairs of the old two-family house in the dark, careful not to slip. The steps were steep and uneven, hidden almost entirely beneath the snow. It had been falling rapidly for hours and there had been too much excitement going on inside the house for anyone to think about shoveling steps for a departing midwife. Perhaps if the fathers of the two babies born had been present, they would have thought to shovel. But the storm had prevented their return, and neither had been home.

She breathed in the cold night air, happy to be outside at last, away from the heat and closeness of the birthing room. How grateful she was for the sudden burst of wind that slammed the door shut behind her, shaking her out of her exhaustion and signaling the finality of the evening. She loved her work and cherished the intimacy of it. But it was not a pleasure outing.

Before today she thought she had seen every permutation of circumstance: the girls who cried out for their own mothers even as they became mothers themselves; the older women who marked themselves as cursed, suddenly bursting with joy over a healthy child come to them at last. She thought she had heard every kind of sound a person could make, witnessed every expression the human face could conjure up out of pain, joy or grief. That was what she thought before this evening.

This night was different. Never before had she seen such long-ing, pain and relief braided together more tightly. Two mothers, two babies, born only minutes apart. She had witnessed tonight what pure woman strength could accomplish, how the mind could control the body out of absolute desperation.

She had watched, and she had ignored. She had taken charge, yet she was absent. She let them believe that her confusion was real, that she was tired. But she was never confused. She was not too tired to comprehend their hopes. The fragile magic of that night had not been lost on her.

She breathed in the air again, crisp and cold, clearing her head. It had been a good night, two healthy babies born to healthy, capable mothers. She couldn't ask for more. What happened now was out of her hands. Wholly and completely she put it out of her mind, said her goodbyes to the house on the steps and made her way home to go to sleep. There would be more babies tomorrow, she knew, and the constancy of her work would keep her thoughts from this place. She promised herself never to think of it again.

Part One

Chapter 1

MORT

(May 1947)

The domestic, feminine scene unfolding before Mort did nothing to improve his spirits. Upstairs, in his brother's apartment, substantial preparations were being made. Not just the brushing of hair and the tying of sashes. Serious words were being spoken from man to man, from father to son. Mort pushed away his breakfast plate and frowned.

Thirty minutes before they were supposed to leave, there was a thudding of footsteps down the stairs and a quick knock on the door. "Got to go! See you there!" Abe's voice rang with excitement. Mort had assumed they would all walk over to the synagogue together. "What do they need to get there so early for?" he grumbled at his wife. Knowing better than to defend her brother-in-law, Rose shrugged her shoulders. "I don't know," she answered.

Mort had been dreading this day, the day of his nephew's bar mitzvah, for months. In the weeks leading up to it, the increased noise and activity of his brother's family overhead agitated him. He found himself imagining different scenarios to go with every thud and thump he heard. Was Abe's wife, Helen, testing out a new cake recipe? Was his nephew Harry trying on his new suit? What were the other boys laughing about? Mort tortured himself in this manner for several weeks. He was a sharp, thin man, and in the month before the bar mitzvah he had lost at least ten pounds. His increasingly angular appearance alarmed his wife, but everyone else was too busy to notice.

Rose had been up earlier than usual that morning to make sure
the girls were ready on time. Hair ribbons were neatened and his three
daughters, clad in matching yellow dresses, were lined up in front of
him after breakfast. "They're like a row of spring daffodils," Rose entreated. "Don't you think so?"

Mort looked up, but he was an unappreciative audience. Judith
was almost twelve and seemed too old for matching dresses. She was
fidgeting in the line, anxious to get back to the book she had been
forced to leave on the kitchen table. Every week, Mort insisted that
Judith present him with her chosen pile of library books for approval.
Every week, Judith asked Mort if he wanted to read one of her books
too, so they could discuss it. Every week, he declined.

Mimi, the prettiest of the three, was the most comfortable on
display. She was only eight, but already she carried herself with a stylish grace that Mort found unfamiliar. Mort thought she looked the
most like Rose. Mimi was forever making cards for friends and family members with pencils and crayons that she left all over the house.
Last year, she found her father's card in the kitchen trash pail the
morning after his birthday. She ran crying to him with it, waving it
in her hand and asking why he had thrown it away. "My birthday is
over," he explained. "I don't need it anymore."

Dinah, the baby of the family, had the most trouble keeping quiet
during Mort's inspection. She was only five, and though she had been
taught not to ask her father too many questions, she couldn't seem to
help herself. "What's your favorite color?" she blurted out, eyes wide
with anticipation. Mimi, hoping the answer might give her some
insight regarding the design of next year's birthday card, seemed
eager for the reply. But the response was of no help. "I don't have one,"
Mort said.

After Mort nodded his silent endorsement of the girls' appearance, the family was ready to go. He usually took the lead during outings like these, leaving everyone else struggling to match his quick
strides. The girls knew better than to try to walk alongside him. Even
Dinah had stopped trying to hold his hand years ago. Instead, they
had taken to walking single file on family outings, like unhappy ducks
in a storybook, with Rose bringing up the rear.

Today, however, Mort was so out of sorts that he lagged behind the rest and stayed at the back of the line. Despite the warm weather, he found himself shivering in his baggy suit. His face grew increasingly gray with each step that he took. Rose walked ahead, slow and uncomfortable in the lead position.

The policy of the synagogue was to seat men and women separately, even children. Once they arrived, Rose and the girls headed upstairs to the women's section, while Mort joined Abe and his nephews on the ground floor. While he was relieved to be unburdened by the flock of women that constantly surrounded him, Mort also felt strangely alone. He had been in the sanctuary countless times, but today he felt out of place and insignificant.

The service continued without incident. It was not a stellar reading by any means, but it was not the worst performance he had heard from a bar mitzvah boy either. He felt a secret burst of delight with each mistake his nephew uttered, but no one else seemed to notice. When Mort looked around the room he saw only smiling people, nodding their heads. They were all on Harry's side.

The walk home was painful. Mort walked behind Abe's family, counting the cobblestones, trying to remember important business matters. He felt strongly that he should be using his time more efficiently that day, not wasting it on celebrations. He counted invoices and orders in his head, thinking about how busy he would be on Monday, and made a promise to himself to work on Sunday in order to get a jump on the week's work ahead. At one point he called out to Abe, offering a reminder of an order that needed to be shipped out in a few days. Abe waved his hand in the air, brushing the reminder aside. Abe would not speak about business today.

Back at the house, Mort said hello to relatives he hadn't seen for months. He accepted compliments on his daughters, praises for their dresses and smiles, but nothing could improve his mood. He took a glass of wine and sipped it. When Rose came over to him with a plate of food, she reminded him to give Harry the envelope they had brought. After that he sat alone, feeling self-conscious and clumsy as he tried to balance the plate on his lap.

The party went on that way, silent and empty for him, until it was almost time to leave. He was on his second glass of wine when he felt a strong arm around his shoulders. It was Helen's cousin Shep, a bearded hulk of a man a few years older than Abe. "Morty!" he said, squeezing with his oversized hands. "Good to see you!" Mort tried to pull away, but it was impossible to escape Shep's grip. "Guess what, Morty? No, you'll never guess. I got married! Never been better! Meet my wife, Morty, and my son!" The next minute Mort was being dragged to meet Shep's chubby wife, Alice, and their even chubbier baby boy. "Nice to meet you," Mort said.

Alice was quiet, a perfect match for the outgoing Shep. "I tell you, Mort," he boomed, "being a father is the best thing for a man! Ah, what am I yapping to you for? You know all about it!" He grabbed Mort for one more stifling embrace. "Nice to see you," Mort muttered, retreating as quickly as possible.

In his haste to escape, Mort turned into the kitchen by mistake. Rose was there with several other women, wrapping up food now that the desserts had been set out. She looked over at him and pointed, motioning through the doorway to Harry, who was standing with one of his brothers.

Mort patted his pocket; the envelope was still there. He might as well get it over with so that he could go home. Over the din of the crowd he heard Shep's booming voice again. Shep, that idiot, had a new lease on life! He was holding up his son, swooshing him around like a kid with a toy airplane. What Mort noticed next confounded him. Men and women alike turned their heads, this way and that, to catch a glimpse of the baby. For a few seconds at least, the guests were transfixed, their eyes tightly set on the infant in the air. For a moment, maybe more, everyone else was forgotten, even the bar mitzvah boy himself.

When Mort looked back at Rose in the kitchen, desire leapt at him for the first time in months. He felt suddenly generous and surprisingly hopeful. He approached his nephew and patted him on the back. "Nice job, Harry," Mort told him, slipping the envelope into his hand.

With his task completed, Mort gathered his family to leave. At the door he let Helen kiss him on the cheek and shook Abe's hand for a moment longer than usual. Abe and Helen looked at each other, but when Helen raised her eyebrow, Mort pretended not to notice. He guided Rose through the doorway, and, with daughters in tow, they left.

Chapter 2

ABE

Abe was a lucky man. He told himself that every morning while he dressed and every night before he went to sleep. Abe wasn't religious but every day he thanked God for his beautiful wife, his four healthy sons, his brother and his business. Sometimes he left out his brother, but only when Mort was being a pain in the ass.

Abe was three years older than Mort, but most people thought he was younger by ten. When people thought of Abe, they pictured him either eating or laughing. It was no wonder, then, that Mort (who rarely engaged in either activity) was so often mistaken for the senior of the two.

The brothers owned a cardboard box—manufacturing company in Brooklyn. It had been their father's company before them, and Abe had started working there in high school. He always wanted to go into the business. Mort, on the other hand, wanted to be a mathematician. Abe wasn't sure what mathematicians did, but he knew Mort was great with numbers. When their father died unexpectedly during Mort's sophomore year at college, their mother begged Mort to take a break from school to help Abe. She had faith in Abe, and she knew he was a good salesman. But she also knew him well enough to understand that his benevolent manner could ruin the business if left unchecked. She was afraid he would give too many orders on credit or allow too many discounts. Mort's head for numbers was necessary.

And she knew that his no-nonsense, tight-fisted nature would balance Abe's generosity.

Months turned to a full year, and the break became permanent. Mort never returned to school. This, Abe knew, had been a horrible disappointment for his brother. It was the point at which he went from a serious but satisfied student to a grim and resentful young man. Abe felt responsible for his brother's unhappiness. He tried to make Mort feel better about working at the company and changed its name to Box Brothers, thinking that Mort might take some pleasure in their bond of fraternity and commerce. He took Mort to lunch every week and tried to set him up with girls. Abe was dating Helen at that point, and she had a lot of girlfriends. But nothing Abe did brought a smile to his brother's face. Mort continued to be somber and unpleasant, and the others at work avoided him.

In his heart, Abe knew that Mort blamed *him* for having to give up school. He had spoken to Mort about it only once, fifteen years ago, after their mother's funeral. She was never the same after their father died, and despite the doctors' insistence that nothing was wrong, she continued to shrink and wither until nothing was left. The funeral took place on a cloudy November morning at an empty cemetery. After the prayers were said; Abe and Mort each shoveled a spadeful of dirt onto the half-buried coffin. Abe was heartsick, even more for Mort than for himself. He had married Helen the year before, and aside from his mother's illness, had enjoyed a blissful first year of marriage with her. He worried about Mort going home to an empty apartment. The clouds overhead gave way, and the rain began to fall. The three of them took shelter under a tree.

Helen had spoken first. "Come home with us, Mort. Stay for a while. You shouldn't be by yourself today."

"We'll be together," Abe added.

But Mort refused. The wind picked up, agitating the tree branches overhead like an angry child shaking a doll. Mort wouldn't look at either of them.

"Come, Mort. Just for one night," Helen pleaded. Abe couldn't tell whether Mort was wincing from the wind or from pain. Either way, his brother wouldn't speak. Mort kicked a rock into the tree trunk and dug his chin farther into the collar of his coat.

Abe took a deep breath. "I've been thinking," he said, "It's been three years. Three years we've worked together. I don't know what I would have done without you. I couldn't have pulled it off. But the company's fine now. It's going great. Our sales are high, the warehouse is paid for. We can hire a bookkeeper, an accountant, maybe. You don't have to work there anymore. You can go back to school."

Mort was silent.

"Go back to school," Abe told him. "It's what you want. You'll be happy. You can keep taking your salary—it'll pay for your classes. We'll keep half the company in your name."

Abe heard the low rumble of thunder, distant in the skies. "It's too late for that now," Mort said, his voice heavy with all the venom he could muster.

"Why? You're only twenty-three years old. Nothing's too late."

"I'm not going back to school to make a fool of myself just so *you* can feel better!" Mort spat the words into the cold, wet air. Lightning flashed overhead, and Abe watched his brother hurry away.

Abe never stopped trying to make it up to Mort. On the surface, their family situations, fortunes and possessions were equally matched: each owned a half interest in the business, each owned a half interest in the two-family house in Brooklyn, each was married and each had several healthy children. As far as Abe was concerned, they were both blessed, with every reason for happiness. But he knew his brother didn't see it that way.

What Abe suspected, what he pushed to the back of his mind during the day, was that Mort not only blamed him but hated him. Some nights, as he was drifting off to sleep, Abe tried to imagine the reasons why. Was he too cheerful? Too eager to show his love for family and his job? Was he too demonstrative with Mort? Did Mort dislike walking to work together every morning? Did Mort object to all of them living in the same house? Abe always thought it was nice for them, nice for their wives to have each other. But maybe Mort felt smothered.

The day after Harry's bar mitzvah, Abe gave up this bedtime theorizing. There were too many other things to think about, and Abe was tired of Mort's sour expression. The guy was a real pill. As a matter of fact, even on the way home from the bar mitzvah Mort had started yammering about one of their shipments, bothering him about orders on a day meant for celebration.

The Monday after the festivities, Abe decided he would walk to work on his own. He would enjoy a quiet stroll for once, unhindered by sales numbers and profit discussions, and think back over the weekend in peace. He whistled on his way, stopping every now and again to smile at a passing acquaintance.

He was almost at the corner when he heard footsteps behind him.

"Abe!" It was Mort, trying to catch up. Abe stopped at the light and waited. As soon as the light turned, he took off again, forcing Mort to match his frantic clip.

"I don't want to talk about the shipment, Mort."

"Of course." Mort was being uncharacteristically agreeable.

"I just wanted to tell you . . . ," said Mort. He stopped to catch his breath. They were walking much faster than usual. "I just wanted to tell you congratulations on the bar mitzvah."

Abe stopped walking. The morning sun came out on the other side of a passing cloud overhead, and Abe's face widened into a happy grin. Forgiveness came easily to him. He grabbed his brother's shoulder and patted him on the back. "Let's get to work," he said.

Chapter 3

HELEN

The day after Harry's bar mitzvah, Helen woke early. When the clock ticked toward 5:00 a.m., she decided it was reasonable to get out of bed. Abe and the boys wouldn't be up for hours, and she would have some time to herself. She walked down the hall to the kitchen, treading softly so as not to wake Rose's family below. Helen often thought she and Abe should live on the bottom floor, especially considering the amount of jumping and stomping that went on in her apartment. She was certain one of her boys was going to end up crashing through the floorboards into Rose's living room one of these days; she just hoped he would end up on the couch.

Helen turned on the light in the kitchen and cringed. There was still so much to clean up from the party. Rows of glasses, left overnight to dry, had to be boxed. Covered plates of cookies and pastries had to be frozen or given away. If they stayed on the counter, the boys would devour them all before lunchtime and have stomachaches for the rest of the day. Helen measured out the coffee for the pot and sat down at the table, waiting for it to brew.

Thank goodness the day before had been a success. Earlier in the week the rabbi had spoken to her quietly, taking her aside to express his concerns. The rabbi didn't usually talk to the mothers, so Helen knew it was important. He assured her that Harry was a wonderful boy, but that she shouldn't expect too much. He tried to tell Helen what she already knew. She just hoped it wouldn't be too disappointing for Abe.

The night before the service, Abe practiced with Harry at the dining room table. Over and over Harry repeated the prayers, just as he had done for months. Harry never got upset when he made a mistake, but he never really improved either. It was, Helen knew, impossible to get upset with Harry because he never got upset with himself. He never uttered obscenities or threw his books or even frowned. He knew the bar mitzvah was something he had to get through, and he was determined to manage it with as little upset as possible. Harry instinctively avoided anything unpleasant.

Girls were *not* unpleasant for Harry. Even at thirteen, he knew how to talk to them. It was a puzzling thing, Helen thought, to be the mother of such a boy. She saw how the older girls, girls of fifteen already, looked at Harry. And even more surprising was the way he looked back at them, meeting their gazes, as if he had answers to questions they had not even thought of.

Helen watched Harry as if she were two people. As his mother she was proud of him, proud of his looks, his confidence. But when she watched him as the young girl she once was, she ached for the girls whose hearts he might break one day. Part of her wanted to warn them against his charms, shoo them away for their own sakes and take their side against him. But the mother side of her held this part back, and she was unable to set any obstacle in front of him. That was why she bought him a tie for the bar mitzvah that set off the color of his blue eyes exactly. And why she never let the barber give him buzz cuts in the summertime.

On the morning of the bar mitzvah, all eyes had been on Harry. The congregation was accustomed to awkward, gangly bar-mitzvah boys, boys made self-conscious by their first burst of hormones and newly grown acne. But Harry had stood in front of the congregation that morning with all the confidence of a rabbi, even if he had none of the knowledge of one. There were many mistakes, of course, but Harry never hesitated for a moment. When it was over, everyone agreed it had been a lovely service. And his father, who heard every mistake with his ears but not with his heart, was beaming.

Family and friends came back to their house for a luncheon that turned into dinner. There had been congratulations for all involved, even Harry's three younger brothers, who didn't quite know what to make of the half-strangers speaking to them. Harry shook each hand and kissed each cheek, accepting the compliments and gifts of every guest.

Halfway through the party, a small group of girls from Harry's class came over to him, giggling. One of them, a pretty blonde named Susan, stood closer than was necessary. "You did great today," Susan said. She whispered something in Harry's ear that Helen couldn't hear and Harry smiled. When he whispered something back, the girl blushed.

Helen's heart, so recently filled with pride, had suddenly deflated. What had Harry said to that girl? She felt disconnected from him in a way she had never experienced and grabbed at the dining room table for support. She found herself breathless, unable to collect enough air in the crowded space.

"Helen? Are you all right?" It was Abe, at her side in an instant.

"I'm fine."

"You look like you're going to pass out. Sit down." He pulled a chair over for her and bent down to look at her. "What is it? What's wrong?"

She had closed her eyes to give herself time to think, to find an acceptable answer to the question. There was no time. She had a house full of guests, platters to bring out, people to feed, a party to run. What could she possibly say? That in watching her son flirt with a girl, she was suddenly terrified, overcome with emotions she could not fully describe? That her knees caved in when she found she could no longer define her role in Harry's life? That the emptiness she felt at that moment was a faceless guest, unwanted and sour, who had snuck into her home and ruined her celebration?

When she didn't answer, Abe told her not to move. "I'm getting you something to drink," he insisted. But he didn't have to. Rose was already there, with tea and a plate. Helen drank the tea and took a few bites. She felt better, and she shook off the emptiness. She was hostess once again.

It had been a wonderful party. The food was delicious. The cake, which Helen made herself, was a spectacle of sugar and love. But no matter how many compliments she received, Helen still hadn't been able to breathe in as much air as she needed. Harry was hers no longer, and the realization of the change had been a terrible blow.

Now, the morning after the celebration, Helen was faced with only a day of housework to look forward to. Her heart ached a little as she filled up her coffee mug. She cut a few slivers off the end of one of the pound cakes, gulped down her coffee and took out her apron. It was time to start cleaning.

When the kitchen was done, the living room was next. Helen wiped and dusted, collapsed folding chairs and card tables, and moved small pieces of furniture back to their proper places. She didn't want to wake anyone with the vacuum, but when she ran her broom underneath the sofa, she found a tiny blue sock that had gotten swept up with the crumbs. She tucked it into her apron pocket and made a mental note to call Alice, her cousin Shep's wife, to let her know she had it. She would put it in the wash tomorrow.

It was only when Helen opened the windows to air out the living room that she thought of it. The idea floated in with the crisp morning breeze, erasing the staleness that had filled her lungs. A new resolve elated her, and she stopped for a moment to savor it. She was only thirty-five, for heaven's sake. Why not?

After that, the rest of her morning chores flew by. By the time the boys woke up, clamoring for food, Helen was giddy with newfound purpose. Abe wandered into the kitchen a few minutes later. "You made a beautiful party," he said, leaning forward to kiss her, already recalling his favorite moments of the previous day. She returned the kiss and played along, but Helen had no interest in reminiscing. The bar mitzvah was behind her, and her heart was hungry for what would come next.

Chapter 4

ROSE

(August 1947)

Rose took the second loaf of bread out of the oven and placed it on top of the stove. The smell made her stomach turn, but she took a deep breath and tried to force the sensation into retreat. She felt awful.

Rose never imagined she would get pregnant again. She assumed that part of her life was over and that Dinah, just turned five, would always be the baby of the family. But she could no longer ignore her condition. And as each day passed, the realization that she was going to have to tell Mort invaded her thoughts more frequently. A month ago, the thought of telling him was like the sighting of a distant ship: a black speck on a remote horizon. Thinking of it that way calmed her. Over the past few weeks, however, an overwhelming sense of dread transformed the picture: the ship grew closer, filling the frame, and no amount of coaxing could turn it back around. Today, she could think of nothing else, and so after the children left for the park, she kept herself busy baking bread.

"Something smells good in there! Open up!" It was Helen at the door, all smiles and pink cheeks. Not just pink, Rose saw, but bright red and dripping with perspiration. She puffed her way inside and saw the loaves cooling on the stove.

"You're baking bread in this heat? It's like a sauna in here, Rose. Open a window!"

Rose slid open the window over the sink. The August morning was hot and still, with no breeze. "I felt like baking bread."

"For heaven's sake, why?"

"I needed to keep busy. One is for you. Sit. You can taste it for me."

Rose set one of the loaves on the table with a plate for Helen and the butter dish. She found the jar of blueberry preserves she had made a few weeks ago and put that down too.

"Oh good, your jam! Don't you want a plate?"

"I can't eat in this heat."

Rose poured two cups of coffee and sat down. She couldn't help smiling as she watched Helen attack the bread. First Helen cut off the end. She sliced a generous piece from the middle, slathered it with butter and jam, and popped it in her mouth, leaving the end piece on the table. "It's so good, Rose," Helen practically moaned. "I swear I could eat the whole thing right now."

"Don't you like the end?"

"What?"

"The heel—you don't like that part? That's Mimi's favorite."

Helen chuckled. She put down the butter knife she was holding and began to laugh harder. When her laughter turned into a coughing fit, Rose jumped up to get her a glass of water. After a few sips, the coughing stopped.

"What's so funny?"

"You never met my grandmother; she died before I met Abe. Anyway, she was from the old country, very stubborn, very superstitious. You couldn't put a hat on the bed, you couldn't eat only one olive—she believed all that stuff. She used to say that if a pregnant woman wanted a girl, she should never eat the end of the bread, only the middle. And if she wanted a boy, she should only eat the end."

"You're pregnant?" Rose was stunned.

"Don't you see what a horse I am? I'm busting out of my dresses! I'm due the first week of January. Five months to go. I thought for sure you knew."

Rose had been so preoccupied with her own pregnancy that she hadn't even noticed Helen's. Of all the babies born to the two women—the upstairs boys and the downstairs girls—Rose and Helen had never been pregnant at the exact same time. There had been a few months of overlap here and there but nothing like this. They were both due in January. "Have you told Abe?" Rose asked.

"Just yesterday. I wanted to wait until it was safe. Boy, was he surprised! You'd think he would have guessed, but men never pay attention."

"I guess they don't," Rose admitted. She filled their coffee cups again and thought how lucky she was to have Helen for her sister-in-law. When Helen was beside her she felt braver, resilient. They would go through this together. Rose felt the terrible feeling in her stomach dissipate. She reached across the table for the bread knife and cut the other end off the loaf. She took the end Helen had cut and the newly cut piece and placed them both in front of her on the table. Then she took a bite from each one.

"You too?" Helen jumped up and put her arms around her sister-in-law. She patted Rose's stomach. "But you're slimmer than ever! You're not showing at all!" Together they went over their symptoms and ailments from the past few months. Rose had been exhausted and Helen had craved sweets.

Slice by slice, Helen polished off the middle of the loaf while Rose nibbled only on the ends. She wanted to believe Helen's superstition would work. She wanted to believe she had some control. She wanted, more than anything, to believe that what lay ahead of her would be better than what had come before. But as she chewed the ends of the loaf she had baked, the dry bits of crust only stuck to her tongue and the crumbs felt like dust in her mouth.

Chapter 5

ABE

Abe couldn't believe it when Helen told him she was pregnant. "Are you sure?" he stuttered. He had left the office early that afternoon because of the heat. Now he was home, sweating even more than he had at work.

"I'm sure."

"Did you see the doctor?" A stream of perspiration was making its way down the side of his cheek, directly in front of his ear.

"Abe!" she scolded. "Of course I did!"

Abe sat down on the couch. He put his head down and tried to breathe.

"What's wrong? Why aren't you happy?"

His head was still down. "I'm happy, I'm happy," he muttered. "It's good."

"Then why do you look like you're having a heart attack?"

Slowly, he lifted his head and looked at her. "I'm just surprised, is all. It's a big shock. It's enough to give anybody a heart attack if you want to know the truth."

Helen sat down next to him and took his hand. "I'm not an old woman yet. It can't be *that* much of a shock. What's the matter?"

"Mmm." His eyes were closed and he was dabbing at his forehead with his handkerchief.

"Stop it!" Helen shook him by the arm. Then she stood up and put her hands on her hips. "Are you happy or not?"

Abe stood up too, a little shaky at first, and managed a smile. "Sweetheart, of course I'm happy. We'll have a beautiful baby." Helen popped a kiss on his cheek and promptly pushed him back down. "Sit. I'm going to get you a glass of water. You look green. I can't raise five children alone, you know. I don't want you to have a *real* heart attack."

Abe closed his eyes again and tried to relax. He should have seen it coming. The way she was looking at her cousin's baby a few months ago—like a kid drooling over a lollipop! That look in her eye, the frantic way she pulled him into bed. He should have known. And here was the result: just when they were able to enjoy themselves a little and get a couple nights of sleep, they were heading back to diapers and midnight feedings.

Abe knew his initial misgivings would fade. He'd get used to the idea and get excited about it, just like all the other times. In fact, he told himself, he might as well get excited about it soon, because Helen wasn't going to tolerate any other kind of reaction from him.

"Drink this. I let the water run so it's cold. Here." She handed him the glass just as he was getting up.

"Where are you going? I thought you felt sick?"

"I'm okay. I'm going to head to the park and hit a few balls with the boys, grab them all and bring them home for dinner in an hour. How's that?"

"Fine. But come home if you don't feel well. And tell them not to pound on the stairs when they come home—it sounds like a pack of animals stampeding!"

"Sure." He paused. "How do *you* feel?"

"Good. Tired. Fat." She let Abe take her in his arms. "A new baby will be good for us," she told him. "I read in a magazine that having babies keeps women young."

Abe was skeptical. "Yeah? What did it say about men? Because all this is making *me* old."

She pulled away and shook her fist at him in mock frustration. "Go to the park already! Go to your pack of animals!"

Abe blew her a kiss and shut the door behind him. He felt like he could breathe again. He wondered if he should tell the boys the news at the park. No, better to do it with Helen at dinner. He'd wait.

Chapter 6

MORT

Mort's sandwich sat on top of a brown paper bag on his desk, uneaten. He wasn't happy. Something was off with the collections for last month, and he was going through the orders one by one until the numbers made sense to him. He had been at it for several hours already, and he was getting frustrated. *Why am I the only one who pays attention to this?* He knew Abe took care of sales and handled the guys in the warehouse. But as far as Mort was concerned, none of that was business. That was just hand-holding and schmoozing. The only thing that really mattered was the numbers. If the numbers didn't make sense, the business didn't make sense.

Mort sharpened his pencil and took down a different book from the shelf on his wall. Mort and Abe had adjacent offices in the back left corner of their building. They were windowless, sparsely furnished and identical in size and shape. But that was where the similarities ended.

For one thing, Mort's office door was kept closed at all times. His desk, bare except for a single black-and-white photo of Rose on their wedding day, was pushed against the far wall. When Mort sat down, he faced the wall with his back to the door. This position suited him best and provided the least amount of distraction.

In contrast, Abe's office was a hodgepodge of clutter and inefficiency. Mort couldn't understand how Abe got any work done there, with his desk smack in the center of the room, facing an open door all day long. Abe's desk was so littered with photos of Helen and the boys that there was barely room for the phone. Plus, Abe never threw anything away, so every card he had ever received was either on the desk, taped to the wall or in a pile on the floor in the corner. Mort considered the ever-growing pile a fire hazard.

He was going over the numbers again when someone knocked. Abe poked his head in the doorway, still chewing the remains of his lunch.

"Mort—we've got a meeting tomorrow morning. Bob Sherman set it up for us." Bob Sherman, a name Mort hadn't heard in years, was their father's old friend. "Bob met somebody in Philly, guy making breakfast cereal." Mort was still absorbed in the pages of his ledger.

"Mmm," he muttered. He had just found the error he had been looking for all morning. He wasn't surprised: Abe had given one of the buyers a discount and had forgotten to record it.

"This is a big meeting. Could you maybe look at me for a minute?"

Mort forced himself to look at Abe. "What's so important about this guy?"

"What's so important is that he's the king of breakfast cereal. Cornflakes, wheat puffs, all that stuff."

"Cereal tastes like sawdust."

"You don't have to *eat* it, for Chrissake! This guy wants us to *package* it."

"Hmm?" Mort had already lost interest in the conversation, his eyes naturally drifting back down to the comfort of the numbers on his desk.

"In cardboard boxes, Mort! Millions of boxes! And the guy needs a new supplier."

Mort was unimpressed. "We don't make boxes for that."

"We can make anything! We make shirt boxes for the laundries now. Why not cereal boxes?"

"I suppose."

"You *suppose*? Mort, do you have any idea how big this could be? How much business we could get from this guy?"

Reluctantly, Mort put down his pencil. He was used to Abe's

enthusiasm, the way he wound himself up over every new client and every new deal. But Mort could never connect with it. He was immune. It had been the same when they were boys. Being the older brother, and the one with more playmates, Abe was always the first to catch any childhood illnesses. Their mother's policy was that if Abe caught something, Mort should be exposed as quickly as possible in order to get the whole thing over with. She had learned this strategy from her own mother, who swore by it. Somehow it never seemed to work with Abe and Mort. When Abe got the chicken pox, their mother forced Mort to sleep in the same bed with Abe. But Mort never got the chicken pox, and he was still resistant to Abe's optimism.

"Listen, I know you don't like meetings, but we both need to meet this guy. He deals with big-time suppliers. What if he asks how many boxes we can get to him every week or how much the monthly shipping is gonna be on this?" Abe's speech was coming faster as he reeled off the issues.

"You don't need me for that. You give buyers quotes for those things all the time."

"Yeah, but not with this kind of volume. These are gonna be big, big numbers." Abe was pacing fretfully around Mort's small office now, pointing at the ledger books and the adding machine to make his point.

"So? Bigger numbers just have more zeroes. They're still just numbers. Don't worry so much."

"Don't worry about the numbers? That's a good one, coming from you!" Abe gave Mort a friendly punch to the shoulder.

Mort rubbed his shoulder and frowned. "You really don't need me for this. You'll be fine on your own." He bent his head back down over his book.

"Come on, Mort. You know I wouldn't ask if I didn't need you. The sign on the building says, 'Box Brothers,' and this guy wants to meet us both." There was only one chair in Mort's office and Mort was sitting in it, so Abe sat down on the corner of Mort's desk. After a few moments Abe put one hand on his brother's shoulder. "Nine-thirty tomorrow. Please?" Mort nodded silently, never looking up. Abe left the office and closed the door behind him.

Abe hadn't asked him to go to a client meeting in years, so Mort knew it was important. It might actually be the watershed deal his brother always seemed to be looking for. It wasn't that the company was doing badly—their numbers were in good shape. But Abe was always looking for the next big thing.

Their father had been the same way. People always needed boxes, he told them. When people are rich they bring home whatever they buy in them, and when people are poor, they use them to carry out whatever they have left. Before the war, boxes had been everywhere, hollow reminders of disposability and eviction. Some people even wound up sleeping in them. And once the war started, well, Mort wouldn't admit it to Abe, but he suspected the business had saved both of them from conscription. Sure, Abe had his heart murmur, and they were both on the older side, but running a company that employed a dozen guys, all sole earners for their families, had to have helped.

Their father always told them that the people getting rich weren't the guys making boxes. They were the guys making the stuff to put in them. But Mort thought maybe his father had underestimated their product. A box could be hopeful, couldn't it? A box filled with something useful, even tasteless flakes, could be important and maybe even make the box makers rich. Mort sighed. It would be a lot of work. And of course, it could only happen if someone paid close attention to the numbers.

Chapter 7

ROSE

Rose felt strangely off balance for the next few weeks. Mort was paying a good deal of attention to her, and she wasn't used to it. His interest unsettled her, and she couldn't concentrate on her daily tasks.

Before Mort, the only man in Rose's life had been her father—a man who never wasted time on frivolous praise or affection. That was the only kind of man Rose knew. Rose's father didn't tell her she was pretty or intelligent because he *knew* she was both, and he found it unnecessary to make it a topic of conversation.

When Rose met Mort, she saw in him a younger version of her father. Familiarity bred a certain fondness. But there was something else, something that drew her to Mort in spite of his overwhelming need for self-control and efficiency, and that was the effect she seemed to have on him.

True, he did not shower her with flowery compliments or romantic gestures, but when she walked into a room, he could not hide his admiration. He was the first man to tell her she was beautiful, and though his voice reminded her ever so slightly of the tone her pediatrician used whenever he made a diagnosis, the compliment was praise in its most sincere form. If Mort took the time to say it, she knew that he believed it.

And then there was the way the color rose in his cheeks every time she came near him. His emotional restraint, so visible in all other areas of his life, seemed to crumble before her. When he held her hand, she could feel it. When he kissed her, she knew. His desire for her was palpable, as real as any number in his ledger books. The fact that he could not control it endeared him to her immeasurably. When he told her he loved her, she knew she loved him too. Their wedding, though modest, was the happiest day of her life.

Things began to change only after they had children. As soon as Rose became pregnant, Mort was clear about his preferences. Abe already had a boy, and Mort wanted one too. Did she think that's what they were having? Wouldn't the doctor have some idea? Mort became increasingly frustrated with Rose's lack of certainty and her inability to decipher the contents of her own womb. When Judith was born, he was clearly disappointed. When Mimi came along, he was despondent. And when he first saw Dinah, swaddled in a pink hospital blanket, he told Rose she was their last. With every daughter she bore, he seemed to desire her less, and he was a little less kind. Over the years, she had grown used to the lack of interest he showed in both her and the girls.

But the past few weeks had been different. Mort called every afternoon to ask how she was feeling. When he took her hand, she felt the same warm tingle she used to feel when they were dating. One night he took the girls for an unprecedented after-dinner walk to the corner candy store. His attention confused her, and she could not get used to it.

Mort's reaction to the news of her pregnancy had surprised her. She had been prepared for hostility, confusion, and silence most of all. Her conversation with Helen had subdued her anxiety, but she still wished there was some way she could avoid the subject for a few more weeks. She knew, however, that once she revealed her secret to Helen, she was obligated to tell her husband. She told him that very evening, as soon as he returned home from work, almost before he was fully through the doorway. With both eyes and hands absorbed in dinner preparations, she mumbled the news in a voice slightly louder than a whisper. Silence followed, and she was afraid to turn around. Her fears were confirmed when she heard Mort leave the room. She took the roast out of the oven and placed the pan on the stove.

When she finally did turn around, Mort was walking back into the kitchen with all three girls. He was speaking in a loud, cheerful voice and smiling. "Girls," he said, "your mother has some news for you." Rose cleared her throat and told them about the baby. Cheers came first, followed by the predictable bickering over who was going to hold the baby first and who was going to be best at feeding and diapering. "You will *all* have a turn to help with him," Mort had told them.

This morning had brought the biggest surprise of all. Rose had walked to the front door with Mort's suit jacket to help him on with it—something she had done every morning of their marriage. Usually he kept his back to her, buttoned the jacket up and left. But this morning, he had turned toward her after slipping his left arm into his sleeve. He turned so gracefully that Rose had actually imagined him for a moment as a dancer on a stage, moving toward her with effortless purpose. And at the end of his turn, this nimble stranger had slipped his left arm around her waist, taken her unsuspecting cheek sweetly in his other hand and kissed her lips goodbye.

So unexpected was the combination of embrace and kiss, so tender the touch on her cheek, that when he was safely down the street and the girls off to the park, Rose sat down at her kitchen table, put her head down on the worn wooden top and cried. It started with a few tears—she had a lot to do that morning and she was determined not to think too much about Mort's behavior. But as she sat, she found she could not stop. Tears streamed out of her as if she were a confused child, with no warning, and seemingly no end to their torrent. What had just happened? As she sat there wondering and rubbing her apron over her eyes, a quick knock came at the door. It was Helen.

"Rose! Are you home? I have no raisins left and I need some for my strudel. Can I borrow some raisins?" Rose stood up from her chair—the door was unlocked and Helen was entering the kitchen. When Helen saw Rose's swollen eyes, she gasped. "What's wrong? Oh my God, Rose, what is it? Is it the baby?" Rose shook her head no, and Helen took a deep breath. "What, then? Oh honey, what's wrong?"

Rose wiped her tears with the back of her hand. "I'm fine," she murmured. "Here, let me find the raisins." But Helen would not let it drop. She grabbed Rose's hand before she could slip away.

"Is it Mort?"

"Oh Helen." Rose hesitated. She was embarrassed to speak of it, to admit that the smallest affectionate gesture from her husband had been so surprising that it had moved her to tears.

"He . . . he kissed me. He held my cheek. He looked at me like he used to, the way he did when we were young."

"Ohhh," said Helen. "I see." She tried to hide her surprise. "Why don't you send the girls up to us for dinner tonight? You and Mort can have some time to yourselves."

Rose couldn't remember the last time she had looked forward to time alone with Mort, but now she didn't hesitate. "All right," she said.

She spent the remainder of the afternoon preparing for dinner. She didn't want to send the girls upstairs empty-handed, so she decided to bake something for them to take. It was so nice to bake whenever she wanted now, without having to worry about cards and rations. As she pulled the flour canister out from behind her spice rack, it toppled over and the lid popped off. Flour poured out onto the counter and floor, leaving a cloud of snowy dust hanging in the air. Rose frowned and took out the broom.

Once the cake was in the oven, Rose tried to come up with something special to make Mort for dinner. What was his favorite dish? She honestly couldn't think of one. Her husband never seemed to care much about food. Not like Abe, who was always asking for seconds. She envied Helen's easy manner with Abe, how he grabbed Helen around her waist by the stove and hummed in her ear when she stirred something. No wonder Helen was such a good cook.

In the end Rose decided on a chicken dish, one she learned how to make from her mother, with dried apricots and marmalade. "A little sweet to sweeten his disposition" her mother used to say when she cooked this chicken for Rose's father. Maybe it would work for Rose too.

"You're being ridiculous," she whispered to herself. Mort had been her husband for thirteen years, and she had eaten dinner with him almost every night of their marriage. Why was she so excited? She hoped the evening would go well. She hoped it would be different from the thousands of dinners that had come before it. Because if this dinner was the same, if the promise of the morning's kiss was lost, the hope she carried would scatter and disappear, like the last puff of flour she had swept off the floor.

Chapter 8

MORT

(September 1947)

Ever since Rose told him she was expecting their fourth child, Mort had been bargaining with God. Somewhere in the dusty bottom drawer of his consciousness, he knew he had not been an attentive father or a loving husband. He knew he had failed. In the quiet of the night, with Rose sleeping beside him, he counted his sins as only a man obsessed with numbers could. He recorded each unkind remark, intentional slight and frown in imaginary columns, tallied the totals and found himself wholly in the red.

Mort's vision of God was the punitive Old Testament righter of wrongs. He convinced himself that with good behavior (as well as good bookkeeping), he could balance his divine account statement and show a profit of virtue. A successful son to carry on his name and his business would be his reward.

So Mort took up the task at hand. He brought his daughters on walks to the candy store. He complimented his wife the way he used to when they were first dating. One morning, as Rose helped him on with his jacket, he decided to kiss her goodbye. As he turned to her, the look of utter disbelief on her face shamed him. He reached out to take her cheek in his hand. It was soft, velvety, like the outside of a peach. For a moment, he forgot about his nighttime tally and breathed in the scent of her.

As the weeks went by, Mort decided it was easier to keep track if he assigned point values to specific actions. He fell into a nightly ritual of calculating his credits and debits, the good deeds and the bad, and silently congratulated himself as his column of virtuous living out-valued the row of unkind words and selfish actions that had so recently defined him.

In his quest to boost his quota, Mort had agreed to an unprecedented outing with Abe's family. The two families spent a lot of time together, but they rarely socialized outside their home. Mort was frustrated. Wasn't it enough that he worked with Abe every day and spent every holiday with his family? Wasn't it enough that he could hear Abe's sons pounding overhead all day long? He had to go out with them on a Sunday too? But saying no for such selfish reasons would compromise his numbers so, reluctantly, he agreed.

Helen had invited them to dinner at a restaurant in Manhattan, courtesy of her older brother Sol. Sol was the proprietor of a candy stand located in the lobby of a large office building on East Thirty-eighth Street. He sold candy bars, newspapers, cigarettes and cigars. Sol also had a notary license and was happy to provide his official stamp for anyone in the building seeking his services. This tidy enterprise earned him a respectable living. But Sol made his real money as a bookie. In the morning, a customer might slip him an extra twenty-dollar bill while paying for a newspaper to place a bet on a boxing match. An afternoon chocolate bar was an excuse to pick a winner in baseball. No one questioned the monetary exchanges or the visits to Sol's stand. Someone paying close attention might have noticed that Sol rarely had to make change for his customers. But if anyone noticed, it never came up. It was the perfect front.

Though he was older than Helen, Sol had married for the first time only a few years ago. His son, Johnny, was two, and lived on a steady diet of chocolate bars and Sugar Daddy caramel pops. Mort thought Sol should take bets on when Johnny would lose all his teeth.

To Mort's way of thinking, Sol's activities were clearly illegal. But Helen adored her brother and forbade anyone from talking about Sol's side business. It was one of Sol's customers, however, who presented the reason for their upcoming excursion.

This particular customer owned an elegant Italian restaurant near the office building and found himself in debt to Sol after getting some bad tips on a horse. Rather than shell out the cash, he invited Sol for dinner at the restaurant. Sol graciously accepted. Knowing the size of the debt, he figured he'd be eating lunch there for a month if he went alone, so he invited Helen and her boys for dinner, and told her Mort's family should come as well.

The girls squealed when Rose told them about the invitation. Dinner at a fancy restaurant! In Manhattan!

"Can we go? Can we?" pleaded Mimi.

Eight pairs of eyes turned to Mort for approval. His initial reaction was to shake his head no. But he nodded his approval instead.

"Will we get to take the subway?" Judith asked her father, obviously excited at the prospect.

"I suppose so," Mort said. He tried to smile. He noted, with satisfaction, that it was his third smile of the day.

"Mommy says the restaurant will be very pretty and everyone will be dressed up. I'm going to wear my best dress and my pink hair ribbon and I'm going to carry my purse!" Mimi spun around as she described the details of her outfit.

Dinah giggled and spun around as well. She approached Mort cautiously, and he patted her on the head.

"Time for bed now," he declared.

As he got into his own bed that evening, Mort began to regret the process he had undertaken. It was only getting harder. The more interested he pretended to be in people, the more they expected from him. A smile one day led to an anticipated "good morning" the next. Just yesterday at work, his warehouse manager, Tom, had cornered him on his way out and asked him what his weekend plans were. Mort was offended. Tom had clearly mistaken his quiet "hello" at the coffee machine a few days earlier as an invitation to discuss all kinds of personal matters. Where would it end? At the rate he was going, he'd end up wasting half his workday with pleasantries and chitchat. The final straw was the dinner with Abe's family. It was too much. Tomorrow, he'd tell them they weren't going.

"Mort?" Rose turned on her side to face him and touched his arm. "Are you asleep?"

"No, I'm awake."

"Thank you for letting us go to the restaurant tomorrow. I know you're not a big fan of Sol, but the girls are so excited. I think we'll all have a wonderful time."

"Well, at least it won't cost us anything," he conceded.

Rose took his hand in the darkness and brought it to her face, where his fingers felt the yielding smoothness of her cheek. Next, she brought the hand to her mouth and kissed it, not just once, but twice, so that a sudden longing overcame him. By the time he kissed her lips and she wrapped her arms around him, he was awash in satisfaction, his nighttime tally long forgotten.

Chapter 9

HELEN

Helen was sitting on the edge of her bed, looking at the two dresses she had set out. One was the blue dress she had worn to Harry's bar mitzvah, and the other was a black three-quarter-sleeve dress she had last worn when she was pregnant with the twins. She loved the first dress, with its soft chiffon skirt and flowing sleeves. She picked it up off the bed, walked over to the full-length mirror that was tucked in the corner of the bedroom and held it up in front of her. Just thinking about squeezing into it made her tired. She would never be able to get it over her hips, let alone zip it up.

She put the blue dress back in the tiny closet and turned to the black one. Helen had given away her other maternity dresses years ago, but she had saved this one because it had been her favorite at the time. "Some favorite," she murmured to herself. It was a dull, tent-like affair in simple black silk, but at least she'd be able to breathe in it. "Looks like it's you and me tonight," she said to the dress. She had run out of lipstick again and decided to walk over to the drugstore before she started to get the boys ready. She was sure she would have to send Abe to the park to round them up. They would never remember to come home in time to clean up.

"Abe!" She called into the living room, where Abe was lying half asleep on the couch, his face covered by the sports section of the newspaper.

"Humm?" He pretended to be awake.

"I'm running down to the corner for some lipstick. I'll be back in half an hour, and then you're going to have to get the boys from the park."

"Mmmm," he mumbled. The paper dropped to the floor and he snored. She would have to wake him later.

When Helen got to the bottom of the steps, she knocked on Rose's door. She wanted to see whether Rose needed anything from the drugstore. Plus, she could use some company. Abe had been asleep for most of the afternoon, and the boys had been at the park all day. She was tired of talking to herself.

Mimi opened the door with her hair pinned up in curlers. She was already wearing her dress for the restaurant, a pink flowered print with smocking on the front.

"Mimi! Don't you look beautiful!"

Mimi nodded as if the observation were a question. "I've been ready since this morning. Mommy made me take off my dress to eat lunch, but I put it back on after. I had to eat lunch in my bathrobe. See my ribbon?" She twirled around so Helen could see the back of her dress, tied in a perfect symmetrical bow.

"Very nice." Helen took a seat on one of the kitchen chairs.

"I can't sit down because I don't want to ruin it. It took three tries to get it just right." She pointed to the curlers in her hair "I'm keeping these in my hair until the very last minute so my curls will be nice and bouncy."

"I'm sure they'll be perfect."

Mimi went to give her aunt a hug but stopped when she remembered her dress. Helen understood. "I'll be careful not to wrinkle you." She breathed in Mimi's little-girl fragrance, all lilacs and peppermint instead of the dirt and sweat her boys always smelled of. The boys hardly ever let her hug them now, and if they did it was only if they were bleeding. Forget about trying to keep them clean. Helen tried to imagine what would happen if she had asked Sam, Joe or George to put on a suit and tie that morning. By now, the jackets would be lost, the shirts would be ripped and the ties would be hanging from a tree branch somewhere.

The boys tired her out more than usual these days. The younger three traveled as a pack, in constant and careless motion. They rarely spoke to her, and if they did, it was all at once and usually because they wanted to be fed. Harry barely looked at her. Most days she felt less like a mother and more like a lonely zookeeper working overtime.

She hugged Mimi a minute too long, letting her go only when Dinah teetered into the room in Rose's heels. The five-year-old held out her wrists for inspection. "Smell!" she ordered.

"Did you use the big yellow perfume bottle or the small clear one?" Mimi asked.

"The little one."

"What! She never lets *me* use that one! *Mommy!*" Mimi was already running out of the kitchen to find Rose. In the meantime, Helen rubbed noses with Dinah. "Are you excited for dinner tonight?" Dinah nodded, then rested her head against Helen's shoulder. She let out a yawn. "If I'm good, I get to have dessert," she whispered.

Helen leaned back against her chair, repositioning Dinah on her lap so they were both comfortable.

A few minutes later, Rose came into the room apologizing. "Mimi just told me you were here—she was so worked up about my perfume that she didn't even mention you came in." Helen scooted Dinah off of her lap and stood up.

"I'm out of lipstick again." Helen frowned. "Everything is swelling. Even my lips! Anyway, I'm running to the drugstore. Need anything?"

"Would you mind taking Judith with you?" Rose lowered her voice. "I think she could use a little air." Helen gave Rose a puzzled look, but it wasn't the right time to say more. "Sure. I'd love some company."

"Judith! Come here!" Rose called.

Judith answered from her bedroom, "I'm reading!"

"I need you to get me some aspirin!"

A few minutes later Judith appeared, cheeks red and eyes swollen. She had been crying.

"Hi, honey," Helen said. "Ready to walk me to the drugstore?"

Judith managed a small smile. "Sure, Aunt Helen."

"Let's go then." The two of them walked out of the house into the crisp September air. Judith was silent, busily picking at a stray thread on her sleeve. She was a full year younger than Harry, but to Helen she was more mature by far.

Helen had a soft spot for Judith, maybe because she was the daughter who always seemed to bear the brunt of Mort's disapproval. Mimi and Dinah were more spirited girls, not as easily flattened by Mort's moods.

When Judith was ten, she had won the poetry award at her elementary school's end-of-year picnic. Helen and Rose had set up their blankets next to each other on the field. Helen still remembered what they brought for lunch that day: her cold fried chicken, Rose's potato salad, homemade cookies and thermoses of iced tea. Helen had felt sorry for the family next to them with their limp tuna sandwiches. After eating, the boys ran off to play kickball, and Dinah followed Mimi to a patch of blacktop where she was playing jacks with some girls from her class. Only Judith remained on the blanket with them, reading one of her books. Rose looked to Helen for reassurance. She's fine, Helen had mouthed, but she could tell Rose was worried.

After all the families had finished eating, the principal walked to the front of the school, where a makeshift podium was set up. The time had come for the awarding of prizes.

The science prize had gone to two fifth-graders for their experiment on tomato plants. The physical education prize went to Benjamin Wareham, for the third year in a row. By the time they got around to the poetry prize, most people had stopped paying attention. When Judith's name was announced, Helen was already packing up their leftovers.

Judith hadn't known about the award beforehand, so when her English teacher asked her to recite the poem she wrote, Judith looked nervous. After a few moments, however, she cleared her throat and began:

> *A friend is like a shining star*
> *That sparkles in the sky.*
> *A friend that's good and kind is like*
> *A twinkle in your eye.*
>
> *But when a friend betrays your trust*
> *The shining light goes dark,*
> *And sadness dims what once was bright*
> *Like water on a spark.*

I told a friend my secret.
My heart was open wide,
Just like a fragile seashell
That shows the pearl inside.

My friend picked up the seashell
She took the pearl in hand.
And once she had possessed it,
She strung it on a strand.

She wore the pearl around her neck
And everyone could see.
She did not keep my secret.
She was no friend to me.

The crowd clapped politely, but they were clearly surprised by the severity of the poem. People were expecting something simpler from a ten-year-old girl—something about rainbows or butterflies. Not Helen. She was impressed.

"I don't get it," said Harry, and Helen had glared at him.

When Judith returned to the blanket with her certificate, the first one she showed it to was Mort. "Very nice," he said blandly.

"Mrs. Curtis said I have a real way with words, and that my imagery is extremely vivid. She said I'm the best writer in the class."

"Who's the best at math?" Mort asked. Rose sucked in her breath, and Judith's smile shriveled. She dropped her certificate on the grass and ran. Rose went after her. The rest of them gathered their things and walked home in silence.

More than two years had gone by since the picnic, but Helen worried that Mort and Judith would always have a strained relationship.

"So, are you excited to go to the restaurant tonight?" Helen asked. She was trying to walk carefully on the uneven sidewalk. The air smelled like onions and potatoes from the knish cart on the corner.

Judith would have preferred to stay at home, but she knew it was Helen's brother who had invited them. "It should be fun," she said. "Mimi and Dinah can't stop talking about it. Especially Mimi."

"I can tell. Did she wear that dress to bed last night?"

Judith played along with the joke. "Nah, that would have wrinkled it." They walked a little longer.

When they got to the drugstore, the bell on the door announced their arrival. "Hi, Mrs. Feldman," Helen called to the woman behind the counter. Helen pulled Judith toward the cosmetics section and grabbed a sample from the counter display. "How's this one?" she asked.

"Too orange."

"This one?"

Judith's eyes widened, and she started to laugh. "It's horrible!" She looked over the choices and handed a different tube to her aunt. "Try this."

Helen gave the tube a twist, put some on her lips and looked in the tiny hand mirror. "Perfect! You can pick my lipstick anytime." She winked at Judith. "Should we pick one for you?" Judith shook her head. "I'd rather have a candy bar."

"Two Hershey bars, one bottle of aspirin and this lipstick, please, Mrs. Feldman," Judith said, piling their items by the cash register.

They walked home together, nibbling on their chocolate bars.

Helen had to ask, "Do you want to tell me why you were crying?"

"It was nothing. Just something about my book. I'm reading a biography of Amelia Earhart."

"Did the ending upset you?"

"I already knew what happened to her. It's just . . . my father didn't like it."

"A biography of Amelia Earhart? What didn't he like?"

Judith sniffed. She was trying not to cry, and her voice was shaking. "He said something about how she had her head in the clouds and look where that got her and how I'd better get my head out of the clouds too."

"Oh honey." Helen squeezed Judith's hand.

"He's just so *mean* sometimes." Judith wiped the tears from her cheeks on her sleeve.

"It's all right. Shhh." Helen patted her back. "We're going to have a nice time tonight—you'll sit next to me." When they got back to the house Helen offered some advice. "When you get inside, take a few tea bags from the kitchen and run them under the faucet. Lie down on your bed and put them on your eyes. They'll take the puffiness away."

"Thanks, Aunt Helen."

"Thank *you* for keeping me company and helping me with the lipstick. You made my day."

"Really?" Judith was surprised.

"Really. It gets pretty lonely upstairs sometimes."

"But whenever I hear you and the boys upstairs, it sounds like you're having so much fun."

"Well, it isn't always a party, believe me. I don't have anybody to talk to up there most of the time. The boys aren't much for talking these days."

Judith nodded as if she understood. She looked down at her candy wrapper.

"You can always talk to me. I mean, if you want."

Helen was touched. "Thanks, sweetheart. I'm going to take you up on that."

By the time she made it up the stairs to her own front door, Helen knew several things she hadn't known half an hour earlier. On the way down the steps, she hadn't realized how alone she had felt or how often that feeling of isolation crept into her days. She hadn't recognized that the tasks that drove her routine had taken over and that the best parts of being a mother—the connection, the companionship—had been missing. As she stood before her door, she knew that she wanted a girl not only because of the clothes she could dress her in or the ribbons she could put in her hair. She wanted someone to laugh with, someone who could cry to her, someone she could comfort and understand. She yearned for a daughter for reasons she had not previously been able to explain. And now that she had the words to express her longing, she knew it would only be more difficult to ignore.

Chapter 10

HELEN

As they walked into the restaurant, Helen was still wondering how she had managed to get the boys ready on time. It was all a blur. Even now they were bickering and shoving each other on the sidewalk. It was only when they pushed through the heavy wooden door and stepped onto the plush green carpet of the restaurant foyer that they were silenced. The light was soothingly dim, and candles left gentle shadows on the mahogany wall panels. A large crystal chandelier hung directly overhead. Harry whistled softly. "Nice," he said. "Think I could bring Susan here?"

"Absolutely not," said Helen.

Sol was waiting for them in the foyer, looking sharp as always. Dark silk suit, hair combed back and nails buffed to a shine that left Helen mildly annoyed. He takes better care of himself than I do myself, she thought. Then again, she wasn't the type of woman who kept up any real beauty routine.

Sol's wife, on the other hand, was exactly that type. Despite a few extra pounds, Arlene looked as eye-catching as ever, in a copper sheath dress that matched her freshly colored hair. She insisted on kissing all of the boys, leaving traces of lipstick on each of their cheeks that closely resembled the shade Judith had warned Helen against in the drugstore.

Rose and Mort entered the restaurant a few minutes later. Mimi's curls were intact, and Judith's eyes had lost their puffiness. Dinah looked tired and couldn't stop staring at the chandelier. Soon all of the girls had Arlene's lipstick on their cheeks as well.

When the maître d' appeared, Sol walked forward and took the man's outstretched hand in both of his own. "We're here for Gino. Just tell him Sol is here with his family." Gino, a short, heavy man in a shiny tuxedo, appeared almost instantly. "Welcome!" he panted, slightly out of breath. Gino gripped Sol in a tight embrace. "And this," he said, turning to Arlene, "must be your lovely wife."

Sol beamed. "This is my Arlene." She gave Gino a smile and held out her hand enthusiastically. Arlene loved meeting new people, even when she had no idea what to say to them.

"Wonderful! But where is little Johnny?" asked Gino. "I told you to bring your whole family!"

"Johnny's still too young for all this. But I brought some other special people." He gestured, and Abe stepped forward to shake Gino's hand. "Beautiful place you have here," he said. Gino smiled and his eyes took a quick count of their party. He blinked for a second longer than normal. His cheeks grew red. "You have a large family."

"Well, Gino," said Sol, "you did say to bring the whole family. I hope it won't be a problem."

Gino cleared his throat and adjusted his bow tie. "Of course not! A big family is a blessing! Welcome, all of you!" He took the maître d' aside, whispered in his ear and practically pushed him through the double glass doors into the dining room.

"My friends, the waiters are setting up a special table for you. The best table in the house!" He led them to a long table set up at the very center of the dining room. The eyes of all the other diners were on them as they crossed the floor. Helen felt like a celebrity. Only Sol can do this, she thought. He just waltzes in and takes over.

When Helen and Sol were young, their grandmother used to come over every Friday after school to watch them. It was the day their mother got her hair done and ran her errands. In the summer when they had no school, their grandmother came on Friday mornings, right after breakfast. On her way, she stopped at Gus's Deli to pick up bologna, water rolls and a small chocolate cake. Helen hated bologna, and every Friday she hid as many slices as she could in her napkin.

When the lunch plates were cleared, Helen's grandmother would bring out the miniature cake box from Gus's. Every Friday she would put the box on the table in front of Sol. Every Friday she would say, "I got this cake especially for you, darling." And every Friday she'd say to Helen, "Of course, it's for you too."

The cake was small, more like an oversized cupcake, perfect for two children to share. Thick chocolate icing held it together, and chocolate sprinkles were scattered on the top. An unnaturally red and shiny candied cherry topped it off.

Every Friday, Sol would call dibs on the cherry, and every Friday, Helen would protest. Every Friday, Helen's grandmother would feign surprise, and every Friday, she'd say the same thing: "Helen, just give it to your brother. It's only a cherry. You can have it next week." After years of Fridays, Helen learned the lesson.

Their table at the restaurant was set with a heavy white linen cloth, flawlessly pressed. Red roses, open to bursting, were in the center. Sol took the spot at the head, with Arlene on his right and Helen on his left. Mort sat next to Arlene, followed by Rose. "Wait," said Helen, remembering her earlier promise. "I'll move down one. Judith, sweetheart, sit here between me and Sol."

Rose was irritated. "Judith should sit here, next to me."

Judith, caught in the middle, stood perfectly still. "Aunt Helen said I could sit next to her tonight," she said.

"Well, *Aunt Helen* doesn't decide where you sit," Rose snapped.

Helen tried to explain. "I told her on our walk today that we could sit together tonight."

Mort spoke up: "I don't want my daughter sitting next to some—"

"Mort!" Rose interrupted before he could say more. "Judith, come sit here. Now."

"Sit next to your mother, sweetheart," Helen whispered, as she moved over and ushered Abe to take the chair on her left. Judith took her place next to Rose, directly across from Harry, who immediately passed her the breadbasket. "The rolls are really good," he said. He was trying to be kind, but Judith was too embarrassed to reply.

Sol was busy lighting a cigarette for Arlene. He was so attentive to his wife that he barely noticed the spat over Judith's seat. When the waiter arrived, Sol ordered scotches for himself, Abe and Mort, and a bottle of champagne for the ladies.

"I don't drink scotch," Mort said, but Sol hadn't heard. He was too busy making sure Arlene could reach the butter for her roll.

"Who do you like in the Dodgers-Phillies game tomorrow?" asked Abe cheerfully.

Sol took a sip of the scotch that had just arrived. "Don Newcombe is one of the best pitchers in the league. Hank Bowery doesn't stand a chance against him. The Dodgers will take them tomorrow for sure."

"I don't think so," piped up Joe from the far end of the table.

"Oh yeah? You don't like the Dodgers?" Sol's interest was piqued.

"They're my favorite team! But I heard Newcombe's got a bum arm. That's why he only pitched one inning in Thursday's game."

"Oh yeah? Where'd you hear that?"

Joe shrugged, "I've got my sources," he said.

Sol laughed. "Did you hear this one?" he said to Arlene. She nodded and sipped her glass of champagne. "He's got *sources.*"

"He's adorable," Arlene told Helen.

"Joe knows a lot about baseball, Uncle Sol," said Sam solemnly.

"Yeah, plus he's got the best baseball card collection in our whole grade," affirmed George.

"Well, Joe," said Sol, "if you're so sure about the game, how 'bout you and I make a little wager?"

"Sol!" warned Helen. "Don't."

Sol held up his hands. "Calm down, calm down, I was only kidding."

"See?" Mort said to Rose, loud enough for Helen to hear. "Do you see what kind of a person he is?"

Abe jumped in: "No one's making any bets. But if I were you, Sol, I wouldn't bet against Joe when it comes to baseball."

Sol smiled. "You wouldn't, huh? Well, Joe, maybe you'll come work for your uncle Sol one day."

"God forbid!" said Mort.

"What did you say?" Sol was agitated now.

"Slow down," said Abe. "Mort just means the boys will work at Box Brothers one day. Just like you'll have Johnny to take over *your* business."

"I want to work in the family business too," interrupted Mimi. "Can I?" she turned to her mother for an answer. Rose just put her finger over her lips. "Shh."

Sol tried to be conciliatory. He held up his scotch glass and made a toast. "To family." He turned to Rose and Helen. "May your new children be happy and healthy."

Sol swallowed his drink, and Mort downed his as well. "I thought you said you didn't like scotch," Helen said.

"I don't," he admitted. "But it's bad luck not to drink when someone makes a toast."

Luckily, Gino arrived then, distracting them all with the menus. Sol handed his back to Gino without even opening it. "Bring us whatever you think we'll like, Gino. You choose for us." Gino made a small bow and collected the menus back from everyone. "It would be my pleasure."

It was a good time for a visit to the ladies' room, so Helen excused herself and left the table. *Why was everything going so wrong?*

When Helen came out of the stall, Rose was sitting at the vanity table, waiting for her.

"Helen, I'm sorry. We shouldn't have come. Mort gets . . . uneasy around Sol. I knew he wouldn't want Judith to sit next to him."

"It's fine," said Helen. "You know Sol just likes to joke. He would never say anything inappropriate with Judith sitting next to him."

"I know," said Rose, though she didn't sound convinced. It bothered Helen that Rose so obviously disapproved of her brother. She knew Mort did, but that was different; Mort disapproved of almost everyone.

"We should get back," Rose said, and she opened the ladies' room door for Helen. There was an awkwardness between them that hadn't been there before, and Helen was surprisingly uncomfortable. Having walked out of the ladies' room first, Helen tried to slow her pace so that Rose could catch up. But no matter how hard she tried, she was always a little bit ahead. For the first time since they had known each other, the two women were out of step.

Chapter 11

MORT

(October 1947)

After the news of Rose's pregnancy became public, Mort became increasingly annoyed with his coworkers. Most of them seemed to think he had nothing better to do with his time than to answer personal questions about Rose's condition and their family life. If it were not for his daily point quota, he would have refused to acknowledge the questions at all. But he knew what he had to do to keep the covenant he had made. It would be so much easier to be nice to people if only they would stop talking to him.

Mort tried to prepare himself as he approached the company coffeepot Monday morning. It was a place where he was often drawn into conversation, and he wanted to be ready.

"Good morning, Mort." It was Sheila, the only woman who worked at Box Brothers. Sheila answered phones and did the typing for Abe and Mort. She arrived on time and was generally pleasant and efficient. Abe referred to Sheila as a "gem." Mort felt she was adequate.

"Good morning," he responded. This was a classic one-point encounter for Mort, but the next moment was critical. He could take his coffee, keep his head down and walk back to his office. Or, he could prolong the meeting with a follow-up remark, thereby creating a multiple-point situation. It was the sort of decision Mort had come to dread. The follow-up remark was dangerous—who knew how much time he might waste if he risked it? On the other hand, the possibility of earning extra points was tempting. The weekend had not been a good one for him. He had made some unkind remarks to Judith about a book she was reading, and his weekend score had plummeted as a result. Here was an opportunity to get himself back on track.

He took a deep breath and spoke. "I hope you had a nice weekend," he said to Sheila.

As the words came out of his mouth, he congratulated himself on his phrasing. He had not made the mistake of asking the open-ended question *How* was your weekend? Through trial-and-error he had come to realize that asking open-ended questions led to long, drawn-out answers from people. The question *Did* you have a nice weekend? was slightly better (if you were lucky, you might get a quick yes or no) but still risky. In stating he *hoped* Sheila had a good weekend, Mort felt certain he had bypassed the need for Sheila to provide any answer at all. The most appropriate way to respond to such a statement, Mort felt, was to nod. Certainly no more than that was necessary.

How wrong he was! "Aren't you sweet for asking," Sheila replied. *Asking?* He had asked nothing. In fact, he had gone out of his way specifically *not* to ask. *Did no one understand grammar? Syntax? The etiquette of language?* He gritted his teeth.

"My girlfriend Pamela and I met for lunch and a matinee on Saturday. They were showing *The Red Shoes*." She sighed. "It was such a wonderful film, Mort. Just lovely. Have you seen it?" Mort shook his head. Why did she feel the need to suffocate him with the specifics of her weekend?

"No? You really should take Rose to see it one of these days. Maybe try to have a night out before the baby comes." *The baby.* There it was. He braced himself for the inevitable interrogation.

"How is Rose feeling?" *What is it about pregnancy that makes people so comfortable prying into personal matters?*

"She's fine."

"When my sister was pregnant, she was sick every day. I'm so glad Rose is having an easy pregnancy."

It might be easy for Rose, Mort thought, but it certainly isn't easy for me. He was having difficulty keeping the "smile" on his face.

The phone rang and Sheila stopped stirring her coffee. "Sorry, Mort, I have to grab that. Can't keep the customers waiting!" She was back to her desk in a flash.

Mort exhaled. He filled his coffee cup. It had taken several weeks for him to learn that if he filled his cup at the beginning of a conversation, his coffee would most likely be cold by the time he returned to his desk. Is this what office pleasantries had come to? Wasting time *and* cold coffee? He was relieved his conversation with Sheila was finally over. He would go back to his desk and decide exactly how to score it. It was lucky for him that the phone had rung when it did.

Chapter 12

ROSE

From the minute Rose got out of bed that morning, she felt changed, lighter somehow. Mort had gotten up early to go to Philadelphia with Abe, and the whole day lay ahead of her, unencumbered. Once the children were off to school, she wasn't sure what to do with herself. Mort was always gone by this time of the morning, so the day shouldn't have felt different from any other. But it did.

The first thing she realized was that she didn't have to make pot roast for dinner. It was Wednesday, and Wednesday night was pot roast night, at least according to Mort. If something else was served, or if she made pot roast on a Saturday instead, Mort would be visibly disappointed. His absence freed her of this restriction.

It came to her then, pot roast and enlightenment entwined: the reason *why* Mort's absence affected her so. She hadn't known what it was until it wasn't there. The daily dread of being judged, of being measured and found lacking in some way, no matter how small, was a burden she carried, compact and profound. It was a too-heavy purse, worn and comfortable on her shoulder, which she did not know the weight of until she set it down.

Ever since Judith was born, Rose realized, Mort had been struggling to maintain control. He could not manipulate the outcome of her pregnancies, and he could not change their daughters into sons. Faced with these setbacks, he was determined to control whatever else was left—what their girls were allowed to read, what they wore, where they went, how much affection he would show to his wife and, though it seemed trivial, even what Rose made for dinner.

Rose opened up the cabinet next to the sink and took out her mother's recipe box. The box was yellow painted tin, with black and red flowers etched onto the sides. The top was copper, faded with brown spots or stains. Some of the recipes were typed onto cards, and some were handwritten on scraps of paper. Others were just torn pieces of magazine pages, folded haphazardly and stuffed inside. None of the recipes was in any particular order, and every time Rose looked through them, she had to spend at least ten minutes searching for the one that she wanted.

That was the fun of it, though. The recipe box was the only part of her mother that Rose had left. When her mother died, Rose didn't care about the jewelry. All Rose really wanted was the box. Their mother rarely wore her earrings or necklaces, but Rose knew she had opened the recipe box almost every day. To Rose, it was her mother's touchstone, and she was certain it had absorbed a small part of her mother's essence. Sometimes, Rose talked to the box as if her mother were inside it, like a genie in a bottle.

She thumbed through the recipes, looking for something to make for the girls that night. Salmon croquettes? Too messy. Chicken Marbella? Too complicated. She remembered there were lamb chops in the freezer, but she just couldn't bring herself to defrost them.

Rose was halfway through the box when her fingertips came upon a white recipe card with frayed edges. The blue printing across the top read, "From the Kitchen of Sylvia Pelt." It was a recipe for cheese blintzes, and Rose's mouth started watering as soon as she saw it. Sylvia had been her mother's good friend.

She couldn't remember the last time she had made blintzes. They were time-consuming and complicated. Plus, Mort didn't like them. And even if he did, he certainly wouldn't approve of having them for dinner. Rose remembered one night years ago when all the girls were recovering from the flu and she had made them scrambled eggs and toast for dinner.

"What is this?" Mort had grumbled as soon as he sat down.

"Eggs. The girls don't feel well and the doctor said to give them something plain when they felt ready to eat again. Eggs and toast is the right thing for them to eat."

"Hmm."

"I'm sorry, Mort. I'll make chicken and dumplings tomorrow. It just seemed like a waste to make it today."

"No, tomorrow is pot roast night."

That was how she knew he expected certain dishes on certain days. And that breakfast food wasn't to be served for dinner. Oh, there were variations for sure. But they weren't usually successful. He would give her a look, close a door too hard or do something else to let her know he wasn't pleased.

She had to admit that Mort had been kinder lately, more attentive, caring. He was no longer indifferent to her. But it wasn't enough. Mort's efforts were because of the new baby—her biggest test yet. If she failed, she knew what it would do to him this time, and what that, in turn, would do to her. It wouldn't be like making eggs for dinner or having pot roast on the wrong night of the week. He would never forgive her. "This has to work out," she said to the recipe box. Rose tried to imagine her mother in miniature, dressed like a genie in harem pants and scarves, but all she could come up with was a vision of her in a housecoat and apron. Whatever her mother was wearing, Rose hoped she was listening. She rubbed the tin box a few times, for luck.

Chapter 13

HELEN

(December 1947)

Why did Abe have to go away today? Over the past few months Helen had grown accustomed to his new schedule of traveling to Philadelphia every two or three weeks. It wasn't so terrible—he'd stay for one night and she could get a good night's sleep without listening to his snoring. But today she wasn't happy about it. It was late December and the weathermen were saying a storm was coming. The idea of Abe driving that far in the snow made her nervous, and the whole thing was giving her heartburn. Of course, everything gave her heartburn now. She was due in less than a month, and whatever food she ate seemed to rest in her esophagus. Today was worse than usual.

Helen had terrible indigestion when she was pregnant with the twins. It intensified right before she went into labor, so that she couldn't eat anything for a few days before she gave birth. She looked up at the clock. It was 10:37. The boys had left for school a few hours ago. By now she was usually sitting at the kitchen table having a mid-morning snack. But she wasn't hungry, and the thought of eating made her queasy. She decided to bring one of the cinnamon coffee cakes she had made last night down to Rose.

When Judith answered the door instead of her sister-in-law, Helen was surprised.

"Hi, honey. Why are you home from school? Aren't you feeling okay?"

"I'm fine," said Judith. "Mom asked me to stay home. She said she didn't feel well and she didn't want to be alone. In case something happens with the baby."

Helen felt that all-too-familiar wave of jealousy again. She wasn't feeling so great either, but the idea of asking Harry or Joe to stay home with her had never even entered her mind.

"Well, I brought you a cake," she said, handing it to Judith. "I'll go say hi to your mom. Is she in her room?" she asked.

"Yes, she's lying down. She's really tired."

Rose was sitting up in bed and knitting, but she frowned when Helen came into the room. "Helen! You're supposed to be resting! What are you doing here?"

"Why didn't you call *me* this morning? I would have stayed with you."

"Yesterday you were having heartburn—I thought you'd be in bed too."

Helen laughed, but there was an edge of bitterness to it. "Who can stay in bed with the boys screaming all morning? Stay right there—I'm bringing you a slice of cake."

A few minutes later, Helen was sitting on the edge of Rose's bed watching her eat. "You're having cake and I'm not hungry," she observed. "That's a switch! There's definitely something strange going on here."

"Maybe it's the weather," Rose said. They both turned then to look out the window, where the sky was growing paler, and the snow was falling faster. When she finished the cake, Rose put the plate on her nightstand. She didn't want to think about the weather any more than Helen did. "Want to see what I'm working on?" She held up two baby blankets and matching hats. One set was pink and the other blue. Helen held out her hands for them. "They're so soft!" she said. "Oh Rose, they're beautiful. You're so smart to make one of each, just in case."

Rose didn't understand. "Just in case?"

"So you have the right color no matter what. I'm so lazy; I would have picked yellow yarn. That way, you'd only have to make one set and it works, no matter what."

"One is for you—the pink set. The blue set is for me."

Helen could tell from the look on Rose's face that she shouldn't argue. She let the issue drop. "You're nesting, that's all. Me too, only I've just been cooking like crazy. That's why I was baking coffee cakes at midnight."

Rose laughed. "Midnight!"

"Yes," Helen admitted. "I made three kugels too. I'll send one down later."

Rose squeezed Helen's hand. "Stay with me awhile, okay? I'm not feeling well again." She leaned her head back against the pillow and took a deep breath.

"Is it starting?"

"It can't be. It's too early still." Rose closed her eyes.

"Should I call the doctor? Or do you want me to call Philadelphia and see if I can leave a message for Mort and Abe? Maybe they should come back tonight?"

"No. Let's wait."

Helen looked out the window. She didn't want to tell Rose, but the wind was picking up.

She patted Rose's hand. "We'll just wait together."

Chapter 14

HELEN

The morning wore on, with both snow and pains holding steady. Rose was happy to have Helen's company, though she told her to go back upstairs after lunchtime.

"I'm fine. You should go. Nothing is happening. I think the pains have stopped."

Helen asked again about whether she should call their husbands in Philadelphia, but Rose insisted she shouldn't.

"Are you sure? What if you go into labor?"

"I won't."

"Do you want me to call the doctor at least? So he can meet you at the hospital?"

"I'm not going to the hospital *now*, Helen. I'm not due for three weeks and the girls were all late! I'm going to have a nice, normal day and I'm not going to interrupt it with expensive long-distance phone calls and hospitals. I'll be fine." Helen had never seen Rose so adamant. She was afraid to contradict her.

At three-thirty the kids came home from school. Helen opened Rose's front door and called to the boys to let them know she would be upstairs in a few minutes. The girls came inside, squealing when they saw the cinnamon cake on the counter. "Girls, your mother doesn't feel well. You have to promise me that you'll be good today. No whining and no crying. You need to help take care of her."

"Yes, Aunt Helen," they chorused.

Helen took Judith aside before she went upstairs. "If anything changes, come up and get me right away."

Judith was worried. "You don't think the baby is coming, do you?"

Helen tried to be reassuring. "Everything will be fine, honey. Your mother and I have had seven babies between the two of us. We know how to handle this. You don't need to worry."

Upstairs, a pile of schoolbags and books greeted Helen at the door. The younger boys were scavenging in the cabinets, looking for something to eat.

"We're starving! There's no food!"

"What about that bowl of apples right there?" She pointed to a yellow bowl on the table, full of Granny Smiths. "Where's Harry?"

"In his room," Sam told her. "He said he doesn't feel good."

"You boys start your homework. I'll go check on him."

"But, Mom! We want to go out in the snow first!" said Joe.

"Mrs. Connors said we're going to have a blizzard!" said Sam.

"Nonsense," Helen insisted. That was the last thing she wanted to hear. "You can go outside now but just for an hour. It'll be dark by then and I want you all back home."

"We will!"

"One hour. And put on your hats and your gloves. And your boots! It's freezing out!"

The boys rushed to find everything they needed and ran outside. Helen went to go check on Harry.

She knocked on the door of the room that Harry shared with Sam. She pushed the door open to find Harry lying on his bed. His back was to her.

"Are you sleeping?"

"Nope." Harry didn't move.

"Are you sick?"

"Nope."

Helen felt her frustration rise. She knew teenage boys weren't much for conversation but the monosyllabic responses were getting on her nerves.

"Harry, what's going on? You never lie down in the middle of the day."

He must have shrugged his shoulders, but it was hard to tell because he was lying down. "I'm going to go start on dinner. If you want to talk, I'm in the kitchen. Your brothers are out in the snow, so nobody's here except you and me." She was closing the door when Harry sat up.

"Susan broke up with me," he said. "She didn't even say why or anything. She just came over to me at the end of school with all her girlfriends and said she had to tell me something. After she told me, that new kid Robert took her books and she walked home with *him*. It was like they had the whole thing planned out. I felt like an idiot." He flung his head back on the pillow.

"Are you upset because Susan isn't your girlfriend anymore or because you feel like she made a fool of you?"

"Both. I hate how *she* got to decide what would happen. And I had no choice."

"Oh honey, I'm sorry." There were so many things Helen wanted to tell him then, things she didn't know how to explain. Like how you couldn't always be in control of your life and how so many things just *happened*, whether you wanted them to or not. She remembered feeling that way when her mother had died. There were no choices then either, except for what dress to wear to the funeral.

It wasn't just tragedy that stripped you of control, Helen wanted to explain. It was the good things too. For one, you couldn't choose who to fall in love with. Before Abe, there had been a wealthy young man from Connecticut she had met at a dance one summer, the cousin of a close family friend. He was handsome and rich, and Helen's father said that if she married *him*, her life would be easy. She knew her father was partly right, and she wanted to like the young man. But no matter what she told herself, she came home from every date lonelier than the one before. When he proposed six weeks later, Helen said no, even though the diamond he offered was ten times the size of the one she wore now. She thought of Rose downstairs, knitting baby blankets, and knew it would be the same for both of them when the babies came: you couldn't choose your children either, no matter how much wishing or knitting you were capable of.

When the phone rang, it was close to five. The boys were just returning, dripping melting snow from their coats and gloves. A trail of icy droplets followed them from the front door to the hall closet.

Helen felt better hearing Abe's voice, but she wasn't sure how much to tell him.

"Everything is fine," she said. But then she couldn't help herself. "There's a chance Rose may be having labor pains."

"What!"

"She didn't want me to tell you. It's probably too early anyway. She's not due for weeks. She doesn't want you and Mort to rush home."

"We couldn't even if we wanted to. There's a foot of snow on the ground here, and it's coming down fast. How's it up there?"

"Not too bad," she lied. "I haven't been outside."

"We're not going to be able to get out of here until tomorrow morning. What should I tell Mort?"

"Don't tell him anything. I don't want Rose to get upset with me. Hopefully nothing will happen."

"How are *you* feeling?"

"Me? I'm fine." That was her second lie. The truth was she had been feeling strange all afternoon. She hadn't been able to tolerate any food all day.

"All right. We'll leave first thing in the morning, as early as we can."

"Drive *slowly*."

"I will."

She was getting dinner ready when Mimi and Dinah knocked.

"Mommy has a stomachache," Mimi told her, "but she said you don't need to come down. Can we have dinner with you?"

"Of course! Boys! Mimi and Dinah are here!"

Helen settled the girls at the kitchen table with some paper and crayons while she finished getting dinner ready. Miraculously, George and Joe sat down to draw with them. It was a sweet domestic scene, even if it was only borrowed for the evening. By the time they were all fed and the kitchen was clean, Helen was exhausted.

So this is what it's like to feed six children, she thought. She looked up at the clock—it was a few minutes past seven. Helen told Harry she was putting him in charge while she went downstairs to check on Rose.

The terrified looked on Judith's face when she opened the door brought Helen to her senses. How could she have left Judith alone like that! For heaven's sake, the girl was only twelve years old! With new determination, Helen walked into the bedroom to confront Rose. "I'm calling the doctor now," she said. "This has gone on long enough."

This time Rose didn't argue. Her hair was wild and matted against her pillow. "All right," she said to Helen. "Call him."

Chapter 15

ROSE

When Helen came back from the kitchen into her bedroom, Rose knew something was wrong. Helen had been on the phone for twenty minutes. It was too long. Rose pulled the blanket up to her chest as far as it would go. "What did Dr. Blauner say?"

"I didn't speak to him," Helen said. "He's not on call today. They've been trying to reach him, but the storm knocked out the telephone service where he lives—on Long Island somewhere." Helen looked lost, like she didn't know where to stand in the room.

"Well, what about Dr. Lowell? Or the other one? What's his name again?"

"None of them are at the hospital. They went home early because of the storm."

Rose tried to slow her breathing. "Well, there are dozens of doctors there. I'm sure they're all good. When is the ambulance coming?"

When Helen didn't answer, Rose pushed the blankets off of her. She swung her legs over the side of the bed and headed toward the closet in the corner. Helen's silence agitated her. "I can be ready in five minutes," she jabbered. "My bag is already packed. Maybe Judith will come with me. You don't mind if Mimi and Dinah stay with you tonight?"

"Rose—"

"Do you think Judith should stay with you? I guess I don't mind going to the hospital alone. I'll be fine. I know what to expect."

Helen took her arm. "It's not coming," she said.

"What's not coming?"

"The ambulance." Rose knew the words that were going to come out of Helen's mouth before they were spoken. But even after she heard them, Rose couldn't believe them. She pulled her arm away.

"What do you mean, it's not coming? That's what ambulances do. If you need them, they have to come!" There was a roaring in Rose's ears that wouldn't stop. The air was thick and she felt a burning in her lungs.

"Rose, *listen* to me. More than half the ambulances are stuck on the roads. The snow is coming down too fast. The drifts are three feet high because of the wind and only getting higher. They can't get the ambulances out. They're sending them only for absolute emergencies."

"This *is* an emergency!" Rose shouted.

"They say it isn't. No one is hurt and no one is dying. They won't send anyone. They probably wouldn't get here even if they tried. Rose, look at me. It's going to be fine. You can have the baby here. People do it all the time. The nurse said there's a midwife—"

"No! I'm not having the baby here! I won't!" She pulled her robe tight and stormed out of the bedroom.

"Where are you going?" Helen ran into the hallway after her.

"To call a taxi. I'll get a taxi to the hospital."

"Rose, I *tried*. I swear, I tried. They're not even answering the phones anymore. I called eight different taxi companies. No one is out on the roads."

Rose started to cry, hot angry tears rolling down her cheeks. She let Helen lead her back to the bedroom, to the chair by the window, where she sat with her head in her hands. Her heart was beating too fast and her frustration turned into a raging wail. "How could this happen? This can't be happening!" Judith came in then, panicked from her mother's screams. "What's wrong? Aunt Helen, what's wrong with her?"

"Shh, shh." Helen was next to Rose, patting her back, trying to calm her, but it had the opposite effect. Rose didn't want to be comforted. She didn't want to be brave. She wanted to pound her fists on the floor and scream at the world. And after that she wanted to ride in a shiny white ambulance to the hospital. She pushed herself up off the chair and left the bedroom again. "I'm calling the hospital *myself*," she hissed.

"I'm telling you, I already called."

"I don't care what you already did!" Rose no longer recognized her own voice, but she couldn't make herself stop screaming. Something she couldn't name or control was fueling her fury, pushing her wrath past every boundary she had ever set for herself. When she got to the kitchen, the phone had no dial tone. She hung it up and tried again, jiggling the receiver frantically. Again and again she tried, but it was no use.

Helen and Judith came running after her, but Rose could only stare past them, stony and unblinking. "The phone is dead. I'm going to have to walk."

Judith was aghast. "You can't walk to the hospital. It's almost two miles away!"

"It's not that far."

Helen tried to reason with her. "There's a blizzard outside—the wind would knock you over, and the snow is up to your waist!" Helen took her by the arm and led her to the window. "Look at it out there. Rose, look. You can't walk for two miles in that! You could get frostbite, you could fall down, you could collapse!"

Rose wouldn't believe Helen or Judith. She wouldn't. She had to stay focused. She had to get to the hospital to have the baby. If she had him at home and something went wrong, Mort would never speak to her again. If something happened to the baby, Mort would never, ever forgive her.

"I can do it. I'll just bundle up."

"*Listen* to me," Helen pleaded. "Before the phone went dead I spoke to Dr. Blauner's nurse. I've been trying to tell you. There's a midwife they know. The nurse said she's excellent. She delivered a baby this afternoon a few doors down from here, and she stayed there because of the storm. The nurse gave her our address. She's going to try to get here, she's going to try to come soon."

Rose shook her head no. How could she make Helen understand? She had to get to the hospital. She had to have this baby in a place that smelled like antiseptic and bleach, a place that was safe and clean, with official forms to fill out and nurses in uniform. She wanted the comfort of cold metal stethoscopes pressed against her back and hospital beds with stiffly starched sheets. She needed to see doctors in white coats walking the long linoleum hallways. Nothing else would be acceptable.

"I've decided," she told Helen. "I'm walking to the hospital. And you're coming with me."

"I can't, Rose. I *can't*." Rose didn't know if it was from anger or exhaustion, but suddenly the color went out of Helen's face. A grimace passed over Helen's lips and she reached backward for the wall to steady herself. For reasons Rose couldn't comprehend in that moment, a puddle seemed to be collecting around her sister-in-law's feet. Everything Rose knew of women and childbirth was gone from her head, and in her grief and her fear she stared, incredulous, at the wet patch on the floor. "What is that?" she wondered aloud.

Helen answered her back in as gentle a voice as she could muster under the circumstances. "Rosie," she said, "my water just broke."

Chapter 16

JUDITH

It always bothered Judith that she never learned the midwife's name. When she thought about that night, whether it was a few months, ten years or twenty years later, the details were always uncertain. She should have found out the woman's name. If she had, maybe the other features of that evening would have stayed with her more sharply. If she had, she might have been able to track the midwife down to ask what really happened. But she hadn't.

In contrast to the time she spent in the midwife's company, Judith remembered the hours leading up to her arrival with perfect clarity. She had a vivid mental picture of her mother, hysterical and angry, screaming about hospitals and taxis. She remembered packing pajamas and dolls for Mimi and Dinah, and bringing them upstairs so the girls would have what they needed for the sleepover with their cousins. Harry had been so unpleasant that night, speaking to her in his condescending way about how *he* was the one who should stay with their mothers and *she* was the one who should be baby-sitting. "But your mother said I have to stay with them," she told him.

"You're lying!" Harry screamed at her, pushing past her and rushing down the steps because he had to hear with his own ears the reason he hadn't been chosen. If Harry had stayed, maybe he would have found out the midwife's name, Judith thought. Maybe he would have paid more attention.

He returned a few minutes later, humbled, but still trying to act like he was in control. "My mother says I should baby-sit the others because I'm the oldest and the most responsible," he muttered. "You can go back down now." He waved his hand to dismiss her. It was maddening, but Judith still felt sorry for him. She knew he was as worried as she was, so she hadn't told him about the little speech Aunt Helen had given her just half an hour earlier. "He can't be here, Judith. This is no place for any man, let alone a thirteen-year-old boy. Men can't handle this sort of thing. Believe me, I've had four children. They're too squeamish to be helpful. They either get in everyone's way or wind up in a corner somewhere sitting with their head between their knees. We don't need that kind of aggravation."

One thing about that night Judith would never forget was the snow. Before that night, she had always thought of snow as beautiful and cheerful, like something you'd see in a Currier and Ives print. Before that night, the very thought of snow had her humming the tune to "Walking in a Winter Wonderland." She would get excited about it, the snowball fights with her cousins and the snow angels they'd make. Snow meant hot chocolate with marshmallows and days off from school.

But the night of the blizzard was the most frightening of Judith's young life. Her mother, usually so docile and kind, turned into someone she did not recognize. Her gregarious aunt became quiet and nervous. The storm, and the isolation it caused, changed them. The snow kept them apart from her father and uncle. It blocked the hospital's ambulance routes, detained the doctors and turned two routine labors into a fearful ordeal. Judith would never see snow again without remembering that night.

Judith blamed the weather for the corruption of her recollections. Its presence was so all-encompassing that it trivialized every other thing about that night, even the birth of the babies. When Judith tried to recall specific details, she felt like she was looking at a distant scene through the glass of a snow globe. Their house and all the people in it were tucked safely inside. But she couldn't see anything clearly because the flakes were in constant motion, covering the house and refusing to settle to the bottom. No matter what angle she approached from, she could never get an unobstructed view.

The last clear moment of the night was when her mother

announced the midwife's arrival. Judith and Aunt Helen were in the living room sitting on the couch. They had just finished getting things ready—putting out clean towels, sheets and diapers—when her mother came rushing into the room. Before that, Rose had stayed in the bedroom, hiding from everyone and staring out the window.

The sight of the single female figure outside in the snow jolted her mother out of her dormant state. "The midwife is here! It has to be her! She's coming down the street—look!" Through the window they were just able to make out the figure of a woman fighting her way through the storm toward their house. For every three steps the woman moved forward, she was pushed back two steps by the wind. When they opened the door a few minutes later, a gust of snow practically blew the midwife into the living room so that she seemed, for a moment, almost to be floating. Snow continued to hover around her until the warmth of the room evaporated it. Aunt Helen hugged the midwife and kissed her, while her mother took the midwife's hand to shake. Judith stood shyly to the side, then headed to the kitchen after her mother asked her to heat some water for tea. The midwife must have introduced herself then.

The midwife was a small, sturdy woman in a navy blue dress with a kind but authoritative air about her. She was neither young nor old and immediately took charge in a way that Judith found comforting. When Judith returned from the kitchen with the tea, the midwife was in the middle of a question: "Which one of you am I here for, then?" Judith set the boiling cup down on the side table. She was the first to respond. "Both of them."

The midwife thought Judith was making a joke. But her mother and aunt confirmed it, nodding sheepishly and explaining the situation. The midwife downed her tea in one gulp.

There was a brief discussion then that Judith didn't follow concerning the timing of contractions, the breaking of water, the number of pregnancies and various other details. The midwife wanted to examine both of the expectant mothers and expressed her desire to set up separate birthing rooms for each of them. "But I want to be with Helen," her mother insisted. "I don't want to be separated from her." It was decided that both women would start off in Rose's room, Rose in her bed and Helen in the rollaway cot. If necessary, they would be separated later.

Judith watched the midwife prepare. Everything she needed was stowed inside her valise. Judith had never seen such a bag before. Fresh blankets and rubber pads materialized from it, as did large bottles of various antiseptic solutions. When the midwife pulled out a lollipop and handed it to her, Judith didn't recognize it because she thought it must have been some sort of medical instrument. The midwife told her what it was and laughed. She took out her gloves and asked Judith to leave the room because she was going to examine the patients.

Judith could still remember the taste of that lollipop. She couldn't describe the flavor, but it was something between grapefruit and peach. It was the most delicious candy she had ever tasted. She wanted to find out the name of it so she could ask her mother to buy some for her sisters, but she couldn't find the wrapper after she removed it. She looked all over the floor, even under the couch, but she couldn't find it.

After the lollipop, the rest of the evening was a blur. Judith lay down on the living room couch with her book. The midwife must have been in the bedroom with her mother and aunt, and at some point Judith dozed off. Several hours later she woke up. The lights were out but someone had lit candles in the dark living room. The lollipop stick was still in her hand and her book was lying on the floor. *What is that noise? Crying? Are the babies born already?*

Judith ran into the bedroom and found her mother propped up in bed holding two tightly swaddled bundles. The midwife was doing something to Aunt Helen that Judith couldn't watch, so she turned away and closed her eyes. "She has to get the whole placenta out or there could be an infection," her mother whispered. "Your cousin was born first but then I had to start pushing. It happened very fast. The midwife delivered Helen but the placenta tore. I couldn't wait anymore so she delivered me and went back to Helen. She'll be fine. Just a few stitches and she'll be all done." The midwife made a satisfied grunting sound when she was finished. Judith sniffed a strong ammonia-like smell, and the midwife told her she could open her eyes. When she did open them, the midwife was almost finished tidying everything up. "I'm going to warm up some water," she announced. "I'll be right back and we'll clean up those beautiful babies."

The remainder of that night was even murkier. Judith took one of the babies from her mother and rocked it in her arms. "Oh my gosh,

I completely forgot!" Judith said. "Which is which? I mean, which one is my cousin and which is my . . . ?" Her aunt and mother looked at each other for what seemed like a very long time. Her mother answered first. "You're holding your cousin Natalie." Then her mother gestured toward the baby she was holding and spoke very softly. "This is your brother, Theodore."

At some point, Judith had left the apartment to tell Harry and the other children the news. The snow stopped, the sky lightened and people began to stir in the streets.

The midwife must have returned from the kitchen after Judith had gone upstairs. She must have cleaned the babies then, written down their names on the certificates and said her goodbyes. She must have. But Judith couldn't remember that part. She could only remember the part that came before. She searched her memory over and over, just as she'd searched the living room floor for the lollipop wrapper. But just like the wrapper, the midwife was gone.

Part Two

Chapter 17

MORT

After the initial excitement of having a son passed, Mort was ambivalent. He decided that all babies were really the same, and that the only thing separating newborn boys from newborn girls was future potential.

The bris had been the highlight. After all the family occasions he had been forced to suffer through, it was finally his turn to be celebrated and honored. When he presented his son to the *mohel* (fulfilling "one of the sacred covenants of our people," as he explained over and over to his daughters), Mort knew he was doing something important. It didn't matter that he turned green as soon as the mohel started. Wasn't it natural to feel queasy during such a significant occasion? He was sure it was. He was able to ignore his brother's loud comments—"You all right there, Morty? Wanna go outside and get some air?"—and focus on the real significance of the day. He had a son to carry on his family's name and traditions. So what if his sole heir was just a recently traumatized six-pound infant? One day Teddy would be much, much more than that. All Teddy needed was time.

At six months old, Teddy was a good deal smaller than Natalie. Mort viewed his lean physique as a positive and Natalie's rolls of arm and leg pudge as repugnant. "What are they feeding her?" he asked Rose. "Bottles of schmaltz?" Rose glared at him when he said such things, but he didn't care. After Teddy's birth, Mort had eased up on his point system and no longer worried about counting every callous remark that escaped from his lips. He still believed his point method had merit—wasn't Teddy proof that it worked? But he was not above making jokes at the expense of his brother's family, especially because he believed he had finally earned the right to do so.

Joking aside, Mort *was* grateful to Helen. He knew she was responsible for getting Rose through the blizzard and the birth of their son safely, and he hated to think what might have happened if she hadn't been there. Though he would never admit it, Mort secretly admired Helen for being so capable.

By the time he had reached six months of age, Teddy had become slightly more interesting to Mort. Mort enjoyed pushing him in his carriage to the park and sitting under the trees on the benches facing the baseball field. Before Teddy was born, Mort had visited the park only rarely with the girls.

The baseball field was in the very center of the park, past the duck pond and to the left of the gazebo. Mort hadn't bothered to attend any of his nephews' games there, but he did love baseball. It was the only sport, in his opinion, that paid due respect to the importance of averages and statistics. He decided to start educating Teddy early by bringing him to watch the local kids play. Who knew what Teddy might absorb? Mort was sure that the baby was paying attention.

"See that kid over there?" Mort would say. "The tall one with the freckles? Watch how he throws the ball. See how he does it? Nice and easy. That's the way to do it." Sometimes Mort's comments were negative. "See that one up at base? He's holding the bat all wrong. You need to turn your body and *bend your knees*." And sometimes Mort would whisper his thoughts, just to make sure that none of the other parents at the field would hear. "You'll be a better hitter than *that* kid by the time you're four," he would say.

Halfway through his first year of life, Teddy was old enough to be interesting, but still young enough to be completely under Mort's control. Mort liked it that way—he couldn't imagine ever loosening his grip on this child. Teddy's future was too important to be left to chance. He would be brilliant, athletic and, one day, the president of Box Brothers. Oh, it would be fine if Abe's boys worked there too;

there were all kinds of jobs for all kinds of abilities—machine operators, truck drivers, shipping clerks, etc. But Teddy would be the one in charge. Teddy would be the brains of the operation. Mort had no doubt about that.

Chapter 18

ABE

When Joe and George were babies, one of them had always been awake. That's how it was with twins. Abe was used to staying up nights for feedings, used to walking in circles around the house with one of the boys in his arms, trying to rock someone to sleep. Half of those nights he was so exhausted that he wasn't even sure which one of them he was holding.

But Natalie was different. The first night he was home with her, Abe got up around three in the morning. It was habit that woke him, not crying. Helen was asleep, and it took a few moments for him to register the silence. His first reaction was panic. Why was it so quiet? He pushed off the blankets and wandered over to Helen's side of the bed, where the bassinet was supposed to be. The room was so dark that he only realized it was there when he stubbed his toe on it. He stopped himself from crying out and waited a few moments for the pain to subside. In the meantime, his eyes adjusted to the darkness and he was able to make out Natalie, asleep and peaceful on her side. He leaned down and put his ear up against her mouth. She was breathing, thank God. But how could she sleep for this long?

Abe got back in bed, but he was restless. He lay awake, listening for the sounds of Natalie's breathing. An hour later, he pulled the bassinet over to his side of the bed so he could hear better. He hoped the movement might wake the baby, but it didn't. At four-thirty, Abe picked her up. He held her up in the air with his hands under her arms and her face directly across from his so he could look at her. Natalie squirmed for a few moments in his arms and opened one eye to stare at him. Abe felt like she was trying to tell him something. *Let a girl get a little shut-eye, will ya?* He put her back down and finally fell asleep. When she whimpered at six-thirty in the morning, Helen jumped out of bed and carried her into the kitchen.

Abe wandered out of the bedroom a few minutes later. "Why did you move the bassinet?" Helen asked him.

"She was so quiet! I couldn't even tell if she was breathing. I got nervous."

Helen widened her eyes at him. "This is our fifth baby, Abe. Our *fifth*. And you're nervous *now*?

He shrugged. "The boys cried all the time. They never slept. I was too tired to be nervous. This one sleeps through the night when she's two days old."

"Since when is sleeping through the night a crime?"

"It's not. But the boys always let us know if they needed something. They were hungry, they cried. Tired, they cried. Needed a change, they cried. How are we going to know what this one wants if she never cries?"

Helen burst out laughing.

"What? What's so funny?"

"You just summed up the difference between men and women, sweetheart. Men kvetch, and women suffer in silence!"

"I'm going to take a shower," Abe said, pretending to be disgusted.

"Bye. Daddy!" Helen lifted up one of Natalie's tiny hands for a wave.

Steam filled up the bathroom, and Abe started thinking. Natalie was only two days old, but she was already making him question the things he thought he knew, even the way he thought about himself. He had been the father of boys. Easy. Sports question? He had it covered. Need someone to play ball? He was always game. War, politics, business, whatever. He could handle whatever the boys threw at him. Guy has a question about a girl? About sex, even? Abe hadn't gotten that far yet with his boys, but he was sure he'd be able to figure out what to say when the time came around.

But Natalie? What was she going to ask him about? He couldn't predict. How was he going to be any help to *her*? He was pretty sure Mort hadn't been much help so far to his girls. Maybe that's why he always seemed so disinterested. Maybe he ignored them because he didn't know how to talk to them.

Well, Abe wasn't going to do that. *His* daughter would have every advantage his boys had. He would make sure of it.

Chapter 19

HELEN

(September 1948)

From the moment he woke up that morning, Joe hadn't stopped complaining. The others weren't happy about the first day of school either, but at least they'd stopped grumbling about it long enough to eat breakfast.

"Are you done?" Helen finally had asked Joe, in a tone that made it clear she wasn't asking. Joe was about to respond, but kept his mouth shut when she began to line their lunch boxes up on the kitchen counter. Helen knew he was smart enough to realize that a nasty response would mean no cookies with his lunch. Missing breakfast was one thing, but no dessert was another, so Helen wasn't surprised when he'd decided to cut his losses and apologize. "Sorry, Mom," he managed.

After Helen handed the boys their lunches she gave them all a final once-over. The last gasp of rebellion came when Sam tried to convince Helen that his stomach cramps might be appendicitis. Her response was to push all of them out the door and to lock it from the inside as quickly as possible. A few minutes later, she heard Natalie babbling in her crib.

With the boys gone and only Natalie at home, everything was easy. Helen was almost ashamed to admit how much she enjoyed taking care of her. With the first baby, Helen had always been afraid she was doing something wrong. When Sam came along it was easier, but Harry had been so jealous that Helen had to sleep with one eye open just to make sure Harry didn't push his brother out the window. And with the twins—well, there were two of them. But with Natalie, Helen could finally relax. The sheer joy Helen felt just from watching her dribble breakfast mush down her chin was sometimes so intense that it brought her to tears.

After she got Natalie dressed, Helen carried her downstairs, pulled the carriage out from its spot in the hallway and knocked on Rose's door. Maybe Rose and Teddy would come with them to the park.

Helen was worried about Rose. She should have been walking on air after Teddy was born. She finally had a son, and Mort was satisfied at last. Helen assumed everything would be perfect. But she was beginning to realize just how shortsighted she had been.

From the start, Helen recognized the signs. She had seen other women act like this after having babies. Rose was withdrawn and she stayed in bed most of the time. The other women Helen knew who had experienced this kind of thing always got over it after a month or so, but with Rose, it seemed to be getting worse. Teddy had been a difficult infant at first, and Rose wasn't used to colicky babies. Helen tried to help—she would stay over a few nights a week downstairs and bring Natalie with her. She spent hours burping Teddy and massaging his tiny body the way she used to when Sam had colic.

After three or four weeks, however, Abe put his foot down. "It's enough already!" he said. "Rose will be fine—it's *her* baby. She has to learn how to take care of him herself!" Helen was furious. For three days she refused to speak to Abe. And for three nights in a row she slept downstairs with Natalie and Teddy.

On the fourth day, George didn't feel well after dinner. When Helen tucked him in that night, he burst into tears. Helen sat on the edge of the bed with him. "Honey, what's wrong? Do you have a stomachache?"

George nodded. Tears were running down his face.

"Don't worry, sweetheart," she said. "I'm going to get a bowl from the kitchen for you and put it by the side of your bed in case you need to throw up." She was about to get up but George grabbed her hand and started to cry harder.

"No! Mommy, don't go! Don't leave me!"

"George!" Helen was surprised. "I'm just going into the kitchen. I'm going to get a bowl for you and then I'll come right back."

"No, you won't!" he sobbed. "You won't come back! You'll take Natalie and go downstairs and leave me up here all alone!"

"George," Helen tried to calm him down, "I would never leave you all alone. Sometimes I try to help Aunt Rose with Teddy, but Daddy is always here if I'm gone."

"No! I want *you* to take care of me! I'm gonna wake up at night and throw up and you won't be here! You're going to leave us and we won't have any mommy at all!"

"George, I'm not going to leave you."

"*It's not fair!* Teddy already has a mommy. Now he has *two* and we have *none*."

"George!"

"You love *him* more than *us*!"

"Oh George, I'm so sorry." Helen had tears in her eyes. She wrapped her arms around him. George choked back his sobs. Then he threw up all over his bedspread.

After that, Helen stopped sleeping downstairs. She missed spending time with Teddy and she felt bad leaving Rose in the lurch. But she had to give it up.

Rose had done a little bit better after that, but during the summer she retreated again. With school out, she relied heavily on Judith and the other girls to watch Teddy and keep him occupied. She cooked dinner when Mort came home, but most afternoons the girls ended up at Helen's house for lunch. Helen started cooking extra food and buying double her usual order of cold cuts on Mondays. She didn't mind. But now that summer was over and school had started, Helen was hoping Rose would get back to normal.

That was why she was knocking on Rose's door now—she wanted to start the school year off on a good note for all of them. They could take a nice walk together and keep each other company. But when Helen knocked, there was no answer. She tried again, but still no response. "Rose? Are you home?" Helen heard crying. The knob to Rose's front door turned easily in her hand so she let herself in. Teddy wasn't just crying—he was screaming at the top of his lungs.

Helen found him in his crib, sitting up and sobbing. His round little face was red, covered in snot and tears from crying for so long. The room smelled of urine; he had soaked through his pajamas. She put Natalie down on the rug and picked Teddy up to comfort him. "Shhh, sweetheart, shhh," she whispered. Teddy rubbed his faced into her shoulder. His whole body was shaking but the sobs were getting softer. "Shhh." He was wet and shivering, and she wondered how long he had been crying like that. Why hadn't Rose heard him?"

"Rose?" she called again.

Still there was no answer. "Mommy must be sleeping, Teddy," Helen said to him. "Did you keep her up last night?" she cooed. He was finally calming down. "Let's change you, okay? In fact, let's give you a nice warm bath."

"BA!" said Natalie, looking up at her mother.

"You can have a bath too, with Teddy! Won't that be fun?"

Helen stripped Teddy out of his wet clothes and put a fresh diaper on him. Then she put him down on the rug next to Natalie, who was busy chewing on a wooden block. She changed the crib sheets and put both of the kids in the crib for safekeeping so she could go check on Rose. That was some nap she was taking! Helen hoped she wasn't sick.

She knocked on Rose's bedroom door, but there was no response. When she opened it, she saw that the bed hadn't been made. Rose was sitting in the chair by the window, staring out at the street. She was still in her nightgown.

"Rose?" Helen spoke again, louder this time. "Are you all right?" Rose didn't move. It was as if she couldn't hear. Helen was afraid of startling her when she touched her arm, but she needn't have worried. Rose looked at Helen and reached for her ears, pulling something out of them. Her eyes were sleepy.

"What's that?" Helen pointed to Rose's hands.

"Earplugs."

"Where on earth did you get earplugs?"

"Hmm? Oh . . . the company picnic." At first Helen thought Rose was hallucinating, but then she realized Rose must have gotten them from one of the employees. Some of them used earplugs to block out the noise from the box-making machinery.

"How long have you been wearing them?"

"I told you, I got them last month at the picnic."

"No, I mean, how long have you been wearing them *today*?"

"Oh. Not too long." Rose turned her eyes toward the window again.

"When Natalie and I got here, Teddy was crying so loud we could hear him in the hallway."

"He's always that way. If I didn't wear earplugs, I'd never get anything done during the day." *What was she trying to get done in her bedroom staring out the window?*

"He was wet, soaked through his clothes. Did you feed him yet?"

"Judith always gives him breakfast. She loves taking care of him."

"I know she does. But it's the first day of school, remember? Judith left early. Maybe Teddy is hungry."

"Then I'll feed him, all right?" Rose snapped. "Will *that* make you happy?"

Helen tried to be reassuring. "All babies cry, you know."

"Ha! Not like him. He's a monster."

Helen couldn't bear to hear Rose say that about Teddy. "Rose, he's just a baby."

"Well, I'm too old to take care of another baby. I can't do it!"

"If I can do it, you can too."

"I'm telling you I can't. I'm not like you. How can you pretend this is all so easy? I can't do this!" Rose's voice was breaking.

"Listen to me." Helen took one of Rose's hands in both of her own. She was pleading with her. "You *have* to. I'm trying to help you, but you *have* to do better than this. Teddy needs you."

Rose shook her head and Helen let go of her hand. "I'm going to give the kids a bath," Helen said. "Then we're all going to the park. *All* of us." She was numb and sick with worry. Don't be angry, she kept telling herself. Don't be angry. She's going through a difficult patch. Everything will work out.

Helen went back to the babies, who were busy chewing on blocks and babbling at each other. When she put them both in the tub together, it reminded her of when she used to bathe the twins. Getting them out was harder than getting them in, but she managed it all right. She dressed Natalie back in her romper and found fresh clothes for Teddy. Then she brought them into the kitchen to wait for Rose.

Half an hour later, after Teddy was fed, Rose appeared in the doorway of the kitchen, dressed and ready for their outing. Teddy started kicking his feet and babbling when he saw her.

"He's excited to see you," Helen said. She took Teddy out of his high chair and handed him to Rose, who held out her arms reluctantly. "Go to Mama," Helen cooed, but Rose's hands were stiff and slow in accepting him. It took several moments before Helen could let go, and it was only when she felt Rose's grip on him tighten that she was sure he was secure. Helen exhaled slowly, picked Natalie up off the floor and followed Rose and Teddy out the door.

Chapter 20

ROSE

(November 1948)

The first few months of school went by quickly, and Rose felt better. She got rid of the earplugs and stopped taking naps during the day. Helen checked in on her every morning. Rose knew her sister-in-law only wanted to help, but she was becoming increasingly annoyed with Helen's little visits.

Living together in the two-family house had always had its benefits. When Rose first moved in, she had been grateful every day for Helen's companionship. Helen taught her how to cook, how to sew curtains, how to bleed the radiator when it started getting noisy. She told Rose where to buy fish and which grocer had the best produce. The two of them had been inseparable back then, more like sisters than some real sisters Rose knew. When the children came along, the cousins had each other for playmates. There was always an adult around if any child was sick or wanted help with schoolwork. And if either Rose or Helen needed something for a recipe, chances were that one of them had the ingredient the other was missing.

But there were downsides too. Rose had been humiliated the day Helen found her in the bedroom on the first day of school. Part of Rose was grateful that Helen had been there. But part of her resented the lack of privacy and boundaries that had developed between them. I should have known this would happen, Rose thought. She began to wonder if they would always live like this, together in the two-family house, never more than a few feet from each other.

Now, the clock struck 10:00 a.m. and there it was, the inevitable knock at the door.

"Rose? Are you home?" Rose had been careful about locking the door in the morning after the girls left. But ever since the first day of school, Helen started keeping the extra key to Rose's house on the key chain she left in her pocketbook. "It's easier," she told Rose. "This way if I need to borrow something from the kitchen and you aren't home to answer, I'll be able to get whatever I need without bothering you. You still have our key, don't you? Or do you need me to make you another one?"

"No," Rose said. "I have it in a drawer somewhere."

Rose preferred to open the door herself, so she rushed over to get to it in time.

When she opened it she found Helen and Natalie, both bundled up in hats and heavy coats. "It's freezing out today," Helen said. "I think it's too cold to go to the park. What do you think?"

Rose shrugged. "We haven't been out yet. But if you think it's too cold . . ." She was hoping Helen would give up their daily walk and leave her and Teddy to themselves for the day.

"Well, maybe we'll come in for a few minutes. The kids can play a little."

"Sure." Rose knew better than to argue. She stepped aside to let Helen and Natalie into the kitchen. Teddy was sitting on the floor, playing with a set of wooden farm animals he had inherited from Dinah. His favorite was the sheep.

Rose filled a kettle with water from the tap and put it on the stove for tea. As soon as Natalie was out of her coat and down on the floor, she crawled over to Teddy and grabbed the sheep from his tiny fist. Then she yelled, "Baa!" in Teddy's face. When Teddy started to cry, Helen pulled the toy away from Natalie and put it back in Teddy's hand. After that, both of them were crying.

Helen didn't know who to comfort first. She took Teddy up on her knee and picked one of the other animals for Natalie. "Here, sweetheart. Here's a cow for you."

"Mooo!" Natalie called out.

"She's smart," Rose said. "Like Judith."

Helen was miffed. "Sam spoke early too."

"I know," said Rose, "but Natalie takes after Judith in a lot of ways."

"She has the same chin as Harry," Helen pointed out.

"True." Rose gave in. "They both have Grandpa Harold's chin." Harold was Mort and Abe's father. Rose knew the conversation was not going in a good direction. She was trying to think of something else to talk about.

Helen must have been thinking the same thing. "What do you want to do for Thanksgiving this year?" she asked. "Do you want me to have it upstairs? It's no problem."

Rose suppressed a sigh. Where was it written that the two families had to celebrate *every* holiday with each other? Rosh Hashanah and break-fast had been in September, but it felt like they had just happened yesterday. Was it really necessary to have Thanksgiving together too?

"We . . . may go to my aunt Faye's place. She invited us." It was only partly untrue. The last time Rose had spoken with Faye was over a month ago. She hadn't invited them specifically for Thanksgiving, but she had told Rose to "come and visit anytime."

"Really? You're going to schlep all the way to Manhattan on *Thanksgiving*? Why do you want to go all the way there?"

"It's not that far."

"I thought Mort didn't like Faye's husband."

"Mort had a nice conversation with Stuart last time."

"Suit yourself. Let me know if you change your mind."

"I will. I'll talk to Mort about it tonight."

"All right. Faye can always come to us. It's just the two of them. Maybe I'll just call and invite her here. That way everyone can be together. Why don't you give me her number?"

"I'll ask her."

"Are you sure? I'd feel rude if I didn't invite her myself."

"I said I'd ask her!"

"All right. *You* ask her." Helen got up from her chair and handed Teddy to Rose. "I forgot how many errands we have to do today," she said. "We need to go to the fish store and the pharmacy and—"

"Don't let us keep you." Rose was visibly relieved. "We'll see you later." As soon as Helen and Natalie were out the door, Rose locked it quickly behind them. She took a small leather-bound book out of her kitchen drawer, found Faye's number and began to dial it.

Chapter 21

JUDITH

Judith was bored. She looked over at her sisters, who were sitting on the other side of the long mahogany table. Dinah's eyes were half closed, like she was falling asleep, and Mimi kept sneaking glances at herself in the enormous gold-framed mirror on the wall. Judith took a spoonful of soup. It was going to be a long afternoon.

Who served soup for Thanksgiving anyway? Sure, they had soup for other holidays, but that was different. This soup was pale green and tasted funny. Aunt Faye said it was cream of celery, but Judith was trying to pretend she hadn't heard. She was afraid she wouldn't be able to eat it if she thought about the ingredients, and she wanted to be polite.

Judith preferred Thanksgiving dinner at Aunt Helen's. There was no celery soup, and Aunt Helen always made pumpkin bread. Judith was pretty sure there would be no pumpkin bread here. She could see only hard, store-bought rolls in the polished silver bowl that sat in the center of the table.

It had taken forever to get from Brooklyn to this fancy apartment building on Park Avenue. There was a stylish-looking doorman in the front of the building who asked them their names and called Aunt Faye on the lobby telephone to announce them. Then another man, also in uniform, rode up the seven floors with them in the elevator. Judith didn't see how a person could make an actual job out of riding in the elevator. How much work did it take to push a button anyway?

Aunt Faye and Uncle Stuart had no children or grandchildren. The floor in the foyer was polished marble (Dinah almost slipped when they first walked in), and there were expensive-looking crystal and china pieces on every surface. The coffee tables were made of glass, and even the couches managed to look fragile. They didn't dare put Teddy down on the floor, for fear he might hurt himself on a sharp corner somewhere or (even worse) break something of Aunt Faye's. Of course Aunt Faye didn't have a high chair. So Teddy fidgeted on Rose's lap.

Aunt Faye was pale and slim, and her gray-blond hair was swept up with silver combs. When Judith's mother asked if she wanted to hold Teddy, Faye didn't hesitate. "No, thank you, dear," she said, wholly unapologetic. "My chemise," she said, motioning to the white silk blouse she was wearing, "is not suitable for carrying babies. It's terribly difficult to clean."

"So Mort," said Faye's husband, Stuart, "how's business these days? Anything new in boxes?" Stuart said this like it was a joke, but Mort answered seriously.

"Absolutely," said Mort. "More and more food companies are using cardboard boxes, so we're focusing production on this trend. Right now we're working closely with a cereal manufacturer in Philadelphia."

Judith could see that Stuart wasn't pleased with the answer. He was frowning, drumming his thick fingers on the dining room table. Stuart was the kind of man who liked to give advice. If no one needed his advice, he became cranky.

"Better be careful," Stuart cautioned. "This cereal fad might not last, you know. You can't grow a business on *trends*, Mort."

"I agree," said Mort. "I'm following the numbers on all of this very closely. Trends come and go, but numbers don't lie."

"Hmmph," said Stuart. He was sitting at the head of the table with Faye directly across from him at the other end. "Faye!" he almost shouted, "When are we serving the damn turkey already? The soup tastes like piss!"

"Stuart! There are *children* present!" said Aunt Faye.

"Well, they probably think it tastes like piss too."

The girls giggled. Rose gave Judith a look, stood up and handed Teddy to Mort. "Take Teddy for a few minutes. I'm going to help Faye in the kitchen."

"Don't trouble yourself," said Aunt Faye. "Lucy can manage." Lucy was Aunt Faye's housekeeper. She was dressed for company that evening in a pearl-gray uniform with a white lace collar. Judith had never seen a real maid before, and having Lucy there made her uneasy. Judith thought her mother must be feeling the same way. They weren't used to sitting around the table and waiting for someone else to serve them.

"Well," Rose said, "why don't I just do a quick check and make sure Lucy remembered to put the sweet potatoes I brought in the oven." Dinah had cried her eyes out when they told her they weren't having Thanksgiving at home. The only way they could calm her down was to promise they would still have the same sweet potato casserole with tiny marshmallows on top at Aunt Faye's house. "Whatever you like, dear," Faye agreed.

"I'll come too," Judith said. That way, she wouldn't have to finish her soup.

"Mom, are you okay?" Judith asked as soon as they were in the oversized kitchen. "Shhh," her mother hushed her. She turned to the maid. "Lucy, I think they're ready for you to clear the soup bowls, if you don't mind."

"Yes, ma'am," Lucy said and hurried out to the dining room.

Rose turned back to Judith. "Stop making this so difficult, young lady," she hissed.

Judith hadn't known she was being difficult. *She* wasn't the one who said the soup tasted like piss. In fact, she had been afraid to say almost anything at all. Aunt Faye and Uncle Stuart seemed like the kind of adults who thought children should be seen and not heard. She was just acting the way she thought she was supposed to.

"What did I do?" Judith asked.

"You laughed at the soup, you've been making faces since we arrived and you've barely spoken to your aunt!"

"I can't think of anything to say!" Judith spoke a little too loudly.

"Lower your voice this instant!"

Judith was quiet. She bit her lower lip and tried not to cry.

"Mommy, I'm sorry. I didn't know . . . I just miss being at home for Thanksgiving."

"Stop carrying on!" Rose glared at Judith. "Poor, poor you, having Thanksgiving in a beautiful apartment with silver bowls and French china and a maid serving you like a princess instead of being back at home with your favorite aunt who makes the world's best apple pie and can do no wrong! Maybe Aunt Helen isn't so perfect! Did you ever think of that?"

Judith was in shock. Not even her father talked to her that way.

Lucy returned from the dining room holding a tray of nearly filled soup bowls and spoons. The maid walked into the kitchen tentatively, humming softly to herself. Judith wondered how much she had heard. As soon as Lucy set down the tray, Rose turned around and left the kitchen without saying another word.

Judith took a deep breath. Had she really behaved as badly as her mother said? Could her mother be jealous of the amount of time she had been spending with Aunt Helen? Judith had only been trying to be helpful, to keep the girls and Teddy out of her mother's way. It was easier to go up to Aunt Helen's than to keep everyone quiet all the time. And over the summer her mother had hardly gotten out of bed. What had Judith done wrong? What could she have done differently? She couldn't think of anything.

Lucy was busy putting the carved turkey slices on a platter. Judith wiped her eyes and opened the oven to check on the sweet potatoes. The marshmallows were golden on top. It was time to take it out. If it burned, Dinah would have a fit. She borrowed the oven mitts she saw on the counter and slowly removed the casserole from the oven. "Would you like me to bring this into the dining room, Lucy?" she asked.

"If you'd like, miss," Lucy said. "Just put it on the sideboard." Judith did as she was told and then made several more trips from the kitchen, carrying out stuffing, vegetables and other side dishes with Lucy. Some of them didn't look too bad. She was happy for the distraction and glad not to have to speak to anyone for a few minutes. Teddy was still fussing on Mort's lap, and her mother was talking to Faye.

On the last trip from the kitchen, Judith carried a white china bowl filled with cranberry sauce. She gripped the bowl carefully but stumbled on one of the tassels of the Persian rug peeking out from under the dining room table. As she landed on her backside, half on the rug and half on the shiny wooden parquet, Aunt Faye gasped. The bowl of crimson sauce was overturned in her lap. Luckily, the bowl was intact.

Lucy rushed over and helped her to her feet. "Come, miss, let's get you cleaned up," she whispered. Judith turned to her mother for support, but Rose wouldn't look at her. Teddy's fussing turned into a full-on wail and Dinah started whining about the sweet potatoes. Mimi was trying to hide her laughter by covering her mouth with her napkin and Mort was glaring at all of them. Uncle Stuart rose to his feet and poured himself a large glass of scotch from the decanter on the bar cart. Aunt Faye called out to Lucy, "Make a note to call the carpet cleaner tomorrow," she said. No one asked if Judith was hurt. No one told her not to worry about the spill. The maid was the only one who took note of her at all.

After she and Lucy did whatever they could to clean off her dress, Judith came back into the dining room. The others had started eating, but Teddy was still fussing.

"Aunt Faye, Uncle Stuart, I'm very sorry for the mess," she said, in as clear a voice as she could manage. "Not to worry dear," Aunt Faye told her. "The carpet cleaners will be in tomorrow." Judith looked at Stuart, but he was busy eating his dinner. She walked purposefully over to the sideboard, made a plate of soft foods and put it down at her place. Then she took Teddy from her father's lap. "I'll hold him," she said. Judith held Teddy tightly on her lap, feeding him spoonfuls of mashed potato and stuffing. He cooed appreciatively, and the room was finally quiet.

"What a helpful young lady you are," Aunt Faye observed. And then, to Rose, "She's very good with the baby."

Judith looked up and saw tears in her mother's eyes. Everyone else was busy eating and didn't notice. *I'm sorry,* her mother mouthed. Judith gave a little nod to show that she understood.

By the time they got home, it was almost ten o'clock and everyone was exhausted. Judith carried a sleeping Teddy into the house and saw that Aunt Helen had left several covered plates of food for them on the table. Judith's stomach started growling—she had barely eaten anything the whole day, and she was only just then aware of how hungry she was. There was turkey, stuffing and the same sweet potato casserole Rose had made for Aunt Faye. There was another plate too, just of desserts, and Judith figured there was probably some apple pie in there somewhere. More than anything, she wanted to take off her coat, sit down at the table and start eating the leftovers.

If her mother hadn't spoken to her that way in Aunt Faye's kitchen, she probably would have. Even though it was late and the cold food would have given her a stomachache, she would have done it. But now she knew better. When she examined her mother's expression, she saw what she was expecting: the tightening of the jaw, the hint of a frown, the squinting of the eyes that was imperceptible to anyone who wasn't looking for it. But Judith *was* looking for it this time, and she could tell Rose was furious that Helen had let herself in and dropped off the food.

If Judith sat down to eat, she knew how her mother would interpret it: even one forkful of pie would mean Judith had taken Helen's side. Judith was too tired for further arguments, so she walked past the table and pretended not to see the heaping plates. She carried Teddy into his room, changed him into pajamas and put him in his crib. Then she went to her own room, put on a nightgown and got under the covers. As she lay awake, she was unable to shake the feeling that something more complicated than a simple fight over Thanksgiving was going on between her mother and her aunt. Judith wanted to know what it was, but she knew she couldn't ask. I'm going to have to start paying more attention from now on, she decided. Her stomach was still growling and she was a long way off from sleep.

Chapter 22

MORT

"Do you have a few minutes?" Abe waited for Mort's nod before entering. He came in and shut the office door behind him. After some fidgeting, he finally said what was on his mind. "Something's wrong with Helen and Rose."

Mort didn't understand. "Rose is fine. Is Helen sick?"

"I don't mean that. Something's wrong with the two of them together. They're at each other's throats. You haven't noticed?"

"No."

"Geez." Abe let out a breath. Mort turned back to his desk. He wanted to get back to work, but Abe wasn't done with the conversation.

"Listen, Teddy and Natalie are gonna turn one in a couple of weeks and I think we should have a party for them."

Mort put down his pencil. "Isn't that something Rose and Helen should work out?"

"That's my point, Mort. If we leave it to them, it could turn into another fight. Like what happened at Thanksgiving. It's gonna kill Helen if we don't celebrate this together. You know how it is."

Mort definitely did not know how it was. He had enjoyed Thanksgiving at Faye and Stuart's apartment. It had been so much more civilized than their usual holidays with Abe's family.

"What am I supposed to do about it, Abe?"

"Talk to Rose. You know, tell her you think it'd be nice to have a little party together. Whatever kind of party she wants."

"Fine. I'll talk to her when I get home."

You would have thought Mort had just handed Abe a hundred-dollar bill—that's how big the smile was on his brother's face. It instantly made Mort wish he hadn't agreed to it.

The truth was, Mort *had* noticed a difference in Rose since Teddy was born. He felt a change in her attitude that shifted something between them, a sense that she no longer cared as much about his approval. Since Rose had given him a son, Mort no longer felt justified in voicing any kind of criticism. What's more, he was sure that Rose had detected this new weakness in his position.

The next morning, Mort decided to leave early to avoid Abe. He had put off talking to Rose and didn't feel like explaining the delay to his brother. Mort was saying goodbye to the girls when two quick knocks at the door interrupted him. It was Abe, ten minutes earlier than usual. Mort's plan of walking to work alone was ruined.

"Good morning!" Abe called into the kitchen.

"I'm ready to leave," Mort grumbled. Abe held the door open for his brother to exit but snapped his fingers quickly, just before it clicked shut. Then he called out to Rose, who was pouring her second cup of coffee.

"I almost forgot! Rose, did Mort tell you the big news about Nat and Teddy's birthday?"

Rose was suspicious. She put down the coffee and crossed her arms in front of her chest. "He didn't mention anything." Mort wanted to disappear.

"Ah, he wanted to surprise you, I guess. I haven't told Helen yet either. But it's too good. You've gotta hear this!"

"I'm sure," Rose snapped. "What's the surprise?"

Abe eased his way through the doorway and back into the kitchen, pulling Mort along with him. "You know Bob Sherman, our father's old friend, the one who introduced us to the cereal guy?"

"I know who he is."

"He called yesterday to see how everything was going. When I told him the babies were gonna turn one, he got all excited. Said his cousin was the manager of some fancy club on Ocean Avenue and he wanted to throw the kids a party there. We have the Blue Room at

Club Elegante booked a week from Sunday at noon and Bob said he's paying for the whole thing!"

"Club Elegante is a nightclub, Abe," Rose said. "You want to have a first birthday party at a nightclub?"

"It's not a nightclub during the *day*." Abe grinned.

"What did Helen say?"

"Like I said, I haven't told her yet. Mort wanted you to be the first to know!"

Rose looked from one brother to the other. Finally she uncrossed her arms and let them fall to her sides. "Fine. We'll have it at the night-club. I'll invite my aunt Faye."

"Terrific!" Abe practically shouted. "Invite whoever you want!"

When they were safely out in the hall, Mort grabbed Abe by the arm.

"What the hell did you do? I'm not paying for some party at a goddamn nightclub."

"Calm down. Bob's paying for it."

"You mean that was true?" Mort couldn't believe it.

"Of course it was true! Bob called me last night at home. I only said you knew because I wanted Rose to think we already decided it together. It'd be harder for her to say no that way."

"I suppose. You handled that quite . . . skillfully."

"I knew one of these days you'd appreciate my talents." Abe winked at him. "I'll see you in half an hour," he said. "I'm going to tell Helen about the party." He turned around and headed up the stairs, whistling as he climbed.

Mort stared after his brother and shook his head. Who would've thought Abe could have pulled that off so smoothly? Maybe he didn't give him enough credit. Sometimes you can't predict what a person is capable of, he thought. Sometimes you just can't tell.

Chapter 23

HELEN

"This stupid room isn't even *blue*," Joe grumbled. "It's *gray*."

"It's sort of a bluish gray," George offered.

"It's not called the Bluish-Gray Room, you idiot!"

"Boys!" Helen shushed them. "Stop it." She tried to sound angry, but she wasn't. The Blue Room at Club Elegante really *was* gray. She had said just as much to Abe when they first walked in. It was pretty in a gaudy sort of way, though. At least a hundred balloons—half pink, half blue—skimmed the top of the vaulted ceiling. Bob Sherman had gone all out.

Helen didn't want to be upset today. She wanted to enjoy herself. But every time she took a step toward Rose, her sister-in-law moved in the opposite direction. She tried a few times to catch Rose's eye, to share a smile or a laugh together like they used to, but Rose kept looking away. Helen wondered whether it had been a mistake to have the party here. Maybe Rose would have been friendlier if they had celebrated at home.

"Attention, please," Mort called out. He tapped his spoon against his water glass. "May I please have everyone's attention?" Helen was surprised. It wasn't like Mort to make speeches.

"A year ago today the road outside this building was blocked with snowdrifts piled six feet high. Twenty-six inches of snow fell from the skies—the worst blizzard to hit New York since 1888." Mort stopped to clear his throat. "Against all odds, my son was born that day, a healthy baby boy. Happy birthday to Teddy." Mort drained his glass and sat back down.

An awkward silence filled the room until someone began to clap. There were so many things wrong with Mort's speech that Helen couldn't decide what aggravated her most. He didn't even mention Natalie! Luckily, Abe stood up next.

"Well, my brother certainly is right about that day," Abe began. "What a storm! And with us away, our poor wives had to deal with everything alone. So first, I think we should all raise a glass to *them,* to Helen and Rose, the two bravest women I know."

"To Helen and Rose!" Bob Sherman shouted, and everyone repeated it. When the noise died down, Abe continued, "You know, when Helen told me she was pregnant again, with our *fifth* child, I was surprised. But imagine how surprised I was when Morty here told me Rose was pregnant too!" The crowd chuckled. "Anyway, it all worked out perfect, everybody happy and healthy. So I wanna say happy birthday to Natalie and to Teddy. Drink up!" Everyone clapped loudly this time, joining together in a chorus of "Happy Birthday to You."

One of the waiters took the cue to wheel out the cake, decorated with yellow and white icing. Rose carried Teddy over to where Mort and Abe were standing, while Helen smoothed the front of Natalie's dress. Someone lit the two candles on the cake, and the babies were held up for photos. Helen and Rose blew out the candles, and everyone clapped all over again.

The crowd broke up as the waiters rolled the cake cart into the kitchen for slicing. Helen couldn't help herself from calling out to Rose as she was walking away, "What'd you wish for?" she asked.

"Hmm?" Rose's back was to Helen and she pretended she hadn't heard.

"What'd you wish for when you blew out the candle? I wished for fifty years more of celebrations like this, all of us together for the kids' birthdays."

Rose turned around. For the first time all day, she looked Helen straight in the eye. "I wished that night had never happened."

Chapter 24

ABE

(August 1949)

Natalie loved steps. At twenty months old, all she wanted to do was climb up and down the hallway steps that connected the floors of the two-family house. Mostly she liked going up. Going down was more difficult, so when she got to the top she'd look at Abe, lift her arms and shout, "UPPY!" at the top of her lungs. Abe would laugh, carry Natalie down to the bottom, then hold her tiny hand while she started climbing all over again. She never got tired of it. Neither did he.

Abe used to worry about what he would do with a little girl. When he tried to picture himself having a pretend tea party or dressing up baby dolls, he started to feel queasy. He didn't think he would be good at it. But this? Walking up and down stairs? *This* he could do.

Helen got annoyed with him. "You're spoiling her."

"Spoiling her? Did I buy some silver spoons at Tiffany's?" The kids were finally in bed and the two of them were talking in the kitchen, trying not to wake anyone up. Helen was drying the dishes from dinner and Abe was putting them away.

"That's not the kind of spoiling I mean and you know it."

"So I walk her up and down the stairs—so what?"

"So, you let her do it *every* morning! You indulge her! Do you know that after you leave for work in the morning, she stands by the front door and cries for you to come back and take her on the steps?"

"Yeah?" Abe was pleased. "What does she say?"

" 'Daddy! Uppy! Daddy! Uppy!' " Over and over."

Abe chuckled. "She misses me, that's all," he said, with a smile as wide as his face.

Helen hit him on the head with the spatula she was drying. He grabbed it from her and gave her a swat on the backside.

"You think it's funny, but it's not. I don't have *time* to walk Natalie up and down the stairs all day! I have to do the breakfast dishes, make the beds and clean the *tornado* the boys leave behind. Plus, whenever we go out she wants to climb every set of stairs she sees! I couldn't get her off the drugstore steps the other day. She thinks it's a game!"

"It *is* a game! Come on, don't get all bent out of shape. Pretty soon Natalie will learn not to cry when I go. She'll understand that when I leave, the game is over." Abe snapped his fingers. "Besides, it's educational. I'm teaching her to count. She says a number for each step. She's already up to ten."

Helen made a face at him. "I don't believe you."

"I'll make you a bet. Tomorrow morning, come with us and see. If she doesn't count to ten, I'll do the dishes tomorrow night. By myself."

"What if she *does* count to ten? What do I have to give *you*?" Abe took the frying pan Helen was drying out of her hands and placed it on the counter. Then he wrapped his arms around her and leaned in for a kiss. "I'll figure something out," he said.

The next day, after the boys left for school, Abe sat Natalie down on the couch and tied the laces on her white leather booties. "Daddy has something important to tell you, sweet pea."

Natalie stared at him, her hazel eyes focusing in on his blue ones. "Daddy," she said.

"Yes. Every morning Daddy and Natalie walk up and down the steps, right?"

"Uppy!" Natalie screeched. She slid off the couch and ran for the door. Abe made her sit back down.

"Every morning we play our special game. But when Daddy has

to leave, that means the time for Uppy is all done. No more crying when Daddy leaves. Do you understand?"

Natalie nodded and whispered, "Uppy."

"I mean it," Abe said, trying to sound serious, even a little angry, to make his point. In response, Natalie kissed his hand and hugged it to her cheek. Abe sighed. *This one's smarter than the other four put together.*

After a few moments, he pulled his hand away. "Let's go," he said.

Out in the hall, Abe carried Natalie to the bottom of the steps while Helen stayed up at the top. Natalie was bouncing up and down with excitement. "Ready to show Mommy how you can count?" Abe asked.

"Who can count?" Mort was coming out of his apartment, briefcase in hand.

"Say hi to Uncle Mort, Natalie. Natalie's gonna count the steps for Helen."

Natalie waved and yelled her name for her uncle. "Mo!"

Mort put down his briefcase and crossed his arms. "Show me," he said, in a tone Abe didn't appreciate.

"You wanna see her go up the steps?"

"I want to *hear* her *count* the steps," Mort corrected.

Abe wanted to smack him, but Natalie kept smiling, repeating his name over and over. "Mo! Mo! Mo!" After she calmed down, she pointed to the steps in front of her. She took the first step slowly, keeping one hand on the wall and the other hand wrapped around Abe's fingers. Once she had balanced herself on the first step, she shouted, "Un!"

"Un?" Mort sniffed. "What does *that* mean?"

"It's how she says 'one,' Morty." Abe tried to keep his voice light. "Give her a break, will ya? She's a baby, for Chrissakes."

"You said she could count. That means she has to be able to say the numbers."

"Shut up and listen."

"Toooo!" Natalie called out on the second step. Mort raised an eyebrow.

"Free, foah, fie, six, sen, ate, nine, ten!" Natalie announced. After she got to ten, she started counting from one again until she reached the top of the staircase. When she was finished, she held up her arms to be carried and buried her face in Abe's shoulder. The climbing had exhausted her, and her breathing became heavy and sleepy. Warm brown curls tickled his cheek and Abe lost himself entirely in the sweetness of the moment. His reverie was broken by a loud sound from the bottom of the stairs. Mort had slammed the door shut, exiting without saying goodbye. By the time Abe looked up, his brother was already gone.

Chapter 25

ROSE

(June 1950)

Rose didn't want to admit it, but she was enjoying herself. She needed a change of scenery, even if the scenery happened to belong to Sol and Arlene. They were showing off their new house on Long Island with a weekend barbecue. Helen and her family were already there, and Rose's family were on their way. Rose rolled down the car window and let the breeze wash over her. It felt good to be out of the house and away from Brooklyn.

When the invitation was first extended, Rose wasn't sure she wanted to attend (she couldn't stand the thought of spending another day with Helen), but as the details of Sol's home were revealed to her (the house was on five acres; there was a swimming pool, a rose garden, woods and a pond), the idea of escaping the confines of her home started to look more and more appealing.

Their bottom-floor apartment, once so spacious, felt cramped and crowded to her these days. And the noise! Even at night, there was never any silence. The late spring days had become unusually hot, and open windows let in the honks and screeches from every passing car and truck. The bedrooms were so close together that the tiniest cough or whimper from one of her children would keep her awake at night. And while Rose felt like she was constantly cleaning and neatening their home, clutter and children seemed to congregate in every corner of every room. She was suffocating. So after a few days of mulling it over, Rose called back to tell Arlene they were coming.

When they turned off the main road onto an unmarked dirt lane, Mort thought they were lost. Rose insisted she had read the directions properly, and in a few minutes the lane gave way to a clearing from which the house was visible. It was an enormous white house with four large pillars in the front. They parked on the semicircular gravel driveway that wound around a perfect green lawn and emerged from the car, anxious to stretch their legs and have a look around. Teddy woke up as soon as the motor was off, and Judith held his hand as they walked to the front door.

Sol's home wasn't an estate exactly, but it came close. There were two other homes that were visible from the driveway, but once the housekeeper guided them through the marbled center hallway to the terrace out back, the view consisted only of trees and a few distant hills. Despite the fact that there were over a hundred people there, the backyard had a peaceful quality to it that Rose wouldn't normally have associated with Sol or Arlene. She wondered what had drawn them to this place.

As Rose crossed the wide stone terrace to say hello to their hosts, the sun beamed down so strongly that she had to raise her hand over eyes to shield them from the glare. Arlene had on a huge pair of sunglasses, and Rose began to see the wisdom in wearing them. She didn't own any, but she certainly wished she had a pair on now.

"Rose! Mort! You made it! Whaddya think of the place? Nice, huh?" Sol gave her a kiss on the cheek and shook Mort's hand vigorously. Arlene hugged them both and thanked them for coming.

"Oh Arlene, you have so much space! It's marvelous!" The words came out so enthusiastically that Mort raised his eyebrow at her. She wasn't usually so friendly to Sol and Arlene, she knew, but she didn't see any point in hiding her admiration.

"Thanks, sweetheart." Sol was enjoying the compliments. "Where are the kids?"

"Oh, right over there," Rose pointed toward the covered pool. "They're excited to see your swimming pool!"

Arlene looked worried. "I hope they won't be too disappointed—it isn't open yet. We couldn't get the pool people over here in time."

"Oh, the kids are fine. It's too breezy for swimming anyway—it's at least ten degrees cooler out here than it is in the city! The air is so refreshing!"

Sol chuckled and elbowed Mort. "Looks like you'll be moving soon too, Morty! Maybe we can get you that house across the street!"

Mort gave him a thin smile. "I guess you never know."

"If that cereal guy of yours keeps up, you'll be ready for a house by next year!"

"We'll see," Mort said.

"Where does that go?" Rose interjected, pointing to the path emerging from the treeline at the back of the property.

"That? Johnny calls it the nature trail! It takes you through a little patch of woods. We got some blueberry bushes back there." Sol called over the waiter and insisted that Mort and Rose each take a drink from his tray. "It's a sloe gin fizz," he informed them. "Go on— you'll love it!"

Mort sniffed at his glass and Rose took a small sip. "What else is back there?" she asked.

"There's a little pond at the end of the path," Sol continued, "Johnny loves it back there. He likes the frogs and the turtles—all that crap."

Rose took another sip. "I'm sure it's very pretty," she said.

"Sol, come say hello to Howard and Connie," Arlene called. She had noticed another couple she wanted to greet, a tall blond pair, both wearing sunglasses like her own.

"Sure, sweetheart." Sol patted Mort on the back. "Gotta go make nice with the new neighbors," he whispered loudly. "Get something to eat, okay?"

"Thanks," Mort said. As soon as Sol's back was turned, he put his glass down on another waiter's tray. "Ugh," he said. "I can't drink any more of that thing."

"Really? I think it's good," said Rose.

"Suit yourself. I'm going to get some food." Mort headed over to the long buffet table set out on one side of the terrace, and Rose decided to look for a bathroom. The powder room she found was as big as her bedroom, and the wallpaper was speckled with cream and gold. The windows looked out over the side yard, where most of the children had gathered, including Judith and Teddy. Rose watched them for a few minutes after she dried her hands. The older boys had brought their mitts and Harry and Joe were teaching Teddy how to throw a ball. Sam and George were helping, and Rose's younger girls were practicing cartwheels in the grass. *They seem to be having a good time.*

Helen was waiting for the bathroom as Rose exited. "How funny!" Helen said when she saw her, "I was just wondering where you were! I saw Mort making himself a plate but I couldn't find you out there!"

"Well, here I am," Rose said.

"Good! I'll just be a minute in here. Wait for me, and I'll walk back out with you." Helen shut the powder room door. As soon as it was closed, Rose walked outside and headed straight for the path by the woods.

Alone on the path she felt like a kid playing hooky from school. She wondered if anyone had seen where she had gone and decided it didn't matter because no one had followed her. The farther along the path she walked, the more distant the sounds and voices from the party became. She passed at least a dozen blueberry bushes, just as Sol had promised, and she was almost certain there were raspberry bushes there as well. It was cooler than on the terrace, and the trees muted the sunlight so that her eyes no longer bothered her.

After a few minutes Rose came to the pond. It wasn't much bigger than Sol's swimming pool, but she spotted two frogs and a lizard on the rocks by the edge. She wondered if there were really any turtles in it, but the water was too murky to tell. A patch of bluebells grew haphazardly near the water, and Rose picked some before sitting herself on a stone bench that someone had placed under one of the trees. The smell of the flowers reminded her of the perfume her mother used to wear when she was little. *What a peaceful spot this is.* The silence was so soothing that she almost fell asleep.

Rose lost track of how long she had been sitting there on the bench. If someone had asked, she would have sworn it had only been five minutes, ten at the most. But then she heard the shouting.

At first Rose thought the children were playing a game. The voices were getting closer and she was annoyed because her private moment was ruined. But after a few more shouts, she realized it wasn't a game. They were yelling her name. They were looking for her.

Isn't this always the way, she thought. *Just when I finally have a few minutes to myself—*

"Rose! Are you back here? Rose? *Rose!*" It was Abe's voice. He sounded upset. "I'm here," she admitted. She spoke it out loud but too softly for anyone to hear. *Helen probably sent him after me because I didn't wait for her at the bathroom. Typical.*

"Rose!"

"I'm here!" she yelled.

Abe appeared on the pathway, dripping with sweat and breathing heavily. When he saw her he froze. "Thank God," he said, gasping for air. He leaned halfway over, hands gripping his bended knees for support. He started to cough, and the words sputtered out: "We couldn't find you when it happened. We looked everywhere for you. They couldn't wait anymore." He stood up straight and wiped his forehead. "They left fifteen minutes ago. I told them I'd drive you there when we found you."

When she stood, the bluebells in her lap fell to the ground. "What are you talking about? What happened? Where are we going?"

Abe took a few steps toward her. "Rose, I don't want to scare you. Everything's going to be fine, but we have to go to the hospital."

"Is it Mort? Did he—"

"Mort's fine, Rose. He's fine. But we have to go now."

"Then who?"

"Come on, we have to get out of here." Abe tried to guide her back to the house, but Rose pushed him away. She screamed at him then, shattering the serenity of the spot she had so enjoyed. *"I'm not leaving until you tell me!"*

"It's Teddy," Abe whispered. "He had an accident. It's Teddy."

Chapter 26

HELEN

Helen was there when it happened. She had walked over to the side yard to check on the kids and saw her boys and at least half a dozen others starting an impromptu baseball game. Teddy was sitting with the younger kids and the girls, watching the bigger boys play. But he got bored with their hand-clapping games and wandered onto the makeshift infield just as Sam was hitting the ball. It smacked Teddy in the eye, and the little boy fell over, crying, from the impact.

Helen had seen her share of playground accidents—she knew enough to know that crying was a good sign. She would have been more concerned if Teddy had been quiet. She ran over to him, scooped him up off the grass and carried him, screaming, to the terrace to find Rose and Mort.

Rose was nowhere in sight, but Mort was there, sitting at a table next to Abe. Both men stood up when they saw her with Teddy. *"What the hell happened?"* Mort yelled, causing Teddy to cry even harder. People were turning their heads, and everyone was staring.

"It was an accident, Mort. He got hit in the head with a baseball."

"What the—"

Abe stopped him. "Calm down, we don't want to make him any more upset."

"Shh. Shh." Helen wiped Teddy's tears. She laid him down on the

closest lounge chair and tried to pry his hands away from his eye
to get a look at it. A few of the women asked if they could help, and
Arlene ran over with a dish towel wrapped around some ice cubes.
Helen whispered to Teddy that she wanted to put the ice near his eye.
"It will make it feel better," she promised. The little boy moved his
hands a few inches but continued to wail. Helen could see the skin
around the eye starting to swell and blacken. Abe politely encouraged everyone to go back to their conversations and food and to give
the little boy some air. Mort just stood by, scowling.

"Where's Rose?" Helen asked him.

"She must be in the powder room."

"I don't think so—I saw her there only fifteen minutes ago. She
wouldn't have gone again so soon."

"Well, maybe she's still there."

"No, she was gone when I came out." *She was supposed to wait for
me, but she didn't.*

"I'll go look for her," Abe told them.

Judith ran over then to see how Teddy was. "Is he all right?" she
asked Helen.

"I think he'll be fine, honey. But we might want to bring him to
the hospital just so they can check his eye and make sure his head is
okay."

"The hospital?" Judith's eyes grew wide and started tearing.

"It's not as serious as it—"

Mort interrupted, his face red and angry: "*You* were in charge,
young lady," he said to Judith. "If you had been watching your brother
properly, this never would have—"

"Mort!" Helen glared at him. "I saw the whole thing. Teddy bolted
onto the field. Judith couldn't have stopped him. This isn't anyone's
fault. It was an accident."

Mort paced around the lounge chair, firing questions at Helen
like artillery shells. She tried her best to answer them.

"Do you think it's serious?"

"I think he'll be fine. Harry got hit like this when he was little
too. They're boys—it happens."

"If he's so fine, then why should we drag him to the hospital?"

Helen took a deep breath. "I'm not a doctor, Mort. They need to examine his eye. Obviously I can't do that. And they should check him for a concussion. To be safe, you should take him."

"Then let's go."

"Don't you want to wait for Rose?"

"What I *want* is for this all to be over so I can get the hell off of this goddamned island. If she doesn't get back here in five minutes, we're leaving."

"But Teddy will want Rose to be with—"

"If Abe can't find her in five minutes, I'll drive and you'll sit with Teddy in back."

"But Mort—"

"*Someone* needs to sit in the back with him," Mort snapped. "If you won't go, Judith will do it."

That's the last thing Judith needs. "Of course I'll come with you. But I'm sure Rose will be back in a minute."

Five minutes passed, and Rose hadn't returned. After ten more minutes, Abe still couldn't find her. Helen had no choice but to go with Mort. She pulled Abe to the side before she left. "Find Rose and bring her to the hospital as soon as you can."

"I will," he promised.

Helen sat in the backseat with Teddy while Mort drove. Teddy had finally stopped crying, and Helen was rubbing his back and patting his hair. His head was in her lap, and she was holding the wet dish towel over his eye. The ice had melted, but the towel was still cold. Teddy's other eye was open, watching her. She smiled at him. "Everything is going to be all right," she said. She said it over and over, like a prayer.

When they arrived at the hospital, Mort pulled up to the emergency room entrance. Helen carried Teddy through the double doors to check in while Mort parked the car. Inside, it looked like every other hospital Helen had seen. The walls were a forgettable shade of pale green and the shiny floors were speckled white linoleum. The smell was familiar—mint and medicine mixed with the faint smell of sickness. Teddy started crying again as soon as they walked through the entrance.

"Shh, don't be afraid." While Teddy sniffled, Helen explained the situation to the nurse at the reception desk and took the necessary forms. She held Teddy to her chest while he closed his eyes. The poor thing was exhausted. Still carrying him, Helen walked over to the most comfortable looking of the four couches in the waiting area and arranged him so that he was lying down with his head in her lap, the same way they had been sitting in the car. He seemed to like that position best. The hard gray leather of the couch was cold against her bare legs, and Helen wished she had a blanket.

Helen's right hand was free so she flipped through the forms. Should she fill them out or wait for Mort? She knew her brother-in-law would want her to be as efficient as possible, but she hesitated. Rose might not like it if she filled out Teddy's forms. *But Rose isn't here.*

After ten minutes passed, Helen decided to start. She wrote down Teddy's birthday and his blood type, his height and his weight, the things he was allergic to (dust and cherries) and the results of his latest vision and hearing tests. She wrote down when he'd had the chicken pox and when he'd had bronchitis. Then she signed the form and brought it back to the desk. "Miss, you forgot something," the attendant called to her as she was walking away.

"Sorry, I thought I was finished," Helen apologized. She walked back to the desk. "Only one more thing!" the nurse chirped. "Just write 'mother' on this line."

"Excuse me?"

"Right here, where it says 'Relationship to Patient,' you forgot to write 'mother.'"

"Oh, but I'm not—you see, I'm just . . ." Helen couldn't get the words out. She cleared her throat. "I'm his aunt."

"Oops! My mistake! Okay then, just put 'aunt' right on that line there." The nurse was unfazed.

Helen wrote in the word. Her hand was shaking. "Am I done now?"

"Yes, you're all set. One of the doctors will call you in a few minutes. It's pretty slow here today, so it shouldn't be a long wait."

"Thank you."

Helen had just settled Teddy on her lap again when Mort finally returned. "What took you so long?"

"I parked across the street, so I had to walk a little bit."

"Why didn't you just park in the hospital lot?"

"They're charging a dollar to park there, that's why! They have you over a barrel, so they try to rob you blind," Mort harrumphed and sat down next to her on the couch. He had just opened a magazine when a nurse called Teddy's name. Dr. Schlatner was waiting for them. He examined Teddy and asked a long list of questions. Had Teddy lost consciousness? Where did the ball hit him? Any vomiting? Blurry vision?

When the doctor finished, he told them Teddy's eye was unharmed and he didn't appear to have a concussion. "I want you to be very careful with him for the next few days" the doctor cautioned. "No running or physical activity for twenty-four hours. If he vomits or complains of blurry vision or headaches, I want you to see your pediatrician immediately." Dr. Schlatner winked at Teddy and rumpled the little boy's hair. "Keep your eyes open, slugger, and don't walk into any more line drives." He dug his hand into his pocket and pulled out a lollipop. For the first time all day, Teddy smiled.

The nurse led them back downstairs to fill out Teddy's discharge papers. Helen spotted Rose and Abe standing by the main desk. Rose was screaming at one of the attendants. "How many times do I have to spell his name for you? How many two-and-a-half-year-old boys could you possibly have admitted in the last hour?"

As soon as Rose saw Teddy she gasped. "Oh my God! Look at his face! What did the doctor say?" She turned from Mort to Helen, demanding answers.

For the first time since the accident, Helen felt a wave of exhaustion overtake her. She was too tired to answer Rose's questions or pretend to be pleasant. She gave Mort the discharge papers and handed him the ice pack the nurse had given her. "Mort can explain everything," she said. "Abe and I have to get back and pick up the kids."

Helen bent down to hug Teddy goodbye, but Rose grabbed her arm and pulled. "You're not going *anywhere* until you tell me what happened."

Helen's reaction was visceral; she yanked her arm free and glared.

"You have no right to speak to me that way!" she shouted. "Where were *you* when Teddy got hurt? Where were *you* when I was comforting him on the way to the hospital, filling out forms and talking to his doctors? You were gone! You were nowhere! You were hiding from your family and feeling sorry for yourself!"

People were staring and the nurses at the reception desk were silent. "Lower your voice, Helen, please—" Mort began, but Helen waved him aside and took a step closer to Rose. "I'm not taking the blame for it anymore, Rose! Not this time! Do you hear me? You can go ahead and pretend you had no part in this, but we both know the truth. For years you've pretended to be the weak one so I would get stuck with the dirty work. You fall apart and I'm the one who has to pick up the pieces. Well, pretend all you want, but you made this happen. *You did this!*" Helen was shouting so loudly that Teddy started to cry. He was frightened and scurried to grab on to Rose's leg.

Rose opened her mouth to respond but closed it without saying a word. For an instant, Helen thought she saw a flicker of remorse pass over her sister-in-law's face, but Rose made no apologies. On the car ride home, Helen decided it was probably just the hospital's fluorescent lighting that made her look that way. Rose wasn't sorry at all.

Chapter 27

JUDITH

(April 1952)

The black-and-white clock on the library wall was oversized and easy to read. She would wait twenty minutes more, until the hands pointed to a few minutes past five. Then she would pack up her books and walk carefully down the pitted stone staircase to the side exit. If she walked at her usual pace, she would reach the front door of her house around 5:25. She had to be home by five-thirty or her mother would start to worry.

That's what Judith told people. "If I'm not home by five-thirty, my mother will start to worry." But "worry" was a euphemism. An entirely truthful girl would have said this: "If I am not home at exactly five-thirty, my mother will start panicking. At five-thirty-one, she will call my father at work. At five-thirty-two, she will call the police, and at five-thirty-three, she will call the local hospitals. At five-thirty-five, she will sit at the table and start crying. She will tell my sisters and little brother that I am most likely dead, hit by a car or kidnapped by a child molester, and that will make *them* start to cry. And then, when I walk in at five-thirty-six or five-thirty-eight, she will scream at me and wring her hands. She will call me irresponsible and selfish. I will apologize and promise never to be late again. She will go into her room, slam the door and refuse to come out. I will hug my sisters and tell them everything is fine. I will rock my little brother on my lap until he isn't scared anymore. I will finish making dinner if my mother has started it, feed my siblings and get them ready for bed. My father, after getting the five-thirty-one warning call, will work late that night and come home between nine and nine-thirty. I will leave a plate for him wrapped in tinfoil on top of the stove. He will eat it alone at the kitchen table, knock on my door before he goes to sleep and call out 'good night.' And in the morning, we will all pretend it never happened."

The first time Rose behaved that way, Judith thought her mother must have been upset about something else. But then it happened a second time and a third. So Judith tried her best never to be late, not from the library or anywhere else. The trouble was, she could never predict when her mother might "worry." On school days, it was settled that she had to be home by five-thirty from the library. But what if she took Teddy to the park? Or walked to the drugstore for a candy bar on a Saturday afternoon? How many times had she come home to find her mother agitated and hysterical, sometimes when she had only been gone for fifteen minutes? She had lost count.

Judith tried to get her mother's attention whenever she left the house, to set a return time so they both knew when she was expected. But half the time her mother forgot the time they had agreed upon and ended up "worrying" anyway. Judith tried leaving notes, detailed and clearly printed with her return time circled in red pen. But her mother claimed she never saw them. "How am I supposed to know that I should look for a letter when my child is dead in a ditch somewhere?"

"But I'm not dead in a ditch."

"How could I have known that? You were twenty minutes late!"

"Mother, please. I'm not late. If you had just read my note—"

"Stop talking to me about notes! I won't be tormented like this!"

Experience taught Judith a few things. She stopped defending herself. She stopped responding to the accusations. She learned that if she apologized right away, the recovery time was faster. So she apologized, over and over, until apologizing felt just the same as having an ordinary conversation. She grew accustomed to it.

In the old days, Judith might have talked to her aunt Helen about the situation. But she felt uncomfortable doing that now. Ever since Teddy's accident two years ago, Judith's mother and her aunt barely spoke to each other. Things had been bad before then, but after Sol's party, they had gotten worse. For years Judith had been trying to figure out the source of the tension between them. She paid close attention whenever the two of them were together. But no matter how attentive she was, she couldn't uncover the source of the hostility. All she knew was that she no longer felt right talking to her aunt about anything having to do with her mother. She talked to Aunt Helen about school, her sisters and even her father. But discussing her mother felt like a betrayal. The topic wasn't difficult to avoid—Aunt Helen never asked about her mother anyway.

Rose started "worrying" about Judith a few months after the accident. She worried about the other children too, but since Teddy was home with her all day and Mimi and Dinah still went to the school across the street, Judith was the primary object of her mother's distress.

Judith knew that if she went directly home after school each day, she might be able to prevent some of her mother's outbursts. But, as much as she wanted to avoid causing her mother additional anxiety, she knew that if she gave up her outings and changed her routine to pacify Rose, her own obedient nature would take over, and slowly the few freedoms she had managed to retain would be lost. There were so many days that she longed to go home—she wanted to play with Teddy and her sisters, or she wanted to have a piece of the apple cake she knew was left over from dinner the night before. But even on those days she forced herself to walk to the library. If she didn't have any homework, she would pick out a book to read or look through the college brochures she borrowed from the school counselor. Eventually she stopped looking for books. The brochures became her escape.

Judith would open the college booklets and imagine herself in the photographs, walking on the campuses and chatting with the students. She would live in a dormitory with other girls her age, and no one would cry if she was five minutes late returning from a class. Her mother wouldn't have to worry about her anymore—there would be dorm monitors to keep track of her.

Judith was just a junior in high school, but one of the counselors had spoken to her in the fall about the possibility of graduating early, in the same class as her cousin Harry. "I really think you should consider accelerating your program here," Mrs. Morhardt suggested. "You've already taken most of the classes we have to offer, and you'll have more than enough credits to graduate at the end of this year. Why waste time reviewing what you already know when you could be expanding your knowledge?" Mrs. Morhardt made it sound so simple. When she asked Judith if her parents had given their permission, Judith told her yes even though she hadn't dared to mention it to them. The few friends Judith had at school didn't know about her plan. In truth, she didn't consider it a plan at all because she hardly gave it any thought. She had gotten some forms from Mrs. Morhardt and applied to a few colleges back in December, but she was convinced that none of her applications would be accepted. Judith couldn't imagine that anyone would actually take the time to reply to her letters. It was already April, and there had been no news. Judith would tell Mrs. Morhardt that she would stay in high school and graduate with her proper class. She was resigned to another year of afternoons at the library.

Judith looked at the clock again: 4:48. She got up to stretch her legs and ran her finger over the top of one of the bookcases. It was caked with dust and turned her finger black. What an uninviting place this was. Three round tables had been thrown between the bookcases, with mismatched wooden chairs surrounding them. The only light source was a dim fluorescent fixture that flickered and hummed every few minutes. The clock ticked. Soon it would be time to leave.

The dull thud of footsteps on the stone stairs startled her. No one ever walked up to the reading area at this hour. Then she heard a familiar voice calling her name. "Judith? Are you here?" It was Harry. Had her mother been so hysterical that she sent him over to the library to find her? The thought of it nauseated her and she wanted to hide behind the bookcases. Instead, she sank back into her chair and covered her face with her hands.

"Are you okay?" Harry asked. He was watching her from the top of the steps. Judith moved her hands away from her face and stood up. "I'm leaving *right now*," she barked. "It's not even five o'clock! My mother knows I don't get home until five-thirty on school days! I can't believe she sent you here to get me!"

Harry stared. "Whoa. Calm down. I don't know what you're talking about, but your mom didn't send me."

"Then why are you here?"

"Because *my* mom sent me. To give you these." He held up two thick envelopes.

"What? Where did she get those?"

"The postman gave her all the mail today when she was outside with Natalie. She was leaving the letters for your parents outside your door when she saw these." Harry smiled at her. He seemed sympathetic. "They were addressed to you. I guess my mom thought they might be important. Thought you might want to open them alone. She knew you'd be here, so she sent me." He handed her the letters. She looked at the return addresses. Barnard and Bryn Mawr. Judith was dumbfounded. She hadn't thought they would ever write back.

"Oh." Judith sat back down.

"What's Bryn Mawr? I haven't heard of that one. I haven't heard of a lot of them, I guess. I don't even want to go to college. I'd rather just start working with my dad, but he says I have to get a degree first so I'm going to City College. Where's Bryn Mawr, anyway?"

"What?" Judith's mouth was dry and her heart was pounding. "Oh. It's in Pennsylvania."

Harry whistled. "Getting out of town, huh? I guess I can't blame you. Hey, why are these places sending you stuff, anyway? You're just a junior."

"Well . . ." Judith hesitated. How much should she say? What should she tell him? She looked at the clock again: 5:05. She had to leave now, right this minute, or she'd risk another frenzied evening of accusations and weeping.

"Let's walk home, okay? I have to get back by five-thirty."

"How come?"

"If I'm not home by five-thirty my mother will start to worry."

Harry shrugged. "Fine by me, but don't you want to open your letters? My mom thought they were really important."

Judith stuffed the envelopes in the bottom of her bag, under her science textbook. "Nope—just brochures. You know. Information in case I want to apply next year. Nothing that can't wait."

"Oh." Harry looked disappointed, and Judith felt guilty for lying. She touched his shoulder and smiled at him. "Listen, Harry, thanks for coming all the way over here to give them to me. That was very thoughtful. I mean, it was really, really nice of you." Harry grinned back at her with big blue eyes and offered to carry her book bag home. They walked down the steps together, and Judith finally understood why all the girls at her school were so crazy over him. He really was handsome, and she had to admit he could be charming sometimes, like today. It would have been nice if she could have opened the letters with him there, at the library. And it would have been comforting to have someone she trusted to tell her secret to. Maybe one day that would happen. Maybe one day she and Harry would be real friends, not just cousins. But for now, she didn't have time to think about that. It was almost five-fifteen, and her mother was at home, waiting for her. Waiting and worrying.

Chapter 28

ABE

Abe whistled as he made his way up the steps to the apartment. Before he could reach for the knob, Helen opened the door from the inside. The look on her face was expectant, excited. *How does she know already?* But when she saw it was him, her smile faded. "I thought you were going to be Harry," she said, "or maybe Judith."

"Well, nice to see you too," he teased, and Helen tried to explain. "I gave Harry some letters to take to Judith at the library and I thought they were back. Why are you home so early?"

"Who's writing letters to Judith?"

Helen groaned, annoyed with having to explain. "Colleges, Abe! And she's not even graduating this year. I've told you, she's a brilliant girl. Mort underestimates her. Remember that poetry award—"

Abe didn't want to get caught up in another anti-Mort tirade, so he cut Helen off. "Which colleges are the letters from?"

"There was one from Barnard and another from Bryn Mawr."

"Where's that?"

"Honestly, Abe! Katharine Hepburn graduated from Bryn Mawr."

"Oh well, if *Katharine Hepburn* went there, it must really be something!"

Helen rolled her eyes at him. "Those letters could be important."

"You said yourself, she's not even graduating this year—the girl hasn't even applied. They're just brochures."

"They're not brochures."

Abe held up his hands in defeat. "All right, fine. Not brochures. I'm going to go wash up."

An hour later at the dinner table, Abe stood up and tapped his fork on his water glass. "Your attention, please," he said. "I have a family announcement." Helen put down her fork but the boys kept on eating. "What's a 'nouncement?" Natalie whispered to George.

"I don't like to talk business at the dinner table, but I think it's important for my family to know that Box Brothers is having a very good year. Last week Bob Sherman's client sent us a five-year contract to become his exclusive supplier, not just for cereal boxes but a lot of other products they're creating."

"That's wonderful, Abe!" Helen was beaming. She started to clear some of the serving plates and made a stack in the sink.

"Sure is," he agreed. "But now we need a bigger factory to make all the boxes, and a different kind of machinery."

"Are you looking for a new factory?" Harry asked.

"Now you're paying attention!" Abe was pleased. "Actually, we already found one. It's perfect—big enough and not expensive."

"Where is it?" Joe wanted to know.

"Out on Long Island, not too far from where your uncle Sol lives."

"Oh," said George. "Are you going to see Uncle Sol when you work there?"

"Well, as it turns out," Abe wiped his mouth with his napkin and placed it on the table, "we're all going to see more of Sol."

Helen was shuttling back and forth between the table and the sink now, grabbing glasses and silverware, even though the boys were still eating. "Is he going to be working with you?"

"Sol and me?" Abe shook his head and chuckled. "You really think Sol would want to work at Box Brothers? Nah, we're not going into *business* with him. We're going to be neighbors!"

Helen stopped short, the last of the glasses still in her hand. "What did you say?"

"Neighbors!" Abe grinned. "We're moving! We're going to buy a house ten minutes from Sol." Helen said nothing, so Abe went on, "I went looking with a realtor the other day and I asked her to show me some houses; I told her I only wanted to see ones with a big room by the front door. Whaddya call that thing again?" He turned to Helen. "Right where you walk in?"

"A foyer," Helen whispered. She was still holding the glass. In a flash, she remembered the day she first met Rose, on the front steps of the two-family house, almost nineteen years earlier. Helen hadn't been thrilled when Abe first told her they were going to share the house with Mort, but the brothers had purchased it together for a price they couldn't pass up. She had been pregnant with Harry, and they needed more space.

A few weeks after they had moved in, Mort met Rose. He didn't tell them much about her, but Helen knew he was in love. Nothing else could explain the way he looked at Rose that day on the steps. Helen had met them coming up as she was walking down with Abe, on a cloudless Sunday afternoon in the middle of spring. She would never forget Rose's sweet smile, the way she congratulated them on the baby, complimented them on the house. She was beautiful and gentle, and Helen wanted to be her friend. She remembered thinking that if Rose married Mort, sharing the house wouldn't be so bad after all.

Abe snapped his fingers, shattering her reverie. "That's it! A 'foyer.' I told the real estate agent I would only buy a house with a nice big foyer because that's what my wife always wanted." Abe walked over to Helen and tried to put his arm around her, but she moved to the sink, turned the glass over and slammed it down, hard. A tiny crack ran its way up from the rim.

"Does it have a television?" Sam interrupted.

Abe laughed. "*That's* what you want to know? Any house can have a television, Sam. We could have a television here."

"Then can our new house have a television?"

"We'll see. Stop asking about televisions. The big news is that we're moving!"

"I don't want to move!" Natalie announced loudly. "I don't want a new house. Everyone will be strangers."

"They won't be strangers once you *know* them," Sam scolded her. "Besides, at least you don't have to worry about changing schools. You don't even go to school yet!" He turned to Abe. "Jeez, Dad. I was gonna have Mr. Ketterer next year—he's the best teacher in the whole school! And now we're gonna have all new teachers and have to make all new friends."

"What if no one likes me at the new school?" George wailed, panicking.

"They'll like you fine, George," Abe insisted.

"This whole thing is a bunch of crap!" Joe got up from the table, eyes flashing. "You didn't even ask us if we wanted to move. This is *crap!*"

"Joe!" Helen shouted. "Don't speak to your father that way! This conversation is over. Go to your room. In fact, *all* of you go to your rooms. Now."

"I didn't even say anything," Harry muttered.

"Now," Helen repeated. The five of them filed out of the kitchen, worried looks on their faces.

Abe was deflated. Everyone was upset and Helen wouldn't even look at him. He knew the kids would take some time to get used to the idea, but why wasn't Helen more excited? How many times had she told him they needed more bedrooms and closets? How many nights had she complained about car horns and truck engines waking her up? For Chrissake, hadn't he specifically told the realtor he would only look at houses with foyers just to make her happy? And even if you took away the foyer, the space and the yard, he couldn't believe she wasn't excited about not having to live in the same house as Mort, for once! He would have thought she'd move anyplace just for that privilege alone!

Was she angry that he hadn't spoken to her about the move beforehand? Did she have reservations about living closer to Sol? If she wouldn't even look at him, how was he supposed to figure it out?

"Look, Helen, if you're angry because I haven't shown you the houses yet, I'm sorry. I wanted to surprise you. But I didn't buy one yet. There are three or four of them we can look at and then you can make the decision. We'll get the one you like best."

Helen was standing at the sink with her back to him. When she turned on the faucet, he could see that her hand was shaking.

"Helen? Look at me. Please."

Helen mumbled something, but he could barely hear her over the running water.

"Helen, I can't hear you. Turn off the water, sweetheart, and talk to me."

When she finally did turn around, Abe barely recognized her. Her eyes were swollen, her cheeks were flushed and her lips were twisted tight in a grimace. She forced her mouth open to speak, but the only sound that emerged was a high-pitched wail. He had never seen her like this.

Abe tried to take her into his arms but she pushed him away, her back up against the sink, her arms wrapped around herself as if she were trying to get warm. "I don't understand," he told her, "Why are you so upset? Please, honey, tell me."

"I can't explain. . . ." She choked out the words in a tangle of sobs.

Abe softened his voice. "I promise you," he said, "I promise you it will be all right." He put one hand on her shoulder. "I know it's a big change, but we're going to have a wonderful new house for our family." She let him take her in his arms then, and wept like her heart was breaking. His shirt was soaked through in moments.

After a few minutes Helen lifted her head. "What about Mort and Rose?" she whispered.

"Mort is telling them tonight," he told her. "He already picked a house. But there's nothing else for sale on that street so we'll be a few blocks away." He tried to make his voice sound playful. "So cheer up—at least they won't be next door!" He thought this would make Helen smile. He wanted to hear her laugh. But the tears only fell faster and her grip on him tightened.

Chapter 29

HELEN

Helen was still shaken the next day. After she got the boys off to school, she was unable to follow her usual morning routine. The dirty breakfast dishes nauseated her. The unmade beds gave her chest pains and the globs of toothpaste on the bathroom counter left her head aching. She needed fresh air, an escape from the drudgery of the morning cleanup. So she left it all—the dishes, the beds, the bathroom—and got Natalie ready to go to the park.

Once there, Helen showed Natalie how to feed the ducks with the stale bread they brought from home. Natalie watched the birds and mimicked their gait. They had been there for half an hour when Helen spotted Rose and Teddy walking through the park gates. Teddy saw Natalie and ran over. Rose had no choice but to join Helen.

"You must have gotten out of the house early this morning." Rose brushed a few leaves off the bench and sat down.

"I couldn't face the breakfast dishes," Helen admitted. It had been a long time since she and Rose had sat together in the park like this.

"That's not like you."

"I know. Did Mort tell you about the move?"

Rose nodded, and Helen's eyes filled with tears. She searched for a tissue in her handbag. "I can't believe it. I don't want to leave the house."

"I do." Rose's voice was hard.

"But it's perfect. The kids can see each other every day. Look at them. They're like brother and sister! Living in the same house makes it so much easier. I can see Teddy and you can see Natalie whenever we want. Why do you want to leave?"

"Do I really have to list the reasons for you? It's too small, for one. You and your family are literally on top of us every minute of every day."

"We'll switch. You can take the top apartment. I'll convince Abe, he won't mind—" Helen was pleading with her. Desperate.

"Listen to yourself, will you? Even if we moved to the top floor it wouldn't solve anything. It wouldn't change the situation."

"What situation?"

"Stop it!" The children looked over from their spot on the miniature bridge that crossed over the pond. They had gotten tired of chasing the ducks and were dropping their crumbs now from the bridge into the water. Rose lowered her voice. "Stop acting like you don't know what I'm talking about. This move will be the best thing for all of us. If we have more breathing room we'll all get along better. Abe and Mort too."

It was warm for April, but Helen pulled her sweater over her shoulders. She was shivering. "But we won't even be on the same street. You and I won't see the children. Days could go by without us seeing them . . . weeks."

"I know."

"I can't stand the thought of not seeing Teddy every day. Don't you want to see Natalie?" Helen beseeched her, but Rose was unmoved. After a few moments she took Helen's hand, just like she used to, back before the babies were born, back when they were still like sisters. "I need to do this, Helen," she said. "I don't know how much longer I can continue on this way, all of us in one house. Some days I feel like I'm losing my mind. Please don't try to stop this. *Please.*"

Helen nodded then—a barely perceptible movement. Still, she knew Rose had seen it because the next instant, Rose let go of her hand. She dropped it swiftly, with complete disregard, as if it were the hand of a stranger or of someone unclean.

Chapter 30

JUDITH

In the excitement surrounding her father's big announcement, Judith forgot about the letters. It was only when she was in science class the next day and took out her textbook that she saw them in the bottom of her book bag. Her heart began to pound. Should she open them at school? No, it would be safer to wait until later, at the library.

In a few hours she was back upstairs in the dusty reading room, basking under the murkiness of the lone fluorescent bulb. She settled herself at one of the empty round tables and pulled out the letters.

Other than an occasional birthday card from a distant relative, Judith rarely received mail. Seeing her name typed across the creamy white envelopes was a thrill in itself, so for a few minutes she was content just looking at them. No matter what they contained, she was buoyed by the knowledge that she was important enough to receive letters like these, and that somewhere, someone in a college admissions office knew her name and cared enough to write to her. Her name was on a list, and whether the list meant rejection or acceptance, in the moments before she opened the envelopes she was overcome with relief that she existed somewhere outside the boundaries of her everyday life and that her name and person were as indisputably real as anyone else's.

But relief didn't satisfy for long. Soon she was tearing at the envelopes. Barnard was first. *We are delighted to offer you admission to Barnard College as a member of the class of 1956. . . .* Next, Bryn Mawr: *It gives us great pleasure to inform you that your application for admission has been approved. . . .*

She read and reread the letters, looking for some sign of trickery or fraud. Were they real? Did this mean she could go to college? What should she do now? Who should she tell?

Judith's initial thought was to bring the letters to Mrs. Morhardt, but it was Friday, and she wouldn't see the school counselor until Monday morning. She could tell Harry, but she was still feeling guilty about lying to him the day before. Of course her parents would have to be told. She hadn't told them she was applying to colleges. She hadn't mentioned that graduating early was even a possibility. What would they think? The library clock read 5:03. She'd find out soon enough.

At dinner everyone was still talking about the news from the night before. What did the new house look like? Were there other children in the neighborhood? Would they walk to school or take a bus?

Judith was surprised by how happy her mother seemed about the move. There was something about the way she acted that reminded Judith of the months right before Teddy was born. Her mother had been so hopeful then. Maybe the move was just what she needed. Maybe her worrying would stop when they were living outside of Brooklyn.

There was even talk of her mother learning to drive.

"You do have a good sense of direction, Rose," her father said, rising from the table. Judith's mother smiled at him as if he had just said the most romantic thing in the world. I suppose now is as good a time as any, Judith thought. When her siblings left the kitchen she cleared her throat. "May I please speak to you both? It's important."

It was not common for Judith to ask for an audience. Her father nodded and sat back down.

"I need to show you something." Judith got up from the table to retrieve the two letters and then placed them in front of her father.

Mort inspected the envelopes. He read the first letter carefully, then turned his attention to the second. Judith waited for him to smile, to congratulate her, but he didn't. He passed the letters to Rose and asked, "Did you know about this?" Her mother shook her head no, her expression unreadable.

"Why didn't you tell us about this earlier?" Mort demanded. Judith was surprised by the severity of his tone.

"The letters just came yesterday."

"Is there anything else you'd like to share?"

"I don't understand—"

He was impatient. "Are you expecting any more letters?"

"No."

"These are the only colleges you applied to?"

"Yes."

"Who else knows?" *Why is he asking so many questions?*

"No one. Well, the school counselor, Mrs. Morhardt. She's the one who encouraged me to graduate early and to apply to colleges."

"You didn't think it was important to tell us?"

"I didn't think it would amount to anything. I didn't think they would accept me."

"You purposefully deceived us."

"No! I didn't tell you because—"

"Because you didn't want us to know." Her father punctuated the sentence with a bang of his fist. The table shook with the force of the blow and Judith pushed her chair back a few inches. She had known that her parents might not react the way she wanted them to. She had anticipated that they might object to her going to school in Pennsylvania. But she always assumed they would be proud of her. She would be the first of their family to graduate from college. Weren't they supposed to be excited?

"I wanted to surprise you," she said, "the way you surprised us with the moving news." This wasn't entirely true, but it wasn't a lie. Still, one look at her father told Judith that she had said the wrong thing. He looked like he was about to explode.

"Do you understand how embarrassing this is? That our daughter went behind our backs without our permission?"

"But I didn't do anything wrong! You're making it sound like I committed a crime!"

Judith's mother finally chimed in. "How could we let you move all the way to Pennsylvania? You're only seventeen years old!"

"But I wouldn't be living by myself. I'd be in a dormitory with supervision and curfews."

"A curfew does not take the place of a mother."

"Of course it doesn't, I'm just trying to explain—"

"You can explain to Mrs. Morhardt, then, on Monday morning," Mort interrupted. Judith did not like the tone of finality in his voice. What had he decided?

"What should I tell her? She thinks I'm graduating."

"Then tell her you'll be graduating. And that you will be joining your cousin Harry at City College in the fall."

"But—"

"It's your choice. You can go to City College in the fall, or you can go to high school for another year. It doesn't make any difference to me. If you choose to go to college you will live at home, and you and Harry can take the train together into Manhattan for your classes."

"What about Barnard? It's in New York too. I'll live at home and—"

"Why should I pay for you to attend a private college when City College is free?"

"They have a wonderful writing program there and Mrs. Morhardt said there are scholarships."

Her father looked at her with absolute contempt. "Do you honestly think you're going to be some sort of famous writer?"

Judith didn't answer, so he continued, "Half the girls in your school will be headed to a steno pool when they graduate and the other half will be headed down the aisle. You are one of the few who will have the privilege of a college education. I hope you know how lucky you are." He got up from the table. "I'm going for a walk," he said, taking his coat from the peg on the wall. He opened the kitchen door and walked out, letting the door slam shut behind him.

Judith's mother folded the letters neatly and placed them in their respective envelopes. She passed them across the table to Judith without a single word, rose from her seat and went into her bedroom.

Judith contemplated ripping up the letters or throwing them away, but she couldn't bring herself to destroy them. The college stationery was too elegant, the envelopes too crisp. She ran her finger over the raised crest on the Barnard letter. Had she been naive to assume she belonged there? She felt foolish now, and relieved she hadn't told any of the girls at school her secret.

She would write to the colleges tomorrow. She would tell them how sorry she was that she could not attend, but that personal matters prevented her. That was the right thing to say, wasn't it? But she would keep the letters. She'd put them somewhere safe, maybe in a scrapbook or a keepsake box. And one day, when she was an adult with her own house and her own family, she would take them out and pass them around, and the people who loved her would look at them and be proud.

Chapter 31

ROSE

(June 1952)

Rose didn't understand why Judith needed to leave for the graduation ceremony so early. If it didn't start until ten, why did Judith insist on leaving the house at nine? "The students have to get there early to line up," she explained to Rose. "We're not allowed to sit with our families. I'll see you there."

Rose sighed. There were so many things about Judith that she didn't understand. For one thing, she couldn't comprehend why her daughter got so upset when Mort told her she couldn't go to Barnard. Was it really worth it to pay all that extra money just for a fancier diploma? For that matter, why did Judith have to go to college when she was still so young? What was the rush?

"I feel like I'm going round in circles in high school," Judith told her. "I just want the next part of my life to start." Judith probably thought her mother had no idea what she meant. But it was the first thing Judith had said in a long time that made sense to Rose. For years, she had felt like she was running around in circles too. She had spent the first part of her married life wasting energy on an impossible task. It was only now that she realized how unattainable her goal had been. Mort would never be happy. There was no test she could pass that would change him.

In the years that followed, Rose nursed her grief with a heady tonic of remorse mixed with the resentment that stemmed from the burden of Helen's constant surveillance. There was no comfort for her in this bitter concoction, but she nearly drowned herself in it just the same.

If Judith's new start would be going to college, Rose's new start would come from leaving the house on Christopher Avenue. As she cleaned out the closets and got rid of her family's worn-out belongings, she pictured an internal purging as well, of her own worst thoughts and habits. When she taped up the boxes of china and crystal her mother had given her, she was Pandora in reverse, putting away her worst anxieties and failures, withholding only hope. She understood the desire for a clean slate more than Judith would ever know.

The graduation that morning was to be held in the high school gymnasium, and there were barely enough seats for everyone in the crowd. It was warm for June, and sitting with Teddy on her lap only made Rose feel more smothered.

Finally the principal stood and tapped the microphone at the podium. When they were done hearing from him, the school district superintendent and a multitude of class officers, they still had to suffer through the presentation of student awards by Vice Principal Kaplan. There was an award for service to the school, service to the community and another for the best scholar-athlete. By then, Rose was more than ready for the ceremony to end. She groaned silently as another speaker she did not recognize stepped up to the podium. "Good morning. My name is Abigail Morhardt, and I am the college counselor for William Wheeler High School." Her name sounds familiar, Rose thought, but she couldn't place it.

The attractive woman in the elegant cream suit continued, "Principal Singer asked me to present the final award to the valedictorian of this year's graduating class. For three years, I have had the pleasure of watching this young woman develop her academic talents. After reading one of her freshman essays, I knew that she was a very special student. She has managed to complete all school course requirements in only three years, and I am so pleased that she will be continuing her journey this fall at City College. Ladies and gentlemen, I am thrilled to announce the valedictorian of the class of 1952: Judith Berman. Judith, please join me at the podium to accept your award."

Rose looked over at Mort, hoping he wouldn't be angry that they hadn't known about the award beforehand. Mort didn't look upset, but his face was difficult to read. He was straining his neck, trying to get a glimpse of Judith, but the graduates were sitting in alphabetical order at the front of the gymnasium and it took Judith a few minutes to make her way out of the crowd. When Rose finally saw Judith, she was relieved. The look of shock on her daughter's face was unmistakable. It was clear she had no idea about the award. Rose watched as Mort leaned back in his chair.

When Judith finally made it to the podium, Mrs. Morhardt shook her hand vigorously and whispered something in her ear. Judith smiled shyly and cleared her throat into the microphone. "This is a tremendous surprise and a great honor. Thank you all so much." Principal Singer stepped forward and handed Judith a wooden plaque, which she carried with her on the way back to her seat.

Teddy was clapping vigorously for his sister, even though he had no idea why. He slid off Rose's lap and clapped until Rose told him to shush. "I told her she should have let me do her hair this morning," Mimi whispered under her breath. "But did she let me? No . . ."

Rose silenced her with a glance, and Mimi went back to her compact mirror. Dinah had woken up just as Judith was headed back to her seat and wanted to know what she had missed. "Your sister was given an award for being the valedictorian," Rose told her.

"What does 'valedictorian' mean?" Dinah asked.

"It means she's the smartest one of all of them," Mimi said.

Mimi loved to tease, so Dinah wasn't sure if this was true. "Is that right, Papa?" she asked Mort. "Is Judith really the smartest?"

The entire family turned to Mort for his answer. "Statistically, she has the highest grade point average," he answered.

"What does that mean?" Dinah asked again. Mimi, sensing her father's impatience, pulled her sister aside and whispered loudly, "It means she's the smartest. Now stop asking questions."

After the last diploma was handed out, the graduates and their families filtered out of their seats and reunited on the small grassy area in front of the school. Rose was happy to be outside, but the boost to her mood was overshadowed by what she saw next. Nearly all the girls were holding small bouquets given to them after the ceremony by their families. Several were holding their bouquets in front of them like bridesmaids as they posed for photographs with friends. Rose felt guilty and then increasingly annoyed. How could she have known she was supposed to buy Judith a bouquet? Why had no one bothered to tell her?

A few moments later Mimi was waving to her cousin. "Happy graduation, Harry!" she called out. Harry, joined by the rest of his family, was walking toward them. Judith appeared at the same time, carrying her plaque, and Rose watched as Harry swooped her up in a congratulatory embrace. "Wow! You're the valedictorian! Can you believe it? That's fantastic!" Judith wasn't used to so much attention— she was speechless. Abe hugged Judith next. Rose didn't notice the small bouquet of yellow roses Helen was holding until her sister-in-law planted it firmly in her own hands. Rose turned to Helen, confused, but Helen motioned for Rose to be silent and take the bouquet. Helen wanted Rose to give it to Judith.

When Abe finally let Judith go and she saw the bouquet her mother was holding, her eyes welled up with tears. "I didn't think anyone would remember my graduation bouquet. I know it's a silly tradition, but it's so beautiful." Judith kissed her mother on the cheek. "Thank you, Mother, thank you!"

Rose accepted the kiss and the embrace that accompanied it. She had never seen Judith look happier, but she wasn't able to enjoy it. Helen had come to her rescue yet again, this time with the bouquet. No matter the occasion, Helen always seemed to be one step ahead of her. The move to their new home, Rose decided, couldn't come fast enough.

Chapter 32

HELEN

They moved a few days after the graduation. Helen had been packing for weeks, and every night Abe brought home a few more boxes for her. "Perk of the job," he'd say when he carried them through the door. The boys groaned, but Natalie laughed every time.

Helen did most of the work when the boys were at school. She would give Natalie a "job" every morning: packing up this or that, collections of spoons, books or socks—anything she could think of that wasn't fragile enough to break. For the most part, it was just monotonous. But some tasks, like going through their photographs, were difficult for Helen. There was a framed picture of Mort and Abe with their father a few years before he passed away; a wedding photo of her own mother and father, now long gone; a photo of her and Rose from Harry's bar mitzvah, before all the quarreling began.

Helen sat on the floor, wrapping the frames in sheets of old newspapers, wondering if she would ever be able to unpack them. Maybe it was better for the pictures to stay boxed up at the new house. They were going to have so much more space—an attic and a basement for storing things. Some of the boxes could go there. There were plenty of other family pictures she could scatter around. Why torture herself with reminders of what had already been lost? After she taped the box shut, Helen wrote, STORAGE, on it with a thick black Magic

Marker she had picked up at the drugstore. She underlined the word twice.

Once the photos were packed, Helen decided to move on to something easier, something less sentimental. But even emptying the kitchen cabinets brought a lump to her throat. The cake pans reminded her of all the birthdays they had celebrated in the house. The pots made her think of all the times she had made chicken soup when someone was sick. Helen was unable to separate even the most mundane objects from her own unshakeable feelings of sadness and loss. It was only after the packing of a vegetable peeler sent her into hysterics that she decided she needed to get some fresh air.

"Natalie, honey!" Helen called out toward the living room. "Get your shoes on. We're going for a walk."

As soon as they entered the drugstore, Helen teared up. She knew it would be the last time she would set foot in it, so she let Natalie pick out a candy bar and decided to buy a tube of lipstick for old times' sake. She remembered back to the day almost five years earlier when Judith helped her pick out a color before their dinner with Sol. She had been pregnant then, hoping for a girl, wondering whether she would ever be able to share a moment like that with her own daughter. And now, here she was, back in the very same spot, hoping again that the next big step in her life would turn out well. "Do you like this color?" she asked Natalie, after applying a generous coat of "Cardinal Sunset" to her lips. Natalie had already unwrapped her candy bar. She inspected her mother's face and shook her head vigorously. "Your lips look dirty," she told Helen. "Take it off."

Helen picked up some candy for the boys and an extra box of Band-Aids. The owner's wife, Mrs. Feldman, was working at the register. She was a thick, unappetizing woman, well into her sixties. "When do you leave?" Mrs. Feldman asked, dispensing with the niceties. She patted the stiff graying mound on her head and slid her glasses down to the tip of her nose to read the price on the Band-Aids.

"The day after tomorrow," Helen answered. "Today is the last day of school for the boys and then they have to pack up their rooms."

"Why you have to move to that *fakakta* island is beyond me, but you should only have health in your new home."

"Thank you, Mrs. Feldman. We'll miss you. Won't we, Natalie?"

Mrs. Feldman leaned over the counter to get a good look at

Natalie. "So long, Mamaleh!" she shouted. Natalie dug her face into Helen's skirt and covered her eyes. She was afraid of Mrs. Feldman. "Hmmph," Mrs. Feldman said, miffed. "That one takes after the uncle." For the rest of the afternoon, every time Helen was tempted to cry, she forced herself to think of the old woman's face.

She packed for the rest of the evening and all the next day. The last night they spent in the house was endless for her, and as she lay awake, listening to the trucks and buses make their routes on Christopher Avenue, she wondered how she would ever sleep once they moved. The absence of noise was impossible to imagine, and the thought of a lifetime of silence frightened her.

When she got out of bed the next morning, her eyes were swollen and her neck was stiff. Abe was still sleeping. She dressed quickly and threw her nightgown into the last open box on the bedroom floor. She took out her curlers and threw those in as well, along with Abe's slippers and the small clock on her nightstand. Then she walked to the kitchen to make a pot of coffee.

Abe came in after her a few minutes later. "Did you sleep?" he asked, even though he knew she hadn't. She shook her head and opened the refrigerator. The only thing left inside was a glass bottle of milk on the top shelf. Helen's refrigerator had always been full, loaded to excess with casseroles and fruit salads, butter and eggs, lunch meats and leftovers. But that morning, all that remained was the miserable bottle, half filled and alone. The sight of it was so discouraging, so contrary to Helen's nature, that she couldn't help but cry. Abe patted her on the back and poured some milk into her coffee.

An hour later, the movers arrived and Helen stood to the side as they carried box after box to the truck. The furniture was next—beds and chairs, sofas and tables. There was nothing for her to do but watch. She was as wooden as the furniture, stiff and dead. Would they carry her out too? But when at last the movers were done, she realized, no. She would have to walk out on her own.

Part Three

Chapter 33

NATALIE

(August 1952)

The summer they moved, Natalie and Teddy hardly saw each other. Whenever Natalie asked to play with him, her mother started to cry. Then, a few weeks before September, the phone rang after dinner. Natalie's father answered it, and even from the other room she could tell that the person on the other end of the line was shouting. "Whaddya mean, he won't come out?" her father asked. There was a pause and then more shouting.

"For Chrissake, why didn't you say somethin' at work?" *It must be Uncle Mort.*

Another pause. "Calm down. Of course she's here. We'll be there in ten minutes." He hung up the phone. "Natalie!" Abe called. "Put your shoes on!"

On the way over to Teddy's house, Natalie's father told her that her cousin hadn't eaten for almost two days. "How come?" Natalie wanted to know.

Her father turned on his blinker to make the turn onto Teddy's street. "He's been sad. Moving is hard, and Teddy misses his routine. He misses seeing you every day and playing with you."

"Me too!" Natalie blurted out.

Abe pulled into Teddy's driveway. "I know, sweetheart. Your mother and I have talked about it." He turned off the ignition. "Let's see what happens with Teddy tonight and maybe we can do something about it."

Abe started to open the car door, but Natalie stopped him. "Daddy, wait! How come we came over so late?"

Her father frowned. "Teddy locked himself in his room. He said he won't come out until he gets to see you. They can't get him to open the door."

Natalie's eyes widened. She scrambled out of the car and took her father's hand. They walked together up the gravel pathway without saying a word. Abe reached out to ring the doorbell, but her uncle Mort was already at the door, opening it for them. Natalie thought Uncle Mort looked worried, and she felt bad for him. She knew her brothers thought he was mean, but there was something about him that she liked.

Mimi and Dinah ran to the door and started talking at the same time.

"Oh my gosh, finally!"

"He's upstairs!"

"Come on!"

They grabbed her by the elbows and pulled her up the stairs to the hallway outside Teddy's bedroom. Judith was sitting on the floor, trying to talk Teddy into coming out. When she saw Natalie she stood up and hugged her. "Teddy!" she said. "Natalie's here!"

Natalie heard Teddy's voice from the other side of the door. He sounded tired. "Nat? Are you there?"

"I'm here!" she called back. "Let me in!"

The lock clicked, the door handle turned and then Teddy's face poked out. "Hi, Nat."

"Come out," she told him. But he shook his head. "You come in." He opened the door a little bit more and ushered her inside. Then he locked the door again.

"Perfect," Natalie heard Mimi say. "Now they're *both* locked in there."

Judith was firm. "Let's go downstairs. They'll come out soon."

After they heard the girls walking down the stairs, Teddy finally relaxed. At almost five, he was small for his age. Two days of not eating had left him frail and exhausted, and his wide brown eyes had dark circles around them. Natalie was a full head taller and felt like a giant standing next to him. She decided to sit on the floor. She had only been to Teddy's house once before, and his room was foreign to her.

"How come you won't leave your room?" Natalie asked.

"I wanted to play with you. I don't like living here. I want to go back to the house on Christopher Avenue."

"Me too."

"But we can't. Someone else lives there now. That's what my mother said. She said we couldn't go back even if we wanted to. She said it's nicer here."

"My mom wants to go back too. She keeps crying."

"Why?"

Natalie shrugged her shoulders. "She cries every time I ask to play with you."

"When I ask to see *you*, my mother yells," Teddy explained. "She won't listen. So I didn't eat dinner last night. And then I didn't eat anything today either. But she still won't listen."

Natalie took Teddy's hand. "Let's go downstairs. My mom sent cookies."

"I'm scared to go downstairs."

"My dad said they're going to figure something out. And I brought you comics."

Finally, Teddy smiled. He couldn't read very well yet, but he loved to look at the pictures. "Which ones?"

"Captain Comet and Marvelman."

"I guess I'll go."

"I'll race you!" Natalie shot out the door and took the steps two at a time. Teddy chased after her, giggling. Abe was waiting at the bottom for them and grabbed Natalie as soon as she reached him. "Look what I caught!" he bellowed, swinging her in the air. "Teddy's all right now, Daddy," Natalie whispered in her father's ear. Abe nodded and put her down. He led the children to the kitchen, where Uncle Mort and Aunt Rose were waiting.

When she saw Teddy and Natalie, Aunt Rose stopped pacing in front of the stove. "Will you eat something?" she asked him. Teddy nodded and took a seat at the table. "Natalie said she brought cookies."

"You have to eat some dinner first. Then you can have cookies for dessert." Aunt Rose didn't bother asking Natalie if she wanted anything. Natalie was used to being ignored by her aunt, but she thought this time it might be different. After all, wasn't she the one who got Teddy to unlock his door and come out of his room? Shouldn't that be good enough to earn a smile or at least a hello? Apparently not—Aunt Rose still wouldn't glance her way. Natalie wondered if she'd be offered a cookie after Teddy finished eating. She hoped so.

After a few moments of silence, Natalie's father coughed. "Now that everyone's calmed down, let's figure out what we can do so this doesn't happen again." Natalie didn't see the need for a long discussion. She got right to the point. "Can Teddy come over tomorrow?" She had taken a seat between Teddy and Uncle Mort, and directed the question to her uncle. He looked over at Aunt Rose, who looked away. Uncle Mort cleared his throat to get her attention, but Aunt Rose ignored him and busied herself with the reheating of Teddy's dinner. Natalie couldn't understand why she was being so rude. Or why Uncle Mort needed her approval before he answered. None of the grown-ups said anything, so Natalie decided to ask again. "Can Teddy come over tomorrow?"

"That's fine by me," Abe answered this time. "How about you, Morty?" Uncle Mort looked at Aunt Rose again, but she refused to make eye contact. "Yes," he answered. "He can come to your house tomorrow."

"Can Natalie come here the day after?" Teddy wanted to know. Aunt Rose put a full plate in front of Teddy. He looked at the food and then looked at Natalie. Before he picked up the fork, he asked again, "Can she?"

Aunt Rose clenched her teeth. "Fine," she managed to say. "But school starts for your sisters next week and you can't play with each other every day then. I'll be too busy." Natalie felt Teddy kicking her under the table. "But we don't want to stop going to each other's houses after school starts," she said.

"Yes!" Teddy echoed. He looked at the plate and pushed it a few inches away, toward the center of the table. Then he looked up at his mother.

Aunt Rose was staring at the plate. "Maybe you can play once a week," she conceded.

Teddy pushed the plate a little farther away. "How about I go to Nat's once a week and she comes here once a week?"

Natalie's father and her uncle, along with Natalie and Teddy, were all turned to Aunt Rose. She threw her hands in the air, exasperated. "Fine!" she said. "Just eat something, will you?"

Teddy pulled the plate closer and began to shovel forkfuls of chicken and potatoes into his mouth.

"You can go to Natalie's house on Tuesdays," Aunt Rose pronounced. "That's the day I do my grocery shopping. Natalie can come here Thursdays." For the first time all evening she looked directly at Natalie. "Thursday is meat loaf day," Aunt Rose warned. Natalie sensed the threat in her aunt's tone, but she was too excited about the prospect of seeing Teddy to care. "Meat loaf is my favorite!"

"Then everything's settled." Natalie's father stood up. "It's late," he said, "and I think we all need to get some sleep. Are we good here?"

"Great!" Teddy said, his mouth full of chicken. Natalie nodded in agreement and got up out of her chair. She wanted to ask for a cookie, but it was more important to leave before Aunt Rose changed her mind.

Chapter 34

NATALIE

(September 1956)

Natalie's favorite day of the week was Thursday. Most of the kids in her third-grade class liked Friday best. The teacher was easier on them and more likely to forgive them if they forgot their homework or fooled around. If you forgot homework on any other day, Miss Murray would take out her red pen and mark you ten points off in her grade book. But if you forgot homework on Friday, Miss Murray would just tell you to bring it in on Monday.

Friday was also kickball day at recess, which most of the kids loved. The boys would line up to pick teams and the girls would stand on the side of the field and cheer. Natalie hated cheering and she didn't like watching the boys, mostly because Teddy was always the last one picked for teams. She knew the other boys wouldn't tease him (she had put an end to that in first grade when she punched Jerry Adler in the nose for calling Teddy a "scrawny weirdo"), but she couldn't force them to choose him. Besides, if she punched Jerry again, the principal would call her mother to pick her up, and Natalie worried that her mother wouldn't be as forgiving the second time.

"What did you do to that boy?" her mother had asked on the way home that day. "Did you know his nose might be broken? Even your *mashugana* brothers never broke anyone's nose."

Natalie didn't respond.

"Honestly, what got into you?"

"He's a jerk," she answered.

"What makes him such a jerk?"

"He was teasing Teddy."

"So you punched him to make him stop?"

"Yup."

"Did it work?"

"I'll tell you tomorrow."

"Let me know what happens." *Was her mother smiling?*

All in all, Natalie didn't think Fridays were so great. But Thursdays—those were terrific. First of all, Thursday was library day at school and she was allowed to take out as many books as she could carry. Second, Thursday was her day to go to Teddy's house. Ever since the night Teddy locked himself in his room, Tuesdays and Thursdays had become their days together. Their mothers knew they couldn't take them on errands or to dentist appointments, and Natalie's mother always baked something special for Tuesday afternoons.

One of the reasons Natalie liked going to Teddy's was that it was peaceful. Her house was too noisy. Harry was gone most of the time, but Joe and George were always yelling or fighting or messing around. Sam was even worse—always teasing her or hiding her schoolwork. But at Teddy's house, Aunt Rose left them alone. She didn't make Natalie sit at the table and talk about her day or her week the way Natalie's mother did with Teddy.

When Teddy came over to her house, Natalie's mother couldn't stop herself from hovering. The older Natalie got, the more annoyed she became with it. Her mother fawned over Teddy, making his favorite foods for dinner and forcing him to take seconds. Once, after a particularly irritating day, Natalie accused her mother of liking Teddy better than her own children. "That's ridiculous!" her mother insisted. But Natalie wasn't convinced.

Aunt Rose was the opposite. There were no special cookies or treats on the days Natalie came over, and Aunt Rose didn't speak to her any more than she spoke to Teddy or his sisters. Natalie liked it that way. Every once in a while, Natalie felt her aunt staring at her when she sat at the kitchen table doing homework. Did Aunt Rose think Teddy was giving her the answers? Or that she was giving them to him? But Aunt Rose never said anything, so Natalie didn't ask.

There was something about the predictability of dinner at Teddy's that was comforting. Aunt Rose cooked on a weekly schedule, so every Thursday night the family ate the same meal. Thursday night happened to be meat loaf, mashed potatoes and peas. The dinner never varied. The conversation never varied either. And there was never very much of it.

"How was your day?" Aunt Rose would ask Uncle Mort.

"Fine. Our shipping productivity is up seven percent from last year at this time. How was yours?"

"Fine. Does everyone like the meat loaf?"

"It's good," Dinah would say. Mimi would nod, push the food around on her plate and then spend the rest of dinner staring at her reflection in the silverware. Judith was never there because her Thursday classes ran late.

"Teddy, what did you learn at school today?" Uncle Mort would ask.

The standard reply to this was "nothing," but once in a while, when he was feeling more confident, Teddy would try to tell his father something about their science experiment or about what happened in a book they were reading. No matter how hard he tried, though, Teddy would end up stammering, coughing and sputtering through his explanation. Natalie couldn't understand why. If you knew someone was going to ask you the same question every night, how difficult was it to have an answer ready? But Uncle Mort made Teddy nervous. Natalie wanted to interrupt sometimes, to clarify something Teddy said or help her cousin get his point across. But she worried that interfering would embarrass him, so she stayed silent. Truth be told, she enjoyed the feeling of sitting at the table and not having to say anything. At her house, if she didn't jump into the conversation, her mother was liable to feel her head and ask if she had a fever. At Teddy's house, she could relax.

One Thursday in the middle of September, Natalie and Teddy were playing outside. Teddy wanted to practice pitching, so they wandered into the garage to look for an extra baseball mitt. "Think there could be one in here?" Natalie asked, pointing to a dusty cardboard box. Someone had printed GARAGE on it in neat black lettering.

"Maybe. Let's open it," Teddy told her. He pulled off the packing tape and pried open one of the corners. "Darn," he said, disappointed. "It's just a bunch of old books."

"What kind of books?" Natalie wanted to know. "Anything good?"

"I can't tell." He pulled harder on the cardboard flaps. "It looks like textbooks. They must be Judith's."

"Are you sure? They look really old. Let's see . . . *Theories of Probability, Calculus, Modern Statistics.* These are all math books. These can't be hers."

"I guess not." Teddy was confused. "I wonder whose they are."

"You know what?" Natalie told him. "I think these are your dad's. My dad told me once how much your dad loves math."

"My dad never talks about it."

"Hey, let's look at this one." Natalie pulled a thick green book out of the box. The silver letters across the front read *An Introduction to Mathematics.*

"Can't we just have a catch?"

"I don't have a mitt, remember? Besides, this one says it's an introduction. Maybe we could figure some of it out. We can ask your father about it at dinner."

"Okay." Teddy was resigned. "Let's bring it to my room."

They brought the book to Teddy's room and sat cross-legged on the floor touching kneecaps. The book was spread open in front of them, half resting on Teddy's lap and half resting on Natalie's. It was full of equations and symbols they couldn't understand. Natalie thought it was interesting, but Teddy wasn't convinced.

At dinner that night, the meat loaf was as dry as ever, and the conversation was just as predictable. Natalie kept waiting for Teddy to ask about the book, but he didn't say a word. Eventually, she kicked him under the table.

"Dad, can I ask you something?"

"You may."

"Can you help me and Natalie with a book we found today?"

"What book?"

"It's a textbook—*An Introduction to Mathematics.*"

Uncle Mort didn't answer.

"It was in the garage. . . . We were looking for a baseball mitt, and then we found it in a box. . . ." Uncle Mort's silence made Teddy nervous. "We looked at it for a long time . . . but the math is too hard for us. . . ." Teddy looked to Natalie for support.

"We want you to teach us how to do the problems in the book!" Natalie blurted out. Teddy gave her a stunned look.

"Um, I mean, please." She lowered her voice. "Please, do you think you could teach us, Uncle Mort?"

Dinah stopped chewing, and Mimi looked up from the back of her spoon. Aunt Rose put down her water glass. All eyes were on Uncle Mort, awaiting his reply.

"What makes you think I know anything about mathematics?" he asked.

Natalie looked at Teddy, but he just shrugged. It was up to her.

"Well," she began, "you're in charge of all the money stuff at the business. And money is really just numbers, so you must be really good with them. With numbers, I mean."

Uncle Mort looked at her expectantly, as if he were waiting for further explanation. Now she knew how Teddy felt.

"And second of all, you always use numbers when you speak. You like to talk about percentages and things that come from math. So you must think about math a lot." She cleared her throat.

He was still looking at her.

"And third, my father always says how careful you are with numbers and how smart you are in math. We figured there's a ninety-nine-percent chance [*did Uncle Mort raise an eyebrow?*] it's your book. You probably still remember a lot of it."

Uncle Mort took a drink of water. Then he asked Natalie a question.

"How did you calculate your percentage?"

She was confused. "Excuse me?"

"You said there was a ninety-nine-percent chance the book is mine. How did you calculate that?"

"I didn't. It was an expression."

"Either the book is mine or the book is not mine. Do you agree?"

"Yes."

"Then isn't there only a fifty-percent chance that the book is mine?"

"Well, if you look at it that way—"

Uncle Mort interrupted her. "There are six people living in this house, correct?"

"Yes."

"If that is the case, then isn't there a one out of six chance that the book is mine?"

"Maybe, but—"

"But what? If there is a one out of six chance that it is mine, then what would that percentage be?"

Natalie took a few moments to think through the answer. "A little more than sixteen percent, I think, but that isn't really right." Natalie felt her cousins stiffen. *None of them has ever had this long of a conversation with Uncle Mort before.*

"Why isn't it correct?"

"Because we know the book *can't* be Teddy's or Mimi's or Dinah's. They're too young. There are really only three people out of the six people living here who could be the owner of the book. Judith, you and Aunt Rose. So it's a one out of three chance."

"Teddy, bring me the book."

"Okay." Teddy got up from the table and returned with the large green volume.

Uncle Mort took it from him and turned to the back cover.

"If you had been more observant, you would have found that there is actually a one-hundred-percent chance that this book is mine."

"Why?" Teddy asked.

"Because I wrote my name on the back cover, right here." He held up the book and pointed to his signature. Natalie giggled. She felt the tension drain out of the room as Uncle Mort's lips formed something close to a smile.

"We can look at this together next Thursday," Uncle Mort said. "Unless you want to study it with me alone, Teddy."

Teddy shook his head. "No, Natalie and I want to do it together. So I'll wait."

"Fine," said Mort. "But I'm only going to do this if you both agree to work hard and pay attention. I'm not going to waste my time unless you both are fully committed."

"We will be," Natalie assured him. She sat back in her chair and exchanged smiles with Teddy. *Dinner is finally getting interesting.*

Chapter 35

MORT

Thursdays became the highlight of Mort's week. In the beginning, he worried that looking through his old math books might bring back painful memories of having to give up school. But his fears were unwarranted.

The first time he read those books, all he wanted was to soak up the information as quickly as possible. Looking at the books with Teddy and Natalie so many years later, he understood what he should have been doing back then: enjoying the study of the subject.

It was only because of Teddy that he was able to do that now. It didn't matter that the books his son found in the garage were much too difficult. It didn't matter that he had never taught math to anyone before. What mattered was that Mort was sharing something he enjoyed with one of his children, perhaps for the very first time.

Mort had never been a father who sat down on the floor and played board games or drank pretend cups of tea. He didn't kiss dolls and he didn't sing lullabies. Mort hadn't known how to talk to his daughters when they were little, and as they evolved into young women he found himself only more uncomfortable. When Teddy came along, Mort had hoped it would be different, but he had already fallen into bad habits. He thought baseball might bring them together, but Teddy was a tentative player, and Mort wasn't exactly sure how to instruct him. Teddy was too young to play on his cousins' team and too shy to ask any of the kids at school to be on theirs. Mort and Teddy listened to the professional games on the radio together, but as soon as the games ended, Mort ran out of things to say.

Every once in a while, Mort would bring Teddy to the factory so he could learn about the family business. But Teddy was still too young to be interested, and he mostly just sat at the receptionist's desk and colored. Sometimes he watched the machinery, but it was loud and monotonous. When Mort stopped asking if he wanted to come along, Teddy never questioned it.

Then the children found the math book. Mort wondered whether Teddy would have had the courage to ask about it if Natalie hadn't been there. He supposed it didn't matter—she *had* been there, and Teddy was willing. Mort knew he would never be great at teaching his son how to hit or throw a baseball, but explaining arithmetic to him was something he knew he could do. The best thing was that Teddy seemed to enjoy it. Having Natalie close by seemed to give Teddy the confidence to ask Mort all of his questions.

"Dad, can you explain square roots again?"

"Absolutely. A square root of a number is a number which, multiplied by itself, gives you the original number. So the square root of nine is three because three times three equals nine."

"Oh." Teddy didn't sound convinced.

"Let's do it backwards. What is two times two?"

"Four."

"Right. So that means the square root of four is two."

"I think I understand."

"Let's pick a different number. Try sixteen. What do you think is the square root of sixteen?"

Teddy scrunched up his eyes to concentrate. "Four?"

"Yes! Because four times four is sixteen. Good!"

This is better than a home run, Mort thought.

Later that evening, when Teddy was in the bathroom, Natalie asked Mort another question. "Uncle Mort? There are really two square roots for every number, right?"

"What do you mean?"

"I mean four is the square root of sixteen but negative four is also. Every positive number has two square roots, right?"

Mort nodded. "Yes, that's true. A negative number times another negative number equals a positive number."

"Good," Natalie said. "That's what I thought."

She never lets Teddy figure out she knows more than he does.

Mort was used to being treated with a mixture of reverence and apprehension by his children, but Natalie was different. She wasn't disrespectful, but she certainly wasn't afraid of him. In fact, she seemed genuinely fond of him and comfortable in his presence in a way that most people were not.

"Uncle Mort, what do you like better, pie or cake?" she asked him one Thursday.

"Cake."

"Exactly!" Natalie practically shouted. "Most people do. So why do books always use pies to show fractions? Why not cake?"

"Yeah!" Teddy chimed in. "I like cake better too."

Mort didn't skip a beat. "It's the layer cakes that are the problem," he said solemnly. "Layer cakes confuse the mathematicians because they have to multiply the fraction by the number of layers. That's why they use pies."

The children stared at him. Then they burst out laughing. "You're so funny, Dad," Teddy said.

No one's ever said that to me before.

The next few months flew by for Mort. Teddy agreed to study with him on Sundays also, as long as they didn't get too far ahead of Natalie. They calculated batting averages for Teddy's favorite baseball players and the ERA of every pitcher in the league. Teddy's work with percentages and decimals was far beyond that of a third grader. The old book was like magic—as long as it sat open between them, father and son could talk easily with each other.

Rose noticed the change and remarked on it to Mort one Thursday after Natalie had gone home. They were in the kitchen, and Rose was drying dishes.

"You seem to be having a nice time with Teddy lately," she said. "Natalie too." Rose hesitated for a few moments, then added, "Why don't you try to get along like that with your own daughters?" She put away some glasses and closed one of the cabinet doors a little too forcefully.

"Excuse me?"

"You have three daughters. You've never taken an interest in them the way you have with Natalie."

He was taken aback. "I'm studying math with Teddy."

"You're studying with Teddy *and* Natalie."

"That's because Natalie comes over on Thursdays. To be honest, I'm not sure Teddy would have asked about the math in the first place without her. She's good for him."

"*Judith* has always taken care of Teddy. But you don't dote on her the way you dote on Natalie."

"I don't *dote* on anyone, Rose! Judith is hardly home!"

"But Judith is so smart. You never encouraged her." Rose was angry.

Mort became flustered. "Isn't Judith in college right now? Studying everything she wants? Isn't she getting a good education?"

"But you don't laugh with Judith, not the way you . . ." Rose's eyes began to tear up.

"What are you crying about, Rose? Teddy and I finally found something we really like to do together. Don't turn it into something unpleasant."

But Rose couldn't help herself. Her sobs only came faster and it was hard to understand the words she managed to choke out between them. "For so long . . . disappointment after disappointment . . . and then *she* comes along and suddenly it doesn't seem to matter. . . ."

Mort couldn't imagine why Rose was so upset. How could she criticize him for spending time with his son?

"I think you need to sit, Rose," was all he could say. He guided her to one of the kitchen chairs. Then he sat across from her and waited.

Slowly, Rose controlled her crying, and her breathing steadied. She wiped her eyes a few times with a napkin and stared down at the table.

Mimi breezed into the kitchen just then. Her hair was in curlers and she had just applied a fresh coat of nail polish. "Hey, Mom, what do you think of this color? Is it too pink?" She looked up from her fingernails to see her mother's tear-streaked face. "Gee, Mom, are you okay? What's the matter?"

"Nothing," Rose told her. "Why don't you ask your father about the color?"

Mimi looked at her mother like she had two heads. "Really?"

"Absolutely," Rose insisted. "Mort, your *daughter* would like your opinion on something." He gave her a confused look, but she ignored him, got up from the table and started to walk out of the kitchen. "I'm sure you two will have a nice conversation," she said. And then she left.

Chapter 36

ROSE

(October 1956)

Rose was putting cereal bowls out on the table when Teddy hobbled into the kitchen. "Why are you limping like that?" she asked him. He sat down and filled a bowl with cornflakes from the box. Rose asked again, "Why are you limping?"

Teddy didn't look up. "My shoes are tight, I guess."

"You guess? Are they tight or aren't they?" Rose was irritated.

"Let me see your foot," she told him. Teddy stuck one foot out from under the table, but looking at the shoe didn't tell Rose much about the foot inside it. "Stand up," she ordered. Teddy did as he was told and let Rose press on the front of his shoes. She could feel his toes pushing up against the edge of his Buster Browns.

"Why didn't you tell me you needed new shoes?"

It took Teddy several moments to answer. "I told you a few weeks ago."

"A few weeks ago?" She shook her head, unable to remember, and made her way to the coffeepot to pour herself a cup. "What did I say?"

"You told me that I had just gotten new shoes and my feet couldn't grow again so fast."

"I don't remember having that conversation."

Teddy stared into the bottom of his cereal bowl. He wouldn't look up. "I told you my shoes were hurting on Saturday too," he whispered.

"This past Saturday?"

He coughed. "Mmm."

"I see. So it's *my* fault that you're limping."

"No, I didn't say—"

Rose silenced him with a look. "I'll take you for shoes today, after school."

"But it's Tuesday."

"So? The stores are open on Tuesdays."

"I'm going to Natalie's house today. I can wait one more day. Please!"

Mort walked into the kitchen just as Teddy's eyes began to well up. "What's all the yelling about?" he wanted to know.

Rose explained, "He can't even walk, his shoes are so tight. I said we'd go shopping this afternoon, but no, he wants to go to your brother's."

Teddy's face was flushed and sweaty. He looked desperate.

Mort had an idea. "Teddy, how are your sneakers?"

"A little small but not as tight as these."

"Wear your sneakers to school then. Tomorrow you'll get new shoes and new sneakers."

Teddy looked happy, but Rose was furious. "You want him to go to school looking like a beggar?"

"Better a beggar than a cripple." Mort held his ground. "He won't make it through the morning in those shoes."

"What is his teacher going to think? That he has a mother who can't even dress her own son? He is *not* wearing sneakers to school!"

"Teddy, go to your room, please. Find your sneakers and give us a few minutes." As soon as Teddy left the kitchen, Mort poured himself a cup of coffee and sat down at the kitchen table. Rose was still standing, glaring at him from her spot by the stove.

"Rose, please. Don't blow this out of proportion. Why can't you just take him for shoes tomorrow?"

"He needs them today."

"One day isn't going to make a difference."

Rose looked like she wanted to throw her coffee at him. Instead, she dumped the remains in the sink, rinsed out the cup and placed it upside down on the dish rack. "You're wrong. One day can make all the difference in the world." She pointed to the clock over the sink. "The bus comes in ten minutes. You'd better call the kids downstairs if you want them to be on it. Otherwise, you'll have to drive them to school. I'm going to get dressed." She walked out of the kitchen, leaving Mort alone with his coffee.

About an hour after the girls got home from school, Rose was in the kitchen making dinner. It was baked chicken night and she was crushing Ritz crackers for the topping when she heard the phone ring.

"Rose, it's Helen. How are you feeling?"

"I'm fine. You?" It wasn't easy to get the casserole dish she needed off of the top shelf with only one hand. "Hold on a minute." Even after she had the dish on the counter, Rose waited a few moments before putting the phone back to her ear.

"Sorry about that. Mort will pick Teddy up at the usual time, all right?"

"Sure. But how *are* you?"

"I told you I'm fine," Rose snapped. "Why do you keep asking me that?"

"Teddy said you weren't feeling well last week. I figured you still must be sick."

"Well, you heard wrong. I haven't been sick." *She always does this. Looking for bad news wherever she can find it.*

There was an uncomfortable silence on the other end of the line. "Oh. My mistake."

"Anything else?"

"Well, one thing. I have some old shoes of George's. They're like new. He wore them maybe for a week before he grew out of them. I'm sending them home with Teddy. They fit. You'll see if you like them."

"Shoes?"

"You know me, I never throw anything away." Helen let out a nervous laugh.

"I knew it. It's always something about Teddy with you."

"No, no. I just noticed last week he wasn't walking so well and he said you didn't get a chance to take him to the shoe store because you were sick."

"I'm not blind, Helen! I wanted to take him for shoes today, but he threw a fit because he wanted to go to your house! He'd have had new shoes by now if it wasn't for you!"

"Me? You're blaming me? I'm *giving* him shoes!"

"Of course you are. You're always coming to the rescue. Pointing out every little thing I do wrong. Keep your damned shoes, Helen! Keep them. Because so help me, if Teddy comes home with them I will throw them in the garbage!" Rose slammed down the phone. Her breathing was heavy and her hands were shaking. What a fool I am, she thought, worrying about the teacher. I should have known Helen would be the first one to notice.

Chapter 37

HELEN

(November 1956)

It had been nine years since they were all together for Thanksgiving. Helen wondered if Rose remembered. After Natalie and Teddy were born, Rose's family started going to her aunt Faye's for the holiday. But Faye's husband, Stuart, had retired over the summer, and Faye and Stuart decided to spend the winter in Miami. When Helen called with an invitation, Rose had no excuse.

At first Helen had been thrilled. After a week passed, however, her excitement turned to regret. She was nervous. They had shared other holidays over the years—there had been Yom Kippur break-fasts, Fourth of July barbecues and Passover seders—but those had always included other relatives or friends. Thanksgiving would be just the two families. Even Sol and Arlene couldn't make it—they had gone to Arlene's brother's place in New Jersey.

Luckily Helen didn't have to worry about the food. Her Thanks-giving menu hadn't changed much in the past eight years. That was one of the best things about the holiday, she decided. People didn't want to be surprised—they wanted the classics: turkey, mashed potatoes, stuffing, apple pie. *Judith always loved my apple pie.*

Helen had seen Judith a few weeks earlier when she'd dropped off a birthday present for Dinah at the house. Helen wanted to stay and talk to her, but there hadn't been time. She was glad she would see Judith today.

"Natalie! Come help me set the table!"

"Coming!" Natalie appeared a few moments later wearing denim overalls handed down from one brother and a faded green T-shirt handed down from another. Helen wasn't surprised. *That's what happens when you have four older brothers.*

"Hey, Mom, what's this?" Natalie was rummaging through the drawers of the breakfront in the dining room searching for extra napkins. She held up a small cardboard box. "I found it under the napkin rings."

Helen looked up from the silverware she was arranging. "I don't know," she said. "Let me see."

Natalie passed the box to her mother. Inside it were four neat stacks of small cream cards. "They're place cards. I think someone gave them to me at my bridal shower. I can't believe I still have them."

"Can we use them?"

"You mean for today?"

"I'm going to write all the names out in orange for Thanksgiving. It'll be so pretty!"

Helen laughed. "All right, if you really want to. But you'd better get started. Everyone will be here in a few hours and you still need to change out of those overalls."

Half an hour later Natalie brought the finished cards into the dining room and started placing them on the table. "Mommy," she asked, "who should I put next to you?"

"Oh, I don't care. Just put me near the kitchen. And separate your brothers a little bit. If they're all together they'll kill each other."

"I know. I put Dinah between George and Joe, and Mimi between Harry and Sam."

"That was good thinking."

"Yeah, but . . . where do you think I should put Aunt Rose?"

Helen knew what Natalie was hinting at from the way she asked the question. *Is it that noticeable? Even to Natalie?*

To be honest, Helen hadn't thought for one moment about sitting or not sitting next to Rose. She had been too busy cooking. But now there were place cards, and she worried that Rose might think she had orchestrated the seating arrangement. "Why don't you sit next to Aunt Rose?" she told Natalie.

"I can't. I'm sitting next to Teddy on one side and Uncle Mort on the other."

Helen was touched. "Oh honey, you can put Uncle Mort next to me. You don't have to sit next to him."

But Natalie was matter-of-fact. "I want to sit next to him."

"You do?"

"Sure! Uncle Mort is really funny."

"He is?" Helen was shocked.

Natalie nodded. "He told us a crazy story about mathematicians and cake. He was making it up but he acted really serious so we believed him. Mommy, what's that called again, when you act serious but you're really not?

"Sarcasm?"

"Yes! That's it! Uncle Mort is great at sarcasm. Plus, he's a really good teacher. On Thursdays after dinner, he teaches me and Teddy from his old math books. He makes up special problems for us because the books are too hard."

Helen was speechless. Mort was teaching them math? Mort was funny? How had such a grim and humorless man captured Natalie's affection? Helen didn't want to think about it.

"Mommy?" Natalie's voice interrupted her thoughts. "Should I put Aunt Rose next to George?"

"That's perfect, honey. Put her there and you can put Judith between us."

Natalie switched two of the cards. "All done!"

Helen pulled her in close for a hug and kissed her on the top of her head. She breathed in her daughter's scent—a mixture of cinnamon gum and Ivory soap. "I am so thankful for you," she whispered in Natalie's ear. Natalie kissed her cheek and promptly wiggled out of the embrace. Then she made a quick dash for the platter of pumpkin bread at the center of the table. "I'm thankful for pumpkin bread," she said. She crammed half the piece in her mouth, waved to her mother and skipped out of the room.

Chapter 38

JUDITH

Judith was uncomfortable sitting between her mother and Aunt Helen. It was reminiscent of the dinner they shared so many years ago at that Italian restaurant in Manhattan—the place where the owner was a "friend" of Helen's brother Sol. Judith remembered her mother and aunt quarreling over where she should sit at the table that night.

Back then, when Judith was only twelve, she assumed that Uncle Sol's restaurant "friend" was just that. She never wondered why he agreed to give so many strangers a free seven-course meal. Harry had explained the truth of it to her on one of their first train rides together into the city for classes, and Judith had been angry at herself for being so naive. How could she not have realized that the man owed Sol money? Harry had shrugged and told her not to worry about it. *You were little*, he had told her. *What does a little girl know about bookies?* Still, the realization bothered her. What else had she overlooked?

A few weeks later on another train ride, Judith had finally summoned the courage to ask Harry the question that still plagued her: *Do you know why our moms don't get along anymore?* But Harry had no insight to offer on the topic. In fact, he seemed barely aware of it.

"Who wants dark meat?" Uncle Abe was passing around a platter of turkey.

"Me!" Natalie was trying to take one of the wings before her brothers grabbed them both.

"I'll take that, thank you." It was Judith's father, gallantly skewering a wing from the platter with his knife and placing it on Natalie's plate. "There you are," he told his niece.

"Thanks, Uncle Mort!" Natalie beamed.

When did those two become friends?

"Cranberry sauce?" Judith turned toward her mother to accept the crystal bowl, but her mother's eyes were focused on the turkey wing occupying Natalie's plate. Judith didn't care for cranberry sauce and immediately turned to her aunt to pass it along, but Aunt Helen's eyes were fixed in the same direction. Both women were clearly unhappy with the show of friendship between Natalie and Mort. The bowl was getting heavy and Judith wanted to put it down.

"Aunt Helen?" There was no answer. Judith tried to tap her aunt's shoulder, but she needed two hands for the bowl. "Um, Aunt Helen?"

"Mom!" It was Harry, shouting from across the table. Aunt Helen almost jumped out of her seat. "Harry, why are you screaming?"

"Judith's been trying to give you the cranberry sauce for half an hour already."

"What? Oh honey, I'm sorry. Here, let me take it from you."

Judith handed over the bowl and gave Harry a grateful smile. He twirled his pointer finger in a circular motion near his right ear to show he thought his mother was crazy, and Judith suppressed her giggle with coughing. Her mother promptly patted her on the back.

"You should cut your meat in smaller pieces," Rose said to her. And then, in a slightly quieter voice, but still well above a whisper, "The meat is dry enough to choke on."

Judith felt her aunt stiffen. "Something wrong with the turkey, Rose?"

"I like the turkey, Mom," George called out nervously, shoveling a piece in his mouth for effect. "Ish derishous," he insisted, still chewing.

"Aunt Helen is a really good cook," Teddy said, thoroughly unaware of the gathering tension. "The turkey is much better than what we usually have on Thanksgiving."

"Thank you, boys," Helen said.

"No one really cares how dry the turkey is," Judith's mother spoke up again. "I'm sure there will be plenty of desserts later for the children to fill up on."

Judith saw Harry's eyes widen across the table. *Now do you see what I'm talking about?* she wanted to say to him. Judith froze in her seat between the two women. Only after Helen left the table and retreated to the kitchen did Judith spot the unmistakable upward curl at the left corner of her mother's mouth. Disgusted, Judith jumped up from her seat and followed her aunt into the kitchen.

Helen was standing at the sink, scrubbing at the roasting pan like her life depended on it. "Want some help?" Judith asked.

"Thanks, honey, but I think this needs to soak." She took off her rubber gloves and filled the pan with Joy and hot water. "You should head back in there and finish your dinner."

"I'm finished."

"I guess your mother *was* right about the turkey."

"No! Everything's delicious! I meant—"

"I'm just joking, sweetheart. Don't worry. Come. Sit down." Judith perched herself on one of the yellow vinyl chairs around the round Formica table and Helen sat down next to her.

"Aunt Helen, I'm so sorry. What my mother said . . ."

"Oh Judy. I'm used to it by now." She clasped her niece's hand and squeezed.

"But it wasn't always this way. You used to be best friends."

"I'm surprised you remember."

"Of course I remember. It hasn't been that long."

"It feels like a long time to me." Aunt Helen sounded tired. There were dark circles under her eyes and her skin looked sallow. Most of her lipstick had rubbed off except for a spot on one of her front teeth. Judith didn't know what to say next. Suddenly her aunt didn't just seem tired. She looked old. Under the unforgiving light of the dull suburban kitchen, Judith finally understood the irreversible nature of whatever had occurred between the two women and the toll it had taken. Even the most skillful tailor couldn't hide a seam once a cloth was torn in two.

Judith decided to put away her thoughts and focus on helping her aunt. "Why don't I start a pot of coffee and get the pies warmed in the oven. The others must be almost finished with dinner in there. Should I check on them?"

Helen slipped on an apron. "Sure, honey. You know I made those apple pies just for you, right?"

"Thanks, Aunt Helen." She gave her a kiss on the cheek and walked through the swinging kitchen door back into the dining room. Harry helped her clear the plates, and for the rest of the evening Judith avoided speaking to anyone but him. Harry acted like nothing had happened—they talked about school and the paper he had to write for his class Monday morning. Later on Judith sat with him in the kitchen, where her mother wouldn't see, and ate two pieces of Aunt Helen's apple pie. When the evening was over, she went home with her family, took off her coat and immediately went to her bedroom.

It was the last Thanksgiving Judith would ever spend with her mother.

Chapter 39

NATALIE

(December 1956)

Natalie had been told the story of the blizzard that struck on the day she was born at least a dozen times. Of course she couldn't remember it. The heaviest snowstorm she ever experienced came a few weeks before her ninth birthday. The weathermen didn't call it a blizzard, but they did say fifteen inches of snow came down.

After two days of sledding and snowball fights with her brothers, Natalie was ready to go back to school. Miss Murray gave them extra homework because of the two days they had missed, but Natalie didn't mind. It was Thursday, so she was in a good mood. At least she could do the homework with Teddy.

When they boarded the bus after school, Mr. Luther, the balding driver, hollered for everyone to sit down. Teddy pulled a comic book out from inside one of his textbooks and Natalie frowned. "Teddy, you weren't reading that in school again, were you?"

Teddy looked guilty, but he couldn't lie to her. "Just for a minute. It's the new *Superman*!"

"Teddy! What if Miss Henshaw catches you again? You'll have to stay inside at recess for a week."

He grinned. "Do you really think I'd mind?"

"I know, but you don't want her to call your parents, do you?"

He closed the comic book. "I guess not. Hey, have you seen your uncle Sol lately?" Sol always brought Natalie candy and comics from his newsstand when he came over, and Natalie always gave the comics to Teddy when she was done with them.

"They had dinner with us on Friday night, but all he brought was the new *Little Dot*." Natalie made a face.

"Why does he bring you those? They're so stupid. And why does she like dots so much, anyway?"

Natalie shrugged. "Who knows? Usually he brings me *Casper the Friendly Ghost*, at least. But he didn't this time. No *Superman* either."

"Too bad." Teddy looked glum.

"He did bring one good thing." Natalie reached into her skirt pocket and pulled out two red boxes, each no more than two inches wide. She handed one of them to Teddy.

"Red Hots! Thanks!" Teddy was already tearing into the box of tiny cinnamon candies. After he poured half the box in his mouth, he opened it as wide as he could to show her.

"That's disgusting," she told him. But she laughed anyway.

The bus stopped abruptly across the street from Teddy's house. Plows had left enormous piles of snow on both sides of the road, and the narrowed streets were full of slick patches. Natalie got off first, and Teddy followed. As he crossed in front of the bus, the *Superman* comic fell out of his textbook and fluttered to the ground. Teddy bent down for it, out of the sight of the driver.

Natalie was already at the front door when she heard the bus lurch forward. Teddy had followed her off the bus, but she didn't sense his footsteps behind her so she turned around to call for him. When her eyes took in the body on the road, her call turned into a scream. "Teddy!"

She was still screaming his name as she ran into the road, screaming on her knees as she shook his shoulders, screaming for him to wake up as she clung to his hands, screaming at the driver as he stepped off the bus, as he took off his cap and cried into the snow. She could hear herself scream, but she still could not stop. Not when a neighbor tried to pick her up off of him, not when she shut her eyes from the glare of the ambulance and not when the long-faced medics whispered in her ear.

She was screaming his name when they took him away from her, took away Teddy, her playmate, her twin. She screamed for him still, long after he left and the pages of his comic blew by her in the wind. The winter dark came early, and she still hadn't stopped when her mother appeared with a blanket to cover her and a hot cup of cocoa that cracked in the cold. Her mother looked surprised as the cup came apart right there in her hand, and the cocoa poured out, hot liquid hissing as it hit the cold ground.

Natalie finally stopped screaming then, to speak. "It's broken," she told her mother, pointing to the cup. "I know it is," said Helen, and together they stood in the snow and they cried.

Chapter 40

ABE

The funeral was the next morning, on Friday. It was the Jewish tradition to bury the dead as quickly as possible, but Abe wished they had waited. It's too fast, he thought.

The last time he had been to the hospital, he had driven Rose there because Teddy had been hurt in a baseball game. Abe had been the one trying to calm everyone down that day, struggling to smooth over everyone's anger. But this time he had driven to the hospital with his brother, rushing from work after a panicked call from a neighbor. Rose was waiting for them, but there had been nothing for him to do. Nothing but to listen, incredulous, to the doctors; nothing but to wait, unbelieving, for Mort and Rose to say their goodbyes; nothing but to accompany them, in silence, out of the hospital doors without their son.

Abe didn't like feeling helpless. When his father died, he had busied himself organizing the office, notifying clients, taking care of his mother. And when his mother died, there had been even more things to do—going through the attic, selling the house, making sure to give each one of her cousins the little tchotchkes she wanted them to have. It was easier to be busy.

But now, he had nothing to do, nothing but to show up in a suit for his nephew's funeral. *His nephew's funeral.* Christ. He couldn't believe it. Teddy wasn't even nine years old.

The truth was, Abe hadn't really spent that much time with him. He saw his nephew on Tuesdays for dinner. But Teddy and Natalie were always busy with something—playing twenty rounds of checkers, watching that *Mickey Mouse Club* show or trying to figure out the math book Teddy lugged over every week. Teddy was a sweet kid; Abe liked him. But if Abe was being honest, he had kept his distance on purpose.

One Sunday afternoon the spring after Teddy turned six, Abe had been at the high school field playing baseball with the boys when he spotted Mort and Teddy in the parking lot across from them. Teddy had been riding one of Harry's old bikes, but Mort had put training wheels on it. Abe had been embarrassed for Teddy, watching him ride around on a too-small bike with training wheels like a toddler. He told his boys he'd be back in a few minutes and headed over to say hello.

"Hey, Mort, Teddy, whatcha up to?"

"Hi, Uncle Abe!" Teddy had called out.

"What does it look like we're up to?" Mort had grumbled.

"Looks like bike riding. Hey, Teddy, how about I take off those training wheels, and you give it a try without 'em?"

Teddy had considered it for a few moments. "Maybe. If Dad says it's okay."

"Whaddya say, Morty? Let's get those things off and teach Teddy to ride."

Abe hadn't exactly waited for Mort's answer. He had found a wrench in the tool kit he kept in the trunk of his car. A few minutes later the training wheels were off and Teddy was trying to ride without them. Abe had run alongside the bike, trying to keep Teddy's momentum so balancing would be easier. There had been a few scrapes and scratches, but in less than an hour, Teddy had done it. He could ride the bike on his own!

Abe thought he was doing a mitzvah that afternoon, a good deed. But Mort hadn't seen it that way. He had moved over to a bench that sat between the field and the parking lot, and ignored them both for the full hour it had taken to get Teddy riding. When they were done, Teddy had ridden the bike all around the parking lot.

"Did you see me, Dad? Wasn't I good?"

Mort shrugged, busying himself with a day-old newspaper

section someone had left on the bench. He hadn't looked up. "Who cares what I think?"

"Didn't you see me?"

"Ask your uncle—he's the famous bicycle instructor."

Teddy was too young to understand why his father was angry, but he understood that something was wrong. His smile faded and he looked like he might cry.

"C'mon, Morty," Abe pleaded. "He did great, don'tcha think?"

But Mort wouldn't answer. He just stared at the newspaper. Abe had a feeling in his gut like he might be sick. He sat down next to his brother on the bench, took hold of his shoulder and whispered in his ear, "Listen, Mort. Stop torturing the kid and cut him a break. You wanna be mad at me for butting my nose in? Be mad at *me*. But don't take it out on *him*. For Chrissake."

Mort refused to respond, and Abe grew desperate. "I won't do it again, Mort. All right? I swear it. I won't go near him. But throw the kid a bone, Mort. *Please*."

Mort had taken his time folding up the newspaper and finally looked at Teddy. "Your uncle is right—you learned to ride quickly. Let's go home and show your mother and your sisters."

Good-natured Teddy had recovered instantly. "Okay! Wait till Mom sees!" But by the time Teddy turned around to thank his uncle, Abe had already been walking away from them, back to the field where his boys were playing. "Take care!" he had called out, waving behind him. Abe wanted to get away from Teddy and Mort as quickly as he could. He hadn't wanted to linger and risk Mort changing his mind.

For the next few years, up to the day Teddy died, Abe had kept his end of the bargain, the bargain he had struck with his brother that day at the school parking lot. He never got too close again. But on the morning of the funeral, one of the many thoughts swirling through Abe's mind was that he wished he had spent more time with his nephew.

"Dad, Mom says we should get in the car. She'll be out in a minute." George walked into the kitchen, still tucking his shirt into his trousers. Abe got up from his seat at the kitchen table and poured his cold cup of coffee down the sink.

"How're you doing, George?"

"Me?"

"Yeah." George was the most sensitive of his sons. Abe wanted to make sure he was all right.

"It hasn't sunk in yet, I guess. Teddy shouldn't have had to die like that, when he was so little." George spoke softly, like he didn't want anyone to hear. "I'm sad for Natalie. He was her best friend—I mean, her best friend in the whole world."

Abe patted George on the shoulder. "I know, Georgie. It's not going to be easy for her. We're all going to have to help."

He gave a solemn nod. "Do you want me to tell her we're ready to go?"

"Let me do it, kiddo. You go round up your brothers."

Abe hesitated for a moment after knocking on Natalie's door, then walked into her room. She was sitting on her bed, reading one of a dozen comic books strewn across the yellow bedspread. Her eyes were red and swollen, but for the moment, at least, she had stopped crying.

"Sweetheart, we have to leave in a few minutes," he told her.

She put down the comic book. "I know, Daddy. I don't want to be late."

"Did Mommy braid your hair for you?" Natalie's hair was set in two neatly braided pigtails. Abe was surprised Helen had found the time to fix Natalie's hair like that. She had barely spoken since the day before but she had been in the kitchen almost all night, cooking and baking.

"I did it. Teddy likes braids. He says braids look like rope."

Her use of the present tense made Abe's heart ache. "You did a good job."

"Are we going to go to the cemetery after the funeral?"

"Yes, sweetheart."

"Is it the one where your mother and father are?"

"Yes."

Natalie's eyes began to tear. "Do you think Grandma and Grandpa know Teddy's coming?"

"Honey, I don't know. It's hard to know things like that."

"But they'll take care of him, won't they?"

Abe wrapped his arms around her. "They'll take care of him." He held her while she cried, until the last tiny sob escaped from her lips, until he felt her exhale, long and slow, and when she finally let go and he looked at her, he saw that something within her had altered. It was like looking at a finished jigsaw puzzle with one piece missing from an undetectable place. No matter what Abe did, he knew he could never replace what had been lost.

Chapter 41

JUDITH

Black dresses made Judith think of funerals. That was why she didn't own any. Now that she actually had a funeral to go to, she realized that what she wore—what anyone wore—didn't matter. In the end, she chose a dark gray skirt and a navy sweater. No one would notice.

Half of the people at the funeral home were strangers to her, but all of them gave her quiet smiles or kind glances. The room was crowded, full of people shaking their heads and dabbing their eyes with tissues. One of Teddy's teachers approached Judith to say what a special boy her brother was, but Dinah interrupted. "We're supposed to go into the chapel," she said. "Rabbi Hirsch wants to talk to us."

In the front right corner of the chapel, Rabbi Hirsch was speaking quietly to her parents. He was the rabbi from their old synagogue in Brooklyn and had traveled to Long Island to be with them. Rabbi Hirsch had been at Teddy's bris and all her cousins' bar mitzvahs. He was in his sixties, with a full gray beard and kind gray eyes. Judith hadn't seen him for years.

Uncle Abe, Aunt Helen and her cousins were in the chapel too, sitting on the long upholstered benches in the back. Aunt Helen's eyes were closed and her head was resting on Uncle Abe's shoulder. As soon as Harry saw Judith, he walked over to give her a hug. He didn't know what to say, but she was grateful he was there. Aunt Helen hadn't seen her come in.

"Judith, dear, come here. Your sisters too," said the rabbi. After Judith, her sisters and her parents gathered together, Rabbi Hirsch spoke to them about *keriah,* the Jewish practice of tearing one's clothes as part of mourning. Hei handed each of them a torn black ribbon attached to a safety pin. "Take this," he told them "and pin it on the left side of your chest over your heart."

Mimi objected. "I'd rather put mine on my skirt. This blouse is silk and it might get a hole and I—"

Rabbi Hirsch cut her off. "Why do we pin it *here?*" he asked her, thumping the left side of his chest with his fist. "We do it because the tear in the ribbon is a symbol, a symbol that our hearts are torn and broken in our grief. In my day, we tore our clothes. But today," he looked at Mimi again, "we use the ribbon."

Mimi replied, "I hope you have more of these because there are a lot of people out there—"

Rabbi Hirsch silenced Mimi for a second time. "The ribbon is not a prize that we pass around the room. It is not an accessory, to be worn wherever we like or by whomever we choose. It is worn only by the immediate family—the spouse, the parents, the siblings and the children of the deceased. No one else." Mimi's face reddened and the rabbi continued, "The death of your brother is a terrible tragedy. A child has no wife or children of his own to mourn him. He has only you." Mimi was silent. She pinned the ribbon to her blouse without another word. The rest of them did the same. The rabbi told them he would begin the service in a few minutes, so Judith walked over to her aunt and uncle to tell them. "We're almost ready to start."

When Helen opened her eyes, they immediately went to the ribbon pinned to Judith's sweater. "Where did you get that?"

"Rabbi Hirsch."

Helen sprang from her seat and began barking orders at Uncle Abe. "We have to put ribbons on before the service. We need to tell the rabbi right away!"

Judith was confused. "Aunt Helen, I don't think he has any more of them. The rabbi said . . ."

Her aunt wasn't listening. "Abe, we have to get a ribbon from the rabbi *now!*"

"Shhhh, shhhh." Abe's voice was barely above a whisper. "The ribbon is for the immediate family, sweetheart. You know that."

"You think *we're* not Teddy's family?" She was frantic now, pacing in front of them, her face flushed with distress.

He tried to soothe her. "Of course we're his family, but only his parents and his sisters can wear the ribbon."

"I was there when he was born! I took care of him and rocked him when he had colic! Every day I watched to make sure she didn't neglect him!" She was yelling now, too loud for the others in the chapel to pretend not to hear.

"I know. I know how much you loved Teddy. But you're not his mother—"

"Shut up!" Judith gasped as she watched her aunt slap her uncle across the face. His hand went immediately to his cheek as the sound of the slap echoed off the chapel's stone walls and floor. When she realized what she had done, Aunt Helen sat back down on the bench and began to sob.

What happened next was something Judith would always remember. She thought Uncle Abe would walk away then, or yell at Aunt Helen for hitting him. Judith assumed he would be furious at what had just occurred. She worried he might retaliate. But Uncle Abe didn't do any of those things. He didn't even look angry, just sad. He moved close to Aunt Helen and brushed her hair gently away from her face. He took a handkerchief out of his suit pocket and wiped away her tears. He kissed her on the cheek, not just once, but twice. And then he held her hand and pressed it to the spot where she had struck him. She folded herself into his embrace and allowed him to comfort her. The rest of them, including the rabbi, looked away. "Love is always forgiving," the rabbi murmured under his breath.

Judith looked over at her mother and father. Pale and silent, they stood at least four feet apart from each other. Each was lost in a place of personal grief, and Judith wondered if either of them would ever be able to console the other.

In a few moments, the rabbi cleared his throat and announced that it was time to begin. Obediently, they followed him out of the chapel and into the main room for the service.

Chapter 42

NATALIE

Natalie threw up on the way to Teddy's house from the cemetery. She asked her father to pull over first, and she managed to avoid her clothes, so it wasn't as bad as it might have been. Mostly she was relieved she hadn't vomited at the cemetery because she thought that would have been disrespectful.

Back at Teddy's house there were crowds of people she didn't recognize. She looked for a drink to take away the bad taste in her mouth, but all she could find in the dining room was wine and a large urn of coffee, so she wandered into the kitchen to find a glass of juice. Mimi and Dinah were in the kitchen too, sneaking cookies from one of the dessert platters, while Mimi's friend Josie rearranged the leftovers to make them look like nothing had been touched. Josie was the chubby, freckle-faced girl who lived next door. Her navy dress was well made but too tight, with buttons that pulled around her waist. Like Mimi, Josie was sixteen, but with none of Mimi's easy beauty. She tended to follow Mimi around, hoping some of her glamour would rub off. It didn't.

"Want a cookie?" Dinah asked Natalie. But Natalie couldn't eat. She shook her head. "Do you have any juice? They only put out wine and coffee."

Dinah opened the refrigerator and took out the orange juice. She handed Natalie a glass from the cabinet.

"Thanks," Natalie told her.

Mimi said something to Josie then about sneaking a glass of wine, but Josie said they might get in trouble, so Mimi just sighed and sat down at the kitchen table. The other girls sat down with her.

"This is so sad," Mimi said, looking up at the ceiling.

"So sad," Josie echoed, with too much enthusiasm.

"The rabbi said it was a tragedy."

"An awful tragedy."

"Jeez, Jo! Would you stop repeating everything I say?"

"Sorry," Josie mumbled, reaching for another cookie. Mimi gave her a dirty look, and Natalie felt sorry for her. "Do people usually call you Jo?"

The girl seemed surprised Natalie had noticed her. "No, mostly just Josie. Short for Josephine."

"I figured," Natalie told her. "Like in *Little Women*."

"Yes." Her face brightened.

"I remember that book," Mimi interjected. "The really poor family with the four girls. And then one of them died. If Teddy was a girl, that would have been exactly the same as us."

"Not exactly," Dinah said. "In the book Beth dies, but she isn't the youngest."

Mimi was annoyed. "The point *is* there are four children and one of them dies. It doesn't matter which one."

"That's true," Josie was quick to agree.

Mimi went on, "If I were one of the sisters in that book I'd be Amy. She's beautiful and she gets to go on a trip to Europe. She's an artist, like me. And she marries the really rich boy from across the street."

Dinah chimed in, "I'd be Meg."

"Who cares?" Mimi rolled her eyes and sulked. "This is so boring. I can't believe we have to do this for a whole week. Dad covered up all the mirrors in the house and this morning Judith started yelling at me just because I lifted the cloth up a tiny bit to check my face."

Josie was Catholic and had never heard of the custom. "Why do you cover the mirrors?"

Mimi was busy examining her nails, so Natalie tried to give an explanation. "When someone close to you dies, you're not supposed to care about what you look like. So we cover up the mirrors."

"Oh," said Josie. "That makes sense."

"It's stupid," Mimi snapped. "And even if it isn't, Judith still didn't have to be so mean about it. Just because *she* doesn't care what she looks like doesn't mean the rest of us have to go around looking hideous."

Natalie thought Judith was pretty, but she didn't want to say so and start something unpleasant with Mimi. "Thanks for the juice," she said. "I'm going to go find my mom now." She put her glass in the sink and went looking for her mother in the living room.

Natalie's mother hadn't said one word on the way over to Teddy's house. Natalie knew she was upset, so she wanted to check on her. Her mother was the only one who truly understood how important Teddy was to her, who knew that he wasn't just a cousin or a friend. Her mother thought Teddy was special too. She knew it.

The living room in Teddy's house was large but dull. It was decorated in monochromatic shades of beige and none of the couches or chairs was comfortable. Over the years Natalie had tried sitting in every spot, so she knew from experience just how uncomfortable all of them were. Once she and Teddy had gone from chair to chair and couch to couch like Goldilocks in the Three Bears' parlor. "This one is too soft," she would say after sitting on one. "And this one is too hard," Teddy would rumble after resting on another. But there wasn't a single place that was "just right" in the whole room.

Natalie spotted her mother on one of the too-hard couches near the fireplace. There was an open place next to her on the right side, so Natalie scooted in and sat down. Her mother's arm immediately went around her, even though her head was turned so she could listen to the woman on her left. Natalie didn't know who the woman was, but her gray-blond hair was swept up in an elegant hairstyle and she was wearing diamond earrings. She was much older than Natalie's mother but still pretty.

"Stuart's brother was eighty-two but still so vibrant. We came north last week for his funeral on Tuesday, and then we got the call yesterday about poor Teddy. It's horrible—two funerals in one week. But I'm grateful we were in New York so we could be here today."

"I'm sure it's a great comfort to have you here, especially for Rose."

"Yes, well, my niece is very special to me." She peeked around Helen to get a look at Natalie. "Now who is this lovely young lady?"

"This is my daughter, Natalie. She and Teddy were born on the same day—I'm sure you've heard the story. Natalie was with Teddy yesterday during the accident."

"Oh dear." The woman took Natalie's hand and held it. She was wearing a lot of gold rings with diamonds and other stones. "That must have been terrible for you."

Natalie wasn't sure how to respond. "Thank you," she managed to say, taking her hand back. "Are you one of the neighbors?"

The woman smiled. "No, dear. I'm Aunt Faye, Rose's aunt. Her mother was my sister."

"You're the rich aunt! With the fancy apartment," she said.

"Natalie!" Her mother was mortified.

"Oh, it's all right, dear." Aunt Faye was amused. "I am rich, and my apartment *is* fancy." She turned to Natalie to explain. "I never had any children, so I never had to worry about buying expensive things. There's no one around to break them."

"That's sad," Natalie told her.

"Natalie! Enough!" It was her mother again. "I'm so sorry, Faye, she really isn't herself."

"Nonsense, dear, the child is perfectly right. It *is* sad."

Natalie nodded. "Did you want to have children?"

"Yes, dear, very much. But, as they say, it wasn't in the cards."

"Oh." Natalie must have looked particularly glum just then, because her mother told her she was going to get her a cookie. Helen got up from the couch, patted her daughter on the head and started walking in the direction of the dining room. Natalie was left alone with Aunt Faye.

"I'm going to tell you something I don't tell a lot of people," Aunt Faye said to her. She scooted a little bit closer on the couch. "Have you ever heard of Emily Dickinson?" Natalie shook her head. "Of course—you're too young. Well, Emily Dickinson was a very brilliant woman. She was a poet and she was also what people call a recluse. She didn't like to leave her house. Anyway, someone gave me a book of her poetry when I graduated from high school. I never even opened it. But years later, after my husband and I were married, I looked at it. I remember the day because it was after I had miscarried for the third time—I couldn't stay pregnant long enough to have a baby. So there I was at home, in my apartment." Aunt Faye paused then and smiled. "My very *fancy* apartment. I had nothing to do so I opened the book and read the poems. And that was when I found a special poem that helped me feel better."

"What is it?"

"I don't remember all of it, but the first part goes like this." Aunt Faye cleared her throat and closed her eyes. " 'I measure every Grief I meet, with analytic eyes—I wonder if it weighs like Mine—or has an Easier size.' "

"I don't understand."

"It *is* difficult to understand, isn't it? Of course everyone has their own ideas, but I think it means that everyone has some sadness in life. Maybe someone they love is sick or died, or maybe someone they love doesn't love them back. Maybe they don't have enough money for something they really need. For me it was that I couldn't have a baby. But for another person the grief could be something different. Something they wish they did or something they wish they didn't do."

"Oh."

"We always think our own grief is the worst—worse than everybody else's. But the truth is, we never know for sure what the people around us are feeling. I have had some bad things happen, but then a lot of wonderful things happened to me, too. An awful thing happened to you yesterday. But you mustn't let it ruin the happiness that lies ahead for you, dear."

"I'll try."

"Good. Now, that's enough talk from a silly old lady."

Natalie got up off the couch and hugged Aunt Faye. "I don't think you're silly," she told Faye. "And you have really pretty earrings."

Faye threw back her head then and laughed. A few of the people in the room turned to see who was laughing so loudly. Maybe you're not supposed to laugh when someone dies, Natalie thought, but I think it might help.

Chapter 43

ABE

Abe was relieved when Natalie threw up on the way back from the cemetery. Nothing felt normal before she got sick by the side of the road. The sight of it finally made the boys in the backseat talk again. *Gross! Who knew she could puke that far?* He was happy to hear their comments, no matter how obnoxious they were.

Abe thought he knew how difficult the day would be for Helen. But when she fell apart at the funeral home he realized he had not fully grasped the depth of her grief. To be told she wasn't worthy of wearing the mourner's ribbon had pushed her over the edge.

Seeing Natalie get sick snapped Helen out of her reverie. She had jumped out of the car to help Natalie clean her face and smooth back her hair. And for the rest of the ride Harry took the front seat next to Abe while Helen crammed into the back of the car with Natalie on her lap. Squeezed in with the boys, Helen was close enough to smell the mint of George's toothpaste and the chemicals from Sam's hair pomade. There was comfort for her in the closeness of her children.

By the time they got to Mort's house, Helen's heartbreak was slightly less visible. Abe saw that it was easier for her to talk to strangers, so he steered her toward people he didn't recognize. Whenever he saw Rose getting close, he purposefully led Helen to the other side of the room.

After an hour passed, Abe decided to go in search of his brother.

He left Helen in the care of Rose's Aunt Faye and walked upstairs to Mort and Rose's room. The door was open and there was no sign of Mort.

Farther down the hall, the door to Teddy's room was shut. Abe knocked softly, then entered. He found his brother, sitting at Teddy's desk, staring down at the collection of notebook paper, baseball cards, marbles and other little-boy paraphernalia precariously piled on top. It was clear that nothing had been touched since Teddy had left for school the day before. Mort's face was expressionless, his eyes blank. Abe approached carefully, not wanting to startle him. "Hey, Mort."

But Mort didn't answer. He sat perfectly still, his body erect, straight against the back of the desk chair. Abe stood behind him and carefully placed his right hand on his brother's shoulder. "How about you come downstairs with me and I'll get you a drink. Or maybe something to eat? Are you hungry?"

There was a barely perceptible shaking of the head. Abe didn't see it, but he felt it. He wanted to lean over and embrace Mort then, to share his brother's burden, but all he could manage was to keep his hand where it was, motionless on Mort's shoulder. Abe was frozen, connected to his brother by only the slightest touch of his fingertips. Five minutes, ten minutes, twenty minutes passed. He had no way to extricate himself. He felt it would have been unbearably cruel.

"Uncle Mort? Are you there?" It was Natalie, bustling up the steps, shattering their silence with movement and sound. This time Mort answered. "In here," he said.

Natalie peeked in, saw Mort in the chair and ran over to hug him. She hadn't been able to get near him at the funeral, and now Abe watched in amazement as his brother accepted Natalie's embrace. For close to half an hour he had stood behind Mort, barely touching him, scarcely speaking, trying to find some way to communicate his sympathy, his solidarity, his love. All that Abe had contemplated, Natalie accomplished in an instant.

"I miss Teddy so much," she told him.

"I do too," Mort said.

She looked over Mort's shoulder at Abe. "Daddy does too. Don't you, Daddy?"

"Yes," he answered. "I do."

Natalie wiped her eyes with the sleeve of her dress. She looked at the mess on Teddy's desk and then back at Mort. "Were you looking for the book?" she asked.

Mort nodded.

"He keeps it under the bed," she said. "So he won't lose it."

She walked over to Teddy's bed, kneeled on the carpet and pulled a large math textbook from behind the navy bed skirt. Abe recognized it. It was the book Teddy brought to their house every week when he came over for dinner. "His best comics are under there too," Natalie told Mort. "In case you want them."

She cleared off an area on the desk and opened the book to page forty-two. "This is where we left off last Thursday. Geometry. Teddy loves the shape drawings."

Abe scanned the pages over Mort's shoulder. "How do you kids understand all this?" he asked. It looked much too complicated for third graders.

"Uncle Mort goes slow," Natalie answered. "We don't do the stuff in here. It's just like a map for us to follow. We do easier problems that Uncle Mort makes up. But we love looking at the book. It used to be Uncle Mort's."

"That's terrific," Abe said.

Tears ran down Natalie's cheeks. "But now it's all over."

"You can still look at the book, honey," Abe told her.

"I can't." She shook her head. "Not without Teddy and not without Uncle Mort."

No one spoke for a long time. Then Mort took in a deep breath. When he let it out, he spoke. "I'm still here," he said.

Natalie shook her head again. "But we can't study together anymore. I can't come Thursdays after school and Aunt Rose would be upset, and . . ." Her words ran together and turned to tears on her tongue. Abe couldn't bear to see her cry again.

"Listen," Abe said. "What if I pick you up from school on Thursdays? You won't take the bus, you'll come back to the office with me."

"Why?"

"Whaddya mean, why?" He tried to smile. "You'll come to the office and you can study with Uncle Mort there." He looked at his brother. "How does that sound?" Abe held his breath. *What if Mort says no?*

Mort turned the pages of the book ahead to the next chapter. "Do you want to?" he asked Natalie.

"Yes."

"All right," Mort said.

Abe took his hand from Mort's shoulder to wipe his eyes. "All right then," he said loudly. "I better head downstairs and check on your brothers before they eat everything in sight. Wanna come down, Nat?"

"Is it okay if I stay with Uncle Mort for a few minutes?"

"Sure, honey. I'll see you down there in a little bit."

The last thing Abe saw before he left Teddy's bedroom was Mort pointing something out to Natalie on one of the pages.

Chapter 44

HELEN

(January 1957)

Helen was making beds when she heard the doorbell ring. Natalie and the younger boys were long gone, but Harry's first class was late that day, and he still had an hour or so before he had to leave for the train. Helen heard the sound of the shower running from the end of the upstairs hallway, so she knew he was awake.

By the time she got to the bottom of the steps, the doorbell had rung several more times. "I'm coming, I'm coming!" she called out. "Hold your horses!"

A familiar voice on the other side of the door answered, "What if I don't wanna hold my horses? What then?"

Helen opened the door to find Sol waving a white bakery box in the air by the strings. "Who wants a Danish? You got a cup of coffee for me?" Helen stepped to the side to make way for him, and Sol breezed past her as if it were his house, not hers. "What are you doing here? It's ten in the morning—why aren't you at work?"

"Whatsa matter, you think somebody fired me? I wanted to see my sister. Is that so terrible?" He placed the box on the kitchen table and took some plates out of the cabinet. In his navy silk suit and bright red tie, he looked out of place sitting at Helen's yellow Formica table. Like a city mouse in the suburbs, complete with a gold pinkie ring.

"You just don't usually visit me on a weekday morning."

"You want me to go?" He picked the box up and pretended to leave, but Helen pushed him back down.

"Don't be such a comedian," she told him. "Sit and I'll pour us some coffee." Sol sat. "I got Ralph covering the early shift at the newsstand," he explained to her, picking a piece of lint off his tie. "God forbid all the lawyers shouldn't have their papers first thing."

"Mornings must be your busiest time."

"How hard is it to sell newspapers to lawyers? They all got their nickels ready. Nah, lunch is when we see all the action. The fellas come over then, grab a candy bar, make a bet—"

Helen didn't want to hear about Sol's side business, so she interrupted. "Here, take your coffee. It's hot." Sol held the cup up to his nose. "Now *that* smells terrific." He took a gulp of the coffee and set down the cup. "All right." He opened the Danish box and looked inside. "I got prune, cheese and cherry. Whaddya want?"

"You know I like the prune." Sol took one from the box and set it on her plate. "Good, I'll take the cheese." He took a large bite and smacked his lips. "Best Danish outside the city. From that little bakery by the gas station on Clark Street."

"They're nice in there. They always give Natalie a cookie when I bring her in."

"Yeah." Sol shifted in his chair and lowered his voice. "Listen, how've you been?" He put his hand over hers on the table and squeezed. Sol's hands were huge, his nails buffed to a brilliant shine. The bottom of his pinkie ring pressed uncomfortably on Helen's fingers.

It had been a month since Teddy's accident. After the first week of sitting shiva, Helen hadn't really known what to do with herself. So she cleaned. Every drawer and closet had been given a thorough going-over. Sometimes she would find things that reminded her of Teddy. A marble that had gotten lost behind the living room sofa, a pair of snow pants in the closet, too small for her boys, that Teddy borrowed when he came over. She would sit wherever she found these things, on the couch or the floor, and cry until her tears ran out. She made sure to cry when the kids were in school. She didn't want to upset them, especially Natalie.

At last, she answered her brother. "I'm all right."

"You sure?"

"I'm sure. It's nice that you're worried about me."

"Yeah, well. It's a horrible thing that happened. A tragedy. And for Natalie to see it—I can't even think about it."

"I know."

"How's she doing?"

Helen shook her head. "Teddy was her best friend."

"Yeah, I knew she'd take it hard." He cleared his throat. "I was a little surprised about you, though."

"Me?"

"Yeah, you know . . . You got a little carried away at the funeral. For a while there I thought you had lost it. But then I said to myself, This is how Helen is. She loves all these kids. She loves them all like they're hers. What if it was Johnny? I said to myself. She'd have been the same way. Worse, even, if Johnny had the accident."

Helen couldn't look at him. Her eyes began to tear.

"Ah, don't start crying. I shudda never said that. All this talk, I shudda never brought it up. I'm sorry." He patted her hand. "Don't get started, okay? I came over to cheer you up, not to make you cry."

Helen took a paper napkin from the holder on the table and wiped her eyes. She stared down at the napkin and began pulling it into pieces. When she realized what she was doing, she got up from her chair, blew her nose with what was left of the napkin and tossed it in the garbage. "I'll be fine. Thanks for the Danish."

"Good, right?"

"I can't believe you left the cherry, though."

"Whaddya mean? I love a cheese Danish."

"I thought you loved cherries." She started wiping the crumbs off the table. "Remember that cake Grandma used to bring us when we were little, from Gus's? You always wanted the cherry from the top. Remember?"

Sol grinned. "Yeah, I remember. Every Friday."

"She always let you have the cherry—you were her favorite."

Sol brought his empty coffee cup over to the sink. "I wasn't her favorite. Cousin Susan was her favorite."

"Well, she liked you better than me."

"You're nuts."

"Then how come she always gave you the cherry?"

"Jeez, Helen, you been stewing over *that* for twenty-five years? A stinking cherry?"

"It was a symbol!" As soon as she said it, she realized how ridiculous it sounded. Sol started to laugh.

"Who are you? Sigmund Freud?"

"She liked you better! You were the boy."

"Bullshit!"

"Sol!" She didn't like it when he talked that way.

"Sorry, sorry."

"Anyway, why'd she give you the cherry every time? How come I never got it?" Helen started rinsing out the coffee cups.

"You didn't need it."

She turned off the water and looked at her brother. "What's that supposed to mean?"

"It means she didn't give it to you because you didn't need it. You were a happy kid, lots of friends. Why'd you need the stupid cherry?" Sol took one of the dish towels hanging from the handle of the oven and started drying the mugs.

"Why did *you*?"

"Because I was a miserable little bastard! Don't you remember me at that age? I was terrible at school—I could barely read!"

"But Grandma always said how brilliant you were!"

"To make me feel better about being so *stupid*! Plus, I used to get beat up every day after school by that Rodney what's-his-name. The kid a few blocks over. Him and his older brother."

"Why'd they pick on you?"

Sol shrugged. "They had a sister, Juliette, Julie, something like that. Beautiful girl. Couldn't take my eyes off her. I gave her a candy bar once."

"That was nice."

"Not to them. Every time they caught me looking at her, they'd practically murder me."

"I can't believe I didn't know any of this. . . ."

"That's why she gave me the cherry. You didn't need it. Pretty, good grades, always smiling. You had it all. Me, I had *bupkis*. So the old lady tried to make me feel special. Gave me the lousy cherry to cheer me up. If I had known it was such a big deal to you . . ."

"I shouldn't have even brought it up. Now I feel terrible."

"Why? That's life, kiddo. Two sides to every story. You gotta look at things from every angle."

"When did you get so smart?" She punched him in the arm and laughed.

"You better watch it, toots . . . ." And then he was chasing her around the kitchen like they were children again, Sol in his fancy suit and Helen in her housecoat. She couldn't remember the last time she'd laughed so hard. She could barely breathe.

Harry walked into the kitchen. "Hey, Uncle Sol." He took in the scene, confused. "Why are you guys running around the kitchen?"

Sol took a deep breath and smoothed back his hair with the palm of his hand. "Just cheering your mom up a little. You want the last Danish?" Sol motioned to the box on the table. "I'll take it with me," Harry told him. "I have to make my train."

"I'll give you a ride in. I was leaving now anyway."

"Thanks! That'd be terrific." He grabbed the pastry from the box and took a bite. "Cherry—my favorite!"

Sol raised his eyebrows at Helen, and she choked back her laughter. "All right, you two. Get out of my kitchen. Go!"

Sol took her by the shoulders and kissed her cheek. "You call me if you need anything."

She kissed him back. "You're a good brother."

Chapter 45

The Box Brothers factory on Long Island was more than twice as big as the old one in Brooklyn. Mort and Abe had larger offices, but Mort still worked with his back to the door, facing the wall. The same wedding portrait of Rose was on his desk, and although Mort's new office had a window, nothing other than a few coats of pale gray paint adorned the walls. A bookcase stacked with neatly labeled rows of brown ledger binders was built into the back right corner, and the left corner was solidly occupied by an ancient metal file cabinet. There was nothing else in the room.

A week and a half after the accident, Mort was back at work. He put the oversized green math book in the center of his desk, lying on its side with the spine facing him. On top of it he placed a new silver frame holding Teddy's school photo from September. In anyone else's office, both items might have gone unnoticed among the ordinary clutter of files, family photographs and paperwork piles. But on the barren surface of Mort's desk, the book and the photograph were painfully conspicuous. Mort knew, but for the first time in his life, he didn't care about attracting attention. He didn't care what questions people asked. Mort had given up his point system a long time ago. Either God wasn't counting, or His adding machine was broken.

The first Thursday Abe brought Natalie to the office after school, the newer secretaries, Rhonda and Maryanne, insisted on opening up a tin of butter cookies in honor of her visit. Sheila, who had known Natalie since she was a baby, gave her a hug and asked whether she might like to help them answer the phones. Did she want to sit in the reception area with them? Use some of the blank typing paper for drawing? The women assumed Helen was busy for the afternoon and that Natalie was still too upset to be left at home without a parent. They wanted to make her feel welcome. But after a few weeks went by and it became clear that Thursday was going to be Natalie's regular afternoon at the office, everyone stopped making a fuss.

Mort wondered what Sheila and the others thought. Did they think it was odd that Natalie went into *his* office to do her homework? He got his answer one Friday morning when he was on his way to get a cup of coffee. Rhonda and Maryanne were waiting for a fresh pot to brew, so Mort headed back to his office. Once he was out of view, Rhonda picked up the conversation where Maryanne had left off. ". . . always so serious," Mort heard her say. "No wonder Natalie does her homework in his office—it's the quietest place in the building!"

Mort wasn't offended. Rhonda was right—his office *was* quiet. The only time it wasn't was when Natalie was there. He remembered the way his niece had frowned the first Thursday when she knocked on his door. "Do you keep your door closed all the time?" she asked.

"Yes."

"Why?"

"I can't concentrate unless it's closed." He had forgotten that she had never been in his office before. Most people hadn't.

Natalie took a few steps into the room, looked around and frowned some more.

"You only have one chair."

"I'll get an extra one from the reception area for you."

"But where do people sit when they come here to talk to you?"

"They don't come here to talk." Why did she have to ask so many questions? When he returned with the chair, Natalie had further observations.

"You need some more pictures. Dinah's school picture was taken the same day as ours, so you should have that one. I don't know about Mimi's, though, because she's in the high school. Do they take Judith's school picture in college?"

"Let's just start with the math." There was no mistaking his brusque tone, and Natalie could sense his frustration. Her smiled dimmed, so Mort tried to explain. "I just don't like a lot of photos and knickknacks around to get in the way. I like to keep my desk neat."

"I understand. The thing is, I'd be really upset if my dad had a picture of one of my brothers on his desk and no picture of me."

"But the girls never come to the office. They don't even know the picture is here."

"I know, but still. Maybe you should put up a family photo. I'll bring you one from home."

And that was that—the slow transformation of his office had begun. After the third week, Natalie suggested he leave the extra chair against the wall. "That way, you won't have to keep lugging it back and forth," she told him. On the fifth Thursday she brought in a framed photo of Mort's family that had been taken at a relative's wedding the year before Teddy died.

"Where did you find that?" he asked.

"My mom had it in one of her albums. She said I could bring it to you. Do you like it?" Natalie looked up at him expectantly and smiled. What could he say? The photograph found a permanent spot on his desk.

After that, there had been no stopping her. She brought a tin of hard candies one week and a dark green pencil holder several weeks later. Natalie understood that he needed time to acclimate to each new item before another one was introduced. She developed a slow-paced yet relentless momentum, and Mort found himself incapable of rejecting her offerings.

He didn't want to admit it, but he found himself enjoying the small changes she made. He put his feet up on the extra chair sometimes when he had his coffee, and he liked how the pencil cup looked when it was filled. There was something satisfying about seeing so many neatly sharpened pencils all in one place.

Every Thursday, Natalie brought some work to do with Mort. Some days she brought equations to solve and some days she brought sketches of shapes she was trying to find the area of. One day she even brought in a story she had written. Mort smiled when he read the geometry-themed fairy tale she wrote about Princess Polygon and the evil dragon Decagon.

"What made you think of this?" he asked.

"Last week you taught me about tangents, and then the next day at school the same word was in our book, but it meant something else. The main character 'went off on a tangent.' It made me think about all of the geometry words I know, so I wrote a story."

"May I keep this?"

She was pleased. "Sure! Do you really like it?"

"It's very clever."

The next morning he pulled the story out from his desk drawer to look at it again. He had just put it down when Abe knocked on his door.

Abe whistled when he found his brother drinking his coffee with his feet up on the extra chair. "Making yourself comfortable there, Morty?"

Mort sprung up from his seat and pushed the extra chair against the wall.

"Don't get up on my account. It's good to see you relax a little. Nice change of pace."

"Hmmph." Mort didn't respond further, so Abe took the chair and sat down. "You know, Morty," he went on, "I don't think I ever sat down in your office before." He stretched his arms out, leaned back and looked at his brother's desk. "Got some new pictures too, I see. Good for you." Abe chuckled.

"What's so funny?"

"Ah, nothing. Glad you finally got an extra chair in here, that's all. Who knows, maybe I'll come around and visit more, now that it's so comfortable in here." Mort gave Abe a look. "Don't worry, little brother," Abe reassured him, "I'm only kidding."

Chapter 46

HELEN

(April 1957)

When the phone rang, Helen had a feeling it was going to be Arlene. Ever since they'd lost Teddy, Arlene had called Helen every day. Having a conversation with her used to be like pulling teeth, but since the funeral, Arlene hadn't stopped talking.

"Helen, sweetie, it's me." Arlene's basic philosophy seemed to be that in order to move past her grief, Helen should be kept as busy as possible. So Arlene called every day with questions, problems that needed solving and tasks she thought might take Helen's mind off her sorrow. Sometimes Arlene referred to her problems as "tiny hiccups" and sometimes she insisted she was just calling for "some practical advice." But whenever Arlene called, Helen knew she would be on the phone for a good long while.

"How are you, Arlene?"

"Fine, fine! I just need a little practical advice."

"Of course. Tell me."

"Well, you know how Sol and I are just crazy about the theater." As far as Helen knew, Sol hated the theater. But she decided to play along. "Mmm hmmm."

"We've been trying for ages to get tickets to see that show about the baseball team, you know the one I mean."

"*Damn Yankees?*"

"That's it! One of Sol's buddy's just called to say he has three tickets for the matinee tomorrow."

"Sounds terrific—what's the problem?"

"Well, Sol and I can't make it tomorrow. We have a wedding, the daughter of one of Sol's old friends from Chicago."

"That's too bad."

"It's just that Johnny is dying to see the show. Two weeks ago, he had never even heard of *Damn Yankees*, but now it's all he talks about. He's convinced one of the *real* Yankees will show up."

"Poor kid. You want me to take him?"

"Sol thought you and Abe could go with him."

"Abe is in Philadelphia, but I bet Natalie would love to go with us. She's never been to a Broadway show."

"Then she'll love it! Now, just one other thing. The wedding starts at noon. Sol and I have to drive out to New Jersey early in the day and Saturday is the housekeeper's day off, so . . ."

"Drop Johnny off any time."

"The reception may run late, so . . ."

"Johnny can stay over with us. Just pack him a bag and bring it when you drop him off."

"I'm so glad this worked out for everyone."

"Always happy to help solve a problem."

"Oh, it wasn't a problem, Helen. Just a tiny hiccup, that's all."

"Of course."

Sol and Arlene didn't even get out of the car when they dropped Johnny off. As soon as Helen opened the front door, Sol beeped the horn and Arlene waved her arm out the half-open window of the pale blue Cadillac. "See you tomorrow!" she called out.

Johnny stood on the front porch, a small duffel bag in one hand and a brown paper bag in the other. He looked at his aunt with an apologetic smile. "They were running late," he said. Helen raised an eyebrow. She wrapped her right arm around her nephew's shoulders. "Come inside," she told him. "I hope our tickets are in that bag." Johnny opened the bag and produced three tickets and a cold piece of toast. "Is that your breakfast?" Helen asked. She took the tickets, threw the toast in the trash and pointed Johnny toward the plate of warm blueberry muffins that sat on the kitchen table.

"Those look good," Johnny said, taking one. He was already taller than the last time she'd seen him, just a few weeks earlier. At eleven, Johnny was just starting to trade his little-boy dimples for more grown up good looks. Helen's boys were all handsome, but Johnny was a different kind of good-looking. He took after Arlene, with his movie-star nose and chiseled cheekbones. Helen was sure he would be a heartbreaker one day.

"Where is everybody?" Johnny asked.

Helen poured him a glass of milk and sat down with him. "Let's see. Well, you know your uncle Abe is out of town. Harry went with him—it's the first time he's ever been to Philadelphia. And the other boys are over at the baseball field. They have a doubleheader today."

"Where's Natalie?"

"Getting ready. She'll be down in a little bit."

Johnny looked concerned. "Is she still really sad? Do you think she'll like the show?"

"Don't worry, she'll love it."

"Can I go upstairs and tell her I'm here?"

"Sure, honey—go ahead."

By the time they got to Penn Station, there wasn't enough time to get lunch, so Helen bought the kids soft pretzels from one of the carts. "Extra salt, please," Natalie piped up, and Johnny said he liked his pretzels the same way. They were all in great spirits until a tall man in a gray overcoat bumped into Natalie on the way to the theater. Natalie ended up on the ground, and so did the pretzel. Johnny helped her up and Helen brushed her off, but the pretzel was unsalvageable. Since there was no time to buy another, Johnny handed Natalie his. "Here," he told her, "take mine."

Helen wanted to cry. It was just what Teddy would have done, and Helen could tell from the look on Natalie's face that she was thinking the very same thing. Natalie stared at Johnny for a moment, then grinned from ear to ear. She broke the pretzel into two equal pieces and gave one of the pieces back to him. "I'm not *that* hungry," she told Johnny. "We can share it."

Chapter 47

JUDITH

Her father wanted to have lunch with her. Alone. The closest Judith had ever come to eating a meal alone with her father had been when her mother was pregnant with Mimi. Rose had been eight months along and exhausted. She had suggested that Mort take Judith for a walk and get her an ice cream cone. "Just remember," Mort had warned, "I'm not buying you another one if you drop it. Understand?" He had said it over and over, so that Judith couldn't even enjoy the cone because of his pestering. The ice cream had melted all over her hand, and he hadn't even thought to give her a napkin!

Claire, Judith's friend from class, couldn't believe it either. She had only met Mort a few times, but Judith had filled her in.

"Do you want me to come with you?" Claire offered.

"If I bring you along, it will look like I don't want to be alone with him."

"You don't."

"I know. But I don't want to make it so obvious."

"Take him to the coffee shop on Amsterdam," Claire advised. "It'll be crowded, but the service is so fast you won't have to linger. They have good sandwiches too. Or did you want something more elegant?"

"No, definitely not. The coffee shop will be quick, at least." Judith was picking at one of her nails and frowning.

"Don't get yourself all worked up, Judith. Maybe he'll surprise you."

"He's not really one for surprises."

Mort had a morning meeting with Abe on 134th Street, so he and Judith had agreed to meet at the stone archway at Amsterdam and 138th Street. "It's called the Hudson Gate," Judith told her father, "in case you need to ask someone where it is."

"I'll find it," he assured her.

Judith's morning classes were over too quickly, and before she knew it, it was time to meet her father. He was waiting for her, just where he said he'd be, underneath the elaborate stone archway on 138th Street. He was standing on the Amsterdam Avenue side, looking in toward the campus. Judith spotted him first and for a moment thought about turning in the other direction. But he looked so harmless standing there, with his brown felt hat and his worn leather briefcase, that she couldn't find the strength to walk away.

"Hi," Judith said to him. She had never called him "Daddy." "Father" sounded strange. It was easiest not to address him at all. She was relieved that he made no move to embrace her.

"Are you hungry?" he asked.

"Claire told me about a place a few blocks up from here—is a coffee shop all right?"

"Fine."

"Up this way then." Judith pointed to the right and the two of them walked together. She couldn't think of anything to say, but her father didn't seem to mind. She couldn't remember the last time she had walked somewhere alongside him.

After a few blocks they saw the coffee shop across the street. It was crowded, but the waitress sat them at the last available booth near the soda fountain. A few of the young women at the counter waved to Judith—she recognized them from her Romantic poetry class.

When the waitress asked if they knew what they wanted, Judith answered quickly that she did. She didn't want lunch to last any longer than it had to. "I'd like a cup of tea, please, with lemon. And a grilled cheese sandwich."

Judith looked over at her father. He hadn't opened the menu either. "Chicken salad on rye," he told the waitress. "And a cup of black coffee." He handed the menu back and straightened his tie. After the waitress left, he pulled his old briefcase onto the seat of the booth and squeezed open the latch. Then he pulled out an envelope and handed it to her.

"What's this?" Judith asked him. He motioned for her to open it. Inside was a photograph of a young man, faded and bent in the upper left corner. It was Judith's father, probably twenty-five years earlier. He was standing in front of the same stone arch where they had just met. "This is you. How old were you?"

"I was eighteen. It was my first year at college."

"You went to college *here*?" Judith's hand was shaking. Her father already knew the campus. It was possible he had already eaten in this coffee shop a hundred times. She put the photograph down on the table. "I remembered you took some math courses after high school, but you never told me you went to college here."

"Just for a little while. I never finished. When my father died, I left to help Abe with the business."

"Uncle Abe asked you to quit school?" Judith was surprised.

"No, he didn't want me to leave school. But my mother worried that it would be too hard for him to run the company alone. They argued about it."

"You majored in mathematics?"

"Yes, but I had to leave in the middle of my sophomore year."

"Is that why . . ." Judith hesitated as the waitress approached their table and put two cups down. Judith put both of her hands around the steaming cup of tea. She was shivering.

When the waitress left, her father raised his eyebrow. "Why what?"

"Why you're always so angry." It dawned on her all at once. "You never wanted to work in the box business." As soon as the words were out of her mouth, she tried to take them back. "I'm sorry, I shouldn't have said that."

The waitress reappeared and set down their plates. Her father picked up half of his chicken salad sandwich and took a bite. *Why isn't he yelling?* She repeated her apology. "I'm sorry."

Instead of answering, he just chewed and swallowed. "I can't believe this place is still here," he said. "They always had the best chicken salad." He proceeded to polish off the first half of his sandwich with a gusto Judith couldn't remember ever seeing before. He usually only picked at his food. "You're right about the business." He wiped his mouth with the paper napkin from his lap. "I wanted to be a mathematician."

Judith was utterly confused. She barely recognized the man sitting across from her. The man who carried around old photographs and liked chicken salad sandwiches. The man who wanted to be a mathematician and wasn't angry at his daughter. The man who wanted to have lunch with her.

She took a sip of her tea and stared at her plate. Yellow cheese had congealed along the edges of the toasted bread. Her appetite was gone.

"Why are you telling me this?" Judith asked her father.

"I was going through some of my old things, and I found the photograph. It made me realize I never told you that I went to school here."

She had so many questions. "Is that why you made me go here? Because you wanted me to go to the same school you went to?"

Her father's face took on a familiar irritated expression. "Look, Judith, I don't want to rehash that old argument. City College is a damn good school, even if it isn't Bryn Mawr or Barnard. When you told us you wanted to go away we were just about to move. We were building the business. We had no idea what we'd be able to afford—"

Painful memories came back to her in a torrent. "Do you know you never even congratulated me for getting into college? Not even for being named valedictorian of my class?" Her face grew hot and she began to cry. She tried to hold back her tears, to spare herself the embarrassment of crying in front of her father in the coffee shop booth. She felt ridiculous. But she couldn't stop.

Her father said nothing. He turned to the briefcase that was still next to him on the seat of the booth, opened it again and fished out a second envelope. Was it another photo? Another piece of his past that he suddenly wanted to share? He handed it across the table to Judith. But this time the envelope was sealed. It was a letter, addressed to her, from Radcliffe College.

She stopped crying. "Where did you get this?"

"It came in the mail yesterday. Your mother hasn't seen it."

But I told them to mail all correspondence to my adviser. Judith had decided to take an extra year at City College in order to continue her studies, but now she was ready for the next phase of her education. Five years had taught her a few things—this time around she was prepared. She had applied for scholarships, housing stipends and work-study jobs, all to secure her financial independence. She wasn't going to ask her parents if she could go away to graduate school—she was going to *tell* them. She would work two extra jobs if she had to, but there was no way she was going to be discouraged this time. She had it all planned. Except the part about Radcliffe mailing her letter to the wrong address.

Her father interrupted her thoughts. "Don't you want to open it?"

"I don't want you to be angry."

"How can I be angry when I don't even know what it says?"

His casual manner only confused her more. She opened the envelope. "Read it," her father urged. So she took a sip of cold tea and began:

" 'We are pleased to inform you that you have been accepted to Radcliffe College as a candidate for the degree of Master of Arts. . . .' " She skimmed the rest of the first page and then scanned the second. "This says I've been accepted as a Mary B. Greenough Scholar."

"What does that mean?"

"It means I have a full scholarship. I don't have to pay any tuition. They're giving me room and board." Judith closed her eyes, savoring the words. "I have a full scholarship. I'm going to Radcliffe." She braced herself for her father's inevitable protest. He would be furious with her. Furious that he had been duped yet again. That she had schemed and withheld information. And this time he would be right. This time she *had* schemed. This time, she thought, he had every right to be angry.

But he wasn't. When she opened her eyes, he was looking at her. Staring straight at her with an expression she had never seen on his face before. An expression that she recognized only because she had seen it on the faces of *other* people's parents. He was proud of her.

"May I?" he asked, pointing to the letter. She handed the pages over to him and held her breath as he read them. When he was done, he handed the pages back to her. "Congratulations," he said. "English literature?" She nodded, and he went on. "This is a tremendous accomplishment, Judith."

She was stunned. Claire had been right—her father had surprised her. She wasn't sure what to say next. But she had to say something. "Did you ask me to have lunch with you today because of the letter?"

He took another sip of coffee. "I found that picture a few days ago. And then yesterday the letter came. I thought we should talk."

"Where did you find the photograph, anyway?"

"Natalie found it in one of my old books."

"Natalie?"

Her father sighed. "It's a math book. Teddy and Natalie found it in the garage last fall. I started teaching them some simple equations. Teddy really enjoyed it. Then after the accident, Natalie wanted to keep studying with me. Abe brings her to the office on Thursdays."

"Natalie comes to your office every week to study math with you? Really?"

For a moment her father looked like he might cry. "Sometimes we talk about Teddy, about the things he liked—comic books and baseball cards. . . ."

Judith could not believe what she was hearing. It was too much to take in, too many revelations in one day. She couldn't put all the pieces together or reconcile the man she had grown up with her whole life with the one sitting across from her in the booth.

"I suppose your mother needs to be told about Radcliffe." Her father was back to practical matters. "Would you like to tell her, or would you like me to do it?"

"Maybe it's best if we tell her together."

"All right," he agreed. "We'll do it tonight."

Judith checked her watch. "I really should go, or I'll be late for my two-thirty class." She got up from the booth and adjusted her sweater. "Do you want to walk back with me?"

"You go ahead. I think I'll stay and have a piece of pie. I used to love the apple pie here."

Judith stared at him. "You know, I love apple pie too. I used to always look forward to Aunt Helen's pie on Thanksgiving."

Judith's father shook his head. "I didn't know that."

"It's something we have in common then."

Chapter 48

ROSE

(September 1957)

Rose still couldn't believe Judith was leaving, but Mort was adamant. "We can't hold her back," he said. Rose knew it wasn't so much the fact that Judith was going away that bothered her. It was the fact that Mort and Judith had decided it together. There was something between them that night, an easy solidarity Rose had never sensed before. She didn't like it.

"You had no problem holding her back last time!" Rose snapped at him after Judith was out of the room.

"Last time we didn't know a lot of things that we know now," he answered.

"So you *know* things now? What could you possibly know?"

"I know how hard Judith is willing to work for her education. How much it means to her."

"If you didn't know those things when she graduated from high school, you were a fool."

"Then I was a fool, Rose." Mort held up his hands in defeat. "But five years ago she was a child. This time she's a grown woman, and she's determined to go. She has a full scholarship. She doesn't need our permission or our help."

"Then why are you so quick to give her both?"

Mort cleared his throat. "Before Teddy died, you told me I didn't pay enough attention to Judith, that I didn't encourage her. Do you remember that?"

Rose wouldn't answer him. "Look, Rose. We both know how bright Judith is. We can't keep her from this kind of opportunity just because we'd rather have her at home."

It's not because I want to keep her home, Rose thought. She walked away from Mort and went upstairs to Teddy's room.

After Teddy died, Rose hadn't been able to go into his bedroom. She kept the door closed and pretended not to notice if Mort or one of the girls wandered into it. It was only a few months after the funeral that she was finally able to muster the strength to go inside. She had been surprised by how neat the room was, until she remembered that Teddy had died on a Thursday. On Thursdays she usually made the beds and tidied up the bedrooms. She must have done that the morning before he died.

That first time she was in Teddy's room, Rose had wandered around in circles. She wanted to touch everything. Did the bedpost feel different? The desk? What should she do with his books and his clothes? Rose had opened the door to Teddy's closet and found the tall wicker basket that served as his hamper spilling over with dirty clothes and sheets from that morning in December. She picked up the basket to carry it downstairs to the laundry room, but on the way down the steps, the scent emanating from the sheets overpowered her, and she let the basket drop. She watched it fall, tumbling down the steps and knocking into the walls of the stairway, until it landed at the bottom with a thud.

Rose never washed the sheets or the clothes. Instead, she folded them neatly and placed them, unlaundered, in the back of Teddy's closet. Teddy's scent was all she had left of him, the last tangible trace that could conjure him to her.

After that day, Rose went to Teddy's room every now and then when she wanted to be alone. She would pretend she was dusting if anyone asked, but the girls never did ask, and Mort never questioned her. She would sit at Teddy's desk and stare out the window, and sometimes, when she was particularly upset, she would open up the closet and pick up the sheets. She would hold them close to her chest and breathe in the scent she had almost forgotten. Sometimes in Teddy's room, as surprising as it was to her, Rose almost felt like she wanted to pray.

Rose had never paid attention to the prayers that were spoken at the services she attended. She was not a religious person, and, like many women her age, she had never learned how to read Hebrew. After Teddy died, however, she found that bits and pieces of certain prayers started popping into her head at different moments. Some fragments had tunes and some were just words. Tidbits from holiday prayers and arbitrary blessings would come together in combinations that made no particular sense to her. Most of the time she didn't even know the meaning of the Hebrew words she was humming.

After her argument with Mort, Rose felt a new incantation composing itself. So she went into Teddy's room and opened the closet door. She clutched the worn sheets and let the words fill her head. This time they came to her as a melody, something she had learned as a young girl, from the end of the Mourner's Kaddish. *Oseh shalom bim'ro'mav, Hu ya'aseh shalom aleinu, V'al kol Yisrael V'imru, V'imru amen.* The melody repeated itself over and over, until part of the Unetaneh Tokef, the prayer the rabbis read every year on the High Holy Days, interrupted it. This time it was in English. *Who shall have rest and who shall wander, Who shall be at peace and who shall be pursued, Who shall be at rest and who shall be tormented . . .*

There was no question that she was being tormented now. And somehow Mort was the one finding peace. How could that be the result after all the trouble she had gone to, all the sacrifices she had made to give her husband what she thought he wanted, and all she had lost in that terrible process?

A few months later, when the time finally came to take Ju-dith to Boston, Rose tried to avoid making the trip with her and Mort. But Helen had offered to take Mimi and Dinah for the night, leaving Rose no excuse for missing the ride. She could express to no one why she wanted to stay home or why her participation in the excursion would be so painful. Soon they were leaving together, bound for Massachusetts to give Judith the education and the adventure that Rose always thought had been reserved for Teddy alone.

Rose watched the miles go by through the dusty patches on the car window. Mort navigated the road and Judith sat behind them in the backseat, carrying on a conversation with her father as if it were the most natural thing in the world. Rose sat in silence, listening to them talk, listening to the familiarity that had sprung up between them like weeds through a sidewalk crack. And all the while Mort drove and all the while Judith chattered, Rose gripped her hands together on her lap and clamped her lips together. She was afraid to open her mouth, even to breathe, because in the car's small space, stuck between her husband and her eldest daughter, Rose felt the anger brewing inside her push its way out of her chest and into her throat. She could feel it, twisting and bending, like smoke on her vocal chords, ready to burn its way up to her tongue. She pursed her lips tighter in an effort to stop it, for if she couldn't, she knew, the truth would burn its way out of her and escape from her mouth in one inexhaustible scream.

Part Four

Chapter 49

NATALIE

(May 1961)

"I'm never getting married," Natalie announced. She was standing on a small wooden box while Mrs. Tuber, the tiny seamstress in an ancient housecoat, pinned up the hem of her bridesmaid dress. The pale blue fabric was stiff and itchy. The skirt was too full, the neck was too low and the waist was uncomfortably tight. She couldn't wait to take it off.

"Mmm hmm." With a mouthful of pins poking out in all directions, Mrs. Tuber was unable to respond. Her gray head was bent over the hemline of Natalie's skirt, and Natalie was afraid the woman might never make her way back to an upright position. "Are you sure you're good all hunched over like that?" she asked.

Mrs. Tuber shuffled forward and bent down further. "Mmm."

This was Natalie's first time at Mrs. Tuber's. The shop consisted of one small room, with a rack of clothes on one side and an old wooden table on the other. Two sewing machines were set up on the table, and spools of thread in every color were strewn across the top. Natalie wanted to leave. She didn't like how people passing by on the street could see her through the shop's picture window. She kept her back to the glass while she stood on the box, but she could see the reflections of the people walking past in the mirror that ran the length of the shop's rear wall. One little boy pressed his face up against the glass and stuck his tongue out at her. She glared back.

Finally the seamstress rose from her spot on the floor. She stood back a little from the mirror and clucked approvingly at the fit. With the pins out of her mouth and tucked into the bottom of the dress, Mrs. Tuber was free to speak at last. "Soon it will be your turn to be the bride!" she told Natalie.

"I already told you. I don't want to get married."

"You're only thirteen," Helen interjected. She was sitting on an old wooden chair in the corner of the shop. "You're too young to say things like that."

Mrs. Tuber agreed. "When my daughter was your age, she wanted to be a dancer. She swore she'd never get married. Then the right fella came along, they fell in love and then she got married—just like that." She snapped her fingers.

"Real love isn't that simple," Natalie protested. "It doesn't just happen all of a sudden." She was tired of talking nonsense with some woman she had only just met. The room was getting hot and she was starting to sweat in the dress.

Mrs. Tuber shrugged. "What's so complicated? You meet a fella. You either love him or you don't."

"You can't just say that. What about Antony and Cleopatra?" Natalie wanted to know. "Or Guinevere and Lancelot?" She threw up her hands in frustration. "What about Bonnie and Clyde?"

Mrs. Tuber stared at Natalie like she had two heads. She turned to Helen. "I thought you said she was only thirteen. Already she's an expert on heartache?"

Mrs. Tuber hadn't known their family for very long. She didn't know what kind of heartache they'd been through. Natalie watched her mother stand up, fish a tissue out of her purse and blow her nose. Natalie calmed herself down and tried to salvage the conversation. "Fine. I might get married someday." Her voice was artificially bright. "When I'm older."

Mrs. Tuber nodded. "Now you're making sense." She took a ticket from a stack on the table and stuck it on a hanger. "Tell me again, who's getting married?" She waved Natalie into the small changing area that was marked off with a curtain in one corner of the room. "My cousin Mimi," Natalie called out. "I'm one of the bridesmaids."

"That's right," Mrs. Tuber said. "The cousin. Pretty girl. Looks like you. She came here last week with her sister. I told her I would fix her wedding dress, but she said it didn't need fixing. Some fancy store did it for her."

Natalie came out from behind the curtain and handed the dress to Mrs. Tuber. Then she walked over to her mother and took her by the arm. "Mimi likes everything fancy, right, Mom?"

Helen agreed. "Lucky for her, she's marrying a rich man. His family insists on paying for everything."

"Good!" Mrs. Tuber said. "She should live and be well."

"She should live and be well," Helen repeated.

Three weeks later Natalie was in the itchy dress again. The bride and groom had just finished their first dance, and Natalie was hiding, sitting on a chair she had dragged to a corner of the cavernous room, behind a pillar and a pair of potted palms. She couldn't bear the thought of speaking to one more stranger or having to smile for one more photograph.

"I can see you, you know." Natalie recognized the voice. She peered out from behind a clump of fronds.

"Johnny? Is that you?" she whispered.

"Yup."

"You weren't at the ceremony. I've been looking for you everywhere! Where were you?"

"My mom took forever to get ready, so we got here late." He tugged gently at the black bow tie that topped off his tuxedo. "What are you doing?"

"Hiding."

"From who?"

"Everyone. Being a bridesmaid is awful. Edward's mother is worse than Aunt Rose. She's so bossy. She wouldn't even let me sit down before the ceremony. She said my dress would wrinkle."

"Who the heck is Edward?"

"The groom! Didn't you read the invitation?"

"Nope. Never even saw it."

Natalie snorted. "Of course you didn't. I guess it's no use asking whether you read the engagement announcement in the newspaper."

"Who reads the newspaper?"

"For Pete's sake, Johnny, your father owns a *newsstand*!"

"Never mix business with pleasure. Besides, who cares which rich guy Mimi married? I just want some food. Come on out of there. Please."

Natalie sighed. "All right. But if Edward's mother comes near me, I'm going back." Natalie stuck one arm out through the greenery. "Can you help me? It's tricky in these shoes." Johnny grabbed her hand and pulled gently, but after she emerged he still didn't let go of her hand. He held it and stared at her.

"What? Is my dress ripped or something?" Natalie took her hand away and looked over her shoulder to see whether the back of her skirt was torn. Her cheeks were flushed.

"You look really . . . nice." Johnny's voice sounded strange. He was probably making fun of her. They always teased each other.

"Ugh. This dress is awful. It's so tight and the skirt is too puffy, and—"

"No. It's nice."

"It is?" She squinted her eyes, trying to read his expression, but he only looked down at his shoes. "Thanks." The silence became uncomfortable.

Johnny recovered first. "Let's head over that way." He pointed across the dance floor. "There's a waiter with those tiny lamb chops."

Natalie stood up on her toes to look and grabbed his hand as soon as she saw the tray. "Let's go," she told him, already running. "I'm starving!"

Chapter 50

JUDITH

"I'm never getting married," Judith said. Her cousin Harry raised his eyebrow at her. "How come? You don't like any of those Harvard boys?" They were moving slowly around the dance floor, neither of them particularly graceful. Harry's wife, Barbara, was dancing with Uncle Abe.

"It's not that," Judith tried to explain. "I just don't want all of *this*." She gestured to the ballroom and the couples dancing around them. "I don't want a big wedding with everyone looking at me and lots of people I don't even know. Mimi likes being the center of attention. But I would never want something this elaborate."

"I don't think you have to worry about that," Harry told her. "Not unless Mr. Moneybags has a brother."

Judith shook her head. "Just Lillian, his sister. Over there." She pointed across the room to a young woman wearing the same bridesmaid dress. It was obvious that the color had been selected to flatter Lillian rather than Judith. Mimi was by the girl's side, and the two of them were laughing and sipping champagne.

"No offense or anything, but Mimi fits in much better with Edward's family than with yours," Harry observed.

"Hmmph," Judith snorted. "Did you know Edward's parents bought them an apartment in their building as a wedding present? Mimi never stops talking about how wonderful they all are. Or about all her shopping trips with Lillian and Mrs. Feinstein to pick out her gown. She didn't bother inviting me or Dinah."

"Did she ask your mom?"

"No, but my mother wouldn't have gone even if they had invited her."

The music stopped and the bandleader approached the microphone. "Ladies and gentlemen," he announced, "it's time for the bride and her father to have their dance."

Judith watched Mimi down the rest of her champagne and hand the empty glass over to Lillian. Mimi and Mort took two uneventful turns around the ballroom before Edward cut in. When her father exited the dance floor, Mimi's face flooded with unapologetic relief. "I'll see you in a little bit," Judith said to Harry, and she followed her father to the bar.

"I didn't know you could dance," she told Mort, as she took the seat next to his. He ordered two glasses of champagne, handed one to Judith and raised his glass. "To your sister," he said.

"To Mimi," Judith agreed, and the two of them touched glasses. Judith was curious. "So what do you think of Edward?"

"He's the kind of man your sister always wanted to marry."

"You mean rich? I guess." She sighed. "I feel like this is the wedding of a stranger, not my sister."

"Well, your mother and I agreed that it was best to stay out of her way while she planned this. Mimi made it clear that she didn't want our input."

"Were you upset?"

"It wasn't unexpected."

"Still, we're her family."

Mort took a sip from his glass. "I think you already know this, Judith, but I've been trying to . . . ," he searched for the right words, "to look at things . . . differently."

"I know, but—"

He held up his hand to silence her protest. He looked tired. "Some things we just have to accept," he told her. Judith followed her father's gaze across the room to where her mother was sitting alone, looking as grim as possible. He turned back to Judith and finished his thought out loud. "So we can save our strength for other problems."

Chapter 51

ROSE

Tradition mandated that Mimi be escorted down the aisle with her father on one side of her and her mother on the other, but Rose had no intention of participating. An hour before the ceremony, while the photographer was taking pictures on the hotel terrace, Rose complained of dizziness. It wasn't a lie—she *had* been dizzy for a moment. But when the moment passed, she stayed quietly seated and kept her eyes closed. She tried to imagine she was somewhere else.

She must have been doing a pretty good job of it, because when the photographer was done, the women and girls all left for the powder room without her. Dinah ran back to retrieve her before the ceremony. "Still not feeling well?" she asked. Rose kept her eyes shut and nodded. She didn't have to say *why* she wasn't feeling well. She didn't have to say anything at all.

Dinah had been given strict instructions. Whether they were from Mimi or Mimi's new mother-in-law, Mrs. Feinstein, it didn't matter. If Rose wasn't feeling up to walking down the aisle, she was to be given a cup of water and brought to the room where the ceremony was to take place. She was to be shown to a seat in the first row on the right, next to the groom's grandmother. Dinah settled her there, gave her an obligatory kiss on the cheek and left to find the other bridesmaids. The wedding was about to begin.

The music started, something classical and elegant, wafting

toward Rose from the string quartet in the corner of the room. Half
a dozen good-looking young men, bow ties carefully knotted, strolled
down the aisle one by one. Rose supposed they were Edward's friends
or cousins—she didn't care. She didn't recognize any of them. Next
came Edward himself, flanked on one side by his father and on the
other by the cunningly coifed Mrs. Feinstein. Mrs. Feinstein's slim
gown was the same pale blue as the dresses the bridesmaids wore. The
same blue, Rose noticed, as the flowers cascading down the sides of
the wedding canopy. No one had told Rose what color dress to wear.
Her dress was gray.

After a few moments the music changed, and the bridesmaids
entered carrying impeccable blue bouquets. The maid of honor took
her place at the front of the room, and the crowd stood in unison,
all hoping for a glimpse of the bride. Rose felt Edward's grandmother
take her hand and squeeze. She tried to pull away—she didn't even
know the woman—but the grandmother's grip was too strong. "Oh
my," she murmured to Rose when she first saw Mimi coming through
the door. The old woman's eyes were watery and bright. "Now I
can die happy," she whispered. Rose managed to free her hand.

A minute later and there was Mimi, floating past in the ivory
gown that Rose had seen for the first time just that morning. Mort
marched beside her, solid and slow, as unremarkable as Mimi was
stunning. The guests let out a collective sigh. Only Rose was unmoved.

The sensation was a familiar one and took Rose back to a day she
had spent with her father at the very first Macy's Thanksgiving Day
Parade. It was called the Macy's Christmas Parade back then, and she
couldn't have been more than ten years old. She had been excited for
the outing, thrilled to see the animals, the floats, the costumed employees. There was a large family standing next to her, the girls in
bright red wool coats and the boys in matching sweater vests. At the
end of the parade, Santa glided past in his red velvet suit, waving to
the crowd from his perch on a giant golden sleigh. The children next
to Rose squealed with delight. "It's Santa! He's here!"

Rose had looked around at the other faces in the crowd. All of
the children were convinced that the man in the sleigh was the real
Santa Claus. Suddenly, she was disappointed. What had seemed so
magical just moments before was only paint and glitter after all. The

parade was not meant for her. She felt the same watching Mimi walk down the aisle.

What if she had done what she was supposed to do? Would she have felt differently if she had walked down the aisle with Mimi and Mort, if she had stood under the canopy with her daughter? She was certain of the answer: it wouldn't have changed a thing. It would only have made her duplicitous. Since Teddy's death, each year that passed found Rose more and more resistant to gatherings of any kind. The wedding was no different.

The rabbi persisted in his musings and the seven blessings were recited. By the time Edward shattered the glass, half of the people in the room were crying. Rose's eyes were dry, but Edward's grandmother passed her a tissue anyway. "Here you go, dear. Don't worry—you know the old saying." She patted Rose's arm in a show of comfort. " 'A son is a son til he marries a wife, but a daughter is a daughter for the rest of your life.' "

Rose wanted more than anything to escape from the doddering old woman, but she was stuck in her seat until the bridal party made their way back up the aisle. Natalie was the last of the bridesmaids to exit, and though Rose had barely glanced at the girl before the ceremony, something in her expression caught Rose's attention in the moment she passed by. At thirteen, she was already a beauty; there was no denying it. But there was something more—the hairline, the eyes—something reminiscent of Rose's own mother as a girl in one of Aunt Faye's old photos. The once-unnecessary tissue, forgotten in her handbag, was retrieved. Edward's grandmother handed her another. "No more tears now," she warned gently, and Rose nodded in agreement. She didn't bother to explain that she hadn't been crying for any of the reasons the old woman imagined.

Chapter 52

HELEN

No one could say Mimi wasn't a beautiful bride. On the outside at least. On the inside, Helen wasn't so sure. As she watched the bride and groom interact, Helen decided Edward was the kind of man who cared more about the outside.

What does Rose think of him? Helen wondered. She's sitting alone, not talking to anyone, not even trying to enjoy her daughter's wedding.

The passage of time had taught Helen some important lessons. A few years ago she would have sat down next to Rose and tried to talk to her. She would have praised Mimi's wedding gown and complimented the lavish celebration, all in an effort to earn back some small bit of affection. It wouldn't have worked, but she would have tried. This time she wasn't going to make the same mistake. She wasn't going to ruin her evening feeling guilty. She was going to keep her distance and keep her mouth shut.

"Hello, gorgeous." It was Abe, wrapping one arm around her waist and waving a waiter over with the other. He kissed her on the cheek and grabbed a handful of mini–lamb chops from the silver tray.

"Abe, how many of those have you had?"

"A few."

She raised an eyebrow and patted his stomach, which protruded visibly from his unbuttoned tuxedo jacket. "Remember what the doctor said? You've put on too much weight, sweetheart. You can't eat like that anymore."

He squeezed her shoulder. "Tonight, I'm celebrating. Tomorrow, I'll have celery." He gobbled the lamb chops in a few bites, left the remains on another waiter's tray and led Helen to the center of the room. "Time to dance with my beautiful bride."

"I'm not exactly a bride anymore."

"You'll always be my bride." The band switched to a waltz, and Helen let Abe lead her. But no matter where they were on the dance floor, Helen could not escape the view of Rose alone at that table.

"What is she doing, just sitting there like that?" She didn't have to say Rose's name. Abe knew.

"Who knows?" He tried to switch topics. "Don't you think that bridesmaid dress is a little grown-up for Natalie? Couldn't they have picked a different dress for her? She's a little girl, for Chrissake."

"Abe, have you seen her? She's not a little girl anymore. And stop trying to change the subject."

"I'm not."

"Fine, then what do you think about Rose? Honestly?"

"Honestly, I think she's starting to lose it."

Helen stopped dancing. "What do you mean?"

"I mean, I'm not joking. Every other week she calls at work and yells at one of the office girls."

"Which one?"

"Whoever answers. She tells them the milk in her refrigerator is sour. Or she can't find the can opener. Then she demands to talk to Mort."

"That's awful." Helen's resolve evaporated and she was overwhelmed with emotion. "What can I do?"

Abe shook his head. "Nothing. *Please* don't do anything, Helen. You know how she gets when you try to get involved. Mort has to deal with her now. It's not for you to do."

"Maybe I can help her."

"No. You can't." He lowered his voice. "You're a good person for wanting to, but you can't. Leave it alone." He kissed her on the top of her head.

What would she say to Rose anyway? Other than saying hello, it had been years since they had really spoken; their last meaningful conversation had been after Teddy's funeral, on the final night of the shiva. Helen was standing by the sink, washing the platters and trying to organize what was left of the food. All the visitors had gone home, and Rose had come into the kitchen.

"You can go home now," Rose said.

"As soon as I'm finished in here." Helen started to pack up the oversized coffee urn she had brought. "I'll call you tomorrow and see if you need anything."

"Why?" Rose's face was blank. It caught Helen off guard.

"I want to make sure you're all right."

Rose didn't answer.

"It takes time." Helen reached for her sister-in-law, but Rose turned away.

"Time can't fix this."

More than anything, Helen wanted to comfort her. "Maybe not, but I think we should try to help each other through this. I'm going to come over tomorrow and check on you."

"Don't."

"But why?" Helen's chest was aching and her face was hot.

"There's nothing left for us to talk about." Rose had made up her mind. "And now that Teddy is dead, there's nothing left for us to argue about either."

Chapter 53

ROSE

Helen should have insisted on a higher neckline for Natalie. The girl may have been only thirteen, but she certainly didn't look it in that dress. Rose noticed more than one of the groom's friends staring at her during the reception. Helen must have seen it too.

It was chilly in the hotel ballroom, and Rose was shivering. She decided to fetch her sweater from the coatroom. It didn't match the dress she was wearing, but she didn't care. The family photos had already been taken, and no one was looking at her anymore.

The coatroom was on the other side of the hotel lobby from the ballroom, miles past the reception desk and down a long corridor. Rose couldn't remember having walked that far when she dropped off her sweater, but when she turned the corner and passed the small restroom on the left, she recognized where she was. The attendant was nowhere to be found, so Rose swung open the waist-high door and began looking through the hangers herself. It was almost June, so there were only a few jackets, and the sweater was easy to find. She pulled it on and decided to sit for a few minutes on the stool she found in the corner. The dim overhead lighting washed over her, and the noise from the reception was muffled. Rose hoped the coat check girl would be gone for a while. She was happy to be alone.

Her thoughts drifted back to the party Helen's brother Sol had thrown the summer before Teddy turned three. She had wandered away from that party too, to a spot by the pond Sol had told her about. She could still see the flowers that grew on the edge of the water— were they bluebells? It had been so peaceful.

Rose couldn't have said how much time had passed when she heard voices approaching the coatroom. She recognized one of them as Natalie's.

"What do you think is back this way?" Natalie was asking.

"I don't know, but at least it'll be quiet and no one will bother us." It was a young man's voice.

What was Natalie doing, going to the coatroom with a man? Rose got up from the stool and stuck her head out the doorway.

"You shouldn't be here."

Natalie yelped in surprise and dropped the plate she was holding. Pastries and wedding cake were strewn across the floor. Cream, berries and frosting were everywhere. The young man frowned and bent down to survey the damage.

"You scared me," Natalie told Rose. Then she looked at the carpet. "This is a mess. Johnny, can you tell one of the waiters to bring a broom?"

"Sure thing." The young man ran back in the direction of the ballroom. Rose thought he looked familiar, but she couldn't place him.

"Aunt Rose, are you feeling all right? Uncle Mort was looking for you when Mimi and Edward cut the cake. Why are you in the coatroom?" Natalie was trying to brush off some of the frosting that had landed on her shoe.

"What am *I* doing here? What are *you* doing, sneaking off to the coatroom with that *man*?"

Natalie laughed. "Man? Johnny's my cousin—you've met him a million times. I told my mom we were leaving the ballroom for a while. The music's too loud and Edward's sister keeps making me dance with people I don't know. Johnny and I wanted to eat our dessert where no one would bother us."

"Hmph. You expect me to believe that the two of you were going to the coatroom to eat dessert?"

"What else would we be doing?"

Rose held up her hands in frustration. "Hasn't your mother taught you anything?"

"Why are you being so mean?" Natalie could see that her aunt was irritated, but she couldn't understand what was making her so upset.

Rose took two steps toward her. "Why do you think all those men wanted to dance with you? I saw the looks they were giving you in that dress."

Natalie took two steps back. "I don't even like this dress. They made me wear it."

"Well, your *mother* never should have let you out of the house in it."

"That's a terrible thing to say!"

"Don't you dare raise your voice to me!"

"Hey—quit yelling at her!" Johnny had returned from the ballroom. He had brought along one of the waiters, and Helen was just a few steps behind. When Natalie saw her mother, she started to cry. Johnny glared at Rose, and the waiter retreated from the scene, saying he would return later to clean up the floor.

"Shhh, shhh." Helen held Natalie and whispered, "It's all right, sweetheart. It's all right." Then Helen turned to Johnny. "Take her back to the party, honey. You two go have dessert. I'm going to stay and talk to Rose."

Once the kids were out of earshot, Helen's composure evaporated. She was livid.

"What did you say to her?" she demanded.

"Nothing." Rose retreated to the back of the coatroom, but Helen followed her.

"Nothing? She's a young girl, Rose. You were *attacking* her!"

"If she's such a young girl, why are you letting her parade around in that skimpy dress?"

"For heaven's sake, Rose, it's the dress Mimi picked! Dinah and Judith are wearing it too!"

"Dinah and Judith aren't thirteen."

"Why do you care what she's wearing all of a sudden? Since when do you care about anything Natalie does?"

Rose almost smiled. "It isn't easy having someone else tell you how to raise your own child, is it?"

"Stop it. I never told you how to raise Teddy."

"Didn't you? What would you call it, then?"

"At least I didn't pretend he wasn't there. You act like Natalie doesn't even exist!"

"She's your daughter, not mine. That was the deal we made thirteen years ago."

Helen's face crumpled, and she put one hand on the wall to steady herself. Her voice dropped to a whisper. "We never made any deal. You know that. We never even spoke about it. That night . . . it was like we were both in a dream. Between the blizzard and Mort and Abe being away . . . it was like it was supposed to happen. I wanted a girl so badly. You needed a boy so much. I thought we'd raise them together in the house on Christopher Avenue. You must have thought that too. I thought we'd be a family—all of us, always, mothers to both of them, and it wouldn't matter. You were like my sister—I thought you would love them both the way I did. I never thought it would turn out so wrong. I never thought you'd end up hating me. I never thought one of our babies would die."

"Stop saying *our* babies. They were *yours*. They were *always* yours. You took Natalie and you never let me have Teddy. You had to have both of them."

"That's not true."

"Yes, it is! I gave you Natalie and you were supposed to give me Teddy. You were supposed to let him be mine. But you never let that happen!" She was so focused on her argument with Helen that she never heard Abe's footsteps coming down the hall.

"What the hell are you screaming about? It's a wedding, for Chrissake!" Abe filled up the doorway of the coatroom, blocking the light from the hallway. How much had he heard? How much had he understood? Rose's legs began to buckle, and she thought she would be sick.

But it was Abe who hit the ground first. Rose felt the tremor from the fall before her eyes even registered it. Helen was on her knees next, shaking her husband's massive shoulders, listening for his breath and yelling to the coat check girl, just returned from break, to call for an ambulance. Rose stumbled back to the reception, amid the chaos and the noise, back to Mort to tell him the news. "It's your brother," she told him. "I think he had a heart attack."

Chapter 54

MORT

In the chaos that followed Abe's heart attack, Mort struggled with what to do next. On the one hand, he was in the middle of his daughter's wedding. On the other, his only brother was being rushed to the hospital. He knew with certainty that Mimi would have no further need of him that evening. He couldn't say the same, however, for Abe. Mort made his apologies and said his goodbyes to the groom's family and guests. Then he left the wedding and drove to the hospital. Rose stayed behind with Judith and Dinah.

The first time Mort had visited the hospital where they brought Abe was when Teddy was two years old and got hit with a baseball. Helen had ridden in the back of the car that day, holding Teddy on her lap. After Mort had dropped them off at the emergency room entrance, he had gone to find cheaper parking because the hospital lot had been so overpriced. When he pulled into the hospital this time, he saw that the rates were three times what they had been back then. This time, he pulled in and parked.

He was almost an hour behind the others in arriving, but he finally found them in the cardiac waiting room on the fourth floor. He was glad Natalie had stayed behind with Arlene and Johnny. The waiting room was grim, and no place for a young girl. Through the closed glass door, he could make out the faded wallpaper, peeling at the edges, and the shabby green tweed furniture that filled the space. Sol was drinking coffee from a paper cup while Sam and Joe paced back and forth under the murky lighting. Harry and his wife, Barbara, were on one of the sofas, talking quietly, and Helen sat with George, wiping her eyes with a handkerchief. Mort hesitated before he opened the door—he felt like he was intruding on their family gathering. But after Helen looked up and spotted him, turning back was no longer a possibility.

Helen motioned for him to come in and got up from the sofa to greet him. "You didn't have to leave the wedding," she told him. "I feel terrible that you left."

"It was almost over anyway." He shrugged. "I wanted to come."

"I'm glad you're here," Helen said, and George patted him on the back. When the other young men came over to shake hands, Mort knew he had done the right thing by coming.

"What did the doctors say?"

"They wouldn't say much, just told us to wait," George answered.

"Then we'll wait," Mort said, and he took a seat in a chair next to Sol. The others resumed their hushed conversations.

Sol drained the last of his coffee and turned to Mort. "Nice wedding, by the way. Beautiful bride."

"Thanks."

After half an hour passed, a middle-aged man in a white coat opened the door to the lounge. They immediately rose from their seats. Helen clutched George's arm. "How is he?" she called out, before the doctor could introduce himself.

"He's stable and resting," the doctor said. He held out his hand to Helen. "I'm Dr. Beineke. I've been treating your husband." The boys all lined up to shake Dr. Beineke's hand, but Mort stayed put next to Sol. He didn't want to waste time prolonging the greetings. He just wanted to hear the report. "Your husband had a mild heart attack," the doctor explained. "We have several more tests that need to be run, but as of now, we see no reason why he won't make a full recovery. We'll need to watch him closely over the next several days, and we'll keep him here to monitor him."

"Do you know what caused it?" Harry asked.

"Any number of factors; heredity, for one. I'd say excess weight is definitely on the list. When he's ready to be discharged, we're going to have to talk about modifications to his diet, as well as specific medications we'd like him to start."

"We'll do whatever you tell us to do," Helen said. "Anything to make sure he gets better."

"We can go over the details tomorrow. Right now, we're just keeping him sedated for observation. We don't want him moving around until we get some test results back."

"Can we see him?" Mort asked.

Dr. Beineke nodded. "Yes, but there are quite a few of you here, so why don't you go in one or two at a time."

Mort waited in the lounge while the others took their turns. He was the last to go in, after Sam and Joe. The room smelled like Clorox and menthol cough drops. Under the dull blue hospital blankets, Abe looked small and pale. He had none of the vigor Mort usually associated with him, and for the first time in Mort's life, he sensed his brother's vulnerability. He sat down on a chair next to the bed.

Mort studied his brother's face. Before this evening, Abe had filled up every room he'd ever entered with motion and sound. His voice, his appetite and his laughter had all dominated. Now that these were dormant and the space around Abe was still, Mort was able to conjure images he had not allowed himself to remember for decades.

He thought back on all the girls Abe had tried to fix him up with, all the parties and dinners Abe had invited him to, the way Abe had encouraged him to go back to school. One thing became clear: Abe had, in his own way, always tried to look out for him. Even setting up the Thursday-afternoon study sessions with Natalie after Teddy died. Sure, Mort knew Abe wanted to cushion the blow of losing Teddy for Natalie. But Abe also understood how much it would help Mort with his own personal loss. Not many men would have been as generous as Abe in the sharing of a child's affection.

The next thing he knew, Helen was patting his shoulder, gently trying to rouse him. When he awoke, he saw that he was holding Abe's hand. He placed it back at his brother's side and rubbed the sleep out of his eyes. "Guess I dozed off for a minute," he told Helen, embarrassed. "I guess so," she answered, looking worried but pleased. "Stay as long as you want."

Chapter 55

JUDITH

Judith wasn't surprised when no one could find her mother for the cake cutting. It was clear to her that Rose no longer worried about keeping up appearances. After all, she hadn't even cared enough to walk her own daughter down the aisle. Judith didn't believe her mother's excuse about feeling dizzy before the ceremony for one minute. She had seen it all before.

Judith couldn't decide if her sisters felt the same way she did, or if Mimi and Dinah were just oblivious to their mother's behavior. As the oldest, she was the only one of them who remembered what Rose was like *before*, back when she still acted like their mother. Mimi and Dinah had no memories of that woman. I lost someone, Judith realized, someone my sisters never knew.

Mimi and Dinah didn't remember that Rose and Helen used to be best friends either, but Judith did. She thought about it all the time: all the Thanksgivings they had together before her mother started making them go to Aunt Faye's, all the school picnics where they sat together eating Aunt Helen's sandwiches, all the times she'd come home from school to find Aunt Helen and her mother drinking coffee and chatting together at the kitchen table.

When she was younger, Judith had tried to trace the change in her mother back to a specific day or event, but all she could ever come up with was the day Teddy was born. That couldn't be right. She knew her parents were thrilled when Teddy came along. Her mother couldn't have been unhappy about *that*.

When Teddy was a baby, Judith had thought her mother was just tired from staying up with a crying infant. But when Rose had stopped caring about the house, the meals, and even whether the younger girls had matching socks in the morning, Judith had decided it was more than just exhaustion. She had picked up the slack as best as she could, but when Teddy's first summer had passed and Rose still wasn't herself, Judith understood that something in her mother had broken.

Rose had grown anxious and irritable. Her outbursts became the norm. It was obvious (at least to Judith) that Rose wanted nothing to do with Aunt Helen. Her aunt continued to invite them over for dinners and brunches, but Rose always had an excuse.

As she grew older, Judith had continued to wonder about the night of the blizzard. She had tried to reconstruct the evening so many times, but nothing ever became clearer in her mind. All she could remember was the snow, and blurry bits of the other details, so over time, she convinced herself that the night wasn't so mysterious after all.

After the photographer finished the photos of the bride and groom with the cake, Judith headed to the ladies' room next to the ballroom. The anteroom was set up as a lounge area, complete with upholstered seating and mirrors. Edward's sister, Lillian, and several of her friends were already there, adjusting their dresses, checking stockings for runs and blotting freshly applied lipstick. Lillian's dress didn't need adjusting and her makeup was already perfect, but a few of her friends needed touch-ups. One of them, a chubby brunette in green taffeta, was sitting on a flowered chaise dribbling raindrop tears. "My father just told me that if Richard doesn't propose soon," she could barely get out the rest of the sentence, "he's going to make me get *a job!*"

Lillian didn't see what all the fuss was about. "Just *make* him propose," she snapped, before turning her eyes toward Judith. "What about you? When are you getting married?" Judith wanted to disappear inside one of the stalls in the next room, but a line had already formed and she would have to wait her turn.

"I thought she was already married," a pale willowy girl in

lavender chimed in. She looked Judith up and down. "Isn't the oldest supposed to get married first?"

"Yes, but Judith is single," Lillian decreed. "Is there someone special I don't know about, Judith?"

Judith tucked back a strand of her hair and met Lillian's stare. "No one special, I'm afraid. How about you?"

The other girls froze, and no one spoke. The prolonged silence became uncomfortable, and it was clear to Judith that she had said the wrong thing.

"You've heard, then." Lillian glared at her.

"No . . . sorry. Heard what?"

"Broken engagements happen all the time," one of the girls said. "He wasn't good enough for you anyway."

"Not nearly good enough," another echoed.

It was definitely time to leave. "I think I'll head back," Judith said, retreating. She wanted to return to the safety of the reception, but she really did need to find a bathroom first. She made her way over to the front desk and asked if there was another one near the lobby.

"Walk all the way down to the end of that corridor," the desk clerk told her, pointing away from the ballroom. "There's a ladies' room at the very end on the left side. If you turn the corner to the coatroom, it means you passed it." The clerk apologized. "It's a little bit of a walk."

"That's all right," Judith told him.

The second ladies' room was much smaller than the first and strictly utilitarian. Luckily, it was empty. When Judith exited the stall, she was still jittery from her run-in with Lillian, so she took her time washing her hands and applied some clear gloss to her lips. Who had Lillian been engaged to anyway? If Mimi knew the details, Judith was sure she wouldn't share them.

When Judith opened the door to walk back to the party, she heard shouting coming from around the corner. She recognized her mother's voice.

"It isn't easy having someone else tell you how to raise your own child, is it?"

"Stop it. I never told you how to raise Teddy."

The other voice was Aunt Helen's. Judith stayed inside the ladies' room and left the door open just wide enough to hear them. She wanted to know what they were saying.

"She's your daughter, not mine. That was the deal we made thirteen years ago."

After that, the voices got very quiet and she could no longer make out what they were saying. Judith heard footsteps coming down the hallway, so she shut the bathroom door. When she poked her head out a few moments later, she saw the back of her uncle Abe turning the corner and walking toward the coatroom. She decided she'd better leave, before any of them thought she was spying, so she exited the bathroom and headed in the opposite direction, back to the party. Her heart was pounding.

What had her mother been yelling about? What kind of deal could Rose and Helen have made? If it had been thirteen years ago, it must have happened near the time when Teddy and Natalie were born. There was something else, there had to be . . . something she was missing.

Back at the reception, Judith took a piece of the wedding cake the waiters had set out on the dessert table and sat down to think. When Harry waved at her from across the room, she thought about him on that night so many years ago. He had been angry, she remembered, that their mothers had chosen her to stay with them, while he had been given the job of baby-sitting the younger children upstairs.

What was it he had said to her just a few hours earlier? *No offense or anything, but Mimi fits in much better with Edward's family than with yours.* He was right, of course. She did. Mimi got along with Edward's mother just like Natalie got along with Mort. But Mimi had rejected her real family. She had chosen another family that she wanted to be a part of, and just like that, the switch had been made.

She's your daughter, not mine. That was the deal we made thirteen years ago.

Just like that. The switch . . .

Natalie and Mort. Oh God. Was it possible? Try to remember, think. Judith's head was spinning as she tried, for the hundredth time perhaps, to reconstruct that evening. She had followed the cries of the newborns to the bedroom. Her mother had been in bed, holding both of the babies, while the midwife had finished up with Aunt Helen.

Then her mother had given her one of the babies to hold and the midwife had left the room. And then, *what happened then?* She had asked which baby was which. Yes. She remembered that part. The women had looked at each other. Her mother and Aunt Helen had stared at each other for a long time. Too long. And then her mother had answered. She had said Judith was holding Natalie. *Your cousin Natalie.* She had said "cousin." Judith had never once questioned it. Why would she? She felt the wedding cake rising up in her throat; she was going to be sick.

"Judith?" Harry was at her side, shaking her elbow. Did he know too? Had he guessed? She opened her eyes. "Judith, listen, my father . . . they think he had a heart attack. The ambulance is pulling up in front now. I'll call you when we know something. I have to go." He was already rushing out the door, running to the parking lot to meet the ambulance for his father. Instantly she was alert, her nausea forgotten, the more immediate crisis taking over. Had Abe had the same revelation, had he put together what she now thought she knew? As the chaos around her shifted, Judith could only wonder what her uncle may have heard or understood. It had taken her thirteen years to piece together what had happened. How long would it take everyone else?

Chapter 56

NATALIE

They wouldn't let Natalie anywhere near her father after the heart attack, and she wasn't allowed to go to the hospital with her mother. The groom's parents told her it was "no place for a child," and that it would be "too traumatic." She wanted to tell them she already knew plenty about trauma, but she didn't want to upset anyone further, so she did as she was told. Uncle Sol went with Helen and Natalie's older brothers to the hospital, and Natalie was pawned off on Aunt Arlene and Johnny. Uncle Sol called a taxi to take the three of them back to his house. Arlene put her arm around her and tried to be comforting.

When her mother called late that night, she told Natalie her father was going to be fine.

"Are you sure?"

"Yes. I promise."

She knew her mother would never lie to her about something like that, so she allowed herself to relax.

Natalie had no pajamas with her, so Arlene said she'd find something for her to wear. She led Natalie into a giant walk-in closet and poked through a wall of drawers. Natalie had never seen a closet like that before—as big as a whole room and carpeted from wall to wall with fuzzy peach chenille. Her aunt chose a long blue nightgown for her, but Natalie was afraid to put it on because she thought she might ruin the silk. "Don't worry, sweetie," Arlene told her, "I've got five more just like it."

Johnny tried not to laugh when he saw her in it. She begged him for a T-shirt and a pair of old gym shorts instead. Arlene didn't mind, so Natalie changed into Johnny's oversized hand-me-downs.

Even though Johnny had stayed at her house a million times, Natalie had never stayed overnight at his. As a result, Natalie realized, he knew her parents a lot better than she knew Uncle Sol and Aunt Arlene.

The first thing Natalie noticed about Arlene was how much shorter she was when she took off her heels. The second was how much younger she looked when she took off all that makeup. There were plenty of mirrors in Johnny's house, so she couldn't understand how Arlene hadn't figured that out yet.

Arlene had an elaborate and fascinating nighttime routine. There were at least ten different tubes of cream on the vanity in her bedroom, as well as an enormous box of chocolates. According to Johnny, she used every cream before she went to bed each night. "Do you have chocolate every night too?" Natalie asked, but Arlene just smiled and winked at her. "Sorry, hon, but I never share my beauty secrets with other women."

The best thing about Arlene, aside from all the candy she kept in the house, was that she seemed to have no sense of time. It was close to eleven when they got home from the wedding, and well past midnight when Natalie's mother called, but Arlene didn't even notice. She gave them potato chips and Cokes and left them in front of the television with no mention of bedtime. "Have fun, kids," she told them. "Don't stay up too late." Natalie's mother would have said it was already *past* too late and that the kitchen was closed until morning.

"Ever watch *The Twilight Zone?*" Johnny asked. She shook her head. "I don't usually stay up this late," she said. "Do you?"

"Just on the weekends," he admitted.

She didn't like the show. It frightened her, but she didn't want Johnny to think she was a baby, so she didn't say anything. He got the idea after she hid her face behind a throw pillow from the couch. He moved closer and put his hand on her shoulder. Her heart was pounding. "Nat? Are you scared?" All she could manage was a quick nod from behind the pillow. When he pulled it away, he saw that she was crying. "Aw, Nat, I'm sorry. I shouldn't have made you watch this junk." He brushed away a few tears with his fingertips. They were softer than she expected. For a few moments he just stared at her, and Natalie didn't know what to do. She felt like she shouldn't move, and then Johnny leaned his face closer to hers. When he kissed her, it felt as natural as writing her name. "Don't be scared," he whispered. "I promise everything's going to be okay."

She didn't know if it was Johnny's first kiss, but it was hers. Maybe she should have felt awkward or embarrassed, but she didn't. She knew he was kissing her more out of sympathy than desire, and she knew it wasn't going to go any further. "I'm not scared anymore," she told him. She knew he would understand what she meant. She had known him all her life.

Johnny put his arm around her and she rested her head on his shoulder. They sat like that, watching repeats of old cartoons, until three in the morning, and when they were done he showed her where the extra blankets were in the guestroom. When she got into bed, it was with mixed feelings about her day. Some of it had been awful and some of it terrifying, but the last few hours with Johnny had managed to soften those parts so she was able to push them out of her mind. She had forgotten to ask for a toothbrush, so she fell asleep with the taste of potato chips and Coca-Cola on her tongue.

Chapter 57

HELEN

The first thing Helen thought of once Dr. Beineke told her that Abe would be all right was that she had been lying to him for thirteen years. In all that time, she had never thought of herself as a liar. But when she saw Abe in the doorway of the coatroom, when she realized just how much she wanted him not to understand the argument she and Rose were having, she understood for the first time her complicity in a terrible deception.

A few years earlier Helen had read an article in the newspaper about a man whose wife discovered he had a second family—another wife and two kids living only an hour away from their home. He had been keeping it secret for fifteen years, telling each of the wives that he had to travel half the week for work. A simple receipt from the dry cleaner had given him away.

Like everyone else she knew, Helen had been horrified by the story. She hadn't been able to fathom how anyone could keep such an important secret from the people he claimed to love. In her mind she bore no resemblance whatsoever to the man with two families. But now, sitting in Abe's hospital room, saturated with guilt, Helen struggled to distinguish her actions from those she had read about. She hadn't planned what had happened. She hadn't been motivated by lust or greed. She was different. Wasn't she?

By the end of Abe's second day in the hospital, Sol finally convinced her to leave for a few hours. The boys had gone home, and Natalie was staying over at Sol and Arlene's.

"Take a shower, change your clothes. Lemme drive you. You need a break from this place for a while," Sol told her.

"But he's barely opened his eyes."

"He's gonna be fine," Sol tried to reassure her. "You heard what the doctors said. They gave him enough medicine to knock out an elephant. His body needs to rest. But he'll be fine."

"I just want him to talk to me." Helen didn't tell Sol how afraid she was of what Abe might say when he finally did speak, of what he might ask.

"He will, just give him a little time, is all."

"Let's just wait until Mort gets here. Then we can go. I don't want to leave Abe alone."

Sol patted her hand. "Whatever you want. We'll wait."

Helen was grateful for Sol's support, but she wished he wouldn't make himself so conspicuous at the hospital. After Abe's condition stabilized, Sol had brought in a flower arrangement so large it wouldn't even fit on the bedside table. The next day, he arrived with a ten-pound cookie platter, wrapped in colored cellophane and ribbons. Helen made him leave it at the nurse's station.

Mort's visits were peaceful by comparison. It was Mort who helped her navigate the maze of doctors and nurses handling Abe's care. It was Mort who dealt with the paperwork and the endless hospital forms. If Helen ever doubted his devotion to Abe before the heart attack, she could not doubt it in the days that followed.

That evening Mort arrived a few minutes after eight. It was a Monday, and he had been at the office to make sure everything was running smoothly. All of the staff and customers had to be notified of Abe's condition. Helen knew how little Mort cared for prolonged conversation with people, so she was not surprised to see him looking exhausted.

Sol stood up and shook Mort's hand. "Listen," he said, "I'm going to take Helen home for a little while. Let her get some things and grab a change of clothes. We'll be a few hours, tops, but she doesn't want Abe to be left alone. Will you stay until we get back?"

"Of course," Mort answered.

"Sol," Helen interjected, "I need to talk to Mort. Give us a few minutes?"

"Take as long as you want. I'll get myself a cup of coffee." He left the room, whistling.

Mort looked nervous. "Did the doctors find anything else? What's wrong?"

"No, no nothing has changed. He just . . . he hasn't spoken yet."

"Sure, he has; yesterday he opened his eyes and said your name. We both saw it. And when the nurse asked if he was thirsty, he nodded and sipped some water from the glass she gave him."

"I know he said a few words," Helen backtracked, "but not even a real sentence. And then he fell asleep again."

"Well, he isn't fully awake yet. They're giving him a lot of sedatives."

"But he might start talking tonight, when I'm not here."

"It's unlikely. I just saw Dr. Marcus on my way in and he said—"

"I know. I know it probably won't happen. But if it does, if he talks to you when I'm gone, I just . . ."

"What is it?"

Helen started to cry. "Before Abe had the heart attack, Rose and I were arguing in the coatroom. We were both yelling, and I'm not sure what he heard or didn't hear, and . . ."

"Don't worry. Abe's heard the two of you argue before."

"But that was why he got so upset, and then—"

Mort was firm. "Our father had his first heart attack when he was thirty-five, Helen. It runs in the family. You know that. It's not your fault."

She was grateful for Mort's trust, but she didn't think she deserved it. "Please, Mort," she begged him, "if I'm not here and he starts talking, please keep him calm. The doctors say he can't have any stress."

"I'll take care of him. I promise."

"I know you will. You're a good brother." Only later did it occur to Helen that it was the first time she had ever told him that.

When Sol pulled into Helen's driveway, the whole house was dark. It didn't feel like her home. Other than the sound of Sol's breathing, everything was quiet. Natalie was with Arlene, and the boys were all at Harry and Barbara's place. She was at a loss.

"Want me to make you some scrambled eggs?" she asked Sol, once they were inside.

"Two days sitting in the hospital, and you think I drove you home for you to make me eggs?"

"Of course not, but we're here and you must be hungry."

"How about you go upstairs and take a shower and *I* make *you* eggs? How about that?"

Helen laughed for the first time since the wedding. "You're going to cook for me?"

"I know my way around the kitchen."

She shook her head. "I'm not hungry and you should go home." When he protested, she opened the front door and practically pushed him through it. "I'll call you if I need you. I promise."

Upstairs, the silence overwhelmed her. She turned on every light in the hallway and her bedroom. *What if Abe knows? Does he think I'm a monster? Will he want to tell the children?*

She went into Abe's drawers and made a small pile of pajamas, socks and underwear to bring to the hospital. She forced herself not to think while she showered and dressed. But afterward, when there was nothing else to do, when she had run out of tasks to complete, she lay down on the bed and turned toward the place where Abe should have been. She lay there, blanketed in remorse, until she fell asleep.

An hour later, the phone rang. It was one of the nurses from the hospital. Abe was awake.

Chapter 58

ABE

When Abe opened his eyes, the first face he saw was Mort's.

"Abe, can you hear me?" Mort's mouth was moving, but it took a few moments for the sound of his voice to catch up.

"I can hear you." Abe started to lift his head, but Mort stopped him. "Slowly," he told him. "Let me get the nurse before you move." Mort walked to the doorway and called down the hall. "Nurse! He's awake!"

"Helen will be back soon," Mort told him. "How do you feel?"

"Tired," Abe answered, struggling to keep his eyes open.

"The doctors keep telling us how strong you are. You had a heart attack, but they say you'll be fine."

"How many days ago . . . ?"

"Just a few. It's Monday. You were admitted Saturday night."

"Too many lamb chops," Abe murmured, and then he closed his eyes.

He was dreaming that he was back at the hotel, in the hallway outside the coatroom. Helen and Rose were arguing, something about Natalie. Rose didn't like what Natalie was wearing. She didn't like her own dress either. Helen said there was nothing she could do about it. "But you took my dress," Rose yelled. "Give it back to me!" "It's mine," Helen told her. "You can't have it." Rose wouldn't let it go, and the screaming became louder. "You have two dresses and I have none. You were supposed to give one of them to me. But you never let that happen!" After that, Abe woke up.

When he opened his eyes, the first thing he saw was that Helen had been crying. She was holding his hand. "Whaddya crying for?" he whispered. He tried to smile, but his mouth was so dry that he started to cough.

Helen brought a cup of water to his lips.

"You're beautiful," he told her.

"Oh my God, Abe . . ." She choked back her sobs.

"What's the matter?" He coughed a few more times. "Can't take a compliment?"

"You're crazy." Helen squeezed his hand and kissed his face over and over. "Don't cry," he told her again, but it seemed like she couldn't stop. He listened to her breathing and felt her tears on his cheeks. "Shh," he whispered. But he didn't think she could hear him.

After several minutes, Helen finally lifted her head away from his. She took a tissue from her purse and wiped her tears from his face, then from her own. She looked into his eyes like she was searching for something, but Abe didn't have the slightest idea what she was trying to find. She looked frightened. "Don't worry, sweetheart." It was all he could think of to say. "They said I'm okay. Healthy as a horse." He wanted to comfort her, but the more he said, the tighter her grip became. *I must have really scared her.*

When she finally spoke, her voice was unclear and murmured. It sounded like she was apologizing, but Abe stopped her before she could go on.

"*You* don't need to be sorry. I'm the one who did a belly flop on the hotel carpet right in the middle of the wedding."

"Do you remember anything?"

"Only a little bit. Natalie came into the ballroom—it looked like she'd been crying. She said you were by the coatroom talking to Rose, so I went to get you."

"And after that?"

"The last thing I remember is Rose yelling at you."

"Do you remember what she said?"

"Just yelling, her dress, your dress, Natalie's dress—who knows. She always has something to yell about."

"That's all?"

"That's it."

"Oh Abe, I'm so sorry." Helen's voice cracked and she broke down. "It's my fault, it's all my fault that this happened. If I hadn't confronted Rose, we wouldn't have been arguing and you wouldn't have had the heart attack. . . ."

"Shh. It's not your fault. Listen to me. You had nothing to do with it. It would have happened anyway."

"You don't know that."

"Listen for a minute. I didn't want to tell you but I wasn't feeling so great on Friday, the day before the wedding. I couldn't breathe so well at work and I had a couple of pains."

"Pains?"

"Chest pains, and running down my arm, just a little bit."

"Why didn't you tell me?"

"Yeah, well, I didn't want to make a fuss right before the wedding. I was gonna go to the doctor on Monday. I guess it wasn't such a good plan."

Abe expected her to scold him, to tell him how stubborn and foolish he had been for neglecting his health. Instead, Helen threw her arms around him and held him close. He shut his eyes and felt the gentle rhythm of her breath against his cheek. In a few minutes, he fell back asleep.

Chapter 59

ROSE

Rose was disappointed that her aunt Faye hadn't been able to come to New York for Mimi's wedding. Faye's husband, Stuart, had died a few years earlier, and after that Faye had stopped coming north for visits. Faye called the week before the wedding to wish Rose *mazel tov,* but Rose didn't like the way she sounded. "Can you believe I caught a cold in Florida *in May*?" she coughed. It was the last thing Rose ever heard her say.

When the lawyer called the Monday after the wedding, Rose couldn't believe that Faye was gone. At that point she hadn't seen her aunt in more than two years.

The lawyer had a lot of information to go over with her. "I'll be sending you the details in the mail, but your aunt's will is very clear. She left her house and her entire residuary estate to you."

"I'm not familiar with the legal terms. What does that mean?"

"Well, aside from some charitable bequests and specific bequests of tangible property—jewelry and other mementos—Faye left you the rest of everything she owned, including her house, bank accounts and stock portfolios."

"What about my cousins in California? Her will must mention them?"

"The will lists all other possible heirs by name, including your cousins, but it states clearly that you are the only one to inherit the bulk of the estate."

Rose had almost no contact with her cousins. None of them had flown to New York for the wedding, and none of them had sent Mimi a gift. Still, she wondered what they would think of her getting all of Aunt Faye's money. She doubted they would be happy for her. "Did Faye say why?"

"The will states that you were the niece who took the most interest in her, and the only one with whom she had regular contact. However, your aunt also left a handwritten letter on file with us, giving more explicit reasons. She referenced the loss of your son several years ago and her hope that this money might bring you some measure of happiness."

Rose couldn't think of anything else to say. "Well, thank you very much for your time."

"There is one additional matter. Faye made a personal bequest to one of your relatives." Rose could hear the shuffling of papers in the background. "Here it is. Your niece, I believe. Natalie. I was hoping you could provide me with an address and phone number for her."

"Natalie?" Rose was stunned.

"It seems Faye met her at your home and was quite taken with her."

"What did she give her?"

"I'll read it to you: 'To Natalie Berman, the niece of my niece Rose Berman, I hereby give and bequeath my Cartier platinum and diamond earrings. I hope she will enjoy them and keep them to remember me by.'"

"Diamond earrings?"

"Yes."

"You realize Natalie is only thirteen years old?"

"I'm sure the girl's parents will keep them for her until—"

Rose cut him off. "Thank you for your time."

"About that address—"

Rose hung up the phone before the lawyer could finish. Let him find the address from someone else. She was furious. *Natalie again!* What made her so damned special? Rose flung the phone across the room.

"What was that?" Judith called down the stairs when she heard the noise. She was home for a few more weeks before she returned to Boston for her summer research position.

"Nothing," Rose answered, trying to sound undisturbed. "I dropped the phone."

"Are you sure?"

"Yes. Everything's fine."

Rose was distraught over Faye's passing, but her anger over the bequest to Natalie superseded her grief. What had Faye been thinking? She hadn't left gifts for the other girls. Why Natalie? What set her apart? And why was everyone always so taken with her?

Rose was up late that night, waiting for Mort to return from the hospital. She was anxious for news, and she wanted to know what Abe remembered from the wedding. She certainly wasn't about to call Helen to find out.

"Abe woke up tonight," Mort told her as he removed his tie.

Rose's heart was pounding. "That's good news . . . isn't it?"

"Yes, very."

"Did he . . . say anything?"

"Not much. I was the only one there at first. Helen was at home getting some clean clothes, but she came later. He was a little woozy still, mumbling about eating too many lamb chops."

"Well, did you see him at the reception? He was shoveling them in like he hadn't eaten in a week."

"Rose, please. He's in the hospital."

"Well, maybe he wouldn't be in the hospital if he hadn't made such a pig of himself."

"Enough!" She had gone too far. Mort looked like he was about to explode. "My brother had a *heart attack*! He could have *died* and all you can do is criticize his eating habits? What's wrong with you?"

She was unprepared for his outburst, but he wasn't done. "I *forbid you* from saying one more word against my brother. Do you hear me?" Mort's voice grew more hostile and ragged. "Or against Helen either! That woman has done nothing but try to help you for as long as she's known you. Do you remember how she used to come downstairs and take care of Teddy when he was a baby? Or how she came with me to the hospital when he got hurt? When Teddy died, Helen was here every night cooking and cleaning. So *what* is so terrible about her? What did she ever do to make you hate her so much?"

The way Mort looked at her then was something she would never forget: like she was a monster from a nightmare and he couldn't wake up. It was awful, but she would have been able to get past it if he hadn't thrown all of Helen's good deeds in her face. If he hadn't held Helen up like some kind of saint against her own awful wickedness. She might even have apologized for the lamb chop comment if Mort just hadn't said what he said to her next.

"Do you know what you're going to do tomorrow?" Mort asked, his voice hard with resolve. "You're going to the hospital to visit my brother, the way you should have two days ago. And when you see Helen there, you're going to tell her you're sorry. Whatever this feud is about, it's gone on long enough. Tomorrow you're going to end it."

Rose's heart was racing. She couldn't do what Mort demanded. The thought of walking into the hospital, of facing Helen at Abe's bedside, made her physically ill. She would not let Mort dictate the terms of her forgiveness.

"I can't go tomorrow. I have to go to the travel agent and book my airline ticket. Then I have to pack. I think I'll bring Dinah with me." She was nonchalant.

Mort thought she had gone crazy. "What the hell are you talking about?"

"My aunt Faye died yesterday," she said.

"What?"

"Faye. She died yesterday of pneumonia. Her lawyer called this afternoon."

She had caught him off guard. "I'm sorry, Rose. I . . . I didn't know."

"How could you know?" Her voice was detached, thoroughly indifferent. "Faye left everything to me: the house, her bank accounts, everything she owned. I need to meet with the lawyer to sort it all out. I'm sure it will take a few weeks at least. So I won't have time to go to the hospital tomorrow. I'll be leaving for Florida as soon as I can arrange the trip."

Chapter 60

ROSE

She wasn't coming back. She wouldn't say that to Mort, of course. She wouldn't say it to anyone. But she knew it to be true. As soon as she recognized it, it became more real than anything else. A calmness settled over her, and she was able to focus her energies with an efficiency she didn't know she possessed. Her anxiety faded into the background, and for the next several nights, she slept better than she had in decades.

Preparations for the trip took up most of her time. Dinah would be joining her at first—she had just graduated from high school and had no summer plans. They would be staying at Faye's house. It belonged to Rose, after all, and she decided that the easiest thing would be to live there. The lawyer had given her the phone number of Faye's longtime housekeeper, and Rose had arranged for the house to be cleaned and groceries to be purchased before they arrived. She had even arranged for Faye's car to be serviced (Faye hadn't driven it for years). "I have it all worked out," she told Mort. "We'll leave next Wednesday."

For the most part, Mort let her be. He didn't bother her with questions about the house or Faye's property. He didn't offer advice about how to deal with the lawyer or the tax implications. There was nothing he could say to change her mind about the trip.

There was one thing he wanted her to do, however. "I'd like you to visit my brother in the hospital before you leave."

She pretended to be busy arranging her toiletries in her suitcase. "I'll visit him when I get back."

"You're staying for two weeks. With any luck, he'll be out of the hospital by then."

"Then I'll see him at the house. I have to pack."

He pointed to the suitcase. "You're finished packing. You've taken care of everything and you don't leave for two days yet. You have plenty of time to see him tomorrow."

Rose had no more excuses. She would visit Abe the next day.

When she arrived at the hospital, she could see Abe through the half-open door to his room. He was propped up in bed, reading the newspaper, and he was alone. *Thank God.* Maybe she'd get lucky and miss Helen altogether.

"Hello, Abe," she said, knocking on the door.

He was surprised to see her. "Rose! Come in, come in." Abe folded the paper and put it on the table next to the bed. He looked better than she expected. Helen must have brought him some clothes, because he was in pajamas instead of a hospital gown. He was freshly shaven but pale.

Rose sat down on the chair farthest from the bed. "How are you feeling?" She couldn't think of anything else to say.

"Good. The doctors say I should be out of here next week." He smiled and looked down at his hands. It occurred to her that he probably couldn't think of anything to say either. She wondered how long she was obligated to stay. Was twenty minutes long enough? If only he had been sleeping when she arrived! She could have just left the gift and written a note. . . .

"I almost forgot. I brought you a gift."

"You didn't have to do that." He winked at her. "But if it's something from that deli down the block, I won't turn it away. The doctor put me on some low-fat diet, and I haven't had a decent sandwich since I got here."

"It's not food." The disappointed look on his face made her want to punch him. Instead, she handed him a rectangular package wrapped in paper from a local bookstore.

"I hope you enjoy it," she managed to say. "It was on the best-seller list for most of last year and some of this year too—it's called *Hawaii*."

"Oh?" It was obvious he hadn't heard of it, but it had given them something to talk about, for a few minutes, at least. "If you don't like it, I'm sure Helen can return it for you."

"No!" he insisted. "It's gotta be terrific if it was on the best-seller list for that long! Geez. I'll start it first thing tomorrow."

"Good." She paused. "Well, I should let you get some rest." She got up from the chair, but before she could leave, Abe reached his hand out. "Wait!"

"Are you all right? Should I call the doctor?"

"No, nothing like that. I just wanted to say thanks for coming to see me. I know you've got a lot to do, so thanks for taking the time."

It occurred to Rose that this might be the last time she would ever see Abe, and that thought, coupled with the vulnerability of his condition, compelled her to take his outstretched hand. In truth, she cared very little about what happened to him once she was gone, but a tiny part of her was glad for Mort that he had a brother like Abe to keep him company. There had never been a man with as little guile and as much forgiveness in him as Abe.

"You're welcome." She held his hand, just for an instant, before she let it fall.

Chapter 61

HELEN

Helen couldn't believe it when she saw Rose leaving Abe's room. What had she said to him? Of course, Rose must have been prepared for the possibility of the two of them running into each other. But Helen was flustered.

"What are you doing here? You didn't say anything to him, did you?"

"Of course not. Mort asked me to come before I left. I'm going on a trip in a few days."

"A trip?"

"My aunt Faye passed away. I'm going to Florida for a while to settle everything with her estate."

"Faye? Oh no. She was a wonderful lady."

"She was. Anyway, I'm leaving on Wednesday."

"How long will you be gone?"

"A few weeks." For as long as the two women had known each other, Helen could always tell when Rose was lying. There was something about the way Rose's upper lip curved inward that gave it away. As much as Helen wanted to know the truth, she didn't want to provoke an argument. The last time the two of them argued, Abe had almost died. Stop asking questions, she told herself.

"Have a nice trip." Helen forced a noncommittal smile and made herself walk past Rose and down the hallway to Abe's room. Her hand was already on the door handle when Rose called after her.

"Helen!"

Even from several feet away she could see that Rose was crying. It took all of her strength not to go to Rose to comfort her, all of her willpower to root her feet to the spot on the floor where she stood in front of Abe's room. She tightened her grip on the door handle and waited for Rose to say something. Silently she counted to ten, promising herself that if Rose was still silent by the time she reached ten, she would open the door and go inside. When she reached eight, Rose spoke.

"I'm sorry. For all of it."

Helen didn't move an inch. She didn't look at Rose. She couldn't trust herself. She couldn't even breathe. Rose spoke again.

"Goodbye, Helen."

She watched Rose turn away from her then, watched her walk back toward the elevator that would carry her down to the first floor of the building. From there, Helen knew, Rose would walk out of the cold sterility of the hospital lobby into the warmth and brightness of the May sunshine. She would go back to her house and finish packing her things. In a few days Rose would board the airplane that would take her south, far away from Mort, from Natalie and from everyone else. Rose would leave every mistake and complication of her life behind, and when she disembarked in Florida, everything would be simple and new. Why, Helen wondered, would she ever want to come back?

Chapter 62

JUDITH

Rose was leaving the next day, and Judith was running out of time. She couldn't speak with Aunt Helen, not with Uncle Abe in the hospital, and there was no one else to ask. She was the only one who suspected. Whether that made her particularly observant or particularly foolish, she would decide after she talked to her mother. Had she finally deciphered the truth, or was the whole idea ridiculous? She wouldn't wait for her mother to return from Florida to find out. She would ask her today.

In the meantime, Judith decided to help Dinah finish packing for her trip to Florida. Judith couldn't figure out why Rose was taking Dinah with her, but she was happy her sister was getting some attention. From a very young age, Judith had taken her place in the family as the most studious of the three sisters. Mimi, as everyone knew, was the beauty. Only Dinah remained undefined. For a few years she had occupied the role of the adorable baby of the family, but only until Teddy came along. After that, she had faded into the background, her personality hazy and her role in the family vague.

Judith found Dinah in her room, folding clothes into neat, square piles on her bed. Dinah had the smallest of the bedrooms, with faded yellow walls and white painted furniture. Other than a carefully arranged display of old dolls on the shelves in the corner, there was no clutter to be found.

Dinah was happy to have company. "You've never been on a plane, have you? I'm nervous."

"No," Judith shook her head, "but they're completely safe." She wanted to say something encouraging, something about how Dinah and their mother would have a wonderful time together, but she couldn't make herself say those words, so she opted for simple truths. "It's going to be so sunny in Florida!"

"Not too humid?"

"Not when you're on the beach! And the food—I bet you'll have stone crab claws."

"Are they good?"

"Delicious. One of the girls on my hall is from Florida and all she talks about are the stone crab claws. Plus you get to stay in Faye's house. I bet it's fancy as anything. Remember her apartment in New York?"

"Of course!" Dinah was finally smiling, and Judith wished she hadn't waited so long to make that kind of effort with her sister.

They were sitting at the kitchen table when Rose returned from the grocery store.

"Is it all right if I borrow the car for an hour?" Dinah wanted to know. "I need to pick up a few things at the drugstore. Want to come, Judith?"

"You go without me. I'll see you when you get back."

"Sure." Dinah took the keys from Rose and headed out of the kitchen with her purse. A few minutes later Judith heard the click of the front door lock. She was alone with her mother.

Rose busied herself unpacking the groceries. She sprinkled a chicken with salt and garlic powder and put the roasting pan in the center of the oven. "There's something I need to talk to you about," Judith told her.

"It'll have to wait. I have too much to do before I leave tomorrow. I have laundry and phone calls to take care of, and I'm just starting dinner." Rose slammed the oven door shut.

"Then I'll talk while you cook." Judith's tone was desperate, but Rose chose not to notice. She slid a pile of chopped broccoli into a casserole dish and poured a can of cream of mushroom soup over the top, all without looking up. "Fine."

There was no easy way to introduce the topic, no smooth transition Judith could employ. "I have to ask you a question, but I don't know how. . . ."

"You don't know how to ask me a question?"

"I don't have . . . the right words."

"Isn't that what you've been studying for all these years? Words?" Rose was exasperated. "I don't have time for this nonsense. I have to start a load of laundry."

Judith stopped her before she could leave the kitchen. "I heard you arguing with Aunt Helen," she blurted out. "The night of the wedding."

"Don't be ridiculous. Helen and I didn't argue at the wedding."

"It was before Uncle Abe's heart attack. I was in the bathroom by the coatroom and I heard you yelling about a deal you made, thirteen years ago, you said. After that, I couldn't hear anything else and I went back to the party."

Judith waited for her mother to speak, but Rose didn't say anything. She took a seat at the kitchen table and smoothed her skirt on her lap.

Judith kept talking. "I don't expect you to explain everything to me. It was a long time ago, I know that. But I think you were talking about the night Teddy was born. The night Teddy and Natalie both were born." Rose still didn't speak, so Judith continued, "You were never the same after that night."

"*I* was never the same? *Nothing* was ever the same!"

"Please don't get angry with me," Judith whispered. "I don't want to argue with you."

"Then what do you want?"

"I just want to ask a question. One question, that's all. And I won't bother you about it ever again."

Rose crossed her arms over her chest and glared. "Go ahead."

The air was thick with dinner smells and it was hard for Judith to breathe. There was nothing to do but to come out and say it. "I think you and Aunt Helen . . . that night. I think . . ."

"For heaven's sake, *just say it*!"

"Is Natalie my sister?"

There was nothing exceptional about the moment that followed. Rose didn't even seem surprised by the question. There were no tears, no shouts, no confessions. There was no hesitation before her mother spoke, and no excuses after. Judith knew the answer before the sound was fully formed. The only thing that surprised her was the flood of oxygen that filled her lungs the moment the word was spoken out loud. "Yes."

Chapter 63

ABE

Abe was glad he was being discharged on a Sunday. After two weeks of hospital food, he couldn't wait to get home and have one of Helen's Sunday night pot roast dinners. She always made mushroom gravy to go with the roast, and those little homemade rolls he loved.

He had never been so happy to sit on the couch and watch the baseball game with his family. Helen didn't follow baseball, but that first day home she wouldn't let him out of her sight. She wasn't watching the game as much as watching *him*, like she wanted to check his pulse. With all her staring Abe couldn't concentrate on the game, so, sweet as could be, he told her maybe she should find something else to do. After that she made Natalie and George check on him and report back to her in the kitchen every fifteen minutes.

Sol, Arlene and Johnny were coming over to celebrate his first night home. Helen had invited Mort and Judith as well. Luckily, Rose was still in Florida.

"I told Mort to come over for dinner any night he likes while Rose is away," Helen told him.

"I'm surprised you want to spend that much time with him."

"I'm sure he won't want to come every night. Judith is headed back to Boston soon and I don't want him to eat alone. Plus, he can tell you what's going on at work over dinner."

"I won't need updates from Mort. I'm going back to work tomorrow."

"Abe!" She swatted his arm, not too hard. "The doctor said no work for at least a week!"

"Yeah, but he meant for people who don't like their jobs."

"He meant for people who had heart attacks! You're not going!" The look on her face told him there would be no negotiating. He held up his hands in surrender.

A few hours later, when Abe looked around the table at Helen and the rest of his family, he felt an overwhelming surge of gratitude. He felt considerably less grateful when he saw what Helen was serving for dinner. "Where's the pot roast?"

She pretended not to notice his disappointment. "The doctor said you have to cut back on red meat. I made a recipe from the cookbook the cardiologist's nurse gave me."

"It looks delicious," George said, without enthusiasm.

"No, it doesn't," said Natalie. "It looks awful. But if Daddy has to eat it, then we do too."

"Thanks, sweetheart." Abe blew her a kiss from across the table. "Did you make the rolls, at least?" he asked Helen.

"Yes, but you can't have butter."

Abe sighed and shook his head. "When I was in the hospital I dreamt about this dinner. Pot roast, mushroom gravy, buttery rolls, pecan pie."

"Well, tonight you can dream about broiled fish," Helen said, "because that's what we're having tomorrow."

Chapter 64

NATALIE

Natalie was excited to have her father home from the hospital, but she wasn't looking forward to a house full of company. She would have liked one night alone with her father and brothers before everyone else was invited. Besides, she hadn't seen Johnny since the night they kissed, and she was concerned things between them might be awkward. It turned out she was wrong: being with Johnny was the same as always. No, the person who surprised her that evening wasn't Johnny. It was Judith.

When Teddy was alive, Natalie wasn't particularly comfortable around any of his sisters, and after he died, she saw them only at large family gatherings. To Natalie, her cousins were "the Three Sisters," like the title of a play George once told her about. She didn't think of them as separate individuals with voices and ideas of their own. Rationally, of course, she knew they were different. But whenever she pictured them, it was always as a group.

Judith was the only one of the sisters to come to Abe's homecoming dinner. Dinah was in Florida, and Mimi was still on her honeymoon. Aunt Rose's absence, coupled with Abe's long-awaited presence, created an unusually festive atmosphere at the table. Maybe it was because of the celebratory mood of the dinner, or maybe it was for some other reason Natalie couldn't fathom, but Judith seemed intent on changing the old pattern between them. She chose a seat next to Natalie at dinner and asked several questions about Natalie's summer plans and her friends. The unexpected attention was confusing but not unwelcome. If Natalie had been asked to choose one of the Three Sisters to spend time with, she would have chosen Judith for sure. Mimi was too self-absorbed and Dinah too wishy-washy. But Judith was more complex; she was smart and interesting. Natalie liked her.

Natalie told Judith about the mother's helper job she had lined up for the summer, and after dinner, they talked about Judith's summer plans in Boston. "I got a position as a research assistant for one of my professors," Judith explained. They were sitting on the floor in Natalie's room, looking at yearbooks from Judith's old high school in Brooklyn. Natalie kept all of her brothers' old yearbooks in her room. The boys didn't want them anyhow, and Natalie liked to read the inscriptions.

Every few pages Judith would remember something about a classmate and stop to tell Natalie the story. Most of them involved Harry and one girl or another. It was cozy sitting together like that, handing yearbooks back and forth. Natalie hadn't realized how much fun Judith could be.

"What are you researching?" Natalie asked.

"I'm looking for religious symbolism in the works of the early Romantic poets. It's actually a lot more interesting than it sounds."

"It's funny," Natalie admitted, "but most people don't think the stuff I like is interesting either."

"You mean math?"

Natalie hadn't known that Judith knew so much about her. "How do you know I like math?"

"My father told me he studies with you. He told me he used to teach you and Teddy from his old math books."

Natalie nodded. "Uncle Mort is *really* smart."

Judith was smiling. "The two of you have a special relationship. I've been meaning to thank you, actually."

The evening was full of surprises. "Thank me? For what?"

"For helping him. When Teddy died, he needed someone to talk to, someone to help keep Teddy's memory alive. Teaching you gave him that, and I think watching you learn made him think differently. You know, when I was your age, my father didn't believe that girls needed the same kind of education as boys. He doesn't think that way anymore."

"I don't think I could have changed his mind about something like that."

"Trust me. You didn't try to, but you did. You were never afraid of him."

Natalie thought back to the day she and Teddy had found the book. "Teddy used to be afraid of him. I'm not sure why I never was. Maybe if he was my father I would have been."

Judith looked upset then, so Natalie tried to explain. "I think everyone is a little bit afraid of their parents when they're young. Kids just want their parents to be proud of them, and it's frightening if they're not."

Judith's expression softened. "Maybe." Then she snapped her fingers. "Hey! What if I ask your mom to let you come visit me in Boston for a few days this summer? What do you think?"

"I'd really like that." Natalie didn't understand why Judith was taking such an interest in her all of a sudden, but it was a wonderful feeling. Natalie had always loved having brothers—they were her protectors, her champions, her family. Still, spending time with Judith made her wonder, just for a minute, what life might have been like if she had grown up with a sister.

Part Five

Chapter 65

MORT

(October 1969)

When Abe had his second heart attack, Mort had not seen Rose for eight years. The day before she had been scheduled to fly back to New York, she had called Mort to tell him she was extending her trip. She needed more time to sort through Faye's estate with the lawyers. Two weeks after that, Mort got a letter in the mail. Dinah had met a very nice young man who was the grandson of one of Faye's neighbors. She was considering enrolling in a two-year college program near Miami in the fall, but she would come home in August for a few weeks. She would either stay in New York and take some classes there or pack up her things and return to Florida for college. Rose supposed the decision would be made based on how things developed with the young man. Regardless of what Dinah decided, however, Rose planned to stay in Florida indefinitely.

The letter was quite specific. Rose didn't want Mort to worry about her—physically she was fine, mentally she was sound and financially she was independent. He should not take her leaving personally, and he should feel free to explain the situation to their family and friends in whatever manner he saw fit. Her reasons for staying in Florida were simple: the ocean had a calming effect on her, and for the first time in many years, she felt peaceful. Rose was sure Mort would not want her to leave such a beneficial environment. She was sure he would be happier without her. She wished him well, but she did not think further extended communication would be constructive or necessary. She hoped he understood.

Mort did understand. He wrote back telling her so, and let her know that he would not contact her further unless he needed to. He packed up the rest of her clothes to ship to Florida. At the last minute he put a picture of Teddy in one of the boxes, but whether it was an act of kindness or cruelty, he was unable to decide.

Mimi and Edward saw Rose whenever they vacationed at Edward's family home in Palm Beach. Dinah eventually eloped with the neighbor's grandson, settled in Florida and saw her father a few times a year when she came north to visit. Of the three sisters, only Judith had no contact with their mother.

Mort wasn't surprised when Dinah told him Rose would not be attending Abe's funeral. He couldn't honestly say that he wanted her there, but her absence forced him to face the finality of their arrangement.

At the funeral chapel, Mort sat between Natalie and Judith. Natalie had grown into an unusually beautiful young woman—she shared a few of Mimi's physical traits, but her eyes were softer and more thoughtful. Judith was attractive in a more typical way, a way that Mort had come to appreciate over the years. The fact that the two cousins had become so close brought Mort a great deal of satisfaction.

Mort had been to his share of funerals, but this was the first one since Teddy's where he was obligated to wear the black mourning ribbon reserved for the deceased's immediate family. He remembered how hysterical Helen had been before Teddy's service when Abe told her she couldn't wear one. Today she wore a black ribbon on her dress, and while its presence over her heart brought no ostensible relief, Mort could see that she was better able to retain her composure in this setting than she had been so many years earlier.

Abe was sixty-two years old when he died. This had been acceptable by the standards of his parents' generation, but it was premature by those of his own. "He was so *young*," the coworkers, relatives and friends murmured to Mort as they shook his hand. At Teddy's funeral, no one had mentioned his age. If sixty-two was too young to die, eight had been too catastrophic even to mention.

"We will now hear a few words from Abe's brother." That was his cue from the rabbi. Helen had asked him the day before if he would speak at the funeral. What could he say? He was a terrible public speaker, he knew, but he didn't want the service to pass without marking the moment in some way. He wanted to honor his brother.

Mort rose from his seat, nervous and slightly nauseated, to take his place at the front of the chapel. Over a hundred people were packed into the seats, and everyone would be watching.

Mort had no notes to rely on, just thoughts he tried to convey. He spoke about how Abe had taught him to throw a baseball when they were children, and how Abe once beat up a classmate for picking on him in school. He talked about Abe's kindness, his generosity, his willingness to forgive all transgressions, and even more remarkable, his ability to forget them. He praised Abe's optimism, his appetite, the interest he took in everyone he met, whether friend or employee. "You know," Mort admitted, "when I was a young man, I used to think Abe didn't pay enough attention to the bookkeeping aspect of our business, that he didn't care enough about the numbers. I used to think that was a weakness. As I grew older, I began to appreciate Abe's contributions more, and I figured that with our different strengths, we balanced each other out. Now, with Abe gone, I know the truth. Abe's role at Box Brothers was much more important than mine. Abe paid attention to the numbers that mattered most: his twenty employees, his infinite friends, his five children, his four grandchildren and his singular wife. I only wish he could have had more than sixty-two years to do that."

Most of the people at Abe's funeral knew Mort, or, if they didn't know him personally, they knew of him from others. His reputation did not prepare them for the warmth of the eulogy he gave. He returned to his seat, unrecognizable.

Later, on the way to Helen's house from the cemetery, Mort could not help but to take stock of his life. His brother, Abe, was gone and Teddy, his only son, had died years before. His wife had left him. Mimi and Dinah were present in his life, but not significantly so. He had two young grandsons (Mimi's boys) whom he hardly saw and no real friends to speak of. Earlier in his life, after measuring such devastating losses, he would have considered himself wholly in the red.

But time had altered his perspective, and there were blessings still left to be counted. Over the past eight years, Helen had become like a sister to him. She invited him to the house a couple of nights a week, where he debated baseball history and game highlights with George and Joe over dinner. He found he enjoyed working with Harry and Sam at Box Brothers. His daughter Judith was a professor at Barnard and was about to publish her second book on modern poetry. Natalie was graduating from Barnard in the spring as a math major and he was looking forward to attending her graduation with the rest of her family.

As Mort considered his situation now, in the autumn of his fifty-ninth year, he concluded that his numbers were steadily improving.

Chapter 66

JUDITH

(April 1970)

Six months after the funeral, Judith met Natalie for lunch between classes. Natalie's thesis was due in a week and she was working furiously to finish it. Judith found the twenty-one-year-old in their usual booth at the coffee shop on 116th Street, scribbling on a stack of papers in red pen. She stopped writing when she saw Judith and waved.

"I already ordered for us," Natalie told her. "Two grilled cheese sandwiches and two pieces of apple pie."

"Perfect," said Judith. She slid into the worn leather banquette and pointed to the paper pile that rested on the linoleum tabletop. "How's it going?"

"Okay, I guess. There's a lot to do, and I'm just hoping it's good enough." Natalie looked as pretty as ever, but Judith couldn't help registering the dark circles under her eyes and the messy pieces of dark brown hair escaping from her ponytail. She had lost weight since Abe had passed away, and Judith was worried about her.

"I understand, but you need to get some rest. Do you want me to talk to your thesis adviser about an extension?"

Natalie rolled her eyes. "Just because Professor Kaplan is your *boyfriend* doesn't mean he should give me special treatment."

"I know, but you've been through a lot this year." She tried to change the subject. "Hey, how's the chemistry major from Columbia?"

Natalie shook her head. "Roger? Physics major, actually. But it's over. There was no *chemistry*." She smirked at her own bad joke and scrambled to move the paper pile over to one side of the table as the waitress set down their sandwiches.

Judith bit into the triangle-shaped half of her grilled cheese. No matter how many she made at home on her own stove, she could never get them to taste this good. "What about that cute Canadian guy from last year? You liked him, didn't you?"

"I did, for a while. . . ."

Judith tried to sound casual. "Have you seen Johnny lately?"

Natalie shoved an entire half of grilled cheese into her mouth and chewed. She wouldn't look up.

"C'mon, Nat. What's going on? All those cute boys calling you, and you don't want to date any of them." Judith paused to give Natalie an opening. But when she didn't stop chewing, Judith continued, "Does this have anything to do with Johnny?"

Natalie paused to swallow. "Are you an English professor or a detective?"

"There are more similarities than you'd think."

Natalie's face flushed red. She finished her sandwich and downed the rest of her coffee. Judith didn't want to overwhelm her with questions, so she tried to be patient. In the meantime, the waitress returned to clear their plates and refill their coffee. When she brought over the two slices of pie, Natalie started talking. "The thing is," she said, scraping the filling out of the crust, "no matter who we date, no matter what we do, it always comes back to Johnny and me. There's so much we've shared together. Teddy, my dad." She put down her fork. "How could I love someone who's never even met my father?"

"Bill is never going to meet my mother."

"It's not the same." Natalie looked annoyed, and Judith regretted her comment.

"I know."

"When Johnny went to college, we said we would meet other people and that we'd try to forget about each other in *that* way. But then he'd come home and we'd see each other again. What's between us just never goes away. Not for him and not for me."

"So you two have been seeing each other?"

Natalie looked sheepish. "Yes. But what can we do about it? We're first cousins, for crying out loud. There's a tremendous stigma."

"It's perfectly legal in New York. Besides, a million famous people have married their first cousins."

"I know, I know." Natalie rattled off a list of names without even thinking. "Charles Darwin, H. G. Wells, Edgar Allan Poe, Igor Stravinsky, Jesse James, Albert Einstein. And that's just a few of them."

"Wow, I guess you've really thought about this."

"Of course I have. Johnny and I both have. But Arlene's great-uncle or something married one of his first cousins and their son had some sort of birth defect. Johnny doesn't really believe that's what caused it, but it worries him."

"Nat, if you love each other, that's the most important thing. Not what might happen ten years from now and not what other people might think."

Natalie wiped her eyes with her napkin. "You say that, but what if my mother doesn't approve? I can't upset her now, not so soon after my father. Judith, I don't know what to do."

Judith wanted to tell Natalie the truth. More than anything, she wanted to take away the burden Natalie carried. *He's not your cousin*, she wanted to say. *You don't need to cry—you're not even related.* But Judith was afraid she would only be trading one burden for another. What would she say? *Our mother and our aunt swapped you and Teddy when you were born?* Natalie might not believe her. She might refuse to speak to her again. And even if it all went well and Natalie was able to accept what Judith told her, the secret was simply not Judith's to tell. If Helen loved Natalie as much as Judith thought she did, shouldn't Helen have that opportunity?

"Natalie, she'll understand."

"How can you be so sure?"

"I've known your mother a long time. She helped me back when my father used to yell at me about the books I wanted to read. She helped me when my parents didn't want to let me go to college. She doesn't shy away from messy situations, and she'll help you now." Judith didn't trust herself to say much more. "Your mother understands how complicated life can be."

Chapter 67

HELEN

After Abe's first heart attack, Helen became vigilant in all matters relating to his health. She changed his favorite recipes so that he stayed on his diet. She forced him to take walks with her every day. She counted out his pills with absolute precision and made sure he didn't stay late at work. Abe lost thirty pounds and looked ten years younger. But the fear of losing him overwhelmed her. She woke in the middle of the night to check on his breathing. She read everything she could find about heart disease. Over time, Helen began to live life partly in shadow.

Abe's funeral was on a perfect October day. The air was crisp and the sky clear and cloudless, as blue as Abe's eyes on their first date. It was exactly the kind of weather Abe loved. Helen knew it was ridiculous to think Abe would have enjoyed his own funeral, but as she listened to the rabbi speak about her husband, that was *all* she could think of: how if Abe had walked into the room right then, his face would have lit up with joy. Abe loved any kind of gathering of people. Put all the people he knew, all his family and friends and coworkers, in one room together, and Helen just knew he would have loved it. That was the thought she clung to when other thoughts became too bleak. Thinking of Abe, smiling and cheerful, was her greatest comfort.

Six months after the funeral, Helen was beginning to recover.

Her sons and her grandchildren kept her busy, and Judith was a great support. Sol came over a few mornings a week to check on her, and Arlene called at least twice a day. Between her family and some of the neighborhood women who had taken an interest in her, Helen's life was busier than ever. The only person she hadn't seen much of was Natalie.

She understood, of course. Natalie was in her senior year of college, hard at work on her final projects and thesis. Helen wasn't exactly sure what a "thesis" was, but Judith described it as a long research paper, the culmination of all of Natalie's studies in mathematics. It was natural that Natalie should be spending most of her time on it. Helen called Natalie several times a week on the phone, but their conversations were always short, and Helen thought she sounded depressed.

Natalie had always been more interested in her schoolwork than her brothers, but Helen hadn't really understood how driven she was until she started college. There was something familiar about seeing her daughter's world widening and her ambition multiplying exponentially as the months and years of college went by. So much change and evolution in such a brief period of time, just like the first few years of Natalie's life. For Helen, it felt like she was watching Natalie grow up all over again. Only this time Natalie wasn't learning how to walk or speak, she was learning (she told Helen) how to *think*.

Abe had been there to see the majority of it. But the fact that he would not be there for Natalie's graduation was a terrible disappointment. Helen was infuriated by the unfairness of it. He had sat through most of the performance, but he would miss the final bow.

When Natalie came home for the occasional weekend here and there, Helen worried even more. Natalie looked tired. She was painfully thin. She slept until noon and only poked at the food Helen made, even the homemade cookies. When Helen asked about her love life, Natalie seemed upset and mumbled about having no time.

The day Natalie's thesis was due, Helen called her in the evening. She may not have entirely understood what Natalie was studying, but she wanted to congratulate her on her achievement. Natalie had mentioned that all papers were to be handed in to the department head by 4:00 p.m. and that there would be a champagne reception for the mathematics department at five. Helen checked the clock. It was almost eight-thirty. There was a possibility Natalie would be out celebrating with friends, but she wanted to try calling anyway.

There was no answer at eight-thirty, so Helen tried again at nine-thirty. On her third try, a few minutes before eleven, someone finally answered.

"Aunt Helen, it's me, Johnny."

"Johnny? What are you doing there?"

"I took Natalie out to dinner to celebrate finishing her thesis. She's been working so hard, I wanted to do something nice for her."

"Well, aren't you thoughtful. Can you put the scholar on the phone, please?"

"Sure. Here she is. Good night, Aunt Helen."

"Good night, dear." There was some rustling and then Natalie was on the line.

"Hi, Mom."

"Congratulations, honey!"

"Thanks." Helen was expecting Natalie to sound happy, elated, even. Instead, she sounded nervous.

"Johnny's leaving in a few minutes. He just took me out to dinner to celebrate."

"That was so nice!"

"Listen, I'm not going to talk long. I want to say goodbye to Johnny, and I'm really tired, so . . ."

"I won't keep you. I just wanted to say congratulations and I'll see you this weekend. Are you still getting the three o'clock train Friday?"

"Yes, I'll see you then."

"All right, sweetheart. I'll pick you up at the station."

"Bye."

Helen was baffled. Why had Natalie been so anxious to get off the phone? She should have been on cloud nine after finishing all that work, but all Helen heard was worry in her voice. *What was going on?*

Chapter 68

NATALIE

"You shouldn't have answered the phone."

"C'mon, Nat. I spoke to her for two seconds. Besides, it's not like she thinks we never see each other."

"Maybe, but now she's going to be wondering why you were in my room at eleven o'clock!" Natalie was pacing now, from the door to the window that looked out over Claremont Avenue. In the tiny dorm room, it wasn't more than a few feet. Johnny took her in his arms, holding her close and tight. Her breathing slowed and she began to relax.

"What are we going to do?" she whispered.

He answered her between kisses. "We. Are. Going. To. Get. Married."

"What will we tell them?"

Johnny kissed her again, longer this time. "We'll tell them I love you. We'll tell them you love me." He was tired of talking. His lips were on her neck, her shoulders, her mouth. His hands were in her hair, at her waist. She didn't want him to stop, she didn't want to think about anything but him. But she couldn't help herself.

"Johnny?"

"Mmm?"

"I told Judith about us."

"Good." Unfazed, he pulled his shirt over his head.

"I'm going to tell my mother on Friday." If he had been anyone else, she would have felt ridiculous bringing up her mother at that moment. But Johnny wasn't just anyone. He was her confidant, her sweetheart, her truest friend. He understood the gravity of her words. The expression on her face, the tone of her voice, none of it escaped him. Putting passion on hold, he held her and spoke to her as gently as the moment required. "She's going to understand," he told her.

"How do you know?"

He spoke with the certainty she needed to hear. "Because she loves you as much as I do and she wants you to be happy."

Chapter 69

HELEN

Natalie's anxiety was palpable when Helen picked her up from the train. Helen tried to appear unconcerned, but the farther she drove, the harder it became to hold her tongue. By the time she pulled into the driveway, Helen was practically bursting. She turned off the engine, but before she opened the car door, she had to speak her mind.

"Natalie, what is it? Please, tell me what's bothering you."

When she had been very young, Natalie had cried no more or less than other children her age. But after she turned five, Helen could count on one hand the number of times she had seen Natalie break down. The first was when Teddy died, and the second was when Natalie was eleven and broke her elbow. The third was Mimi's wedding, when Rose yelled at her in the hallway, and the last time was six months ago at Abe's funeral. Natalie was an exceptionally composed young woman. So when she burst into tears in the car, Helen knew something was very wrong.

"Do you want to go into the house and talk?" Helen asked, but Natalie couldn't answer. She shook her head back and forth, sobbing. It was a side of her Helen had never seen. What could make a girl like that, so strong, so sure of herself, cry like her heart was breaking? The moment she asked herself the question, of course, was the moment Helen had her answer. Natalie's heart *was* breaking. Natalie was in love.

Through choked-back tears and weepy breaths, Natalie managed to express that she had something important to tell Helen and that she wanted to get it over with before getting out of the car. Helen could barely understand her, but she stayed put and rolled down the window for some fresh air. She handed Natalie some tissues from her purse and patted her hand. After fifteen minutes passed, Natalie was still unable to speak. By that time, Helen had already figured it out. Perhaps it was the confined space of the car's interior that helped to focus her thoughts, or, more likely, somewhere inside, Helen already knew. Either way, the clues she had overlooked for years suddenly became obvious to her.

"It's all right," Helen consoled her. "I think I know. You're in love with Johnny." After she said it out loud, Helen couldn't remember not knowing it. Had she purposely ignored the signs for her own selfish reasons? Natalie was miserable, inconsolable, all because of a decades-old secret that Helen couldn't bring herself to tell. *What kind of mother lets her child suffer like that?*

"Sweetheart," Helen said, as Natalie's breathing returned to normal, "it's going to be fine. Let's go inside—I'm getting a crick in my neck sitting here for so long. Besides, I have a few things I need to talk to you about."

Chapter 70

NATALIE

More surprising than the fact that her mother had guessed she was in love with Johnny was the fact that she didn't seem phased by it one bit. Was Helen really going to be so supportive of the relationship? Was it all that simple? Natalie couldn't shake the feeling that something more was going on. Even if Helen really understood about Johnny, why wasn't she angry that Natalie had kept her in the dark for so long? Natalie supposed she'd have to tell her mother the whole story, no matter how convoluted.

Natalie walked into the house and dropped her overnight bag in a corner by the kitchen table. Ever since she had started college, the house had felt a little bit less like home each time she visited. She unzipped her duffle and pulled out a copy of her thesis. "I thought you might like a copy."

Helen weighed the heavy bound volume in both hands. "It's like a book! You didn't tell me you wrote a whole book! No wonder you've been working so hard."

"It's really just a long research paper. Maybe I'll write a book one day. I'm not sure anyone would want to read it, though."

Helen flipped through the pages, but the equations and explanations were indecipherable to her. "Of course people will read it. Not ordinary people like me, maybe. But mathematicians will—professors and students. I'm going to read every page, even if I don't understand a word. Did you make a copy for Mort? He's dying to read it."

"I have an extra for him. I'll bring it to him tomorrow." Natalie took a seat at the kitchen table and ran her fingers over one of the scratches in the yellow Formica. Helen filled a kettle with water from the sink. "I'm going to make us some tea. Sol brought over some Danish yesterday. How about one of those?" At the mention of her uncle's name, Natalie could feel herself panicking again. She was worried about how Sol and Arlene would react.

"Do you think they're going to understand? What are they going to say?" Natalie started to tear up again. "We want . . . we want to get married. We tried to stop ourselves from feeling this way, we *tried*, but it never worked. He's the only boy . . . the only *man* that I've ever loved." Natalie wiped her eyes with the back of her hand. Helen sat down, put one arm around her and rubbed her back like she used to when Natalie was little.

When the kettle whistled, Helen jumped up to fill the mugs. She brought them to the table, along with the white bakery box. Natalie didn't touch the Danish.

"I'm sorry I didn't tell you about Johnny before," she said. "I don't like keeping secrets from you." When her mother didn't reply, Natalie got nervous. Helen's face was hard to read. She looked hopeless.

"We need to talk about Johnny," Helen said. "We need to talk about a lot of things. After your father recovered from his first heart attack, I promised myself I would never let my . . . actions . . . hurt you or anyone. I got lucky with your father, but now . . . look what I've done. *You're* being hurt, and it's my fault."

"Mom, you're not making any sense. I don't understand what you're saying."

Helen took Natalie's hands in hers. "Sweetheart, I have to tell you a story. It's a very long story about my life years ago, before you were born, before even some of your brothers were born. I need you to be patient with me. I need you to listen to the whole story before you say anything."

"You're scaring me."

"Don't be scared. Will you listen?"

"Yes."

Natalie listened. She listened to her mother talk about her life in

Brooklyn, her friendship with Rose, Rose's marriage to Mort. "You need to understand," Helen told her, "Mort didn't used to be the way he is now. Honey, he used to be awful to Rose. Every time Rose had another girl, he would say such cruel things to her. He ignored the girls and Rose, just to punish her for not giving him a son."

"I can't imagine Uncle Mort acting that way. Judith has told me some things, but it's so hard to believe."

"Judith knows better than anyone."

"You mean, because he didn't want her to go to college?"

"Partly. Of course, everything is different now. He's so proud of Judith and what she's accomplished. He's proud of you too. But I want you to understand what it used to be like for us, for Rose and for me, when we were young mothers. Uncle Mort was so jealous of your father. And Rose, she got a little bit . . . smaller somehow, day by day. She was afraid of disappointing him."

"But you and Daddy weren't like that."

"Never. Your father was a prince. Your brothers were a handful, though, with all the fighting and running around. Sometimes all I wanted to do was just go downstairs and be with the girls. Mimi would play dress-up and she used to love for me to do her hair. Dinah was little then, she only wanted to cuddle. And Judith . . . well, Judith was like a grown-up. Even when she was ten, I could talk to her. *You* were that way too, you know. Brilliant, both of you."

Natalie smiled. "Let's hope the thesis committee agrees with you."

"Don't worry about them. I'm sure they're going to see right away what a genius you are."

"Sure. Anyway, go on."

"I know this sounds terrible, but sometimes your brothers would drive me crazy. Rose had three sweet little girls, and I was jealous because I knew they would all be close to her when they grew up and I would be alone. I used to worry that your brothers would all move away and get married to girls who hated me."

"Meanwhile, Sam lives the farthest, and it's only twenty minutes from here! And no one could ever hate you. Everyone loves you."

"Well, I've been lucky. But back then I worried. Anyway, I was thirty-five when I got pregnant again. My grandmother used to say if a woman waited more than seven years between babies, her body changed and she'd have the opposite of whatever she had the last time. I thought for sure I'd have a girl.

"Rose got pregnant at the same time. Our pregnancies had over-lapped before, but we never had due dates as close as that. We were so excited. Rose and I were like sisters back then. But she was worried. The whole time she was pregnant, she was scared of having a girl."

"She told you that?"

"She didn't have to tell me, honey. It was obvious. Uncle Mort was convinced they were having a boy. He called the baby 'he,' he told the girls they were having a brother, he told everyone who'd listen. He started paying more attention to Rose and the girls—and that only made her feel more pressured. I don't think she would have been able to bear it, to disappoint him again."

"Geez. Lucky for her she had Teddy."

Helen's face reddened. She looked away. There was something amiss in her silence. "Mom?"

"Natalie, Johnny isn't your cousin."

"What?"

"I don't know how else to tell you. Johnny isn't your first cousin. You love him and you're going to marry him and have healthy babies and you *don't* need to worry about those stories Arlene tells about her uncle's children."

"What are you *saying?*" Natalie stood up from her seat and started pacing across the kitchen floor. "*What are you saying to me?*"

"I'm saying, the night you were born, the night of the blizzard, Rose and I . . . she was so distraught, we . . ."

Natalie's ears were ringing and her hands started to shake. She stopped pacing and fell back, limp, into her chair. Her eyes were blank, and when she spoke, she was incredulous.

"Rose and Mort are my parents?"

"Yes."

"And Teddy was your son?"

"Yes."

Natalie shook her head. Her brain was filled with a buzzing static so that every thought was muddled. "But how? How is that even *possible?* How could that *happen?*"

"You were born first and then Teddy was born a few minutes later.

Rose was absolutely crushed, hopeless. She didn't speak. And then Judith came into the room and she asked us which baby was her mother's and which baby was mine. Rose looked at me then, and she was so . . . I don't know. So *desperate*. She stared and stared at me, pleading, and I . . . I nodded. I agreed. And then it was done. Without a single word it was done."

"What do you mean, it was *done*? You decided to switch your children without even discussing it? How could you have known what Rose was thinking? How could she have known that you agreed?"

"We just knew."

"But what about the midwife? Didn't she see what you were doing? Didn't she *say* anything?"

"No. She was out of the room when it happened, and when she came back I was holding you and Rose was holding Teddy. The midwife filled out the forms the way we told her to. She knew, but she didn't stop us."

"Did Daddy know? Does Mort?"

"Only Rose and I know. And now you."

Natalie lifted her knees to her chest and rocked back and forth in her chair. "Oh my God. *Oh my God.* Why are you telling me this now? *Why?*"

"Because I can't let what I did control who you marry or how you live the rest of your life. I want you to be happy, even if it means you hate me and you never speak to me again. Even if it means everyone finds out the truth. Even if it means you know I'm not your mother."

Natalie's lungs were burning. A terrible tightness gripped her chest, and her thoughts turned suddenly to Abe. If she shut her eyes tight, she could conjure Abe's face, she could summon his smile. She could hear his daily complaints about the diet Helen kept him on, about the tub of margarine that had been substituted for his beloved dish of butter. "Why do you make me eat this crap, Helen?" he would ask. "Because I love you," Helen would answer. "Now eat it."

Natalie tried to picture Abe sitting with them, listening to the true story of the night she had been born. She tried to imagine him pounding his fists on the table, screaming his outrage and walking away from Helen, the same way Natalie wanted to now. But when she tried to conjure the scene, she found that she could not. All she could see was Helen and Abe together in the funeral chapel on the day they buried Teddy. All she could picture was Abe cradling her mother in his arms after Helen had just slapped him across the face. All she could hear were the old rabbi's words, words she had then been too young to understand—"*Love is always forgiving.*"

After several minutes, Natalie opened her eyes. She sat up straight in her chair and looked at Helen, at the woman who had given her everything and had asked for nothing in return. She could not chastise her for her choices. She would not condemn or find fault. Her mother had lost a son and a husband. She had lost a best friend. Natalie would not make her suffer the loss of a daughter as well. "Please don't ever say you're not my mother," Natalie whispered. "You will always be my mother and Teddy's mother too. No one ever loved either of us more than you."

Helen stared at Natalie, eyes wide with disbelief. She had never expected to be forgiven. "It's going to be all right," Natalie said, in a voice so authoritative she did not recognize it as her own. Her energy was renewed, her mind overflowed with plans for how to proceed. "I have to tell Johnny right away," she said. "I don't want to keep any secrets from him."

"Of course," Helen agreed. "He's going to be your husband."

"I think we should tell Uncle Sol and Arlene too so they won't worry about Johnny and me being together."

Again, Helen nodded in agreement.

"But all the others . . . I don't think anyone else should know. It would be too painful, too confusing for all of them."

"Not even Mort?" Helen asked.

There was no hesitation when Natalie answered. "No. He's at peace with his life now. I don't want to ruin that for him."

"I think you're right."

Natalie hugged her mother then, folding Helen into her arms the way her father had so many years ago. When Helen lifted her head, Natalie could see the toll that keeping the secret had taken. The invisible veil that had shrouded her mother's face every day since her birth was finally lifted. For the first time in her life, Helen spoke her greatest regret out loud. "If I hadn't done this . . . if I had kept Teddy, he might not have had the accident. He might still be alive, here now, with us."

"No." Natalie spoke with gentle sureness. "You can't think that way." She brushed her mother's face with her open palm and held her hand against the softness of her mother's cheek. "It wouldn't have mattered which house Teddy lived in, he would have bent down for his comic just the same. I knew him better than anyone. I was there."

"Do you really think so?"

"Yes." Natalie's lower lip trembled and her voice became a whisper. "You couldn't have saved him. But you did save me."

Chapter 71

ROSE

Helen had sent Rose a brief letter along with the clipping from the local newspaper announcing Natalie and Johnny's engagement. She wanted Rose to know she had told Natalie the truth. When Rose finished reading, an unexpected feeling of relief washed over her. The photograph that accompanied the clipping showed a jubilant young woman with a life full of promise.

When she finished Helen's letter, Rose sat down at Faye's old desk to write a reply. Her writing was shaky, and a few tears stained the page. She wrote that she was sorry about Abe, that she would always remember him as kind and forgiving. She wrote that Natalie and Johnny made a lovely couple and that she wished them a long, happy life together. Before she finished the letter, Rose slid open the left-hand drawer of the desk. There, in the back, was a jewelry box containing the diamond earrings that Faye had left to Natalie in her will so many years before, the earrings that Rose had never been able to bring herself to send. Tomorrow, she would go to the post office and mail them with the letter. They would look perfect with a wedding dress, Rose wrote to Helen, and she hoped that Natalie would enjoy them.

Epilogue

(June 1970)

Whenever Johnny tried to cut a name from the guest list, his parents added two in its place. "I'll get a bigger tent," Sol insisted.

"They've known you since you were a *baby,*" Arlene gushed.

Eventually, Johnny gave up any hope of having a small wedding. Natalie was so grateful for the family's support that she couldn't care less who was invited. "Your mom can ask the whole neighborhood," she told Johnny. "As long as we're together, who cares?"

Natalie had been particularly worried about telling Mort. She knew Mort and Sol hadn't always gotten along over the years, and she was afraid Mort would disapprove of the marriage as a result. It turned out Johnny and Mort had more in common than she knew. All those years of listening to his father talk about the odds he'd pay on horses, and the interest his late-paying customers owed, had rubbed off on Johnny. He had a combined appreciation for numbers and sports, and he knew the stats for more baseball players than Mort. The fact that he *wasn't* going to work for Sol helped too. "I like him," Mort admitted.

"That's a relief," Natalie replied. "Because I want you and my mother to walk me down the aisle together at the wedding."

Mort was speechless. He never imagined Natalie would include him in her ceremony in such a significant way. His experience at

Mimi's wedding had left him feeling out of place and unwelcome, and
Dinah had eloped. "I would be honored," he told her.

Natalie was sitting in his office when she told him, in the extra
chair she had made him leave against the wall during her first visit, all
those years ago. "Your father would be very proud of you," he said. "I
hope you know that."

"I do," she answered, smiling. "I know my father is proud of me."
On her way out, Natalie forgot to close the door to Mort's office.

For the first time, he decided to leave it open.

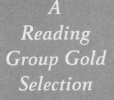

Reading
Group
Gold

THE TWO-FAMILY HOUSE

by Lynda Cohen Loigman

About the Author

- A Conversation with Lynda Cohen Loigman

In Her Own Words

- "The Story Behind *The Two-Family House*":
An Original Essay by the Author

Keep on Reading

- Recommended Reading
- Reading Group Questions

Also available as an audiobook
from Macmillan Audio

For more reading group suggestions
visit www.readinggroupgold.com.

🦁 St. Martin's Griffin

A
Reading
Group Gold
Selection

A Conversation with Lynda Cohen Loigman

The Two-Family House *is your first novel. Had you always wanted to be a writer?*

I have always had a passion for words. But as a child, it didn't occur to me that becoming a writer was really an option. I didn't know any professional writers, and writing novels seemed like something out of reach and far away—something only famous people did. If you had told me when I was young that I was going to be a writer, I probably would have guessed that I would write poetry or song lyrics. I've always loved poetry, and though I am far from musical, I used to be obsessed with memorizing the words to old Cole Porter and Irving Berlin songs. It is because of those early interests that now, as a fiction writer, I probably pay too much attention to individual word choices and the rhythm of my sentences.

"[This] is a story I thought about for at least ten years before I ever wrote a word."

In the fall of 2010, I started taking classes at the Sarah Lawrence Writing Institute. I had always wanted to write, but I didn't know how to get started on my novel. Writing didn't seem real until I had a community of writers for support. The first day I read my work out loud in class was the first time I felt like I actually was a writer. I read the prologue from *The Two-Family House*, which I had been playing with for years. It was an amazing feeling to begin to share it and to hear and see how other people reacted to the story.

Talk about your writing process: How did you find your way into the story? What challenges, if any, did you face along the way?

Writing *The Two-Family House* has been life-changing for me. I am in my late forties and I feel like I have only now found the thing I am supposed to do. It has been such an exciting process because when I sit down to write, even if I think I know exactly what I am going to put down, something always surprises me. For *The*

Two-Family House, I had the outline of the story in
my mind before I began. Despite my planning, the
characters changed and developed in ways I had
not predicted. The story went in directions I had
not outlined. To me, writing is as good as reading
something new—I am always in a state of anticipation,
wondering what is going to happen next.

*Could you share some details about your writing life in
the day-to-day?*

I write throughout the day, at all different times. At
first I wrote mostly when my children were at school,
but now that they are both in high school, I write in
the evenings as well. Ideas come to me often when I'm
driving, so I keep a small notebook with me in the car.
I don't write actual pages then, just plot points and
character details.

When I write at home, it's always at my kitchen table.
Half the time people are talking and eating around me,
but that is where I'm most comfortable.

The Two-Family House *unfolds from multiple
perspectives: male and female, adult and child. Why
did you decide to write in each perspective, and can
you describe how you were able to channel each
character's voice and perspective so vividly?*

The Two-Family House is a story I thought about for
at least ten years before I ever wrote a word. I spent
countless hours over a full decade thinking about how
Rose, Helen, Abe, and Mort would behave in difficult
situations, and how they would feel when faced with
tragedy or joy. By the time I found the courage to start
writing, I knew those four characters as well as I knew
any person in my real life. With four distinct voices in
my head, it seemed wasteful to combine them into one
omniscient narrator.

Although I originally intended to tell the story only from the perspectives of the four adults, when the time came for me to write about the night the babies were born, I realized I had to add Judith's voice. As the oldest female child, Judith bears the brunt of Mort's disapproval, and I knew she would also be the one most burdened by Rose's eventual postpartum depression. She is too young and innocent to understand or question the events of that evening, so she is the perfect unreliable witness.

As the story progressed, I also added Natalie's point of view. I did this mainly because I wanted to contrast Judith's opinion of Mort with Natalie's view of him. I was fascinated by the idea that Judith and Natalie could have such different childhood experiences with Mort.

Brothers Mort and Abe live with their families in a two-family house in Brooklyn. How much do you feel the physical setting of the families in the two-family house contributed to the story?

For me, the house is critical to the narrative—so much so that it is almost another character. Would Helen and Rose have formed the same bond as young mothers if they hadn't lived in such close quarters? Would Mort have been as resentful of Abe's brood of boys if he hadn't heard them pounding overhead day after day? Would Rose and Helen have made the same choice on the night of the blizzard if they hadn't thought they would always live together in the two-family house? I think the answer to all of these questions is no. Without the house, the characters, the conflicts, and the resolutions could never develop the same way.

Helen and Rose make a misguided choice on a dramatic winter's night that is alluded to in the prologue of the book. While you don't come out and reveal the secret directly, most readers will have figured out what happened very early on. Was that intentional?

I always assumed that readers would guess the truth of what happened on the night of the blizzard fairly quickly,

or that they would at least have strong suspicions. It was never my intention to make the novel a mystery, but I felt that to reveal the truth outright would have stripped the story of a portion of the tension I wanted to create. I wanted the secret to wear on the reader, to be the same burden for the reader that it is for Helen and Rose. As a result, you know in your heart what happened, but, just like Helen and Rose, you are powerless to do anything about it. Instead, you are forced to bear witness to the way the choices made on that mysterious night affect the characters' lives. For me, that is the most compelling part of the story.

The Two-Family House *leaves readers with a lot to think about: motherhood, nature vs. nurture, longing, love, betrayal, regret, and the consequences of long-buried secrets. What do you hope people take away from the book? What have you taken away from it?*

Several early readers have referred to *The Two-Family House* as an "old-fashioned story." I hope this is true because to me, an "old-fashioned" story is one that is satisfying and readable—one that people can't put down. More than anything, I want readers to care about the characters in this novel and to miss them when the story is over.

I hope this is something I have achieved. One of the reasons I used alternating points of view to tell the story is that I wanted readers to appreciate the individual motivations and emotions of each character. I wanted to give readers the background necessary to understand why Mort behaves the way he does, where Helen's longing comes from, and how Rose's regrets can lead her down such a bitter path.

Writing the book was, in many ways, an exercise in compassion. Don't get me wrong: there is no question that I tortured my characters. But presenting them at uncomfortable moments and forcing them to deal with so much pain and loss gave me greater understanding and empathy for them.

What type of research, if any, did you perform for **The Two-Family House?**

The research for my next book is much more extensive than I did for *The Two-Family House,* but even so, I did a good amount of it. In addition to learning about the blizzard of 1947 in New York City (important for describing a pivotal scene in the story), I researched the songs, movies, books, and clothing of the era, all so I could accurately describe the time period. My husband is very detail-oriented, and after reading a scene in which Helen wore rubber gloves for house cleaning, he asked me whether I was sure that rubber gloves were around in 1947. That led to a lot of research concerning the popular cleaning products of the day. A lot of my baseball research didn't make it into the story, but I did use some of it. One of the biggest surprises was the cardboard box business—it was a fascinating topic, especially because it was so important to the food industry at the time.

Why do you think readers are so drawn to historical fiction and books about families?

Because my book isn't based on a specific historically significant event, I didn't think of it as historical fiction at first. The more I spoke with readers, though, the more I realized how much the history of the 1940s and 1950s meant to them, and how important it was to capture that era in terms of their connection to the story. I think readers are drawn to historical fiction because they recognize something familiar in it. Either it reminds them of their own past or it relates to an area of personal interest for them. In both instances, the reader's experience is enhanced and enriched by their individual knowledge. I think it's the same with books about families. We all have family stories and we can all relate to the broad spectrum of emotions that accompanies family interactions. Our parents, siblings, spouses, and children are the most influential

"We can all relate to the broad spectrum of emotions that accompanies family interactions."

people in our lives. Those relationships make for fascinating and engaging stories.

Are you currently working on another book? And if so, what—or who—is your subject?

I am working on my second novel now, and I'm really in love with it. The story takes place in Springfield, Massachusetts, and focuses on two estranged sisters who grew up in Brooklyn. This time, I'm really earning that "historical fiction" classification because much of the story takes place at the Springfield Armory at the beginning of World War II. The Armory was actually established by George Washington, so there's a tremendous amount of history there, but during World War II, it was a critical production site of M1 rifles for American troops. More than twelve thousand people were employed at the Armory then, and many of them were women. Exploring the changing role of women in that time period is fascinating, but the relationship between the sisters is really the focal point of the story. Each sister is keeping a shocking secret from the other, so tensions run very high!

Who are some of your favorite authors?

Edith Wharton, Charles Dickens, Herman Wouk, J. R. R. Tolkein, Betty Smith, John Irving, Anthony Doerr, Helene Wecker, J. K. Rowling, David Liss, Alice Hoffman, Geraldine Brooks

(Please see the Recommended Reading section to learn more.)

"The Story Behind *The Two-Family House*"

Before he slept with the fishes, Luca Brasi delivered
his most famous line to Don Corleone on the wedding
day of the Don's daughter. If you've ever seen *The
Godfather*, it's a line you probably remember: "And
may their first child be a masculine child." I have
always been irritated by the sentiment.

For at least sixteen years, I have carried the notion
of *The Two-Family House* with me. Long before that,
I carried only the questions that would eventually
lead me to my narrative. Why did my grandmother,
the mother of three daughters, repeatedly tell me how
much she had longed for a son? Why, in the earlier
generations of so many cultures, from Jewish to Italian
to Chinese, were boys valued more highly than girls?
Was a mother's love for a daughter truly different
from the love she felt for a son?

In the summer of 1999, when my first child was
six months old, I read an article by Lisa Belkin in
The New York Times Magazine called "Getting the
Girl." "We care about the sex of our children," Belkin
wrote. "Some of us care more than others, but we all
care. It is the first question asked about a baby, almost
from conception, certainly at the moment of birth.
Any preference has always been but a wish, a dream,
sometimes a throbbing unspoken regret." The article
examined Microsort, a company that allowed clients
to choose the sex of their infant through a complicated
sperm separation process. According to the company,
more parents were requesting girls than boys. The tide,
it seemed, had turned.

Belkin's article resonated with me. Before becoming
pregnant, I had struck a deal with my husband—he
wanted two children, and I concurred. "But if the first
two are boys," I insisted, "we'll try once more for a girl."
My terms were nonnegotiable, and I was lucky enough

to get what I wanted: I am the mother of one girl and one boy. But why was I so adamant? Where did my need for a daughter come from, and how far would I have gone to fulfill it?

In the sleep-deprived haze that followed the birth of my daughter, the story of *The Two-Family House* truly took root. Inspiration came from a collection of near-mythic stories I had heard throughout my childhood. Like the families in my novel, my mother and her two younger sisters grew up in a two-family house in Brooklyn. They lived on the top floor while my grandmother's brother, his wife, and their three daughters lived on the bottom. The girls were raised together, almost as siblings. My grandmother, Tillie, and her sister-in- law, Diane, were always close—in part because they were so different. Tillie was a traditional wife and homemaker while Diane, by all accounts, was a woman ahead of her time; she was the first of her contemporaries to learn to drive, and she didn't like to cook. My grandmother loved telling stories of how her three nieces would come upstairs when they were hungry. "They'd bring two slices of bread," she used to tell me, "and ask for something to put in the middle."

In the two-family house of my mother's childhood, there were no sons to be found, no reason for the kind of envy that Mort felt in the book to develop. But as a young girl with a grandmother who made no apologies for her preference for grandsons, I often wondered: what if there had been?

In my mind, a new family emerged. Abe would have four boys, and his brother, Mort, would have three girls. Their wives, Helen and Rose, would be close in the way my own grandmother and her sister-in- law always were; and the children, all seven of them, would be raised together. With a family of boys, Helen would yearn for a daughter, while Rose, meek and miserable, would crumble under the constant pressure she felt to produce a son for her husband. Aside from their environment, the characters bore no significant resemblance to the members of my family. But for me, they became real.

The house itself—where both families lived on separate floors, yet had unlimited access to each other and minimal privacy—was vital to the story. Living in tight quarters created a bond between Helen and Rose that couldn't have been formed otherwise, but it also inflamed Mort's feelings of anger and resentment toward the brood of rambunctious boys upstairs. Were it not for the house, Helen and Rose wouldn't have been capable of making the decision, in secret, to switch their babies. Because they lived under the same roof, both women inhabited a world clouded with just enough denial to make their shocking choice acceptable.

"The house was a necessary percolator for the narrative. . . ."

Without question, the house was a necessary percolator for the narrative. But once the scene was set, I no longer felt the need to dwell on the outward details. At that point, I was free to focus inward on my characters, their temperaments, their beliefs, and their motivations. My need to expose the full spectrum of each character's emotions propelled certain aspects of the plot. How could I ignore the opportunity to explore Rose's postpartum depression, Helen's anxiety over filling out a hospital form, or Abe's concern over the rift between the two mothers? What would happen if the families ever moved? How would a funeral of one of the children play out? My objective always was to reveal, in small, domestic moments, the cumulative layers of tragedy that could result from a single misguided choice made by ordinary individuals.

Although none of the main characters in the novel were modeled on my relatives, personal tidbits and fragments of family legend slipped in here and there. I really do have my mother's recipe box that I talk to from time to time. And the inspiration for the

restaurant scene in the first part of the book came from stories my mother and aunts used to tell about their family dinners at a restaurant in Little Italy.

Of all the anecdotes in the story, I included only one from my own personal experience. Every Saturday afternoon when my mother got her hair done, my grandmother really did come to my house with bologna, rolls, and a miniature chocolate cake with a cherry on top for my brother and me. Every Saturday afternoon, she would tell my brother that she had brought the cake especially for him. Ask any of my relatives and they'll tell you. My brother got the cherry every time.

In Her Own Words

Recommended Reading

A Tree Grows in Brooklyn
Betty Smith

This book probably had the greatest impact on me growing up.

Marjorie Morningstar
Herman Wouk

If you haven't read this classic, I highly recommend it. I can't wait for my teenage daughter to read it!

The House of Mirth and **The Custom of the Country**
Edith Wharton

These are two of my favorite books. I have always loved how Edith Wharton gets inside the heads of her characters. It is something I am always trying to do.

The Golem and the Jinni
Helene Wecker

I can't say enough wonderful things about this book. Helene Wecker captures old New York in such rich and layered detail. I love books with mystical aspects to them, and this book certainly has that! I can't wait for the sequel!

All The Light We Cannot See
Anthony Doerr

Another book with mystical bits to it. This book is one of my all-time favorites. I am in awe of his writing, and the sense of place he is able to create.

The Marriage of Opposites
Alice Hoffman

This book was comforting and disturbing all at the same time, in the very best of ways. Hoffman's descriptions of colors are breathtaking.

The Coffee Trader
David Liss

I love everything David Liss writes. He has such talent for capturing a fascinating moment in history and making the reader care about it. Every time I read one of his books, I am utterly swept away.

The Autobiography of Mrs. Tom Thumb
Melanie Benjamin

This book is my favorite of hers. It's such an imaginative premise and the story is so touching.

March
Geraldine Brooks

I loved this story, a sophisticated sequel to Louisa May Alcott's *Little Women*.

Eloise
Kay Thompson

My favorite children's book of all time.

*Keep on
Reading*

Reading Group Questions

1. We learn early in the story that Abe's relationship with Mort is a complicated one. Would you try as hard as Abe does to maintain a positive relationship with your sibling if he/she acted the way Mort does? Why is it so easy for Abe to always forgive and forget?

2. Do you consider Mort to be emotionally abusive at the beginning of the novel, or is he just disinterested? Does Mort's behavior justify Rose's actions?

3. Do you think either Helen or Rose thought about switching babies before the night they were born? How does living in the two-family house affect their decision? Do you think the same choice would have been made had the families lived in separate homes?

4. Does Helen interfere too much in Rose's daily life once the babies are born? When Helen and Rose have their argument in the coatroom, Rose says that Helen took both babies and left her with none. Is there any truth to this?

5. How do you feel about the way Mort and Rose handle Judith's college news? Were you surprised that Rose didn't stand up for Judith? Is Rose's anxiety the main reason she doesn't want Judith to live away from home, or are there others?

6. The theme of nature vs. nurture runs throughout the novel. Which prevails in terms of shaping the identities of Natalie and Teddy? What qualities do the children take from their natural parents vs. their adoptive parents?

7. Discuss the ways in which each of the four adult characters cope with their grief after Teddy's death. Whose reaction do you find the most surprising? For whom do you feel the most sympathy?

8. After Abe's heart attack, Helen realizes for the first
    time how deceitful she has been. If Helen had
    told Abe the truth, do you think he would he have
    been able to forgive her?

9. Rose and Mort are the characters who change
    the most throughout the course of the book.
    Whose transformation do you find to be the most
    compelling? Is Teddy's death, Natalie's influence,
    or Judith's forgiveness the most important factor
    in Mort's metamorphosis?

10. In the novel, Judith continually has the feeling that
    she is missing something. Is it realistic to think
    she would be able to figure out the secret? Do you
    think she has an obligation to tell Natalie or Mort
    once she knows the truth?

11. Rose is obviously bothered by the attention Mort
    pays to Natalie, but why is Rose so upset when
    Mort finally becomes close to Judith? Which
    relationship bothers Rose the most?

12. Do you think Mort gets off too easily at the end
    of the novel? Would he suffer more if he knew the
    truth about Natalie and Teddy?

*Keep on
Reading*